Praise for the novels of Adele Ashworth

Stolen Charms

"An utterly and overwhelmingly magnificent read ...
one of the most breathtakingly beautiful relationships I
have ever had the pleasure of reading in a novel ... I
can't recommend *Stolen Charms* highly enough."

—*The Romance Journal*

"Charmingly written and filled with passion and adventure."

—*Romantic Times*

"Teases and tantalizes ... fast-paced and entertaining. I
became involved in the conflict, felt the pressure of the
tension, and basked in its romantic afterglow."

—*Rendezvous*

"Well written ... an exciting, fast-paced tale of famous
jewels, a beautiful spy, and enough twists and turns to
keep the reader interested."

—*Old Book Barn Gazette*

"Readers who enjoy a humorous Victorian romantic intrigue will relish *Stolen Charms* ... A delightful tale."

—*Affaire de Coeur*

continued on next page ...

My Darling Caroline

Winner of the RITA Award for Best First Book

"Smart dialogue, complex characters, and complicated plot twists . . . a joy to read."

—*Booklist*

"A stunning debut." —*Affaire de Coeur*

"Some of the best sexual tension I've read in a long time . . . a five-heart book." —*The Romance Reader*

"Remarkable . . . an emotionally enthralling story."
—Arnette Lamb, author of *Threads of Destiny*

"[An] entertaining debut novel . . . fine storytelling, beguiling characters, and a charming romance . . . Adele Ashworth has a fine future ahead of her."
—*Romantic Times*

"A tantalizing blend of seduction and intrigue. She brings us characters that we can relate to and fall in love with."

—*Under the Covers Book Reviews*

"Some great plot twists . . . strong characters. . . . The author ties everything together with great skill, producing a very rewarding read."

—*All About Romance*

"Historical romance readers of all eras will be totally enthralled by this absorbing drama, which also happens to be the debut novel of tomorrow's superstar."
—Harriet Klausner for *Painted Rock Reviews*

Jove Titles by Adele Ashworth

MY DARLING CAROLINE
STOLEN CHARMS
WINTER GARDEN

Winter Garden

ADELE ASHWORTH

JOVE BOOKS, NEW YORK

WINTER GARDEN

A Jove Book / published by arrangement with
the author

PRINTING HISTORY
Jove edition / July 2000

The Penguin Putnam Inc. World Wide Web site address is
http://www.penguinputnam.com

ISBN: 0-515-12866-X

A JOVE BOOK®
Jove Books are published by The Berkley Publishing Group,
a division of Penguin Putnam Inc.,
375 Hudson Street, New York, New York 10014.
JOVE and the "J" design
are trademarks belonging to Penguin Putnam Inc.

PRINTED IN THE UNITED STATES OF AMERICA

10 9 8 7 6 5 4 3 2 1

*For Jane Kleitsch, Robin Bentley, and Michele Adams—
three amazing friends who support me through each
and every book, and who I have finally managed
to thank in one of them.*

*A special thank-you to Yvette McClelland, my cousin,
who always has an E-mail shoulder to cry on;
Gail Poole, her mother,
who supports my efforts from afar;
and my mom and dad for always being there.*

*Also, I'd like to thank all of my journalism professors at
the University of Utah. Their patience and skill taught me
how to succeed with continued work and belief in myself—
after my freshman English teacher, who gave me a solid
B, suggested I switch majors because I had no talent
and would never make it as a creative writer.*

*And, as always, this book is for the greatest loves of
my life—Ron, Andrew, and Caroline.*

One

The cold, late-November wind slapped her face and whipped her lightweight skirt against her legs as Madeleine DuMais stepped down from her hired coach and onto solid ground at Winter Garden. She breathed deeply of the crisp afternoon air, briefly closing her eyes and pointing her face toward the sun as she wrapped her traveling cloak tightly around her, bracing herself against a chill to which she was unaccustomed.

England. At last she was back in England. The smells of home fires burning and rich, damp soil lingered in her senses and her memory. The rustle of trees, the clopping of horses along the graveled road that meandered through the village teased her gentle thoughts of family, of where she belonged. This was her father's country—*her* country as she liked to think of it—and where, if she could live anywhere on earth, she would reside for the remainder of her days.

Alas, she was French, and life was not so simple.

With a nod of acknowledgment to her driver, he placed her things—just two trunks—beside her as she stood roadside, then he returned to his seat to move on to the next stop. He could get the coach no closer to the cottage on the narrow lane, and since she couldn't carry them herself, her possessions would momentarily have to remain where he had stacked them. No bother. The trunks were locked, and Thomas Blackwood, her new associate and a man she was soon to meet, could retrieve them for her in only a matter of minutes.

The instructions given her yesterday had been clear. For the next few weeks she would be working and living at the southern edge of the village, in the last cottage on the right. From where she stood now she could see the waist-high, wooden gate, painted the color of spring daffodils, that surrounded the property. Madeleine pulled her hood forward to rest loosely on her head, tucking fallen strands of her windblown hair behind the dark fur trim. Then, holding the collar securely against her neck with one gloved hand, she lifted her skirts and lightweight valise with the other and began her short walk down Farrset Lane.

This assignment had come as a surprise to her. She'd been wondering about it with building anticipation since she'd received the urgent note from Sir Riley Liddle, her immediate superior, only ten days earlier. It communicated no details, just: *You're needed at home. Come quickly, alone.* And she had, without question, because she longed for any excuse to return to England; but more importantly, she came because it was her work, and her work was all she had, was all in the world she cherished.

Sir Riley, however, had had little to add to the scant information she possessed already. Her moments with him in London yesterday had been brief, for there wasn't much known beyond scattered rumors of an unusual smuggling operation being conducted in or perhaps just through this tiny, enchanting winter retreat. Conveniently, smuggling happened to be her area of expertise, and the reason her superiors had chosen her to help with the investigation. It was also quite probable that they needed a woman for the work, since sending another man might have looked unusual, even suspicious, to village residents. Mr. Blackwood's assumed identity of a retired scholar could be better maintained if he were sent someone to pose as his companion or nurse—any number of plausible occupations. She would leave the decision to him, and he would enlighten her with the details. She eagerly awaited the meeting between them that was soon to occur.

Madeleine, in her own very worldly, sophisticated, elegant way, worked as a spy for the British government. She'd been performing in that capacity for nearly seven years, and she was extraordinarily good at what she did. Her position was unique, and she knew it. It also made her valuable. A Parisian by birth, she usually worked for the good of England from the quaint town of Marseille where she now lived. Her fabricated identity as the young widow of the mythical Georges DuMais—a trader of fine teas, lost at sea—was intact and believed by all who knew her. Her function involved differing interests, although most often it concerned uncovering various secrets on both local and national levels in the broad and sometimes dangerous realm of trade smuggling. Those in top English government positions had set her up in a beautiful home, near the center of the Mediterranean city where she was needed most, and from there she relayed all pertinent information to Sir Riley. Of course, this mission to England was a first for her, given the fact that she had been told very little regarding the circumstances, and because she'd never used her skills outside of France.

She knew only a little about the village of Winter Garden. It was located just a few miles north of the southern coastal town of Portsmouth, nestled between low hills on all sides, which in turn kept it protected from harsh winters. Its lush grounds and mild, year-round climate made the location a haven for the English gentry, as half of the village's population were those of the upper classes who journeyed there only for the winter months, using it as a sort of seasonal retreat. This in itself was unusual, especially during such hard economic times. As in France, most villages were inhabited by peasants, their conditions typically harsh and dreary. But Winter Garden had the reputation for difference, and from her first look, Madeleine could understand why. Loveliness surrounded her; the well-dressed walked the streets. Even cold as it was now, some greenery still flourished. It never snowed in Winter Garden, or so she'd heard.

Still, she had to remember the serenity was an illusion, or she wouldn't have been assigned there at all. Beneath the surface of this village a scandal brewed, waiting to bubble over. She would be the one to uncover it, with the help of Thomas Blackwood, a man about whom she knew even less than the mission itself. The only information about him provided to her was that he was a large man of thirty-nine years, he had been working for the government for roughly the last ten of them, and that he'd been in Winter Garden for several weeks already with no luck in learning much at all about illegal activities. He had requested help, and she had been sent.

Madeleine neared the end of the road as the cottage came into view. It faced the morning sun and appeared to be a small, square, two-story structure, charming in its simplicity, and constructed of clean, white brick. Yellow shutters that matched the gate, open to allow daylight beams inside, defined large beveled windows. Empty window boxes in hues of rose and blue stood out as the only decoration aside from lilac shrubs and dormant rosebushes to trim the property, constant reminders of the warmth of spring to come.

Madeleine unlatched the gate and followed the stone path to the porch partially obscured by an ivy-covered trellis. She placed her valise on the ground to her side, knocked twice on the front door and stepped back, glancing down her figure and straightening her skirt with a palm brushed against her cloak. Silly that she should worry about her appearance here, she considered; but then it had always been her greatest asset, and she did want to make a good first impression on the man in whose company she was soon to be spending a great deal of time.

For moments she waited, but the door didn't open, neither by a dutiful servant nor Mr. Blackwood, confusing her a little because she knew she was expected. Then she heard the dull smacking noise of someone chopping wood from behind the cottage. Leaving her valise on the porch, she turned, pulled her full skirt up to her ankles to step cautiously onto the grass, and followed the sound.

Tall pine trees hugged the property on all sides, enclosing it intimately from the observance of watchful neighbors. Lilac bushes lined the brick walls of the house itself. As she rounded the back corner, she took notice of both flower and vegetable gardens, recently upturned and laying dormant for the coming season. It was a lovely, secluded place, with thickly shaded areas for protection from heated summer sun, for insulation from brisk winter wind, made especially for retreat from the burdens of everyday life.

Then she saw the man.

Madeleine came to an abrupt halt and stared open-mouthed. It was a ridiculous reaction on her part, she realized at once. Yet she'd never before, in her very experienced life, seen anyone like him. The graphic sexual thoughts suddenly rolling through her mind actually startled her.

He stood along the far end of the property, probably only ten feet away. His back was to her, legs spread wide in a chopping stance, naked from the hips up as he effortlessly lifted an ax and slammed it into the brush in an attempt to clear the overgrowth. He was huge of stature and beautifully muscled from his bunched shoulders and sculpted arms, through the cords of strength along his back, to his lean, tapered waist that disappeared into tight black pants hugging long, thick, booted legs. His skin shone with the sheen of exertion, from the sun on his shoulders, and although it was cold enough outside for breath to crystallize, he didn't seem to notice the icy, autumn air as he leaned over and wrapped one enormous hand around a wayward vine while slicing the base of it with the other.

Large didn't begin to describe him, was Madeleine's first coherent thought after once again taking control of herself. Sir Riley had understated the obvious, which seemed to be a continuing occurrence she probably needed to discuss with him. Or maybe it was just that Sir Riley hadn't clarified that by large he meant strong, tall, broad. Not rotund as she'd assumed and expected. This man didn't look thirty-nine or scholarly, either, at least from the view of his firmly muscled backside.

The breeze shifted, blowing into her eyes the soft fur

that lined her hood. Madeleine reached up and adjusted it, and it was at that moment that he realized she stood behind him.

He tensed, the ax in midair. Then he let the handle slide through his fingers as the head of it dropped to rest against his fist. With a very deep inhale he raised his face to the setting sun. Five seconds passed. Ten. Then he turned his head to the side so that she only saw his profile as he spoke to her over his shoulder.

"I've been waiting for you, Madeleine."

His voice, so smooth and deeply vibrant, resonated a kind of poetic . . . longing. His words expressed only irritation at her late arrival.

"Monsieur Blackwood," she returned confidently, although her hands were clutched in front of her, fingers coiled tightly together.

He drew himself up, standing rigid, and very, very slowly he finally turned to look at her.

His eyes, thickly lashed and honey brown, probed hers with intensity. But it was the full sight of his face and immense bearing that took her breath. She wouldn't call him classically handsome. Indeed, he was not. He was brutally so.

His skin, darkly bronzed, gleamed from sweat; his hair, thick and nearly black, fell in waves behind his ears and down his neck. With bone structure perfectly proportioned in hard, set angles, his clean-shaven face drew attention to a deep, two-inch scar running vertically just to the right of his harsh, well-defined mouth. He looked like a warrior, sleek and untamed, sending signals of rugged masculinity as finely tuned as a concert piano.

What made her strangely uncomfortable in his presence was not his overpowering size but his immediate and explicit disregard for her own physical assets. She wasn't used to that. This man in front of her only stared unswervingly into her eyes. He never regarded her figure, her face, nor did he glance down to her breasts. He stared at her, into her, with unreadable features—big, square, hard—his gaze magnetic. Drawing. Madeleine shivered involuntarily.

For seconds nothing happened. No further word was spoken, no thought conveyed. Then at last he lowered his eyes and placed his ax on the ground beside him. "I expected you by noon."

She composed herself as he tempered the mood. "The train was late departing the city this morning, and I missed the first coach. I only just arrived." She licked her lips. "It's a lovely village." A ridiculous thing to say. She was a professional, here as his working colleague, no complications, and yet he unnerved her.

He reached for his shirt of white cotton, hanging from a tree branch, and proceeded to pull it over his head and onto his perspiration-coated body. She watched the movement, studied the dark curls on his chest as they gleamed in sunlight when his muscles flexed, unable to look away.

"Your accent is thick," he said, stating an obvious fact.

She almost smiled. "But my English is exceptional."

"Indeed." He scrutinized her mouth. "The combination can be very seductive."

She shifted from one foot to the other, squirming from a suggestive comment for the first time in her life, delivered low and thoughtfully.

He placed his hands on his hips as his gaze met hers once more. "We can use it."

It was so blunt a statement after one so telling that she had to blink, unable to formulate a suitable reply. Still, he hadn't moved from where he stood, hadn't asked her questions, and although he seemed genuine enough, he didn't appear to react to her on a physical level. She wasn't sure if that bothered her or not.

She took a step toward him. "Perhaps, Monsieur Blackwood—"

"Thomas."

She stopped moving and nodded once. "Perhaps, Thomas, you wouldn't mind retrieving my trunks? There are only two of them, but my coach driver couldn't get any closer to the cottage, and they had to be left at the top of the road."

The dark planes of his face tightened just enough for her to recognize hesitation on his part. Or was it just continued irritation? She couldn't be sure. If she had to choose one word to describe him that word would be *powerful*, and with his obvious strength he should be able to carry her possessions easily. Yet he seemed reluctant.

He reached for the ax beside him and lifted it again. Then in a one-handed thrust, he drove it into the hard earth at his feet. "I'll get them," he said in a tone of quiet reservation. "Then we'll go inside and talk."

"Thank you." The bright sun spread across her cheeks in its deceptiveness, but the icy wind blustered around her, down her neck, up from the bottom of her skirt. It was going to be a frigid winter, inside the cottage and out of it.

With another quick glance into her eyes, he took his first few steps toward her, and that's when Madeleine understood his reluctance all too clearly.

His limp was pronounced, shocking her in a measure he probably noticed. Or expected. At first impression, she concluded it wasn't a recent, healing injury. Thomas favored his right leg, although both appeared to be afflicted. From the way he moved, she knew it had to be an old wound that had likely left scars.

"Thomas—"

He paused in midstride, effectively cutting her off, but he didn't meet her gaze. "It's all right, Madeleine," he replied in a deep whisper.

Then he brushed by her so closely she felt the heat from his body, and she instinctively took a step away. He continued, though, without observing her unusual preoccupation with his physique, rounding the corner and heading toward the front road.

Madeleine, who prided herself on her poise and constant attention to detail, found herself thoroughly embarrassed by the exchange. More so than he, she thought. Her reactions to the man were so out of character, her blunder so tactless, their first meeting so odd. As she thought about it she became increasingly annoyed that Sir Riley hadn't mentioned her new business associate to be an invalid. That really was something she should have been told.

Madeleine turned, shoulders back, cheeks burning, and retraced her steps, walking through the grass and along the side of the house. Thomas hadn't waited for her to follow but had already stepped onto the road and was well out of sight. She moved to the porch and stood silently, hands folded in front of her, refusing to watch him collect her things, although she was inexplicably drawn to do so—not because his injuries intrigued her but because the rest of him did.

Within minutes she heard his uneven footsteps on the gravel. Then he reappeared from behind the trees that lined the road, and in his hands he carried both trunks, one atop the other, as if they weighed nothing more than ounces. Incredible strength.

She moved her gaze from him to regard the freshly

painted trellis as he stepped past the gate and onto the
stone path.

"Open the door?" he requested in a solid voice lacking
any sign of strain.

God, what was wrong with her? She should have done
that already. Appearing to be a gawking, witless Frenchwoman was not at all how she wanted to begin their
working relationship. He'd wonder at her competence.

Forcing a confidence she didn't feel at all, she lifted
her valise with one hand and reached for the knob with
the other, pushing the door open easily, then stepping
quickly to the side to allow him ample room to enter.

She followed him into the cottage, finding it at first
glance to be more spacious than it appeared from the
outside. Past the small foyer, vacant but for a brass coat-
rack, she entered the parlor, the only visible room for
entertaining, decorated sparsely in shades of brown and
green. In the center, facing the grate on the west wall,
sat an ordinary sofa in muted teal brocade, beside which
rested the only chair, also of the same material, high-
backed and padded generously, with a matching footstool in front of it. There were no paintings on the floral
papered walls, although long windows took up most of
the space along the north wall to her right. The hard-
wood floors were also bare save for the brown oval rug
running the length of the sofa in front of the grate, held
in place by a sturdy but ornately carved oak tea table.
Between the sofa and chair, on top of a matching end
table, sat a marvelous chess set, chiseled beautifully in
coral and brown marble—the only thing in the room
besides a few potted plants and scattered books that
made the cottage actually look lived in.

Thomas rounded the corner to his left when he entered, continued down a short hallway, and disappeared
into a room she assumed would be hers. She noticed a

narrow staircase leading to the second floor on her immediate left, and underneath it, at the edge of the hall, a doorway opening to the kitchen. She stood silently where she was, waiting for an invitation to sit, although she knew this was now essentially her place of residence, too.

It was much smaller than her home in Marseille where she lived alone, and she saw no servants here, another essential to which she was probably far too accustomed. In Marseille she had only one personal maid, the very efficient Marie-Camille, who took care of meals, the house, and even her wardrobe. Normally Marie-Camille traveled with her, but the instructions from Sir Riley had forbidden that. She would have to make do on her own in Winter Garden.

Thomas returned after only moments, his head almost touching the ceiling as he ducked to keep from hitting a beam with his forehead. This appeared to be out of habit, though, since his eyes were once again focused solely on her.

"The room on the right is yours," he informed her quietly. "Beth Barkley, the vicar's daughter, comes in every other day to cook meals, clean, and collect the laundry. I had her put clean sheets on your bed this morning."

"I see." She pulled her blue leather gloves from her fingers, still feeling mildly uncomfortable for reasons unknown to her. At least he didn't appear to witness her discomfiture. "And where do you sleep, Thomas?"

He stopped about three feet from her, hands on hips, apparently finding no underlying significance to her question. "I've taken the room upstairs. You'll have plenty of privacy. The water closet is next to your room, at the end of the hall. We have no tub for bathing, but the local inn charges a minimal fee for the use of theirs, and it's clean."

She attempted a smile and began to unbutton her cloak. "Thank you." She really wished he would stop looking at her with such hard, assessing eyes, as if he didn't recognize at all how feminine she was but instead found her . . . something of a contradiction, maybe? Certainly Sir Riley had told him what to expect of her. Yet he appeared to be studying her closely rather than admiring any part of her.

"Would you like tea?" he asked politely, cutting into her thoughts.

"Yes, please," was her quick response as she lifted her cloak from her shoulders.

He reached out and took it and her gloves without comment, only briefly scanning her figure clothed in an ordinary traveling gown of sky-blue muslin. Then he turned and disappeared into the hallway once more.

Madeleine shook herself and breathed in fully, trying to relax, fighting a tired, aching head and binding stays that had been wrapped around her middle for nearly ten hours. She needed to keep her mind clear and remember her purpose. She was here on government business, and so was he. His thoughts of her, his impression of her person, were irrelevant. Where he was concerned she couldn't understand herself either, or her reactions to him upon first meeting. Usually, when choosing male companionship, she preferred dashing, sophisticated men of gentle breeding. Thomas Blackwood was unlike any she'd ever been attracted to before, yet that in itself intrigued her.

She heard him rattling dishes in the kitchen but didn't feel like walking in there herself. What would she say to him? Of course, they had plenty to discuss, but she felt more comfortable letting him lead the conversation, which he would undoubtedly do over tea. And she was far too restless to simply retire to her own room so early in the day.

Instead, Madeleine entered the parlor proper. She liked the spacious feel of it, surprisingly light and airy considering the dark furniture, and windows that only faced north and west. The embers in the fireplace were low but would soon be stirred, coal added, to warm the house for the coming evening. Above the grate, on the mantel, she noticed a gold-faced clock indicating the time was nearly four, and next to it what appeared to be a wooden music box. She wondered if these were his things, if anything in the room was his. Certainly the chess set was. She didn't know this for a fact, but the hardness of it, the solitude it implied, seemed to suit what little she knew of him.

She stopped in front of the set and picked up a brown marble knight, rolling it between her thumb and fingers. It felt heavy, cold, sturdily sculpted. Yes, this was his.

At the sound of his booted feet on the hard wooden floor she looked up. He walked into the room carrying a silver tray complete with china teapot and matching cups on saucers, a sugar bowl and pitcher of cream. He looked straight at her, into her eyes again, his expression flat and unreadable.

She sank slowly onto the sofa, holding his gaze and trying not to smile at the picture he presented—the enormous, warrior god-man, dark and sensually arousing, carrying a tray to serve tea to her personally. Instead, she maintained a neutral expression and managed a general question. "Who owns this cottage, Thomas?"

His brows rose fractionally. "I'm not certain." He set the tray in the center of the tea table, reached for the pot, and poured two cups, placing one in front of her. "Sir Riley offered me only the key and directions. The few things in this room are mine that I brought with me from home. The bedroom furnishings and kitchen items were here when I arrived."

Madeleine adjusted the hem of her skirt, pulling it in so he could take a seat in the chair next to her without stepping on it. He lowered himself stiffly, cup and saucer in hand, regarding her.

"Then you're not from here," she commented rather than asked, keeping her eyes fixed on his face.

"I'm from Eastleigh, several hours to the north of here," he returned without pause or pretense. "I've been to Winter Garden twice on holiday, although it's been six or seven years since my last visit. I knew nobody when I arrived this time, but I've managed to meet several people and make some acquaintances during the last few weeks."

"I suppose that will be helpful to our cause," she responded thoughtfully.

"Mmm."

An awkward moment passed silently. She glanced back to the marble piece she still held in her palm. "You're a chess player, Thomas?"

He raised his cup to his lips, taking a small sip of his steaming tea. "I play frequently. It helps me think, sometimes to relax."

His tone had dropped as her questioning grew personal, but she ignored the significance. "I imagine you play with someone from the village, then?"

He was quiet for so long she felt compelled to raise her gaze back to his. Almost at once his expression had become clouded, intense.

"Only with myself, Madeleine," he answered through a low, thick breath. "I've had no one to play with for quite some time."

She had absolutely no idea how to take that, feeling

warm suddenly from the closeness of his body and the
heat of his eyes. Did he have any idea how suggestive
that sounded to her? Like a secret, sensual remark between lovers. Without question, she knew that if they
were in a room with ten people she would be the only
one to find that statement erotic. Was he thinking the
same?

He watched her, his sculpted lips pulled back vaguely
in challenge, his eyelids lowered just faintly. The muscles in her belly tightened, but she couldn't turn away.
Oh, yes. He knew. He knew exactly what he'd said, and
he knew exactly how she'd interpret it.

"Do you play?" he questioned, his voice dark, quiet.

Madeleine blinked quickly and straightened, turning
her attention to the chessboard beside her, very gently
replacing the marble knight. "I can, although it's been a
while since I have," she admitted with a diffidence that
surprised her. "I assume you're good, Thomas?"

"I'm very good."

She hesitated. "Do you . . . usually win?"

"My skills haven't failed me yet."

He hadn't touched her at all, and yet she felt him, felt
his puncturing stare—blatant, probing, daring.

"I think I might enjoy the challenge," she conceded
quietly, looking back at his face with forced candor.
"But perhaps you should know I also play to win."

He lengthened his body in his chair, stretching one
booted leg out to rest on the footstool. "And do you?"

"Win?"

He nodded negligibly.

She fidgeted on the sofa cushion, running a moist
palm slowly along her thigh over her gown. "Usually,"
she confided, her throat dry, tight.

For a fleeting moment she was certain he almost
smiled, something she had yet to see him do. Then he

brought his cup to his lips again with slow, calculated precision, taking a long sip, never averting his eyes from hers.

"I'm sure you'd agree," he said seconds later, "that it's always better when both players have the opportunity to win, to keep the game . . . mutually enjoyable." He paused, then added in a soothing whisper, "I think it would be fascinating to watch the jubilation on your face when you do, Madeleine."

She couldn't believe he had said that and she couldn't take any more. The room felt stuffy to her suddenly, thick with a tension she couldn't describe. She wished she had a fan. But it was nearly winter. The heat she felt was entirely from within, brought out by a man she hardly knew as he caressed her with innocent words having vivid, sexual meaning they both clearly understood. All in the guise of playing chess.

The clock on the mantel chimed four, startling her. Madeleine was the first to look away, quickly reaching for her tea, stirring in a trace amount of sugar and cream with uncommonly graceless fingers, taking special note of the intricate detail in tiny purple tulips etched into the dainty china cups.

"Would you like to hear about our assignment?"

She felt jittery in her skin, but he'd become indifferent again, almost formal. He was good at this, she considered, and obviously quite the expert in masking his thoughts, feelings, and probably his emotions. She read that in him immediately. She was good at it, too, but he did seem to have the advantage when it came to the time it took to compose himself. Certainly he wasn't flushing as she was right now, something he no doubt witnessed. For a second or two she wondered if he'd been as stimulated by the exchange as she had, but it was difficult to tell and she tried not to think about it.

"Please," she replied, laying her spoon on the saucer.

He placed his cup and saucer on the table and sat back, leaning his elbow on the chair's padded armrest. "How much do you know already?"

She shrugged, taking a sudden great interest in her steaming tea as she lifted her cup and lightly sipped. "Only that there is a rumor of smuggling activity operating from or through Winter Garden. Beyond that, I know nothing."

Cautiously he asked, "What did Riley Liddle tell you about me?"

She glanced at him sideways through her lashes as she took another swallow. What remained of the setting sun shone through the west window, casting a stream of light across his face and body, the scar at this mouth. A thick, dark curl hung low over his forehead, but he didn't appear to notice these things, remaining curiously focused on her.

Madeleine placed her cup and saucer next to his on the table, then angled her body so that she faced him directly, folding her hands properly in her lap, trying her best to push from her mind the sexual thoughts brought out only moments ago. As he apparently had.

"He said only that you were a large man, thirty-nine years old. That you have been living here at the cottage for several weeks without learning anything. That you requested help and would be the one to give me details. That's all really. I only saw him for a few minutes yesterday."

"I see." He rubbed the backs of his fingers along his chin, scratching the skin with his day's growth of beard. "Do you know what's being smuggled?"

Her brows rose. "No, although I assume it to be something important or valuable. I'd never be requested to come here from the south of France to investigate a trivial matter."

"Opium," he revealed quietly.

Madeleine stilled as a cold darkness swept through her. Of all the memories of her childhood to leave a lasting black impression, her experiences with the effects of opium abuse caused the greatest pain. But he didn't need to know that.

"Opium," she repeated softly. "How does one smuggle something legal to own and conveniently purchased?"

"By stealing it randomly, before it's properly taxed and distributed." He grew focused as he collected his thoughts to carry on. "Our suspicions first surfaced about eighteen months ago when it came to our attention that very small supplies were disappearing soon after arrival in Portsmouth. Intelligence was slow to start an investigation because the amount taken was not, in the beginning, worth the effort. During the last four or five months, however, this amount has steadily increased to a point that it can no longer be ignored. The loss is becoming valuable. So, an official inquiry began, but after a few weeks of learning nothing, the decision was made to send me here to integrate myself into the town and work covertly."

Intrigued, Madeleine sat forward, forearms laying flat along her thighs, hands folded together. "They think the opium is being smuggled through Winter Garden?"

He leaned toward her over the armrest, eyes bright, face taut. "The trail leads to the *vicinity* of Winter Garden, where it subsequently vanishes. Normally we should be able to see activity, or hear something useful through infiltration and boastful gossip, but so far nothing." His lids narrowed shrewdly. "I think the opium is being brought here because the village is unsuspecting, and once here it's divided and transported north into England proper for sale and distribution. The reasons are unclear, and we're completely ignorant of the means, but we believe whoever is taking the risk is selling it to be smoked, not drunk, and that he—or perhaps even she—is making a profit by selling to a select clientele. I also believe that the operation is maintained, or at the very least organized, by someone who lives here permanently, since shipments have been taken during summer months. But the two questions yet to be answered are who, and how this person is able to carry out the dispersion in absolute secrecy."

Madeleine reached again for her tea, starting to feel the slow burn of anticipation envelop her as it did so often at the beginning of a new assignment. "Since the opium is stolen, it's undoubtedly a lucrative operation for the supplier," she speculated aloud, staring at the table in front of her. "He wouldn't take such a great risk otherwise, and because there is no initial expenditure, the income from the sale would be entirely his. But he is not working alone. The process is too complicated." She took a long sip from her cup. "He is aware of shipments coming into port, organizes the theft, somehow arranges for it to be brought here, then ships it out again to sell to those in need, for either a low cost or the price of discretion. Maybe both. And if his clients are addicted, and wealthy, the income could be substantial." She looked back at him, eyes sparkling. "Remarkable operation. And smart."

"It's also very dangerous."

She agreed with a nod. "So he must be quite arrogant or desperate. Any suspects?"

Thomas sat back once more, relaxing as he studied her. "I've got two of them, but no proof, and I'm not sure how to go about getting it. That's why I requested assistance."

"I see." She leaned her shoulder on the soft sofa cushion and swallowed the rapidly cooling contents of her cup. "And they are?"

"Lady Claire Childress, a widow whose husband died of mysterious causes two years ago. And Richard Sharon, Baron Rothebury."

Her lips turned up in droll amusement. "A lady and a baron—both members of the gentry."

He tilted his head, his thick brows lifting in question. "You don't think the aristocracy can be as deceptive and greedy as the middle and lower classes, Madeleine?"

She smiled fully at that, beginning, for the first time since they'd met, to feel comfortable in his presence. "I know from experience that they can, Thomas. In fact, they usually have more opportunity and desire for riches since they are closer at grasping those things, especially if they have come from wealth and have somehow lost it. It's also true that anyone can cheaply buy laudanum, but not everyone of good birth wants an addiction to be known. It's likely that the smuggler is selling to his, or her, social class."

He dropped his chin in acknowledgment of her reasonable deductions. "My thoughts exactly."

A warmth of communication passed between them. "Why these two?"

He paused to consider that. "Lady Claire is . . . harsh. You'll understand when you meet her. It wouldn't be above her to lead a group of smugglers, but that's just my opinion. She recently began refurbishing her estate, although she's had only a small income provided her by her late husband. I don't know where she's getting the money to do so." He pursed his lips, thinking, then said softly, "I also think she's an addict."

The partial smile died on her mouth. Madeleine turned to face the tea table, gently placing her empty cup and saucer on top of it as thoughts and memories she'd so long kept hidden deep within came gushing to the surface, surprising her with an intensity she thought had cooled. "And the baron?" she carried on, voice steady, giving nothing away.

He pulled his leg up from the footstool and planted both feet on the floor to sit forward, elbows on knees, fingers tapping together in front of him. "The baron is a more likely suspect," he disclosed, finally moving his gaze from her and resting it on the fireplace. "Partly because he's a mystery and smooth as oil. I met him only once. He didn't like me, although I'm not sure why."

"Perhaps you intimidate him," she offered more seriously than jovially.

"Rothebury is certainly nothing like me," he acknowledged with a trace of annoyance. "He's handsome, charming, full of good humor. The ladies adore him. He's also thirty-two years old, unmarried, and considered Winter Garden's most eligible prize."

Madeleine eyed him candidly. "Is that why I was sent for, Thomas?"

He turned his head sharply and stared hard at her. "No."

The force of that one quietly spoken word took her a little by surprise. In truth, during all the years she'd worked for the government she'd never used her body for information. Her charms absolutely, but her body never. She'd been with her share of men, but never for personal or professional gain of any kind. It soothed her a little to know Thomas Blackwood didn't expect this of her, and had even seemed a bit irritated that she'd mentioned it.

"You are to work with me, Madeleine," he explained coolly. "I need the help of a professional, and being a woman is an advantage on two fronts. First, you'll be more perceptive where Lady Claire is concerned. Second, the baron will be more receptive to you. Flirt if you must, but don't consider compromising yourself. It's not worth it."

His concern for her was a little overwhelming, and quite unnecessary. "I'm very good at taking care of myself," she maintained, composed and sitting erect. "I think I can handle the baron."

He continued to regard her for a moment or two, then looked back to the grate, apparently deciding not to argue.

"You can start with Lady Claire," he said at last. "If we can rule her out as a suspect, we can work on the baron with fresh energy."

"And you?"

"I'm going to concentrate on Rothebury's property, his house, and get closer to it and him if I can without being observed. I want to determine his doings and dealings, who visits regularly and at what time of day."

"Spy on him rather than integrate yourself into his life," she said pensively. "Is that prudent under the circumstances?"

His lips drew back into a half smile. "He'll never become a friend, if that's what you mean, so I can't have a go at him from that angle. The man has no close friends and keeps the villagers at a distance to a certain degree unless he's formally entertaining many at once. I've stayed in the background until now, just getting acquainted with the area and people, but since you're here to help, I think we can finally move in and become a little more aggressive in approach."

That was logical, she supposed, although the risk of

being discovered was always greater when working in shadow rather than in open, friendly confrontation.

"Have you given thought to my identity?"

He hesitated just long enough for her to realize he had, and that he was uncomfortable with it. That piqued her curiosity.

"Thomas?"

With his hands on his thighs, he pushed himself to a standing position, very stiffly, and she took note of the tiny grimace along the lines of his mouth, through the tightness of his jaw. His injuries pained him, perhaps only a little, but pained him they did.

"I've given it considerable thought, Madeleine," he quietly replied, walking slowly to the mantel, peering down to the music box, running his fingertips along the wooden edge. Seconds later he turned back to her. "Have you?"

She hadn't expected him to ask her, accepting instead that he would have it planned and ready to adopt. He seemed intent on her opinion, though, and maybe it was something they could decide together.

Standing to meet his gaze levelly, she murmured, "I thought perhaps a companion of some kind, but you're really a bit too . . . robust to need one. After meeting you that doesn't seem plausible."

His cheek twitched in mild amusement. "No."

She gave him a dash of a smile in return as she looked his enormous, masculine body up and down. The top half of him was in perfect shape, but he did have a limp, an obvious injury, one undoubtedly noticed by villagers. Posing as his nurse might be believed, although she didn't really look like much of one. Still, it was the best she could think of.

"Your mistress?" she suggested instead in a deep whisper.

She had no idea where that had come from. Neither did he. He actually looked stunned.

Madeleine reached up with one hand and covered her throat with her palm, hoping he couldn't see the pounding pulse she could feel beneath her fingertips, wrapping herself with her free arm in a measure of defense. But she never took her eyes from his face.

His lids thinned, and once again she felt that same strange magnetic pull from him, charging the air between them, palpable and thick.

"I don't think that would be believed, either, Madeleine," he whispered huskily, and very slowly.

She was on the verge of asking why, as it seemed perfectly reasonable to her, when he carried on with a more logical concern.

"It might also give us problems socially, and we need to be free to accept invitations."

She should have considered that before blurting her thoughts. Word would spread that they lived together and alone, however, and eventually people would suspect a deeper involvement between them. Certainly he'd thought of that.

"Of course, you're right," she agreed with a shade of embarrassment. She sighed, sagging a little. "Have you any ideas, Thomas?"

He stared sharply into her eyes with obvious reluctance. Then he groaned softly and raised a palm, wiping it harshly over his face.

"I fought in the Opium War, Madeleine," he revealed soberly. "That's where I received my injuries." He shifted his body uncomfortably on the rug. "I thought maybe you could pose as the French translator of my memoirs."

Sympathy coursed through her. She understood so intimately the pain of a past one could never change.

He'd fought in a war of questionable merit, sustaining injuries that had left him maimed, and he'd been averse to tell her. And the Opium War had ended six years ago, which meant that if his legs hadn't healed by now, he would live with his suffering for the rest of his life. Tragic, and yet he carried on, just as she had in her life when faced with misery.

"You don't really look much like a translator," he proceeded when she didn't comment, "but it's the best I can think of. Certainly better than posing as a companion, and it will probably be believed."

You're right, Madeleine thought with mounting confusion, clasping her hands behind her back. *I don't look like a companion or a translator. I look like a mistress. Why haven't you noticed that about me, Thomas?*

"I agree that makes the most sense of all, and should be convincing enough," she remarked aloud, feeling somewhat defeated. "I will be your French translator."

He stood only a few feet from her, their bodies divided by just the tea table. He searched her expression for several silent seconds, with a deliberation she could feel, then ever so slowly he dropped his gaze to her breasts, lingering there long enough for her to grow warm from the visual caress.

"I'm sure you're hungry," he said abruptly. "I'll see what Beth arranged for dinner, and perhaps we'll eat early." Without further comment, he turned away from her and walked toward the kitchen.

Madeleine watched his back until he disappeared from view, finally allowing a wide grin of frank satisfaction to grace her face. His sexual innuendoes earlier could have been misinterpreted on her part, but now she was certain they weren't. At last it was obvious that he'd noticed her as a woman.

•   •   •

The wind had grown to a roaring pitch, causing tree branches to scrape against the cottage's brick walls, slamming the shutters against his window. Thomas was oblivious to it all.

He lay flat on his back in bed, only the sheet covering his body, hands behind his head on the pillow as he stared vacantly at the ceiling. He'd been in this position for nearly an hour, too restless to relax, too absorbed in his thoughts to move. She was probably already asleep, as she'd been very tired during dinner, eating only a little. They'd talked of trivial things—her home in Marseille, her trip to England, the climate differences between the countries. Then she'd said goodnight and had retired for the evening. He'd remained sitting in front of the fire for a while, listening to her footsteps as she moved around her room, imagining her manicured fingers unbuttoning her gown, her petticoats slipping from her tall, curved body. He'd heard her bed creak as she climbed into it. He had wondered what, if anything, she wore when she slept; if she braided her hair or wore it down; if she lay between the sheets opened sensually, as if waiting for a man, or curled up from the chill like a soft kitten aching to be stroked.

God, she was beautiful. He'd known that, though, before she'd arrived, knew much more about her, in fact, than she knew of him. Born Madeleine Bilodeau twenty-nine years ago, the illegitimate daughter of Captain Frederick Stevens of the British Royal Navy, and Eleanora Bilodeau, a less than talented, opium-addicted actress of the French stage. She'd become a spy for the British government at her request after disbelieving Englishmen disregarded her until she'd single-handedly prevented the escape of two French political prisoners by informing Sir Riley before it occurred. She'd proven her worth over the years. She was glamorized in England by those who knew about her, adored in Marseille, and celebrated across the Continent as one of the greatest beauties of their time.

He didn't know how long she'd stood behind him in the garden that afternoon before he'd realized she was there. She'd been watching him, he was sure of that. Her scent had reached him first as the breeze lifted her perfume and mixed it with the particular essence that made her a woman, carrying it to him, rousing him, making his heart pound. It had taken moments to gain control before he could look at her. When he'd finally gathered the nerve to do so, she had entranced him instantly with her glossy, chestnut hair coiled around her ears in thick plaits, her heart-shaped face so soft in an expression of innocent question, her flawless, ivory skin that begged to be caressed. And those eyes. Her eyes shattered resolve—ice-blue but the most sensual thing about her somehow. Eyes that could cut and wound deeply, or melt a man as they shimmered in pools of longing arousal, vivid hope.

Oh, yes, he'd been immediately affected by her, as any man would be. And, God, the conversation over chess! How had he started that?

Thomas expelled a long, slow breath, turning on his side at last and shoving his arm beneath the pillow, staring at the swaying trees as they moved in shadow across the moonlit wall.

He'd never expected to be so forward with her and yet she'd caught his mood, had been so perceptive as to understand the meaning behind his words. He knew she'd lost her virginity years ago, and had spent time in the company of men far more charming and attentive than he, far more exciting, far more worthy of her beauty. But she had responded to his sexual suggestions, regarding him with a confused fascination she couldn't hide, gauging his response, teasing him in return without really trying to, making his body succumb to that delicious ache as it hadn't in years.

She was attracted to him. He knew it and relished that knowledge in wonder. Madeleine DuMais, the belle of France, the darling of the English government, the smart, polished, engaging woman, who had sat across from him at dinner and licked her fingers so sensually of honey, was attracted to him. To *him*—Thomas Blackwood the ordinary man; Thomas Blackwood the huge, intimidating recluse; Thomas Blackwood the cripple.

She was attracted to him.

Smiling, Thomas closed his eyes and, for the first time in ages, fell into a deep, restful slumber—no pain in his body, no thirst in his soul, no hurt in his heart.

Two

Madeleine woke badly. Her head ached, her nose was stuffy, her body freezing, and for seconds she had trouble remembering where she was. Perhaps her momentary confusion was due to the fact that a murky darkness filled the room, and the cottage seemed unnaturally silent. The wind had died down sometime during the night, and unlike her warm house and bed in Marseille, with the sound of street traffic always just below her bedroom window, she heard only the creaks of the cottage itself as it settled into the damp earth.

It had to be mid-morning, although she had no idea of the time, probably due to the thick, overcast sky she could barely discern through her bedroom window. Usually Marie-Camille woke her by seven if she didn't wake herself. Nobody would rouse her here, however, and Thomas certainly would never enter her room.

Since the moment she'd stepped foot on British soil just three days ago, she'd had little time to contemplate her immediate situation and surroundings. She was back in England and essentially alone. Although accustomed to solitude, her life in recent years had been spent in the company of others, albeit only because her work had put her there. At home she was known in social circles, granted invitations as the respectable Widow DuMais, an acquaintance to many, friend to few—all ignorant of her deep-seated hatred for her French heritage and the childhood of near servitude she was forced to endure at the hands of an ignorant, ill-bred mother. But that seemed another life to her now.

In England, she was unknown, which, as she thought about it, could be a challenge or an asset in the weeks to come. She could create her own character and be any person she chose, using her charms or subduing them. Above everything else, though, she was a professional, and would be exactly who she needed to be to accomplish this mission for the love of her father's country. It was time to go to work.

Shivering from the damp, chilly air, Madeleine pushed back the sheet and blanket and slowly sat upright, rubbing her pounding temples and brows with her fingertips. Tea would help the head pain; but, of course, she'd need to dress fully before entering the kitchen.

At last she forced her eyes to remain open, placed her bare feet on the cold floor, and stood on stiff legs. Her room was small, with only a bed for one and a petite dressing table, painted white, with a raised mirror attached to it to accommodate her toilette. The walls were papered with the same flowered print that lined the walls of the parlor, but nothing hung from them. The only window, draped with white lace curtains, framed the head of the bed, and a full wardrobe closet sat across the floor at the foot of it.

Closing her arms around her shivering body, Madeleine walked to it. She'd only brought four gowns with her—one for traveling that she'd worn yesterday, one

morning gown, one for day, and one for evening dress.
Unfortunately she had had no room to carry a full wardrobe all the way from France, and suddenly she felt unduly conscious about that. She would be wearing the
same gowns again and again. Not very flattering, but
then Thomas hadn't appeared to notice what she wore.
The villagers would expect nothing more from a translator.

Madeleine discarded her linen nightgown and dressed
quickly in her morning gown of canary-yellow muslin
over full crinoline. The sleeves were long, the neckline
modest though tightly molding to her bosom, which
pleased her since that was the only part of her anatomy
Thomas had seemed to regard, however briefly. She
looked becoming but unassuming, and for the first time
in her life she was grateful for the layers of petticoats
against her skin that warmed her body.

She brushed her hair, plaited it, then wrapped it in
loops around her ears. At home she was used to wearing
face color to accentuate her features, but she supposed
she'd have to abandon that indulgence in Winter Garden.
The English were rather staid about the application of
false color, preferring their ladies to look pale and flat
instead of ripe and sensuous. Sexless in her opinion, but
then her opinion hardly mattered. She'd no doubt get a
better response from the villagers if she chose to forgo
even rouge.

Madeleine splashed her face with cold water from the
pitcher, dried herself with a soft face towel, pinched her
cheeks, and gently bit her lips. Then with shoulders back
she left the privacy of her room and walked into the
parlor.

It was dark save for the light from the roaring fire and
one small lamp. Thomas sat in the chair, facing the grate,
his head bowed, his mind engrossed in a book of

considerable thickness. In this position, poised with one leg resting on the footstool, his body clothed in black trousers and a white linen shirt buttoned to the neck, he looked casual but every bit the gentleman scholar he professed to be.

He turned when he heard her footsteps, his gaze scanning her attire then meeting hers with approval. She brushed off the sudden, overpowering feeling of being scrutinized within and smiled into his eyes. Just a simple look from him gave her pause.

"Good morning, Thomas," she said congenially, hands folded in front of her as she moved toward him.

"Good morning, Madeleine," he replied in a voice of deep smoothness.

She pulled her gaze from his to glance at the clock on the mantel. Half-past nine. She'd overslept by hours. "I'm sorry I woke so late," she said, sitting comfortably on the sofa and arranging her skirts. "Usually I'm up very early."

He closed his book without looking at it. "I'm sure you were tired after several days of travel. Did you sleep well?" he asked politely.

"Yes, very well, thank you." That was a lie he could probably read through. Feeling the tension ease from her shoulders, she leaned heavily against the sofa back. "Actually my head aches, and I was rather cold."

For once he looked amused. "I'll find you another blanket for tonight. In the meantime let's get you some tea. Then we'll walk the grounds." He placed his book, *The Complete Works of Alexander Pope*, on the table in front of him, then pushed himself up to a standing position. "The fresh air might help your head as well, and Richard Sharon takes his morning ride at about ten. He'll be in the distance, but you'll get a good enough look at him. Then we'll talk about plans for today. If you're feeling up to it, of course."

He was attending to business already, seemingly unaware of her desire to start the day slowly or perhaps to just engage in a few minutes of intimate conversation. But she could think of nothing to say for the moment that would be of a more casual or personal tone, which left her to do nothing but follow his lead.

She gave him another vague smile. "I'm sure I'll be fine."

"Good."

He walked toward the kitchen, and she stood again, trailing him into the room boldly painted in colors of bright yellow and leaf green. The sink had been placed in front of one of the large, wide windows, having its own well-water supply—rather a luxury for them as they wouldn't have to haul it into the cottage from the village well. Nestled against the far wall was the stove and next to it a small, square table of dark pine surrounded by four chairs. The scullery took up the space under the staircase that led to the second floor.

They would have no servants, he'd informed her last night, for the simple reason that they wouldn't be able to talk candidly with others in the house. That meant, of course, that although the vicar's daughter would do the cooking, it would be up to them to set the meals and clean up after themselves. The good thing for her was that Thomas seemed ready enough to help and didn't expect her to wait on him. Unusual for a man, but again, she supposed they were partners, not a married couple or even just lovers. Their relationship was nothing more than functional, and she wondered for an instant why she had to keep telling herself that.

Thomas put the kettle on, and she helped herself to thick bread and raspberry jam. They sat together at the table for a few minutes, discussing with casual reference the dreary weather of the day and the general changes in season. Then he left her sitting alone to eat in silence, returning a few moments later wearing his own black twine coat and carrying her cloak in his hands.

"I put your gloves in the pockets. I thought you could first just carry your mug and let the tea warm your bare hands."

"Thank you," she murmured, licking her lips of jam, noticing with satisfaction that he focused on the movement. She repeated it, unnecessarily and quite without intention—at least she thought so—and a slight frown creased his brows.

"The water is boiling, Thomas," she said very softly.

His gaze shot back to hers, held it for a breath, uncomfortable in assessment, which she found uniquely gratifying. Then he apparently caught himself and swiftly looked away, laying her cloak across the chair and turning his attention to the stove.

Madeleine finished eating, watching as he poured her mug nearly to the brim, adding sugar and cream for her as he'd obviously observed her do yesterday.

Seconds later he placed her mug on the table in front of her and reached once more for her cloak. "Are you ready?"

She nodded and stood, turning her back to him, and he draped it over her shoulders. She buttoned the front and then reached for her tea.

Together they walked out the front door and into the cold, gray morning. The chill stung her cheeks, but with her body wrapped in her fur-lined cloak and her hands and fingers clutching her hot mug, Madeleine felt relatively warm on the inside.

Thomas led her along the side of the cottage and into the garden area where they'd met yesterday. She followed a pace or two behind his slow but steady stride as he moved to the rear of the enclosed property. She could see nothing in front of her but trees and a wall of thick brush, although he knew exactly where to go. Finally he stopped at the edge of the cluster of bushes he'd been clearing yesterday.

"You'll need to hold my hand," he remarked matter-of-factly.

She looked up to his face. His gaze was once again forthright and unreadable, features neutral, as he held his palm out for her. She had never touched him physically, and she hesitated before doing so, for reasons not entirely clear to her. And yet, for him, it seemed a decidedly necessary action, meaning nothing of any significance whatever.

She extended her left hand, but immediately they both realized she couldn't step through the trees and bushes in her wide skirts without lifting them. Devoid of comment, he reached for her mug, gently pulled it from her grasp, then took her hand with his free one, wrapping his fingers solidly around hers. The contact was wholly unremarkable yet struck her with overt awareness. She held to him tightly, pretending indifference to his warmth and strength as she raised her skirts and followed him.

She stepped cautiously along the narrow path well concealed in dense forest and covered with brown, moist leaves, avoiding mud as best she could, and within a few yards they came to another opening. Thomas pulled her through after him, and as he moved his broad form to enlarge her view, Madeleine found herself in a clearing of breathtaking loveliness.

She stood at the edge of a small lake, shining a vivid dark blue, surrounded on all sides by bare oak and maple trees, and luscious green pines. To her immediate right she noticed a wooden bench, weathered but sturdy, facing the water in an enchanting spot where one could sit to enjoy the peacefulness of summer or winter, listening to the wind through the trees, the lapping shore, birdsong.

"It's beautiful," she whispered, still clinging to his hand.

"Yes."

Madeleine glanced up. He watched her intently for a second or two, his hair hanging low over his dark brow, his warm eyes crinkled in a privately felt satisfaction. Then he leaned very close to her.

"That's Rothebury's manor house," he said, nodding toward the opposite shore. "He lives there year-round, and each morning at about ten he rides along the perimeter of the property, which encompasses the entire southern edge of the lake and stretches all the way up here to the left. The path takes him near the water, and he should be coming along shortly."

Madeleine carefully surveyed the home in the distance, assessing detail. She only saw the top of it through the trees but could tell it was old, three stories in height, made of light brown stone, solid of structure, and that it faced the water. From her vantage point it looked well tended and larger than most of the homes she'd seen in Winter Garden thus far, although the owner being a baron and permanently living in the area would explain that.

Gently Thomas pulled her toward the bench. She stepped lightly on grass and leaves then sat gracefully on the hard, wooden seat, adjusting her body and skirts to give him ample room to join her. It was then that he finally released her hand, offering back her tea at the same time, then squeezing in beside her. She lifted the mug to her lips, taking a swallow or two, feeling his

eyes on her but avoiding them with her own as she gazed
out over the water.

"I've accepted an invitation on your behalf for Thursday afternoon," he continued formally. "Mrs. Sarah Rodney, the town historian, is hosting a gathering of local
ladies for tea. She does this once a month or so, and
members of the gentry and those of adequate social class
are always invited. I called on her several days ago for
something insignificant, with the underlying intention of
informing her of your arrival. And, of course, she said
she'd be delighted to meet you." His tone lightened in
conspiratorial amusement as he dropped his head close
to hers. "Naturally, the invitation stems from Mrs. Rodney's curiosity more than anything else. There will be
plenty of gossip for you to garner, and they'll all wonder
about you since the only information I supplied Mrs.
Rodney is that you are French."

She glanced up at him again. He was sitting very near
to her on the bench, the edge of his muscled thigh lost
beneath the folds of her gown; his shoulder brushing
hers; his eyes bright with anticipation; his thick, dark
hair still hanging loosely over his brow, which he didn't
appear to notice. Madeleine's breath quickened from
nothing more than his proximity, his deeply smooth
voice and the virility he exuded with his overpowering
stature. She wasn't used to such a sudden sexual awareness of a man, and frankly didn't understand her body's
response to this one in particular.

"It sounds as if I will be enlightened," she replied with
only half interest in the topic, clinging to her cup, and
the hope that he'd not realize how taken with him she
had become in one short day.

His forehead creased in frown. "Have you something
appropriate to wear? I didn't think of that."

His pragmatic concern waylaid her fears, and she

smiled wryly. Just like a man not to recognize the attraction. "I brought one gown for each possible social occasion, but with minimal trunk space I could only carry three of them in addition to the one I wore yesterday." Without thought, she admitted, "You will likely tire of seeing me wear the same things repeatedly."

"I doubt it," he countered very quickly.

That small compliment, coming from his mouth in honest disclosure, warmed her more than the tea in her hands. She stared into his eyes, almost brazenly watching him as he gradually became aware of what he'd said. Then he grew serious and looked away. "A translator wouldn't have a spectacular wardrobe anyway. It will better fit your role if you appear less sophisticated and extravagant."

A marvelously reasonable answer, she mused; and what she herself had rationally considered.

"As for today," he continued before she could comment, "I thought we could walk through the village so that you can get a feel of it and learn something about the area, perhaps even call on one or two prominent residents."

"A very good idea," she agreed pleasantly, taking another sip of her tea. Slowly she lowered her cup, studying the creamy liquid for a moment in contemplation. "Thomas, we've been together for nearly a day, sleeping under the same roof, taking meals at the same table, and yet we have discussed nothing more than our assignment and the weather." She paused for effect, then added, "Don't you think we should learn a few things about each other if we are to be living together indefinitely?"

He turned back to her, and she raised her lashes to peer into his eyes, offering him a small, challenging smile.

"What would you like to know?" he asked pensively.

She was really hoping for more than that. "Are you married?" she inquired, trying to keep the tension from her voice and knowing that the question had been driven by agonizing curiosity on her part. It surprised him, too, but she really knew that only intuitively.

"No," he murmured in quiet diffidence, "although I was once."

Her eyes grew round with interest she couldn't hide. She was also thankfully relieved he couldn't possibly be aware of her enormous satisfaction.

"I see," she responded sedately, hoping he'd clarify. He didn't disappoint.

Breathing deeply, he leaned forward on the bench, elbows on knees, rubbing his fingers together to ward off the cold as he shifted his focus to the lake. "Her name was Bernadette. She died twelve years ago, giving birth to my stillborn daughter. I have one living child, William, now fifteen, who's enrolled in a Viennese boarding school." Faintly he concluded, "There's really nothing else about me to know personally. I fought in the war, I work for the government now, and I live a very quiet life in Eastleigh."

"I suppose you miss your son," she said rather than asked. "And your wife."

"I miss my son every day," he admitted through a sigh, "but he's a gifted violinist and needs to be where the great tutors are if he is to become great himself. Sometimes I miss my wife as well, but she's been gone for a long time."

Madeleine grew cautious. She didn't want to pry and yet she fully believed there was more to him than he chose to disclose. He was a complex man, that much she'd gathered, and his silence was a shield. Her best option for getting him to confide was to open up to him.

"I was never married," she revealed too brightly, raising her mug to her lips again. The contents were nearly cold, and she drank what remained then leaned over to place it on the forest floor. "I've never wanted to bind myself in such a manner, and I've never wanted children. I enjoy the life of challenge and excitement offered me by the British government without the necessity of being tied to a husband."

He gazed down to the thick grass, twisting his foot and pushing the sole of his boot into hard wooden twigs and fallen pine needles until they cracked. For a moment she was certain he almost smiled.

"I would like to marry again," he thoughtfully admitted. "There are many advantages that come with such a union—"

"For a man," she cut in, eyes glowing as he lightened the mood. "As a woman I would prefer those advantages outside of wedlock."

He glanced at her sideways, studying her face. "I'm not sure we're discussing the same advantages, Madeleine."

She smiled companionably and sat straighter on the bench. "I'm sure that we are. I'm twenty-nine years old, Thomas, and French. I wouldn't call myself naive. I refuse to be someone's property to enjoy him."

Her first thought upon that admission was that he might be shocked by her very frank tongue. He wasn't. For seconds he just looked at her, and then, for the first time since they'd met, his mouth grew broad until he grinned fully, showing near-perfect teeth and a face that looked years younger. Boyish. In that instant, sitting on the edge of the woods near a shimmering, peaceful lake, Thomas Blackwood charmed her, and she felt a slow rising heat within, deliciously comforting and ridiculously capricious.

"Perhaps you've simply not met a man who warms

your blood with the kind of desire that lasts, Madeleine," he suggested in a deep, intimate whisper. "The kind that's never satiated but instead makes you always yearn for more. The kind that makes you want to hold on and never let go."

The fact that he hinted at something she nearly felt made the heat rise to her cheeks. She blushed fully, which she almost never did. He recognized it, too, as his eyes once more grazed her features, his expression soft.

She dropped her lashes and fidgeted on the bench, reaching into the pockets of her cloak for her gloves with more of a need for something to do rather than for the warmth they provided. She pulled one first over her left hand, then the other. "You talk as if you've felt that kind of devotion for a woman."

"Do I."

It wasn't a question but a simple statement void of implying a needed response on her part. That made her slightly uncomfortable and even more inquisitive. She wanted details but bit her tongue to keep from probing, and in the end he offered nothing else.

She sighed purposely, turning her attention to the lake. "Perhaps you're right, Thomas. But I've accepted my station. I'm too old for marriage, and as I have never experienced that kind of devotion to or from a man, I have serious doubts that I ever will. I'm not sure I would even recognize such romantic feelings at my age. Passion, yes. Romance, no."

He shrugged lightly, which she perceived more than saw. "One can feel it at any age, Madeleine. Of course, it won't happen if you close yourself off and never allow it into your life, but then that would be your choice."

His tone was casual, but his words were explicit, cautionary in a manner not meant to insult, vivid with meaning.

"My work means too much to me, Thomas," she countered somewhat defensively. "That must always come first."

He sat back, relaxing against the bench once more, crossing one booted leg over the other. "I understand that kind of devotion as well."

She was sure he meant that assertion. Yet he couldn't possibly know the depth of hers, and she had no idea how to explain it to him should she try.

Abruptly her attention shifted to the opposite side of the lake where a man emerged from a thicket, sitting atop a large gray horse as it meandered along the path toward them near the water's edge.

"Is that him?"

"That's him," Thomas answered warily.

Prior conversation abandoned, Madeleine leaned forward earnestly and focused on the baron, assessing him as well as she could over the distance. He wore riding clothes of dark blue, but he was too far away for her to determine their quality. His hair was sandy red and cut in standard fashion, his skin pale and clean-shaven aside from long side whiskers, body average in size although his legs and arms were strong. His expression was hard with effort at that moment, but she could visualize him as the handsome charmer at social functions, and he rode with the experience of one well trained.

As if on cue, his concentration faltered. He peered out over the water, slowing his horse's gait as he became aware of them for the first time. He stared at them while continuing to move slowly along the forest path, no nod or wave of acknowledgment, no smile on his face, eyes black and shrewd. Calculating.

He's clever. And he's watching me.

A gust of icy wind unsettled the air, lifting fallen leaves and stirring them, rustling trees, rippling the water. Still he never took his eyes from them, from her. For the first time since she'd walked outside that morning, utter cold seeped through her clothing, chilling her skin, and she shivered.

Thomas either felt or saw her reaction. In one even movement he reached behind her and lifted the hood of her cloak, slowly, running his palm along the edge then pulling it tightly in at her neck. The fur caressed her face, and she grasped it herself, her gloved hand touching his for several seconds until he dropped it again at his side.

She pulled her attention from the baron and once more regarded the man beside her. Their eyes met, and a glimmer of something passed between them—not sexual exactly, but something with grave meaning she couldn't quite grasp. Then, in a bolt of clarity, it was there before her, and her eyes grew wide in comprehension and amazement.

The gesture he'd innocently made in raising her hood was more than simple gentlemanly behavior. It was as calculated as the look she'd witnessed from Richard Sharon, an overt move of direct intention. It meant possession, in a silent communication from one man to another. It meant possession. Thomas had acted, and the baron had seen it.

"Are you ready to go inside?" he asked gently.

She blinked then wavered and turned back to the lake. Baron Rothebury had disappeared into the low trees.

"I suppose so," she mumbled, feeling the dull ache in her head again, flustered by her own concerns.

He stood, offering his arm which she took without thought. She reached down for her empty tea mug then walked silently behind him through the tunnel of foliage, wondering at her confusion, wondering if he was as inexplicably attracted to her as she was to him, wondering if his show of possession was actually something he felt or was only just performance.

Three

Madeleine's impatience made her uncommonly fitful. For the good part of forty-five minutes she'd been a guest at Mrs. Sarah Rodney's lavish country home, nibbling dry pudding cakes that certainly lacked pudding, and sipping weak tea, listening to her hostess and four other ladies gossip outrageously while they fairly ignored her presence except for an occasional remark and glance at her person as if she were an unwanted but highly intriguing and colorful insect. Granted, they had little in common with her beyond the social graces one needs to commune in genteel fashion. Madeleine herself had learned her grace not from growing up with discipline and training like these ladies, but by observance, practice, polishing, and then becoming. She was essentially one of them and they didn't like it, not that they could find anything wrong with *her* precisely. But she was French, and they simply found that affronting, irrationally unforgivable, feelings they tried only superficially to hide. This made her burn inside. She was half English as well, but that was a secret she couldn't reveal without also revealing, to some degree, her scandalous birth. Doing so would draw questions she wasn't prepared to answer, and foster a pity she couldn't bear. This was primarily why she chose to live her life in France instead of England, despising her French heritage and all that the culture stood for while using her assumed station in life to help the country she loved, and its people who would always consider her an outsider because they didn't know.

Madeleine sat on a small, white, wrought-iron chair, straight-backed with a hard, rounded seat, into which her body fit snugly though the others were undoubtedly squeezed painfully. That gave her a fair amount of satisfaction. She helped herself to her second pudding cake—not because she wanted another but because it gave her something to do with her restless hands.

Together, the six of them had taken their places around the matching wrought-iron table, now covered with a white lace tablecloth, fine pink china, and wedged into the southwest corner of Mrs. Rodney's sweet smelling, flower-filled conservatory. It was the first sunny day since the afternoon of her arrival in Winter Garden nearly one week ago, and although it was cold outside, the large conservatory windows absorbed the sunlight and warmed the air as if it were summer.

She sat with her back to the sun, in her day gown of pale plum silk that, although rich in fabric and modest in cut, had a medium full skirt accentuated by two large, flowing bows in creamy yellow near the hem, and a square neckline and tapered waist fringed with lace of the same color. The bodice fit snugly but conservatively, the wide cuffed sleeves were at three-quarter length, and with her plaited hair coiled becomingly at the back of her head, she looked every bit the conventional young widow dressed for an afternoon of calling.

The Lady Isadora Birmingham sat to her right. She was a vibrant woman in her midsixties, pink-cheeked and lively, softly rounded in figure, probably lovely in her early years, and the only one of the group to allow Madeleine any kind regard, as she'd asked a question or two of her with actual interest in the reply.

Mrs. Catherine Mossley occupied the next seat, a corpulent woman who continued to stuff pudding cakes into her mouth while she talked, which was incessantly. She was a lady in only the broadest stretch of the word, for she had the table manners of a country hog, in Madeleine's opinion. But undeniably, making her worthy of an invitation, she also had wealth bestowed upon her by her late husband who realized a fortune in the gas industry before his untimely demise in an industrial fire that fortunately left his money and good name intact.

Next to Mrs. Mossley, and directly across from Madeleine, rested the sober but erect figure of Mrs. Penelope Bennington-Jones, followed by her daughter, Desdemona Winsett. Mrs. Bennington-Jones possessed shrewd black eyes, coarse brown hair streaked with silver, and a nose like a hawk's. She was large of stature, though not particularly fat, and not in the least attractive. She was, by far, the keenest of the bunch, however. She looked upon Madeleine's presence as an intrusion, occasionally glowering at her with a scorn she couldn't hide. She was the greatest threat at the table.

Desdemona was entirely different from her mother. A rather homely, fair-haired bride of nineteen, she'd been married only two months to an Army officer now away on duty, but she was already showing signs of pregnancy. This would probably be one of her last outings before socially retiring to await the birth, as her baby, by Madeleine's estimation, would arrive sooner than the expected and normal nine months of carrying. Of course, the family would be saved from direct scandal by declaring the child early but amazingly strong, large, and healthy, which would likely go unproved but not unheeded as society whispered about it secretly. Desdemona bore a particular shyness of personality that, when coupled with a domineering mother, encouraged pity. And although she'd hardly spoken to anyone beyond initial introductions, Madeleine knew the youngest lady found having a Frenchwoman in their midst strangely fascinating. Desdemona stared at her continuously from across the table while sipping her tea.

To complete the circle, Sarah Rodney, the acknowledged Winter Garden historian, and their hostess, sat at Madeleine's left. She personified an Englishwoman in every sense of the word, down to her pale skin, generous bust and hips, soft demeanor, white hair and exquisite manners. Madeleine thought Mrs. Rodney to be outwardly charming and intelligent, but inwardly flawed in that her invitation to a socially acceptable Frenchwoman was predicated not on kindness or hospitality, but on curiosity and the underlying desire to discover flaws.

The conversation had been about nothing that mattered so far, starting with superficial chatter about the unusually cold autumn weather and everybody's health, including that of Lady Claire Childress, who had been invited but was feeling too poorly to attend, which apparently had become a frequent occurrence. The topics from there flowed naturally into more confidential gossip regarding Winter Garden residents and those just coming south for the season. Madeleine listened raptly, adding her own comments where appropriate, though being generally ignored where it wasn't socially required to acknowledge her opinions. Finally, after two cups of tea, filled for her by the ever present but silent servants who stood between the rhododendrons and African violets as if nothing more than decoration for the colorful room, she wanted to turn the talk in a direction to help her.

Lifting her lace napkin and pressing it gently to her lips, effectively informing them all that she was about to speak, she turned to her hostess.

"Mrs. Rodney," she started thoughtfully, "I was wondering who owns the large house on the far shores of the lake? It's a lovely piece of property, and quite unlike the other homes I've seen in Winter Garden."

Silence ensued, and Madeleine feigned ignorance to the fact that they all seemed rather taken aback by her audacious interruption and outright turn in conversation. Or maybe it wasn't the manner of her questioning but the desire to discuss the baron?

Mrs. Rodney cleared her throat and leaned slightly to her left. "I believe you mean the manor house owned by Richard Sharon, the Baron Rothebury," she said rather than asked.

"Such a charming man," Mrs. Mossley interjected quickly.

Mrs. Bennington-Jones raised her cup to her lips with delicate fingers and took a slow sip of her tea. "Indeed he is, Mrs. Mossley. I would have been very happy had he chosen my lovely Desdemona to wed, but alas, she had her mind set on marrying Mr. Winsett." She gave her daughter a guarded look, hard as steel. Desdemona, flushing scarlet, lowered her eyes to her lap, fidgeting with the peach lace on her skirt.

"The baron is Winter Garden's most eligible bachelor, Mrs. DuMais," Lady Isadora properly explained. "He is a year-long resident. Of course, he is titled, handsome, and not without a good family name and substantial means."

Madeleine smiled and nodded as expected. "A marvelous prospect for any family." She glanced again to

Desdemona now sitting rigidly in her chair. Subduing her irritation at the lady's mother who, like so many others, including her own, used her daughter as a pawn, she added, "Any lady would be fortunate to marry a baron, I suppose. But young ladies today, and even some young gentlemen, are more often marrying for love instead of financial and social stability. At least it seems to be that way in France."

Desdemona's gaze shot up to meet hers, and Madeleine couldn't decide if the lady looked frightened or appalled. The others had no idea what to say in reply, which was exactly what she'd anticipated.

Mrs. Bennington-Jones took the cue. "I suppose you married for love, then, Madame DuMais?"

The Englishwoman's use of the title "Madame" instead of "Mrs." had every intention of reminding them all of Madeleine's place at the table. But more significantly, she recognized the underlying suggestion that as a Frenchwoman she might somehow be whimsical by nature, perhaps even loose. It gave her the opening she needed.

"Goodness, no," she said with some surprise, staring the woman straight in the eye. "My marriage was arranged, Mrs. Bennington-Jones, as my husband was from an excellent family—tea traders all of them—with sufficient means and respectability. I have been most fortunate since my wedding day, although from time to time I miss my dear Georges. He was lost at sea several years ago."

"How very sad," Mrs. Mossley remarked with feeling.

Madeleine shrugged negligibly, dropping her gaze and reaching for her fork to slice another piece of cake. "Yes, but the sea takes many souls each year, Mrs. Mossley," she said frankly, "and I was not unaware of the risks when I married him."

Ever the practical widow, well mannered and well married. One or two ladies nodded with genuine, growing approval of her.

After swallowing a very small bite, she turned back to her hostess to revert to her original query. "And the baron's house, Mrs. Rodney? Has it always been in the family?" If the woman noticed she was pressing for information she didn't show it.

"Oh, yes, it's been the Rothebury estate for . . . nine or ten generations now. It's lovely inside, and parts of it are quite old actually. The family has enlarged it through the years." Her wide forehead crinkled gently as her eyes focused on pink carnations in the center of the table. "I recall that it was once a monastery of some kind, or at least the foundation upon which the house is now built was part of a structure belonging to the church several centuries ago." She glanced up to her guests again and lowered her voice. "Some records indicate, or rather"—she patted her lips with her napkin—"rumor suggests it was a haven for those not afflicted with the Black Death."

Madeleine glanced around the table. Everyone's attention was now thoroughly engaged, as was hers, but, of course, for different reasons.

"To hide from those individuals who were diseased?" Lady Isadora asked with genuine titillation.

"To keep from succumbing themselves, I should think," Mrs. Mossley corrected with an air of assurance, wiping crumbs from her mouth with her fingertips. "If one secures oneself from the outside world, disease can be avoided."

Mrs. Bennington-Jones scoffed. "Nonsense. If God chooses to cast down affliction, nothing can be done to avoid it."

Quiet filled the room for a moment as those words

were absorbed. Then Lady Isadora shook her head slowly. "But who would take shelter there? Clergy?" Her own answer satisfied her, and she sat back in her chair. "I suppose that would explain who was inside and why they lived through the Death. Men of God would not be afflicted."

Madeleine reached for her tea, bringing her cup to her lips. "But men of God are still men. They succumb to temptation, illness, and death as do laymen."

Every woman at the table looked stung by that.

Mrs. Rodney cleared her throat again, this time purposely. "I believe, Mrs. DuMais, that with the good Lord's help and guidance, men of the cloth would have sense enough to close themselves off from the outside world until the threat of danger is passed."

Madeleine took another sip. "You're suggesting, Mrs. Rodney, that the baron's home once posed as a fortress of sorts for those seeking shelter?"

"Precisely," she returned with a drop of her thick chin.

"But they would still need to eat and provide for essentials," she argued pleasantly. "The Black Death lasted for several years. Surely those inside could not go that long without food and supplies."

Mrs. Bennington-Jones smiled at her flatly. "Monasteries are equipped with the land and means to provide, Madame DuMais. I should think they are the same in France?"

Madeleine nodded once in acknowledgment, holding her tongue graciously of a retort that food alone wouldn't be the only thing needed for survival, but also firewood and oil among the many, as well as messages from the outside world that would allow those inside contact with others. She didn't need to say anything. Everyone else knew it, too.

Mrs. Mossley stuffed her mouth with the last of her

cake. "Maybe they all died." She smiled broadly at her own sense of humor as she chewed. "What I mean is that it's just a story. Mrs. Rodney even said it's more rumor than fact. The Black Death occurred five hundred years ago. One cannot be certain of events that took place so far back in history."

There was silence for another long moment, then Desdemona offered softly, "I've heard . . . rumors of lights in the night and ghosts on Baron Rothebury's property. Maybe they're all dead clergy—"

"Oh, for heaven sake, Desdemona," her mother interjected, annoyed. "There are no ghosts. Clergy do not become ghosts. Your imagination is beyond the incredible."

Desdemona sank lower in her chair, looking sufficiently scolded. Mrs. Rodney attempted to clear the air.

"I really think there is little fact behind it after all," she admitted, sitting straighter in her seat and reaching for a third slice of cake. "I don't know if anyone even lived in the Winter Garden valley so long ago. Records are vague at best, and only kept though the church that far back. One could trace the history, probably, but Baron Rothebury likely only has information regarding his family after the time of purchasing his estate."

"I should think Winter Garden existed then, being so close to Portsmouth," Lady Isadora remarked with drawn brows. "That the baron's property is as old may be in some doubt, but I imagine there were people here."

"Perhaps, Madame DuMais, you could ask the gentleman with whom you are living if he knows," Mrs. Bennington-Jones murmured with a calculated twist of her mouth. "I've no doubt the two of you are . . . sufficiently acquainted by now. And he is, after all, a scholar, is he not?"

An awkward pause followed. A servant shifted feet

on the creaking wooden floor, someone dropped a fork to her plate clumsily. All but the Englishwoman who had so brazenly asked the question looked elsewhere—to their tea, to the flowers, anywhere but to her.

So that was it. She lived alone with Thomas in a small cottage, and in less than one week speculation as to the depth of their relationship had started. Quicker than she'd expected, or than it would have in France, she had to admit, and probably with more scrutiny and concern. In France, Thomas would be considered fortunate to have an attractive widow in his company; she, at the worst, would be ignored. Here, in this small village, he would be snubbed and she would be scorned, at least by respectable women. He had been right. They could never pose as lovers. Already these ladies questioned her scruples. But they also, for now, had nothing more enticing to go on than assumption.

Madeleine folded her napkin in her lap, meticulously, thinking with care as she spoke. "Mr. Blackwood is a scholar, Mrs. Bennington-Jones, but he is not from Winter Garden. I am uncertain whether he knows anything at all of its history."

"Indeed," Mrs. Rodney inserted with interest.

Madeleine smiled dryly. They were all certainly aware of this and yet they chose to carry on as if ignorant. "He is also a rather quiet individual. I know very little about him other than what I have learned while translating his memoirs."

"And how on earth did he ever find you among all the translators in France?" Mrs. Bennington-Jones asked with pointed meaning. "Naturally I don't mean to be insulting, but surely there must be other individuals who are better able to do the work."

Madeleine gazed at her directly, pretending innocence

as she clutched her napkin with both hands. "How so, Mrs. Bennington-Jones?"

The woman shifted her large body in her chair. "Well, I'm sure there are men—"

"Ahh . . . I'm sure that there are," she cut in, composed and in flawless form. "But I've always wanted to travel to England, and this seemed a prime opportunity to spend some time here. I am, of course, well-qualified for the position as I was extensively educated in the language during the six years I spent in a Viennese finishing school for young ladies, run by the very famous Madame Bilodeau. I'm sure you've heard of her?"

Mrs. Bennington-Jones blinked, taken aback by a question she had not foreseen. "I imagine so, yes."

Madeleine lowered her chin, smiling tightly. "When I read Mr. Blackwood's advertisement in a Parisian newspaper requesting aid from a person of skill and good breeding to translate his memoirs, I wrote him with recommendations and a list of my credentials, and he chose me from among several. I left France only a few days after receiving word. As I am widowed, Mrs. Bennington-Jones, and without children, my time is my own. And now I am here."

There was another pause of piercing quiet. Nobody moved or replied. Then Desdemona leaned forward in her chair, her blond ringlets spilling forward onto the table and into the crumbs on her plate. "Are you not a bit frightened of him, Mrs. DuMais?" she asked in near whisper.

Her eyes widened. "Frightened of Mr. Blackwood?"

Desdemona hesitated. "He's rather . . . ugly."

Madeleine was shocked, not so much by the young lady's candor and gross breach of decorum, but by the idea itself which had not struck her. Dark and formidable he was, his face and body scarred, but "ugly" would never be a word she'd use to describe Thomas.

"Desdemona, really," her mother rebuked with some obvious embarrassment, fairly yanking her daughter back into an upright position.

"Of course, he is a large man, isn't he, dear?" Mrs. Mossley corrected with the first touch of grace she'd shown since sitting at tea. "Intimidating I'm sure is what you meant."

"Yes," Desdemona replied tautly, staring now at her cup.

Madeleine pressed her lips together and smoothed her skirts, cautiously choosing this moment to correct all assumptions. "He is large, and perhaps intimidating to many, women especially. I don't find him at all frightening, Mrs. Winsett. I don't suppose he is dashing, either. But he has been a gracious host, charming to an appropriate degree, and I find him quite appealing actually. Handsome in a very rugged way."

Confusion lit the room. They didn't know how to interpret that, which was exactly her intention. They'd been sure of a deeper involvement between them, perhaps even a beginning love affair. All but Desdemona, who seemed still lost between childish fantasies and the realities of the adult world.

Mrs. Rodney reached out and moved the cake platter, which didn't need moving, to a better position. "I don't find him particularly handsome, but he is a gentleman, and quite . . . virile. Wouldn't you agree, Mrs. DuMais?"

"Oh, yes, he is a gentleman," she responded accordingly. She lifted her spoon, stirring more sugar and then cream into lukewarm tea she had no intention of drinking. "However, there are some . . . indications that Mr. Blackwood's injuries reach far above his legs, which are noticeably impaired, although I have not seen them to know this as fact."

Not a sound could be heard above breathing. She waited, knowing she had their full attention, and that nobody would speak again until she elaborated. The information they all hoped she'd reveal was far too captivating.

Madeleine placed her spoon on her saucer, then sighed and raised her lashes to regard them. "Without sounding indelicate," she carried on very quietly, "and since we are all married ladies, I think I can safely inform you that Mr. Blackwood and I have no particular interest in each other beyond the work I was hired to accomplish." She leaned into the table and lowered her voice to a whisper of intrigue she knew they all but felt. "You see, Mr. Blackwood also suffers from injuries that, well, make it difficult for him to enjoy the . . . intimacies associated with marriage."

They all sat rigid as stone, unblinking and staring at her with varying degrees of fascination and utter disbelief that she would mention something of such a personal nature. Then again she was French, and they knew without doubt that the French spoke frequently and far too openly about marital relations. And naturally such incredible news was a great deal more invigorating than any hint of a love affair. They would not stop her until she finished.

"How on earth would you know this?" Mrs. Bennington-Jones pursued in a gruff exhale.

Madeleine smiled again and lifted her fork, slicing another piece of cake as they all watched. "It really is only a conclusion on my part, Mrs. Bennington-Jones. But consider this. His injuries cause him to limp markedly, and he has not the slightest interest in me as a woman. As women, I'm sure we'd all agree that we know when a man shows us interest in that way. I also know we're all ladies of quality sitting here today, and understand perfectly the consequences of gossip."

There was a sharp intake of breath at her understated warning. Madeleine noted with satisfaction how they all at once were so very interested in their tea—except for Desdemona, who gaped at her, uncertain but blushing a brilliant red as she suddenly grasped the meaning inferred.

"Mrs. Mossley," Lady Isadora moved on at last, "are you playing the organ in church again Sunday or is Mrs. Casper feeling well enough to return?"

They'd reverted to safe conversation, and Madeleine sat back, listening politely, marvelously pleased at the turn of events. They couldn't dislike her—all but Mrs. Bennington-Jones—and even found her intriguing. She would be invited again. She may be French and a bit too free with her tongue, but she was also polished, educated, respectable, and absolutely not whoring for Mr. Blackwood. They believed that much, or at least had their doubts. She'd stifled the indecent talk.

The gossip had been steered in a different direction. By nightfall Winter Garden would be stirring with the details regarding the scholar and his war injuries that had left him impotent. Her only concern now was how in heaven she was going to tell Thomas.

Four

Madeleine sat comfortably on the sofa with her bare feet tucked under her gown and a woolen shawl wrapped around her shoulders, staring into the slow burning fire. She'd returned from Mrs. Rodney's tea only a half hour ago, but it was already growing dark, and Thomas had yet to appear from an afternoon of observing Rothebury's property from afar. Clouds had gathered overhead again during her walk home, and she'd been sprinkled with the first of the evening rain, dampening her hair and clothes. Now drops tapped the rooftop in a soothing, steady drone.

She'd been watching the low flames for twenty minutes or so, contemplating all that she'd learned in the last few hours, but in truth thinking mostly about Thomas. Their first week together had been unremarkable as he'd kept his distance from her to an almost obvious degree. She knew he didn't find her presence irritating or unwanted, but she had no idea whether he found her pleasing to be around or desirable as a woman. It had taken her days to concede that although his regard of her personally was quite irrelevant and that she really shouldn't care, it bothered her that she didn't know. The central problem, however, aside from the fact that her straying thoughts were interfering with her concentration on her work, was that an intimate relationship with Thomas really wasn't something she could just discuss with him over breakfast. Frankly, she wasn't altogether sure she wanted one. It would no doubt complicate their business association, and her work, regardless of personal circumstance, always came first and always would. She would never do anything to jeopardize that. Lovers might come and go, but her work was her only true form of lasting satisfaction in her life.

Growing warm at last, Madeleine pulled the shawl from her shoulders, draped it over the arm of the sofa, then looked behind her toward the door because she suddenly felt his presence in the room.

She hadn't heard him enter. The steady rainfall had covered the sound. But his commanding figure blocked the entryway from her view as he brushed water from his overcoat while plainly regarding her.

"Hello," he said softly.

An innocent word, implying nothing.

"Hello," she returned, studying the sparkling water droplets in his hair, his slightly furrowed brows as he lowered his eyes to concentrate on unfastening large, black buttons, his damp, glistening skin shining a dark bronze in dim firelight.

"Any luck today?" he inquired, hanging his coat on the rack, then running his fingers once through his hair.

Quickly, before he caught her staring, she shifted her attention to the rug where she'd placed her shoes. "Actually, yes," she said, squeezing her feet into soft brown leather. "It was a typical social gathering, so much of the conversation was little more than gossip. But I did

learn some things worth noting, one or two of them interesting." She heard him stride toward her, his gait slow
and uneven, and she repositioned herself on the sofa to
face forward, folding her hands in her lap. "How was
your afternoon?"

"Cold," he replied. "Generally uncomfortable. Sur-
veillance is the part of this work I like the least."

"So you didn't learn much of anything," she acknowledged aloud.

He lifted the iron poker and stirred the embers in the
grate. "I didn't expect to after only three days, although
it's clear that Rothebury doesn't get many visitors. He
keeps to himself and rarely leaves the house." He sighed
and lightly shook his head. "Still, without much surrounding property to manage, it does make me wonder
what he does each day."

"He probably does what the nobility usually do, I
imagine," she submitted with a hint of humor, noticing,
even through his white, linen shirt, how the muscles in
his back smoothly flexed. "He no doubt relaxes as he
should, orders servants to draw his bath and cook his
food and polish his shoes, while he basks in his accu-
mulated wealth and the luxuries of his social class."

She couldn't see his features clearly but she knew that
amused him.

"Is that what you think the nobility do each day, Madeleine?" he questioned in light amazement, replacing the
poker and turning to face her, his backside absorbing the
heat.

She lifted one shoulder in a shrug. "That, or they carefully manage lucrative smuggling operations." With an
understanding smile into his eyes, she added, "It will
probably take some time, Thomas. We might be here
working together for several months."

He smiled in return, vaguely. "I'm aware of that."

"Would that bother you?" she pressed. Before he could answer, and because she didn't want the question to seem too personal, she clarified, "I mean, are you anxious to return to Eastleigh? To your home, family?" *To your lover?* It dawned on her suddenly that she hadn't considered that before. If he had a lover at home, someone he cared for deeply, it would explain his reluctance to respond to their obvious physical attraction to each other. Then again, during their first conversation about chess he'd implied that he hadn't been with anyone for some time. Neither had she. She squirmed on the sofa.

He stood very still for a moment, his dark eyes fixed with hers. "I'm not anxious to go home when there is work to be done here, Madeleine. I'm an extremely thorough man, and I intend to stay in Winter Garden until my objectives are at least tried. I take them very seriously."

Objectives are tried? She had no idea what that meant, and she would have brushed the phrase off had he not seemed to plan with care exactly what to say in reply. If there was one thing she knew about Thomas already, it was that he did not ever mince words.

"Well, then," she expressed through a loud exhale, "I suppose it's just you and me alone indefinitely." She looked over his left shoulder to the clock, rubbing her fingers along her skirt at the waist, feeling the prickling of lace on her skin. "I assume no one in Eastleigh will care that we're working so closely together."

She said that as a statement of fact, watching the second hand pass the five, then the ten.

"I don't have a lover, Madeleine," he revealed very softly.

Her gaze shot back to his face as her palms grew moist and her belly fluttered and her cheeks became hot.

His expression was intense and centered, though giving nothing away.

"Nobody will care that we're together intimately or otherwise," he continued, subdued, "except for those in the village. I trust that came up in conversation today and I'd like to hear what you learned."

Madeleine blinked. Her mind floated to thoughts of seduction while his returned to the business of work. He always so smoothly returned to the matter of work. Why was that? Because he was uncomfortable discussing them personally? A creeping warmth descended from her shoulders to her toes as she also realized that by doing so he'd just saved her the embarrassment of explaining herself. Instinctively she knew he'd done that on purpose.

He crossed his arms over his thick chest, waiting.

"My day was very enlightening," she explained at last, hoping her voice didn't sound as dry as her mouth felt. "There were five ladies present at tea: Sarah Rodney, Penelope Bennington-Jones and her daughter, Desdemona Winsett, Catherine Mossley, and Lady Isadora Birmingham."

"I've met them all," he interjected.

Her body relaxed again as her thoughts focused on the events of the afternoon. "They were gracious, but suspicious of me at first. French, you know. For a time they ignored me, and then I made my presence obvious by asking them who owns the house on the lake."

He passed her a look of approval in a very slight nod, and she carried on, placing her elbows on her thighs, hands together as she dropped her chin to rest on her knuckles.

"Mrs. Mossley and Lady Isadora know nothing of any significance. I'm sure of that. Mrs. Rodney knows a good deal about Winter Garden obviously, and the baron's home. She's convinced it was originally a monastery. Rumor suggests it was also a haven for those not afflicted with the Black Death, although she did admit this is unproven and probably far-fetched."

That grabbed his interest. "It's also fascinating."

"I thought so as well, but I can't imagine what this might have to do with Rothebury and any illegal enterprise the man might be engaging in now."

He considered that, then shook his head minutely. "Likely nothing, maybe something. The original house structure is very old."

Her eyes brightened, and her mouth lifted in mischievous smile. "Maybe Baron Rothebury has found the burial ground and is hiding stolen opium inside the ancient tombs of dead clergy."

For a second or two he seemed confused by her sudden attempt to be droll. Then his lids narrowed. "Madeleine . . ."

She liked the way he said her name. A brandy-rich voice drawing the sound out in playful warning. She grinned fully now and he did the same.

"Perhaps they're angry about it," she continued. "Desdemona says she's heard rumors of lights in the night and ghosts on Rothebury's property."

His smile faded. "What?"

"Bizarre, is it not?" Her tone grew serious again. "I think, however, that if there are any lights to see and ghosts to hear, she's seen and heard them herself. And they are not dead clergy."

He stared at her for a second or two, concentrating. Then he dropped his arms and began to slowly walk away from the grate, allowing its brightness and heat to fill the room again. She straightened, adjusting her skirts a little and angling her body toward his chair, but he didn't sit there as expected. Instead, he moved around the tea table and lowered himself onto the sofa, only a foot or so away from her.

The fire hissed and crackled, and the rain came down harder still, thumping the windows in steady rhythm, and she found the intimate atmosphere and his unexpected nearness momentarily disconcerting.

"Anything else?" he asked, stretching one booted leg out and under the table.

She pulled away from him a little. "Desdemona is a bride of two months, but I'm nearly positive she's carrying a child she conceived before her wedding night. Other than that I don't have any conclusions about her except that I don't think she is the innocent, demure lady her mother presents her to be. But she is naive."

His brows drew together, and he studied her. His gaze lingered on her hair, her cheeks and lips, then met hers again. He leaned his side into the sofa back, raising his arm to lay it lengthwise along the top, his hand at a right angle to her body. With any other man the action would have meant nothing; with Thomas it seemed somehow provocative.

"And her mother?"

"Her mother didn't like me," she replied levelly. "Even after I explained my position as a properly raised lady and respectable widow, as well as my very functional reason for being in Winter Garden, she was the only one to remain openly hostile."

"You threaten her," he said simply.

"Probably, although I'm not certain why."

"Work on Desdemona."

"I intend to."

He nodded as if he expected that. "What happened to Lady Claire?"

"Invited but under the weather." His fingers were now less than an inch from the top of her bare shoulder, but she tried to overlook that. She lowered her voice and added, "Apparently it's becoming a regular occurrence. If she's addicted, it's the opium affecting her life, and it will only get worse."

He started rubbing the cushion very gently with his fingertips, brushing her sleeve almost imperceptibly. She had no idea whether he did it on purpose, but the closeness, without obvious further action or intent on his part, felt invasive. He pondered her words, though, with no indication that he even realized her uneasiness, or what he was doing.

"We need to see her," he maintained. "I want your impressions, to rule her out if nothing else. I'll arrange a luncheon with her on Saturday."

"You'll arrange a luncheon at her house?" Her lips curled up at one corner. "You're that confident she'll invite you?"

"Us, Madeleine," he corrected. "And yes, we'll get an invitation. She enjoys my company and finds me . . . charming."

"Charming," she repeated flatly.

He cocked his head. "Don't you find me charming, Mrs. DuMais?"

She was fairly certain he was teasing her now, his tone low and coaxing, his body so close she smelled outdoor woodlands mixed with the freshness of rainwater and his own individual, male scent.

"You flirt with her," she clarified unsteadily, ignoring his question while trying to ignore the desire to reach for him.

His warm eyes narrowed as he continued to caress the sofa beside her. And then his fingers grazed the skin on her neck, just once, barely felt. The touch shot her through with tingles, jarring her inside, disorienting her because she wasn't so sure it was accidental. But she didn't move.

"She's lonely, and I flatter her," he explained quietly, every bit in control. "I don't have the personality or appearance to be flirtatious."

Yet in a manner Madeleine knew he was flirting with her now, teasing her, exciting her physically. She sensed it all as she felt his nearness. She was experienced. She recognized the various forms.

"I wonder what the lady will think of me?" she asked a bit impishly, one brow raised, knowing she was pushing.

His eyes scanned her face again. "I imagine she'll be jealous—of your beauty and your presence at my side."

She flushed but didn't look away. Neither did he, which she found oddly gratifying. She couldn't stop there, though. "You think she'll be jealous when there's obviously nothing between us?"

Without pause, he whispered, "She's not blind, Madeleine. She'll see it."

That made her pulse quicken. *What exactly will she see, Thomas?* she wanted to ask, but couldn't. She gazed at him in speculation, trying to keep a sharp focus on the issues as her thoughts strayed to his hard, mesmerizing features: his magnificent eyes centered intently on her; his large, powerful hands so close to her body, and the vivid intrusion of what they might feel like grazing the skin on her throat and shoulders, the tips of her breasts.

Madeleine wavered, lowering her lashes and turning her gaze to the fire, wishing he'd sat in his chair like he was supposed to do.

"I'd be more inclined to believe Rothebury is smuggling the opium," she argued pointedly.

He didn't respond right away, and whether he was

surprised by her abrupt return to the topic of their concern, she couldn't guess.

"No conclusions, Madeleine," he said at last. "Not yet. We have a great deal of work to do and much to learn before we can draw any."

He was right, of course. But he didn't know how much she knew about opium. "Thomas, if Lady Claire is addicted, as you suspect, even if it's just to laudanum, I find it difficult to believe she could remain in charge of an organized group of smugglers." She inhaled deeply and looked back into his eyes. "I've seen opium addiction before, and its effects. If she is using it daily, her mind is otherwise occupied. She is not smuggling."

"Then we will observe and learn what we can," he replied, completely serious.

It took her a moment to realize he was not discarding her opinions, nor disbelieving her account. He was being thorough. She had no idea what to say so she just nodded faintly.

An invisible wave of tension passed between them— hot and thick and silent. Thomas recognized it as she did, noting her discomfiture, the sullen look in her beautiful eyes, the grim line to her mouth. He knew her worries, her past fears, and it took all that was in him not to lean forward just six tiny inches, blend his lips with hers, and kiss all her troubles from her forever. And she would respond. He knew that, too. The wait to make love to her was physically painful now as she was here, alone with him in the cottage, by his side every day. He wanted to move forward with his intentions, but that would never do. She wasn't prepared for the acts and consequences, and neither was he. He needed more time.

He'd thought of her all day as he'd crouched uncomfortably in the cold brush, watching nothing happen, wondering at her success, what the English ladies would think of her, how she would react to their baiting and veiled insults. She was regal and polished and smart, and gifted in the art of deception. He would have loved to see her in action.

Now she sat so very close to him, so lovely in firelight, so exposed to him in her feelings, so confounded by their mutual attraction to each other that she wasn't sure he noticed. She wondered if he'd touched her neck on purpose, and if he would touch her again. The thought made him smile, and she glanced to his mouth. He would take care of her confusion eventually.

She stirred a little and adjusted her skirt, pulling the silk away from his thighs so as to keep them from coming into physical contact. Her deliberate action puzzled him, as they'd sat touching from shoulder to knee by the lake only days ago, and it hadn't seemed to bother her then. Now she appeared uncomfortable, nervous about something.

"Anything more I should know?" he inquired rather casually.

Without looking at him, she reached up behind her head and pulled the comb from her hair, tossing it on the tea table, releasing her long, thick braid to slide over her shoulder and down her right breast. It looked like silk the color of dark autumn leaves. Someday he would weave his fingers through it, put his face against it, and inhale the fragrance he could only now faintly detect.

"Yes, there is something more to tell you, Thomas, and I'm not sure—" She stopped, and after a moment's hesitation, she stood and gracefully walked to the hearth, staring at his music box on the mantelpiece. "I'm going to be blunt with you about this and I hope you'll not be angry."

"Angry about what?"

She gathered her thoughts, then straightened her

shoulders so that her gown tapered perfectly down the curve of her spine. "Through no intention of my own, the conversation at tea turned to you."

He leaned back, watching firelight reflect off the smooth, milky-white skin at her neck. "I assumed it might."

She raised her gaze to the ceiling briefly, then turned around again to face him squarely, though defensively folding her arms across her stomach.

"Forgive me, Thomas," she expelled quickly, "but the ladies were suggestive, asking questions and offering comments that were not of their concern. I had to put a stop to the rumors so I started one of my own."

Thomas didn't know how to take that precisely, but his curiosity was building. "Explain it to me, Madeleine."

She licked her lips. "Desdemona asked me if I were frightened of you. I told her no. Then Mrs. Mossley observed how large you were—are—and that prompted Mrs. Rodney to ask me if I found you virile."

His body tensed from both nervous anticipation and pleasure-filled hope. "And how did you respond?"

"I said that I did," she confessed softly, her eyes simmering as they gazed boldly into his. "I also said I found you appealing."

Slowly he lowered his arm so that he could sit forward, forearms on thighs, listening to the steady thumping in his chest, biting the inside of his bottom lip to control the grin that threatened to escape his blank expression. "I see."

She cleared her throat. "That's not all."

"I assumed as much, since the fact that you find me virile and appealing isn't something that would make me angry, Madeleine."

Her eyes widened, and she shifted her feet on the rug, though otherwise ignoring the remark.

"Thomas, they were cold to me initially," she continued dauntlessly in a bright, clear voice, "because they already suspected we were lovers and had been gossiping about it. The only way I could think to save both of our reputations so that we could remain together long enough to finish our work was to discreetly tell them that we have no sexual interest in each other."

He said nothing, just looked at her.

She raised her chin a fraction and untangled her arms, running her palms nervously down her hips. "And the only way I could think of to make them believe that was to inform them all that you are impotent."

The clap of distant thunder cut through the shock that followed, and Thomas's only thought was that he'd never been made speechless in his life until now. He gaped at her for a slice of a second, a sliver of fury digging into his skin at her audacity, but then it dissipated just as fast while the humor of it all invaded instead.

It was actually a very smart response on her part. Brilliant, really. He didn't live here. Nobody knew him personally, so it didn't matter, except to his masculinity, which was flagrantly damaged. But as a woman she probably hadn't considered that. And he didn't need to ask how she'd explained to five prominent Winter Garden ladies that he couldn't perform. His injuries would be accepted as proof enough.

She eyed him carefully for reaction, fidgeting, although she tried to hide it. She stood almost directly in front of the fire, hands clasped behind her now, her body silhouetted from the glow behind her as the room grew dark with coming nightfall. He rubbed his hands together and cleared his throat, at last attempting to find his voice.

"Well," he said, and couldn't think of anything else appropriate for the moment.

She closed her eyes. "I'm sorry, Thomas. I know that's something deeply personal and none of my business—"

"No, it's *our* business, Madeleine."

She raised her lashes again, frowning delicately, unsure.

He waited, thinking, and then he stood with hands on thighs and slowly strode to her side, facing the fire as she faced away from it. She didn't move her feet, but her body stiffened beside him.

"We have to be able to work together," he finally admitted, soothingly, looking not at her but into the burning embers. "If others suspect our involvement sexually, it will make it that much more difficult for us to succeed. I believe I've mentioned this before."

"Yes."

The word came out raspy.

"We will have to be careful," he added quietly.

Perplexed by that, she turned her head sharply to look at him, and he did the same.

"Not everybody will believe the lie that my war injuries are severe enough to keep me from desiring you as a woman, Madeleine. Or reacting physically to your presence."

Her eyes were huge, the blue of them dark and liquid soft. The skin on her face shone radiantly, half shadowed, half golden as light from the glowing fire played upon it. Her full lips were moist as she licked them from an expectation of a touch she wanted but couldn't comfortably take. At this moment in time he would give all his worldly possessions to know what she was thinking.

"I'm . . . glad you're not as mad as you could be," she whispered, partly in defense, partly in continued confusion. "I feared that."

"Really?"

"You're imposing, Thomas."

It was meant as a compliment, and he knew it. He nodded and turned his attention back to the fire. Seconds ticked by. Then in a husky whisper, he acknowledged, "Your decision to explain our relationship that way was well timed and rational. It was smart, Madeleine."

He could feel the anxiety ease from her body, her arms relax at her sides.

"I hope you don't think I've damaged you for all the marriageable ladies in Winter Garden."

She was trying to lighten the mood in her quest to understand him, and he had every intention of letting her. He wanted her to know. But he didn't want light. He wanted dark desire between them, uncertain excitement, unmatched sensuality and erotic thought. Potent passions she could draw on with eagerness in the weeks to come.

Turning to face her fully, his side to the fire, he took a step closer. Then he raised his arm and rested it across the mantel, behind her shoulders, running his fingertips along the music box as he stared into her eyes. She didn't move, but the smile had left her mouth.

"Nobody concerns me but you, Madeleine. What I really fear is that you might begin to believe that because of my injuries I won't be able to perform as a man."

His tone had darkened, and she'd noticed it. It startled her, too, very much so. She stood so still suddenly that he could no longer tell if she breathed.

He inched closer so that he towered over her, his body feeling the static charge of hers, his nose inhaling the pure woman scent of her he'd already come to recognize, his legs lost in the folds of her flowing gown, his heartbeat discernable to him now as it thundered from thoughts of touching her, of raising his hand and closing it over her breast. Just enough to caress the swell beneath silk and lace. Just for a second of pleasure.

She saw the heat in his eyes. "Thomas . . ."

His breath quickened, his jaw tightened, and above all else he wanted to feel her. Slowly he leaned over her, into her, his face near the slender curve of her neck, just an inch away from touching. He detected the warmth from her skin, inhaled deeply of her, then exhaled very gently so that his warm breath caressed her cheek and ear. She shuddered, and that reaction, one she couldn't control, impaled him with a sharp, powerful charge of satisfaction.

"I'm not impotent," he disclosed in a rough whisper. "I've never been, and near you I never could be. Even now the evidence is within your reach."

A slight sound escaped her throat, barely heard.

"I react to you, Madeleine, respond to the sight of you. But we cannot be lovers. It would complicate things." He closed his eyes, and in a harsh breath against her ear, he added, "I just wanted you to know you're not fighting desire alone. I feel it just to think of you."

Gradually he backed away from her. She trembled now, but her eyes were squeezed tightly shut, and she didn't open them when she felt him move. Her breathing came as quickly as his, her lips parted seductively, begging contact, and Thomas couldn't take any more.

"The fire is burning, Maddie," he said gruffly, standing erect beside her again. "I need to walk in the cold for a while."

He left her then, swiftly and silently.

Five

Opium was the drug of the ages. First used in the ancient world, the wonders of the poppy plant had been proclaimed through time from Europe to the Far East. Because the plant grew well in only warm climes, a vast and growing trade through the centuries resulted in relatively easy access to all who partook. Extraction of the juice was difficult, so early users either ate parts of the flower or mixed them with liquids for drinking. In the early sixteenth century, Philippus Paracelsus, an unconventional Swiss physician, arbitrarily named a remedy based on opium *ladanum*, later to be called laudanum—a liquid mixture made primarily of opium and alcohol. This was the miracle cure for many, and easily and cheaply obtained. Nearly everyone consumed opium in some form, for its calming affect and its ability to deaden pain. All except Madeleine who knew its destructive properties better than most. She'd seen them, had experienced them firsthand for nearly twenty years.

Her mother had smoked it daily, along with her friends, becoming an addict at a very young age. Smok-

ing opium—as opposed to eating or drinking it—created
a far more intense rush of pleasure. It also produced
more irrational behavior when the pleasure dissipated,
sometimes even physical pain and vomiting, and ultimately a growing dependency, which her mother had
experienced early. Madeleine was always there to see it.
This was the primary reason she'd become the victim of
her mother's anger, shifting moods, and the outright center of her distress and years of depression. Jacques Grenier, initially a friend to her mother and fellow actor, and
Madeleine's first lover when she was no more than fifteen, had smoked it, too. But Jacques had controlled his
intake as her mother had not. He'd also never physically
and mentally punished her, as her mother frequently did
when the affects wore off.

Because of her childhood experiences Madeleine despised any medication or product of consumption that
impaired the mental faculties, including even wine,
which she rarely more than sipped. She knew her limits,
just as she well knew addiction when she saw it. Sitting
now in Lady Claire Childress's dark and eclectically fur-
nished dining hall, she was looking it straight in the face.

The lady had positioned herself for their luncheon at
the head of the long maple wood table, now covered
with a burgundy lace tablecloth and what remained of
their meal on exquisite white china. Thomas sat at her
right, followed by Madeleine. She'd inwardly questioned
being seated next to Thomas rather than to Lady Claire's
left, and then it occurred to her that this was intentional.
With this arrangement the woman received Thomas's
undivided attention, as he couldn't talk to both of them
at the same time, while Madeleine, in the seat behind
him, was placed as if at an inferior station. In a manner
of speaking, it was clever manipulation on the woman's
part, albeit obviously so.

Expressionless footmen stood nearby to lend assistance should they be needed, but aside from their silent presence, it was only the three of them to be seen or heard. And as the lady was somewhat inebriated herself and didn't seem to care what her household employees were privy to, she spoke freely, and almost entirely to Thomas.

Conversation during a surprisingly delicious meal of salmon mousse, cheese soufflé, chilled corn salad, and baby peas, had generally consisted of talk about Lady Claire herself, her late husband, her estate, which upon first glance was quite impressive, and naturally about Madeleine's employment in Winter Garden. The lady had been quite frank in her disapproval of that. To put it mildly, she loathed her female guest upon first sight, and Madeleine understood why. Lady Claire fancied Thomas to a noticeable degree and she didn't appreciate another woman in his company. Just as he had speculated would happen last Thursday.

Madeleine and Thomas hadn't spoken to each other much at all since then, since the evening he'd so aroused her with nothing more than implicit words and stimulating smells and his deep bass voice resonating a superbly controlled lust. Their topics of conversation had become formal again, almost awkward, largely about work and insignificant subjects. He'd left early on Friday only to return in time for dinner. But they were keenly aware of each other. She'd caught his eyes upon her whenever he was near, and from an experience she'd been drawing on a great deal recently, she knew his thoughts were about her. She only wished she knew what those thoughts were precisely.

Finally this morning, after her first long bath at the Kellyard Inn, she'd dressed for their luncheon in the same day gown she'd worn to Mrs. Rodney's tea, swept her hair up in conservative fashion, and together she and Thomas had walked side by side in silence, through the village teeming with Saturday activity, to the north end of town and onto the lavish private estate of their hostess for the afternoon.

Thomas, gracious in manner and word, had introduced her as his translator, of course; and she'd been received coldly, as expected. At first sight it would be evident to anyone that Lady Claire had at one time been beautiful, probably spoiled, and raised with selfish expectations like many in her class. Now she was wispy thin, frail to the point of collapse, and the aging of her skin was most apparent. She couldn't be more than forty-five by Madeleine's estimation, and yet she looked a good fifteen years older. She wore a well-made, expensive gown of deep bronze satin that would no doubt look smashing on someone whose figure curved becomingly from bust to hips. On her, however, the excessive fabric looked heavy, and hung off her body like loose drapery. Her light brown hair, pulled up neatly into a large chignon at her crown, had only just begun graying, but it had faded to dullness and was probably brittle at the ends. It was her skin, though, that had suffered the most at the hands of her indulgences. It had turned pale, lifeless, and wrinkled, and sagged at the neck and around the eyes, which she tried to hide with a severe application of powder that only made it more noticeable.

Lady Claire was dying, in Madeleine's opinion. Even now she slouched in her chair from too much wine, conversing with Thomas somewhat clumsily, ignoring Madeleine as well as her food, while her fingertips toyed nervously with her small, crystal glass of ruby-red medicine she waited impatiently to take at the end of her meal. She was certainly a habitual user, and the routine of mixing it with alcohol would one day likely be fatal.

It was only a matter of time before her death from either taking too much at once, or the giving out of a lifeless body that could accumulate no more excess.

Thomas must have known it, too, known far more than he'd intimated during their first conversation the day of her arrival in Winter Garden. That's why he flattered Lady Claire, as he put it. The woman was indeed lonely, drowning in drink and laudanum. And Lady Claire detested her, Madeleine assumed, because she was French perhaps, but probably more likely because she had stolen, to some degree, the only attention the woman received from an attentive man.

The two of them were speaking now of the Childress library across the hall from the grand music room they'd already discussed, of its large and unusual assortment of books collected by her husband's family for more than three generations. Thomas nodded where appropriate and listened courteously as Lady Claire carried on about something entirely insignificant. Madeleine imagined he smiled at the woman with sparkling soft eyes but she herself couldn't see them to know.

Madeleine leaned back so a servant could remove her empty plate, while another dutifully placed dessert in front of her—bubbling baked apple cobbler topped with whipped, sweet cream. If she learned nothing at all today, at least she would depart well fed.

"They're part of such a magnificent collection, Thomas, that the good Baron Rothebury has been buying them from me from time to time these last few months," Lady Claire announced proudly, lifting her spoon and stirring the cream on her cobbler. "I thought you'd find that interesting since you are a scholar. Perhaps you'd like to see them, too."

At the mention of the baron, Madeleine concentrated on the discourse once more, lifting her spoon and dipping it into her cobbler, saying nothing for a moment because she wanted to see where Thomas would take it.

"Baron Rothebury is buying your books?" he asked casually to clarify.

Lady Claire smiled enough to reveal yellowed teeth. "It's a hobby of his."

"Is it?" He appeared quite interested. "What do you suppose he wants with old books?"

The lady's eyelids sagged as she tipped forward and placed a small, gaunt hand on his coat sleeve. "These aren't just old books, Thomas. Some of them are worth quite a penny. And he's a collector himself, you know." Her forehead creased. "No, that's not right. Actually, I think he's more of a dealer."

Now Madeleine found herself intrigued. The peculiarity of such a preoccupation by a certain suspect was more than could be ignored.

"A book dealer," Thomas repeated. "How fascinating. I've only met the man once, though, so I really don't know him."

He leaned back in his chair, and Madeleine had to wonder if Thomas was trying to pull away from the lady's obviously tight grip. Of all the things she could read in him, she knew he was certainly not attracted to this woman.

Lady Claire's groomed brows lifted in forced surprise. "Goodness, I thought everybody knew the baron." She gave a nervous laugh and dropped her spoon from her left hand loudly on her china plate. "But perhaps you haven't lived in Winter Garden long enough. I shall have to invite you both to tea someday."

"I'll look forward to it," Thomas said, turning to his cobbler.

It would never happen. Madeleine knew that, and so did he.

"Do you know Baron Rothebury well, Lady Claire?" Madeleine interjected at last.

The woman's features waxed brittle as she shifted hard, bloodshot eyes to her for the first time in minutes. "Not nearly as well as I know Thomas."

"I wouldn't imagine so," she returned quickly, politely, scooping an apple slice onto her spoon. "But I have heard a great deal about him in recent days and I think I would like to meet him."

Without a second of pause, the woman sneered. "I don't think that will happen. He is not of your class, Mrs. DuMais."

A footman coughed. Thomas shifted a booted foot across the polished floor. Caught completely off guard, Madeleine nearly choked on the smooth, rich cinnamon-flavored confection sliding down her throat. Never had anyone of gentle breeding been so pointedly rude directly to her person.

She stiffened and slowly lowered her spoon to her plate. "I realize he and I probably have little in common—"

"I think that is an understatement," the lady cut in. She finally lifted her hand from Thomas's sleeve and sat up, reaching for her wineglass, gripping it gracelessly enough to splash a few tiny drops over the side. "I suppose where you are from women of all kinds express familiarity with well-bred gentlemen, but it doesn't happen here."

Even in France, familiarity meant a great deal more than acquaintance. Madeleine remained composed, but her appetite had floundered. Seconds of uncomfortable silence passed, then Thomas cleared his throat and leaned a little toward her, shielding her in a manner with his broad shoulder.

"I think what Mrs. DuMais means is that she would

like to meet a number of people during her stay in Winter Garden," he offered very smoothly, his voice and smile conveying charm and reason. "Baron Rothebury is only one. And perhaps it won't happen. She won't be in England very long."

Lady Claire's gaze narrowed as she looked from one to the other. Then she took a long swallow of wine and set the glass back on the table. "I'm sure that's for the best. He hosts a ball each January, you know. The annual Winter Masquerade. A beautiful party every year. Perhaps you'd like to escort me, Thomas?"

"I should find that most enjoyable, Lady Claire," he answered thoughtfully. "But in truth, I doubt I'll receive an invitation. I'm not especially of his class, either."

She looked stung. "Of course you are. You are an educated man." Waving a hand in irritation, she dismissed it. "Anyway, it doesn't matter in the least. I shall take you as my guest."

Thomas nodded very slowly, spooning a bit of his cobbler. Then with deliberation, he murmured, "But what of Mrs. DuMais?"

The lady's expression tightened. "What about her?"

Thomas shrugged subtly. "Who will escort her if she is still in town?"

Madeleine knew he was intentionally provoking the woman. There were an assortment of reasonable responses already discussed, not one of them needing to be spoken again.

Lady Claire bristled in her chair, making the bones in her shoulders even more pronounced. "She is not worthy of an invitation, Thomas. She is your employee and nothing more."

The air grew stifling suddenly. Madeleine folded her hands in her lap, waiting, refusing to speak in her own defense and ignoring the insults for the good of her profession.

Thomas took another bite of his cobbler then laid his spoon to the side. "But she is also educated, Lady Claire, and as Englishmen we should be hospitable while she is visiting our country, don't you agree?" He smiled again and leaned forward over the corner of the table. "Maybe the baron would find her company charming. That would leave more time for you and I to spend together."

The tops of the lady's cheeks and nose reddened; her thin mouth curled. She refused to look at Madeleine. "The good Baron Rothebury would naturally find her charming, Thomas. Just to look at her is to see what she is."

Madeleine stilled as the first wave of outrage pulsed through her. She supposed for a moment that such an incredible statement uttered in total disrespect bothered her so much, as it never would have before, because she was in some small regard afraid that Thomas would believe it. But he played his part perfectly.

"Lady Claire," he said easily, "I'm sure Mrs. DuMais is of good family—"

"I'm sure she is not. And she is not for you, Thomas."

That was enough. Her embarrassment was thorough; the rudeness overwhelming. "You are right, Lady Claire," she affirmed brazenly, tilting her chin and staring into the woman's vicious eyes. "My mother was an actress."

The instant satisfaction beaming on the Englishwoman's face was at first laughable, then suddenly unimportant because at that moment Thomas reached out, under the table, and placed his palm high on her thigh.

Her first coherent thought was that it was a large palm, warm even through the layers of her skirt and petticoats, with long fingers that reached into the gentle crease between her legs.

She didn't move, and he didn't look at her. With his left hand he reached for his wine, took a large, slow swallow, then lowered it back to the table.

Ignorant to the rising heat in the room, Lady Claire lifted her wineglass and did the same. "Was your father also an actor, Mrs. DuMais?" she asked with harsh sarcasm, seconds later.

Thomas squeezed her slightly. Whether it was a warning or just a show of understanding, she couldn't guess, but right at that moment she didn't care, for he still hadn't made a move to release her from his grasp.

She tried to speak with confidence. "I didn't know my father, Lady Claire." An outright lie, and one that would only solidify the lady's delight, but she refused to degrade the memory of the only bright part of her life by revealing it to a woman who would no doubt ridicule it.

"I see," Lady Claire replied with exaggerated concern. "Then they were never married?"

Madeleine felt his fingers move. He didn't say a word, but she took the action as warning this time. Even now she felt his large body so close beside her, the warmth of it radiating through his brown woolen suit, his palm scorching her leg as his fingers pushed very close to the center between her thighs. Then her heart began to pound, because it occurred to her that although he could feel nothing directly, he was quite aware of exactly where he touched her.

Her cheeks flushed, and perspiration broke out between her breasts, but she knew he wanted to witness her continued composure. That had to be his point. She thanked God that he hadn't yet looked at her because she was certain if he did she would fail.

With arms as heavy as thick tree branches, she pulled

her hands from her lap. One she raised to rest on the arm of her chair, the other she placed lengthwise across her thighs, under the table, closing her palm over his knuckles.

He didn't move.

"Naturally my parents were married," she murmured, her tongue thick and dry as she tried to balance her thoughts. "He was English, Lady Claire, and a sea captain. He died in the West Indies before I was born."

Their hostess visibly cringed from the revelation and lifted her wineglass for a final time to gulp the remaining contents. "Were you aware of this when you hired the woman, Thomas?"

He drew in a very long breath before he shared his concern. "Yes, but in choosing a translator, I felt education to be more important than a background one can never change."

Lady Claire put her glass down hard and gaped at him, appalled. "Good breeding means everything."

In a very cool voice, he countered, "I think what one makes of one's own life is far more significant in the end."

Madeleine felt an immediate swell of pleasure from his defense of her, especially since there was such a risk to their work in his expressing such opinions.

The lady glared at her, and then her eyes turned lifeless with acceptance. "Her appearance has bewitched you, Thomas."

He shook his head. "I'm not easily bewitched, madam. I know exactly who she is."

A tremor passed through her at the decisiveness in his voice, but he still hadn't looked at her, and he had yet to move his hand from her leg. The tone of the conversation was starting to turn against them both, however, and she couldn't let that happen with so much at stake.

"My mother only took to the stage, Lady Claire, because she had no other options," she explained gravely, recovering her poise and working the lie splendidly. "I shall be grateful to her always for raising enough money in such a degrading profession so that I could be educated in Switzerland and eventually find a suitable match in my late husband."

Thomas, at long last, turned his head to face her, but she couldn't meet his eyes. Not yet. She felt their warmth on her skin, knew she was reacting to his touch by the blush in her cheeks and that he saw it.

"And what of your family now, Mrs. DuMais?" the lady gruffly pursued, once again fingering her crystal glass of laudanum. "Is your mother still *working?*" She drew out the last word as if it were something despicable. Evil.

Madeleine had regained her senses and was ready to respond. Until Thomas moved the fingers on her thigh even closer, then covered her thumb with his. She was now certain he touched, just minutely with the tips, the intimate center between her legs.

She grew hotter still and finally, bravely, chanced a glance into his eyes.

He knew what he was doing. He knew, and she liquefied from the gentleness and pleasure those honey-brown circles conveyed. His expression remained neutral to the best of his ability, but she read his thoughts. He wasn't at all worried that they would be discovered. He was enjoying this.

She tried to faintly push his fingers aside, but he refused to withdraw them. What annoyed her, though, was that he wouldn't do this at the cottage when they were alone, but he would do it here. He insisted they couldn't be lovers, and yet he purposely aroused her in Lady

Claire Childress's dining room while they worked. She didn't understand his motives at all.

"Mrs. DuMais?"

Sharply she looked back to her hostess, who waited patiently for an answer.

"I—" She straightened a little and shook herself to carry on. "I've not seen my mother in years, Lady Claire." It was now time to get to the point, before she gave herself away. "Over time she grew to enjoy the addictive qualities of opium and ceased to function rationally. I'm not at all sure whether she still lives."

Thomas felt the instantaneous shift in mood. Excitement of several orders ran thick in the air and, mingled with the friction between the women and the contact of his skin to her gown at the point where sanity reached the entrance to paradise, it created the most incredible wave of desire in him. Unlike anything he'd felt in years. She was marvelous—in action, in beauty, in cleverness, and the ability to disguise her feelings. This couldn't be easy for her, and yet she remained in perfect form. The need to lose himself in her eyes, in her embrace, to tease her body in escalating pleasure was overwhelming. He wanted her desperately, but the only time he could allow himself to touch her was when she couldn't respond. It was safe now, and although he'd never planned to confuse her with such a forward act, he just couldn't bring himself to pull back.

"I'm sure she overindulged, Mrs. DuMais," Lady Claire said in a disgusted, ragged breath, interrupting his carnal thoughts like a callous slap to the face. "Living such a-an unrestrained life will do that to a woman."

Madeleine was tight beside him, but she remained totally self-possessed. "Opium in any form can be addictive, Lady Claire, and can kill. Even the laudanum at your fingertips."

Thomas shifted his gaze to the head of the table. That was the knife thrust. The woman's eyes blazed, her face grew red beneath sagging skin. Then it hardened with a rage she couldn't hide.

"This is medicine, Mrs. DuMais. I have a heart condition that requires attention. I take neither more nor less than my physician prescribes."

Madeleine shifted her bottom in her chair, lifting her hips and squeezing his knuckles at the same time so that he couldn't budge them. He clenched his teeth; drew a sharp inhale. There was no mistaking her actions. She had purposely taken the advantage away from him. His fingers now grazed the place of his ageless hunger, and even through her clothes he felt the heat of her there, felt the outline of soft, luscious curls that would one day beckon him to bliss. . . .

That was impossible. She was fully dressed in layers, and he could feel nothing. He was a starved man, and his imagination carried him to a feast he couldn't yet taste. His heart pounded, and although he faced away from her, he still closed his eyes momentarily to regain control. He could take no more and he was certain she knew it. Gently he pulled his hand away, and she let him go.

"I am sure you need your medicine, Lady Claire," Madeleine acknowledged softly, her thoughts unreadable in her level voice. "I was not speaking of you but of my mother. It is true, however, that opium, when taken too much in any form, is deadly."

The woman had nothing to say. For seconds intense hatred flowed without discretion from a lady of quality who knew to behave better. But she was drunk and nearly incoherent. Thomas had seen it in her before.

Quickly Lady Claire raised her crystal glass to her mouth, closed her eyes, and drank the contents, allowing it to slide down her throat before she licked her lips of the excess. When she looked at them again, her focus was clouded, her face tired. Old.

"It is time for me to rest, Thomas," she mumbled sadly. "As always I have enjoyed your company and wish you to return. Perhaps next time I'll show you my extensive library, and hopefully some of the other private rooms in my extraordinary home."

It was meant to be an intimate invitation, clear to all of them, but he wouldn't respond to it now. Madeleine sat beside him, and he sensed the anxiety in her. They'd seen enough, and they'd been clearly dismissed.

After placing his napkin on the table he buttoned his jacket to hide what remained of his rigid need, then stood with some grace. Lady Claire offered him her hand in expectation, and he took it in his, lowering his head to brush his lips against the back of it.

"It is always a pleasure to visit you, madam. Lunch was superb, as usual."

The woman dropped her chin graciously. He released her and turned toward Madeleine, pulling her chair out and helping her to rise. "Shall we go?"

"Yes, Thomas," she replied pointedly, gazing into his eyes, revealing nothing. "I think we should return to the cottage and discuss what we've started."

And it had started. *He* had started it, and there was no turning back. She was confident and determined, and he was, in part, feeling the gravity of it all beginning to sink in.

"Thank you for a delightful luncheon, Lady Claire," Madeleine said to their hostess.

She was ignored.

With that, Madeleine straightened her shoulders,

turned, and strode regally from the dining hall as he followed, his palm to her back. Lady Claire certainly noticed him touching her, and at that moment it was exactly what he wanted.

Six

They walked to the cottage in silence. The sky had turned a dark, smoky gray, the day bitter with cold, and the village square had emptied of all but those who needed to be there for essentials.

Of course, they had many things to discuss, but Madeleine was lost in her thoughts, and he didn't interrupt them. He wasn't sure what he would say that wouldn't sound evasive or gauche, and another discussion of work seemed trite. He realized she intended to bring the subject of his gross breach of decorum to his attention as soon as they were safely inside the cottage walls. At least that gave him a few more minutes to conjure up an excuse of some sort, although for the life of him he couldn't think of one other than that he craved so badly to touch her intimately that she should be pleased he hadn't leaned in and sucked the skin at her throat in front of Lady Claire and all of her servants. Madeleine probably wouldn't be amused to know that, though. He couldn't decipher her mood exactly, but he was fairly certain she was annoyed, as her step had been nearly a pace in front of his for the entire return trip through the village, which had to be purposeful since he couldn't walk as fast as she could anyway.

As they reached the gate to the property, she waited for him to unlatch it and hold it open for her to step through. A frigid gust of wind whipped around them, knocking her hood from her head, and she shivered.

"It's cold," he murmured, then felt ridiculous announcing something so inept.

She stopped abruptly on the stone path and whirled around, nearly causing a collision between them. He reacted by grabbing her shoulders with gloved hands to steady her.

Her eyes were blazing, huge and accusatory as she stared into his, but she didn't push him away.

"Yes, Thomas, it is cold," she agreed matter-of-factly. "And since the weather is something you feel especially safe discussing with me, let's discuss this aspect of it." She tipped her head slightly, her features flat. "My lips are freezing, and I would like you to warm them for me."

His breath caught in his chest. He'd never expected that. Instinctively he dropped his arms to his sides and took a step back.

She clearly didn't like that response to her demand. Her glare hardened, and her eyes narrowed to thin slits. She gripped her gloved hands together in front of her so tightly the leather pulled at the knuckles.

"We are a man and a woman physically attracted to each other, Thomas, and you are quite aware of it," she said soberly. "Decide what you want from our relationship, and I will honor it, but I think it's time you stopped teasing me."

He blinked, startled so much she probably noticed it. She wasn't just annoyed with him now, she was infuriated. Was he teasing her? Is that how she perceived his actions? He supposed it had to be. He'd stood so close to her two nights ago, breathing heavily at her neck while telling her they couldn't be lovers, then boldly caressed her inner thighs without permission less than thirty minutes ago.

The icy wind blew a strand of her hair across her cheek, and he reached out and touched it with his fingers, drawing it back behind her ear. She shivered again but she held his gaze squarely, daring him to deny her.

His nerves charged at the thought of kissing her at her request. His body, even in winter chill, grew tight again with need. Suddenly he'd never been more desperate to do anything. It was time to move forward, to openly acknowledge his interest where touching her surreptitiously and stroking her with words did not. He grasped her elbow firmly through her cloak, turned her toward the cottage, and led her along the path to the front door.

"Thomas—"

"If I am to kiss you, Madeleine, I can't do it outside where anyone can see."

That logic subdued her a little, at least enough to silence her, but he knew without looking that she smiled with satisfaction.

He stopped at the door but didn't release her as he fished into his coat pocket for the key. Smoothly, surprised he wasn't shaking noticeably, he unbolted the lock, pushed the door open, pulled her inside behind him, and closed it with a loud *thud*.

He turned to her then, standing in the entryway, and although his pulse was pounding in his ears from the most intense anticipation he'd ever felt, his body remained remarkably calm.

They stared at each other, the sound of their breathing ringing hollow in the empty foyer. For a brief moment he hesitated because he hadn't done anything like this in years. Nervousness pierced him with uncertainty and a shade of embarrassment. But she was waiting, her cheeks and nose pink from cold, her beautiful blue eyes challenging him to change his mind, to withdraw.

He had no intention of withdrawing now. This would be the contact of his fantasies, the beginning of his dreams.

Still bundled in winter layers, standing a foot apart, he bent toward her, pausing only a second when he watched her close her eyes. Then he tilted his head and closed his.

He first noticed the coolness of her face, the scent of flowers on her skin, and then he felt the sweetest softness against his mouth—cold, inviting. Perfect.

A very slight, utterly feminine sound carried on the exhale that left her throat at the initial joining. His breathing grew shallow, his heartbeat raced from that small response of contentment, and he was instantly transported to the brink of heaven.

He lingered with his lips just barely pressed to hers, warming them as they warmed his, drinking in the pleasure, and she didn't immediately push for more. He wanted to savor it all for memory, and she was allowing him. She reached up gingerly with her hands, lightly encircling his neck with her palms, the leather soft and cool on his skin. He closed his arms around her waist, pulling her toward him a little, absorbing the feel of her as he gently began to move his lips against hers.

She followed his lead, opening for him, picking up the rhythm, leaning into him until their chests touched. Her breathing began to quicken as well when he ran the tip of his tongue briefly along her upper lip, and that ignited him inside.

He groaned and crushed her to him, raising one hand

from the curve of her spine to the back of her head. She did the same, her arms around his neck, hands on his hair, clutching him now with intensifying need. Her tongue mated with his, their breath mingled, and the sounds of their joining echoed loudly in the small, empty foyer.

Thomas pushed her back a foot or so until she rested against the wall, the air quickly charging with a consuming, physical hunger as his lips now moved frantically against hers, tasting, savoring, craving more.

She lowered her arms, her fingers reaching for the buttons on his coat. But he wanted the control, and he grabbed her hands and forced them back, positioning them on either side of her head, her knuckles flat against the paneled wood behind her.

He pinned her there, supported by his greater strength, deepening the force of his mouth, his heart thundering, sweat beading at his neck and forehead, gloved fingers wrapped around hers in a vague display of his command. And then he plunged his tongue into her farther still, searching, finding, sucking hers, burning inside.

She lifted her body to his, held powerless but desperate to feel. She kissed him back for moments, hours it seemed, expertly, passionately, giving as he gave. Then finally she gasped against his mouth and broke free, jerking her head to the side, pushing her breasts into his chest, pressing her lips to his jaw.

"Touch me, Thomas," she begged in a raspy, hot breath against his skin.

God, how he wanted to touch her! To feel her naked flesh scorch his, to stoke the flame between her legs, to envelop himself in her wet heat, to love her until she climaxed around him, in his arms. His body begged him to drag her to the floor and take her here. Now.

But he couldn't. It would be an act without emotion

on her part, the beginning of casual interludes between them, Madeleine leaving him in the end, expecting and wanting nothing more. He'd risked too much already to allow that to happen.

At that moment determination overtook sexual urging, and he slowed his actions, remembering his purpose, his reasons for bringing her here. He drew his lips across the milky softness of her cheek, sucked her earlobe, grazed it with his teeth, felt her tremble against him.

"Please—"

"Not now," he whispered with a restraint he couldn't believe possible. They were the hardest words he'd ever said in his life.

She whimpered from frustration, from unfulfilled want, and he traced the curve of her throat up and down with his parted mouth, inhaling the scents of soft wool and woman for a final time before squeezing his eyes shut and withdrawing his touch.

She turned away from his face, and he lowered his forehead to the cold, hard wall behind her.

For nearly a minute they stood like that, their heartbeats drumming loudly in the otherwise silent house, their breathing irregular and fast. He still held himself firmly pressed against her, and she didn't immediately try to move.

"Madeleine," he whispered, and could think of nothing more to add.

She attempted to inhale deeply, and he pulled back enough for her to draw breath, releasing her hands at last which she dropped to her sides. He coiled his into fists and shoved them against the wall behind her head, keeping his eyes shut.

"You are marvelous, Thomas," she murmured shakily, the words barely heard.

That wrapped his heart in exquisite warmth.

"You don't know me," he countered huskily.

He felt her turn to look at him. Then she reached up with her gloved fingers and drew a line down the scar at his mouth.

"I will in time."

The certainty in her voice captured his imagination, and let free the possibilities implied.

Slowly he pushed himself up and rotated his body, falling back against the wall to stand next to her, allowing his eyes to open finally as he stared at the dark, polished wood paneling across from him.

"You are not practiced, are you?" she asked quietly, seconds later.

She was attempting to measure the awkwardness of their kiss, the depth of his experience, and for the first time since they'd met, he considered lying outright. In the end he decided against it. "It's more accurate to say I'm out of practice, Madeleine."

For moments nothing happened. Then she sighed and reached for his hand, squeezing his fingers gently. "Do something for me, Thomas?"

He turned his head to glance down at her at last, swallowing forcefully at the sight of her heightened color, the heat of arousal still in her eyes, the playful smile lifting her full, sensuous lips.

"You called me Maddie once before," she whispered very slowly. "I would like you to call me that again."

Before he could respond, she released him, stood upright, and entered the parlor as she headed to her room.

Seven

At precisely half past nine, as he did seven days a week without exception, Richard Sharon strolled into his well-lit and lavishly adorned dining room to find his usual steaming breakfast of three poached eggs, ham, and toast awaiting him. Pouring tea from the silver pot, his butler, Magnus, bid him a prosaic good morning without looking up, then placed the pot on a sideboard and pulled a chair out for him at the head of the table. Richard sat comfortably, and without a word, Magnus laid his napkin in his lap, bowed his head once, and quit the room. Lifting his fork, Richard speared a thick slice of ham and began to eat in earnest.

Life was good, he decided, spreading a newspaper before him across his new and elaborately embroidered Spanish table linens. He perused the front page, noting nothing in particular of any great interest—more worker discord at the docks, a fire on the north end, the usual irregularities at Parliament. Alas, it was rather old news by several days, but then that couldn't be helped when one lived in the country. And, of course, he would never dream of moving from his family home to the city. In Winter Garden his assets were many, his business lucrative, and with his latest endeavor he now reaped rewards beyond his first imaginings. Yes, life was very good indeed.

Cutting into his eggs, he continued to skim over mostly trivial information when his butler returned to the dining room and cleared his throat.

Richard peeked up in acknowledgment, knowing it had to be important because he had strict rules about being disturbed during meals.

"Forgive the intrusion, my lord, but Mrs. Bennington-Jones is requesting a moment of your time. Are you receiving?"

Richard hid his smile well. He always received Penelope Bennington-Jones, and Magnus knew this. But it was the man's station to ask, and Richard invariably placed high value on servants who kept to their station. His excellent butler had been with him for six years and tirelessly followed direction without question—exactly as he should.

Looking back to his plate, he placed a bite of ham on his tongue, chewed slowly, and turned another page of the paper while Magnus waited, hands behind his back. After swallowing and reaching for his tea, he directed, "Send her in."

Magnus once again left the room, and it was Richard's turn to wait, partly in anticipation and partly in dread. He'd sent a note yesterday requesting a visit with Penelope today, and although he didn't think she'd arrive so early, he knew she would come. He found the lady irritating beyond words, but she was his favorite Winter Garden busybody, mostly because she didn't realize how much value he placed on her nosy observances. Indeed, the woman had no idea he used her thus. Even so, she was remarkably adapted to the work.

Moments later he heard the click of her heels on his parquet floor, and he resigned himself to the meeting, though refusing to indicate his anxiousness. He continued to eat and read his newspaper as her ample figure filled the room.

"Good morning, Lord Rothebury," she said brightly.

He raised only his lashes to regard her, catching the false smile upon her lips, the suggestion of mischief in her shrewd eyes, taking in her full, extravagantly designed gown and matching feathered hat that now inclined unnaturally on her head due to the force of the outside wind. The woman was a sight, and not for the first time Richard wished his best spy was a trifle more appealing to look at.

"Mrs. Bennington-Jones, how good of you to call," he responded nonchalantly, shifting his focus to a jar of blackberry jam. With his elbow he gestured to an adjacent chair. "Please join me."

It was a command, not a request, and she obliged, squeezing her large body and wide skirts into the seat beside him.

"Tea, madam?" Magnus asked, standing beside her with the pot and an empty cup.

"Yes," she replied stiffly, not looking at the help when she spoke, but at Richard's food and his hands as he spread jam on his toast.

He knew she waited for an invitation to dine; but she didn't need the nourishment, and he refused to feed her. Good food was costly.

Magnus poured, then returned the pot to the sideboard before taking his leave for a third time.

"So," Richard started, indicating cream and sugar on the table, "how is your family?"

It now became apparent to her that he wasn't going to offer breakfast. She sniffed and reached for the sugar spoon. "Very well, thank you," she answered curtly. "My lovely Hermione will make her debut come spring, if you'll recall, so we're already planning our visits to the city, engaging the services of only the best dressmakers, hatters, jewelers, and such. It's a very busy time."

Naturally, he mused, deciding not to comment. He understood perfectly Penelope's intention of drawing him into a courtship with the second of her three homely daughters, and he refused to honor her remark with any indication of interest. "What of Desdemona?" he inquired instead, scooping up the remainder of his eggs.

Penelope bristled. "She and her weasel of a husband are expecting."

He nearly dropped his fork. Desdemona and Randolph Winsett were expecting a child? Extraordinary. So much so he was suddenly quite nervous about the revelation. "How wonderful for them," he mumbled after swallowing a thick coating of yoke. He lifted his wide, cloth napkin to his mouth to hide his stunned reaction. "When is the blessed event to occur?"

She sighed, obviously annoyed by the entire matter, but she didn't look up as she stirred a generous helping of cream into her tea. "In June, I expect."

A rather equivocal reply. Richard wiped the corners of his mouth, making the calculations quickly. A birth in late June would put conception close to the time of the wedding night he supposed, if they'd had one at all, but then what other answer would her mother give? Still, regardless of the predicament, Desdemona was now safely married so it really didn't matter that she carried.

"My congratulations, then," he offered, dropping his gaze once more to what remained of his breakfast. "I'm sure you must be quite happy at the prospect of having a grandchild."

She ignored that, adjusting her large skirts in a vain attempt to find a more comfortable position at the table. "I'm sure you've heard the news about the Frenchwoman who has invaded our village and is now living alone with the scholar in the Hope cottage."

Invaded? Richard nearly snorted at the ridiculousness of it. She made it sound like the whole bloody French Army had descended upon them. If there was one thing Penelope Bennington-Jones most assuredly did not possess it was the gift of subtlety. What struck him, though, was that she'd brought this to his attention before he'd requested the information, which, as it happened, was the sole reason he'd invited her today. The Frenchwoman was creating quite a stir in their little community, and Penelope was greatly bothered by her.

"I haven't heard a thing, actually," he maintained with a casual air, "but I have seen the lady from a distance."

"She is *not* a lady."

The strength of that assertion took him aback, but he didn't reveal any thought beyond indifference. "And why do you say that?"

"Well," she huffed, "not only is she living alone in a small cottage with a man who is not her husband, but I've met her, my lord. I find her quite . . . invasive."

"How so?" he asked, biting into the last of his toast, noting with interest that she'd used the same word choice twice in as many minutes.

Penelope's lips stretched thin as she stared hard at him. "She is obviously immoral."

He nodded as he chewed, understanding that this broad statement was nothing more than conjecture, that she had no conclusive evidence of anything. He decided not to pursue it.

Penelope lifted one of her thick hands and tried to push her hat back up on her head without success. "She is a widow," she added accusingly, "and not unattractive to look at, but frankly, I find her presence here suspicious."

From what he'd seen of her in the distance, the Frenchwoman was lovely; and, of course, that's what bothered Penelope the most. What bothered *him*, for reasons unclear, was that such a woman spent her time with Thomas Blackwood: thirty-nine, Cambridge scholar, war veteran, and cripple. *That* is what he found suspicious. Odd that a lady of her background and beauty would intentionally reside with a man who couldn't possibly please her in any way.

Richard lifted a silver bell and rang it twice to inform the servant standing directly behind him that he required more tea and that it was time to collect his empty plate.

"So, madam," he carried on through a deliberate sigh, "what do you gather she's doing among us in our small village, hmm?"

Penelope scoffed with an exaggerated toss of her hand. "She says she's here as Mr. Blackwood's employee. That she's translating his war memoirs into her native tongue."

An intriguing piece of news he'd need to absorb, though not entirely implausible, he supposed. "When did you meet the woman?"

"Thursday last, at Mrs. Rodney's tea."

That had to have been an interesting affair. "What were your impressions of her?"

She straightened. "I found her to be quite French."

How outrageously *profound*, he wanted to shout. Instead, he stirred more cream and sugar into his full, steaming cup, then leaned back easily in his chair.

"What do you know of the scholar?"

Her brows lifted. "Mr. Blackwood?"

What other scholars were they discussing? He nodded once, smiling tightly, withholding his impatience.

She shrugged nimbly, lifting her cup. "I've only spoken to him briefly, but he seems to be a regular gentleman, quiet, educated. A bit of a recluse."

Again, not much substantial information. But something uncertain about it nagged at him, and Richard began to tap his fingers on the table, thinking. "What do you suppose *he's* doing in Winter Garden?" he pressed, voice lowered.

Penelope seemed genuinely surprised at the question. Truthfully, even he hadn't considered this until just now, but, of course, he had no intention of making her aware of it.

"He's never said," she replied after a long sip of her tea. "I just assumed he was here because he wanted to spend his time in the solitude of our village, to retreat to a simple but socially adequate community." Within seconds her lids narrowed, her lips puckered, and she eyed him conspiratorially. "That seems odd now, doesn't it, Lord Rothebury?"

He had to ask. "How so?"

"Well, it's not as if he's from Northumberland, or even London," she explained gravely. "He's from Eastleigh. That's a rather quiet community in itself, isn't it? Small and lovely, and not too far from Winter Garden." She leaned toward him, dropping her voice, to add, "Why should he come to our village to do what he could just as easily do at home?"

Why, indeed, Richard pondered with mounting qualm. If the scholar had spent a week or two—even a month—on holiday here, he would think nothing of it. Many of the gentry retreated to Winter Garden for its seclusion and beauty, especially during the cold season. But Tho-

mas Blackwood had arrived from a town with a climate
not unlike their own, had been here for nearly three
months with no sign of leaving anytime soon, and was
now even taking employees into his rented cottage. Penelope had posed a magnificent question, infuriating him
immediately because she'd thought of it before he had.
No reason to allow her to know that, however.

Smoothly, he said, "I've wondered this very thing myself, madam."

"Have you?"

The intrigue in her tone and the widening of her dark,
piercing eyes made him pause. This was a sensitive time
in his prosperous business, and the consequences would
be extreme should he fail. He didn't want her snooping
openly into something that was starting to give him serious question.

With a blasé grin, he waved his palm to brush the
matter off, then lifted his cup again. "But I'm sure
there's nothing to it. He probably needed a change of
scenery for a season, and the Hope cottage is peaceful
and has an excellent view." *Of my home*, he suddenly
realized like a strike to the face. Something else that
seemed enormously coincidental to the moment. Something else he'd need to give more extensive thought.

Penelope's forehead crinkled skeptically with his casual explanation, so Richard subtly, and quickly, reverted to his original topic. "What about Mr.
Blackwood's relationship with the Frenchwoman? Are
they . . . friendly, to your knowledge?"

If she found his endless questions unusual or prying
she didn't show it. Indeed, a look of embarrassment
overcame her as a flood of color crept up the sagging
skin at her neck. She squirmed uncomfortably, lowering
her gaze and once more attempting to fix the ugly hat
on her head, once more to no avail.

He waited for her answer, sipping his tea, watching her with marked interest.

"According to the Frenchwoman," she revealed at last, staring now at the embroidered leaves on his table-cloth, "there is no chance of a romantic involvement between them because of the . . . of his particular war injury. He cannot—he does not find her appealing."

Richard blinked quickly and sucked in his cheeks to keep from laughing. He didn't believe this absurd bit of female gossip for a minute, although he conceded that the ladies of Winter Garden likely did. Most amazing was that the Frenchwoman had discussed this socially.

He took another full swallow, then placed his cup back on the table to fold his hands in his lap. "What is her name?"

Penelope drew a long breath and squarely met his gaze again. "Madeleine DuMais," she said succinctly. "And if that doesn't sound like a name one might use on the stage . . ."

She let the statement linger, her eyes now sparkling with implication, and it had its effect. Mrs. Bennington-Jones was a nosy bitch, but she was keen with perception and usually chose her words carefully. He knew that, and it had served him well in the past. But did she mean an actress literally or figuratively? Or just that the Frenchwoman was living indefinitely in Winter Garden using a false name for a purpose they didn't yet understand? He'd never ask Penelope to clarify for fear of appearing ignorant, or worse, stupid. It hardly mattered anyway, as he would no doubt discover the French-woman's intentions on his own eventually. For now, though, Richard acknowledged that regardless of the scholar's reclusive nature and Mrs. Madeleine DuMais's beauty or background, both of them had come to Winter

Garden under very odd circumstances and at a very peculiar time.

Raising a fingertip, he traced the rim of his china cup. "I suppose it would be in our best interest if I made her acquaintance."

He read a mixture of feelings as they crossed Penelope's face—doubt, irritation, disgust, and even flattery that he had included her as somewhat of an equal in his statement. Then she masked her expression once more and nodded in agreement. "I'm sure you'll not invite her to the Winter Masquerade, Lord Rothebury," she readily advised. "The woman is not of our class, and her presence at the ball would certainly be pernicious."

Pernicious? *Only by stealing the attention from your own ugly daughters*, he wanted to insert but had the good breeding not to. Still, he couldn't ignore the remark. He had the power, and she needed to remember that.

"Mrs. Bennington-Jones," he began directly, his smile charming, "I'll do what is necessary to discover what I can about her. If she is beautiful, that will make my efforts all the more enjoyable, and I should be delighted to extend her an invitation."

He watched her blanch, then color profusely in the cheeks. She couldn't say anything to counter without being rude or insolent, and they both knew it.

Placing his napkin on the table, he stood. "I'm sure you have other social calls to make, madam, and I am anxious to begin my morning ride. I'm so pleased you were able to visit."

Reluctantly she also raised her body to a standing position, because there was nothing else she could say or do.

"Thank you for the *tea*, my lord," she murmured tightly.

He supposed he had to give her credit for that one.

She extended her hand, and he squeezed her knuckles gently, choosing not to raise them to his lips, which she clearly noticed. Then abruptly she turned, and with a *swish* of her skirts and a hard tug at her hat for good measure, she regally strode from the dining room.

Richard remained where he was for a solid minute, staring at the empty doorway. For as long as he'd lived in Winter Garden he'd never trusted anyone, and to do so now would be a wild risk he refused to take. Too much was at stake. But it was apparent that he needed to meet the Frenchwoman soon, and the avoidance of wild risks certainly didn't preclude his socializing with a beautiful woman. Or from starting a discreet investigation of his own.

Eight

It was well after ten when they left the cottage. Darkness prevailed, save for the glow of a three-quarter moon directly overhead, the air cold, moist, and very still. The lingering scent of an early-evening rainfall and damp earth roused her senses as Madeleine silently walked behind Thomas into the backyard toward the cluster of bushes that would lead them to the path beside the lake.

During the last few days their suspicions about Richard Sharon had been building. Madeleine believed him to be the smuggler, more out of intuition than anything else, and that she trusted. She worked from intuition frequently, and hers had yet to fail her. She did, however, understand rationally that facts were far more important in the end, and now they had facts anew and were acting upon them.

For the third consecutive night of what could turn out to be many frigid hours in dark silence, they were sneaking onto the baron's estate to observe what they could clandestinely because Thomas had received urgent word from Sir Riley that another shipment of opium had been stolen from the docks at Portsmouth only five days ago. It had been several weeks since the last theft, and this bit of news couldn't have come at a more fortunate time for them in their investigation. It also gave Madeleine the opportunity to accompany Thomas to Rothebury's property as she hadn't before. Of course, they had no idea if they'd witness anything at all, but by their estimation the stolen crates would be making their way to Winter Garden within the next several days, and it was more likely that they would be smuggled in at night. If she and Thomas saw or heard anything at all, the proof would be at their fingertips.

They cleared the brush at that moment to stand side by side at the edge of the lake. It shimmered like thick, black ink, and from the moon's reflection off the water she could see the manor house in the distance, now dark and looming, silhouetted in shadow. Whatever else the baron did, he retired early. Not a light could be seen in any window.

Thomas took her hand in his companionably, to help her along the unfamiliar path, she supposed, and she raised her eyes to regard him. He stared out across the water, his harsh, warrior-like features etched into lines of calculated contemplation. Then he glanced down to her, and a ghost of a smile lifted his lips.

Her heart fluttered from anticipation—an uncommon feeling for her. She'd been stimulated within by men before, but never by one so ruggedly masculine, and certainly never by a simple look. Suddenly she felt the most intense desire to kiss him again.

He obviously had other ideas.

Holding her hand firmly, he turned, and together they began to make their way through the dense brush in a southerly direction toward Richard Sharon's Winter Garden home.

They'd talked little to each other during the last few days. Thomas had kept to himself, and so had she, each of them going about their business for the good of the government. She'd worked the village market, meeting a few of the common people with the pretense of purchasing goods, while Thomas, for his part, had called on and visited with a few members of the local gentry. Together they had attended church service, which many had found so peculiar that they'd concentrated more on Madeleine and Thomas's presence than on the vicar and his lengthy lecture on forgiving one's neighbor of trifle irritants. They'd also watched the baron's home from the distant trees for the last two nights, but so far they'd neither seen nor learned anything of real significance. She wouldn't go so far as to say the limited conversations between them since their kiss had been a kind of avoidance. Rather, it would be more correct to say they were simply returning their concentration to the issues that had brought them to Winter Garden in the first place. Madeleine also realized, work aside, the days since their kiss had been uncomfortable for Thomas. This was why she hadn't pursued a discussion about it specifically. Until now.

"I've been doing some thinking, Thomas," she said, broaching the subject thoughtfully, breaking the silence at last as they ambled along the path.

He lifted a long tree branch, holding it away so she could pass beneath it, but he didn't release her hand. He didn't respond immediately, either, so she carried on. There was nobody around to see or hear them, and the baron's property was a good walk away.

Confidently she expounded. "I've been thinking about the kiss you gave me last Saturday."

"Have you?" he replied quietly, giving no indication

of being surprised at her choice of topic. "And what are your conclusions?"

So like Thomas to be pragmatic. Smiling, voice steady from an imminent triumph, she answered, "Aside from the fact that it was rushed and somewhat awkward, I found it to be quite . . . consuming."

He tossed her a fast glance that she felt more than saw as she fixed her eyes on the darkened thicket straight ahead.

"Did you," he responded rather blandly. After a brief pause, he added, "Consummation can be a marvelous thing when it happens because of total will. And between two people who want it desperately."

That confused her a little because she wasn't entirely sure what he meant, and she was almost equally certain he wanted it that way.

"It was also obvious that there wasn't any artistry involved in your maneuver," she carried on, "but then, neither was there a casualness about it."

He chuckled lightly but didn't interrupt.

"So, after days of reflection," she concluded, "I decided that this was strictly because you were so centered in it. Our kiss totally consumed you—not in style or the desire to please, but in its sheer intensity. You put everything into it while restraining yourself from going farther physically, even after I practically begged you to." Madeleine dropped her voice to a husky whisper. "I don't think I've ever before witnessed such a singular response in a man."

He hesitated briefly in his stride, drawing a long, slow breath, and she took advantage of his momentary unsureness.

"And do you know what else I think, Thomas?"

"No, but I'm beginning to fear it."

She grinned broadly and squeezed his hand. "I think

it was the most wondrous of any kiss I've experienced in years."

That comment, uttered in absolute honesty, drew him to a standstill. He turned to face her, gazing down into her eyes, his voice and features heavy with caution. "If that's a compliment, then I'm very flattered. But I have my doubts that a woman as sophisticated and lovely as you would consider an awkward kiss from me to be wondrous."

"You find me lovely, Thomas?" she pressed softly, instantly filled with satisfaction, knowing he'd said this before, but sighting deeper meaning in it now.

Without pause, he whispered, "I find you breathtaking beyond adequate words, Madeleine."

Her satisfaction turned to sublime warmth so subtly fulfilling she had trouble responding to it immediately. How many men in her twenty-nine years had remarked on her beauty? Yet not one, until tonight, had ever left her feeling so overwhelmingly pleasured inside.

The lingering smell of rain and the chilly nighttime air blanketed them as she moved up against his body, nearly touching.

Very slowly, clinging to his hand and staring into his eyes, she whispered, "I am hoping, Thomas, that we will kiss over and over again in the days and weeks to come. Because you see, what made your kiss so wondrous was not your style, experience, or lack of it, but the fact that it so totally engaged you. Until last Saturday I had never, in my life, been kissed by a man and felt, for that brief moment in time, as if I were the center of his universe."

She watched his smile fade, his lips part just slightly, and silently she pleaded for him to lean over and take her mouth again, to feel that heady power between them once more.

"Will you kiss me again?" she asked in a small, challenging voice.

His eyes narrowed as he focused intently on her, his scar twitching as the side of his mouth curled up. "You seem to be doing all the thinking, Madeleine," he returned dryly.

She fought the urge to laugh. Instead, she reached up and touched his face with a gloved palm. "I think you will."

His smile deepened. "Confidence becomes you."

She did laugh at that, very softly. "Have you thought about our kiss since Saturday?"

"Constantly," he said forthrightly.

Again she felt that sudden rush of warmth. "And?"

"It went beyond my dreams, Madeleine."

That took her breath away. She sighed audibly, faltering in her stance, unable to offer a suitable reply.

He reached up and grasped her palm that still lay across his cheek. Then without further comment, he rubbed the knuckles of both gloved hands, released one, turned, and began to walk again, pulling her along with him.

They paced themselves, rounding the corner so that they were finally heading west, nearing the property line where they would pick up the well-drawn path Baron Rothebury used when he rode each morning.

"I am not a virgin, Thomas," she said moments later, deciding it might be best to bring that into the open.

He never slowed his step although he was silent for several seconds before responding. "I can either say that I assumed as much, Madeleine, in which case I would be implying that I think you are loose. Or I can act surprised and say I don't believe it when we both know you're a twenty-nine-year-old, independent woman who is merely being honest. In either case I'm insulting you."

The perfect answer. She grinned again as the tension left her. "You should have been a solicitor."

"An upstanding profession that would better pay my living expenses, I'm sure." As an afterthought, he added, "But then I wouldn't be here with you."

That made her insides turn from warm to hot. He wanted her physically but he also enjoyed her. He could never know how much that meant.

"How did you feel when you learned you'd be working with a Frenchwoman on this assignment?"

He straightened just enough for her to know the question put him a little on edge.

"It was my decision to bring you here, Madeleine," he murmured.

She had no idea how to take that revelation either. "Why?"

He continued to stare straight ahead. "Your professional reputation is excellent. I also thought help from a woman would be invaluable, and that although you'd draw some attention of your own, as a Frenchwoman you'd never be considered a serious threat. You'd . . . rouse the social scene in this community without being suspected for more than you are."

Another logical answer, and probably correct. "Why won't you call me Maddie as I asked you to?"

He hesitated. "It's rather personal."

An owl hooted in the distance; a small gust of cold wind came from nowhere and rustled through the trees, rippling the water on the lake, creating waving lines of black and moonlit silver. His shoulder brushed hers as they had to move closer together on the path, and she reached up with her free hand to grasp his coat sleeve, holding his arm against her tighter than was probably necessary. He made no move to disengage her.

"Personal because your reasons are private in nature," she probed with growing interest, "or personal because it would imply a greater intimacy between us?"

He thought about that for a moment. "When my feelings are centered, I imagine I'll call you Maddie again."

His feelings? "I'm certain I don't understand that explanation at all, Thomas."

He stopped short and turned to face her fully once more. Staring down at her with shadowed eyes, he stated softly, "I have reasons for not getting intimately involved with you, Madeleine."

"And they are?"

"Personal," he repeated.

That annoyed her a little. "And the fact that it would complicate our working relationship, as you said before."

"Yes."

"But you want to," she goaded brusquely.

Slowly his gaze swept what he could see of her face. "Yes, I want to," he whispered. "But not now."

"Thomas—"

He lowered his lips to hers. It wasn't the kind of kiss she'd been hoping for after a discussion of one so heated, but it was a lingering one, gentle enough to silence her rebuttal and weaken her legs. Then without warning he withdrew.

"Time is short," he said through an unsteady breath. "We're getting close and shouldn't risk the talk." With fingers still wrapped around hers, he resumed walking.

She didn't argue. They didn't speak from that moment forward as they traveled along the edge of the water, now on Rothebury's estate and nearing the house from the east. A thin layer of clouds had begun to move in to partially conceal the moon, forcing Thomas to keep his full attention on the path.

The problem the two of them shared, Madeleine decided, was the lack of emotional intimacy of any kind between them, and it suddenly occurred to her that maybe Thomas was reluctant to pursue a deeper physical involvement without it. Two reasons for this came to mind. Either he held much sadness over the death of his wife, having loved her deeply, and refused to give in to quick sexual desire out of respect for her memory; or his insecurities got the best of him because he considered himself too physically impaired to attract the attention of a vibrant woman. Perhaps he feared rejection, or being hurt in the end. She'd never known a man who didn't place great value on his masculinity. Then again, she'd never met a man who couldn't accept a physical relationship without emotional involvement.

Still, one fact was paramount. He desired her as she desired him. There was no question now. He possessed a strong self-control and he never would have kissed her if he'd intended to keep their relationship perfunctory. They would be lovers eventually, and she was equally certain he knew it.

Abruptly he halted beside her, shaking her from her pleasant thoughts, pulling her tightly against him and hushing her quickly with a finger to her mouth.

She glanced to his dimly outlined face, and he nodded once to the left.

And there it was. A faint glow of light in the distance, moving jaggedly through the far cluster of trees to the south of the main house, probably a good three hundred yards from where they stood on the baron's riding path.

Thomas left the trail and began to move toward it, his pace careful and slow as he assessed the brush, his body cautious, his gaze as intent as hers.

At closer observance she realized it had to be lanterns. Two of them, their dull yellow glow cutting into the surrounding darkness, with no voice to accompany them through the quiet, nighttime forest.

Then suddenly, just as quickly as they saw them, the lights disappeared—first one, then the other—into the blackness of night.

For a moment Madeleine was baffled. Those holding the lanterns weren't yet close enough to the house and certainly not on any distinguishable trail. Why extinguish them in the middle of the forest? Unless they'd detected intruders, heard some sound she and Thomas were trying so carefully not to make. But she didn't think so. Then the memory of Desdemona's comment came to mind.

I've heard rumors of lights in the night and ghosts on Baron Rothebury's property.

It wasn't a rumor, nor were there ghosts. This is what Desdemona herself had seen. Madeleine was sure of it. But when? Under what circumstances? And why was an innocent young woman out in the forest at night?

Thomas continued to walk very slowly until they were nearly on the main house grounds. The lights had been to their immediate left as they stood there now, gazing out into the distant trees. He guided her to a large, round stump, and she sat upon it while he knelt beside her, waiting.

Nothing happened. No movement, no sound, and no more light as the minutes ticked by.

Finally, shivering from the crisp, cold air, surrounded by darkness as the moon dropped in the western night sky, they wordlessly returned to the cottage at nearly half past two in the morning.

Nine

For five nights in a row now, before they'd set out for the baron's estate, they'd played chess. The first night he'd let her win, and she knew it; but their subsequent games were played fairly on his part, and she'd very nearly beaten him. She was out of practice but she was very good. Her mind worked with careful evaluation and logical thought, which he supposed she'd learned and perfected during the years she'd served England in her profession.

Madeleine relaxed on the sofa, facing him as he sat in his chair, wearing her morning gown because Beth Barkley had taken her day gown to launder when she'd left earlier that evening. With only a dim lamp and bright firelight to illuminate the shiny strands of reddish-brown in her plaited hair and the tiny creases in her forehead, she concentrated on the chessboard between them. Thomas knew, as she probably did from simple observance, that he had the most difficult time taking his eyes from her and her beautiful form. That made him smile to himself. Let her speculate on his appraisal of her, on the depth of his attraction. He would intensify their relationship soon, kissing her again tonight if luck was on his side.

"I keep thinking about those lantern lights, Thomas," she tossed in from nowhere.

That's what he admired about her intelligence. She could concentrate on the game as she pieced together complications regarding work. She was thoroughly polished.

He moved his bishop forward to the left five squares, in line to take her queen. "Thinking again, Madeleine?"

"Haven't you been thinking about it?" she asked with only a trace of excitement to escape her steady tone. "Something very strange goes on in that house, and Desdemona Winsett knows more than she told me."

He drew a full breath and nodded minutely. "Probably. Although it's not ghosts or any other nonsense."

She lowered her eyes back to the chess pieces and moved a pawn to block his bishop. "He's smuggling."

"Probably."

"He is," she stressed, "and although it might be a very organized operation, he's not very careful."

"You deduced all this from lantern lights we saw for thirty seconds two nights ago?" he teased, capturing her pawn.

"And other things," she replied, trying to hide her smile as she studied the board.

"Oh, yes, those other things," he said with feigned remembrance. Then, "What other things?"

She shrugged but didn't look at him. "Intuition, for one."

"I often work from intuition," he admitted freely at once.

"So you agree with me."

He shook his head. "Not exactly. Hard evidence is

what we need. The problem with relying on intuition is that it changes one's focus without facts."

Slowly she ran her fingers up and down her long braid as it draped over her shoulder and down her right breast. "Explain that to me."

He paused for clarity of thought, watching her movements. "The baron probably is smuggling the opium for reasons unknown, likely for nothing more than monetary gain. But if we decide he's the smuggler based on intuition only and a few unusual happenings we've chanced to witness, we might be shifting our focus for nothing if it's not him—"

"It *is* him."

Thomas smiled. The woman in her was clearly shining through. "I agree that we need to find out what Desdemona knows. Beyond that I think we should refrain from drawing any conclusions."

"We also need to get into his house."

"We will."

"Soon."

"We will," he repeated.

Her brilliant blue, mischief-filled eyes shot up to meet his. Then with a triumphant grin that melted his heart, she moved her knight forward to capture his bishop. "Check."

He looked at the board again. He was in trouble.

"I believe, Mr. Blackwood, that you are nearly defeated," she noted with radiant pleasure. "Is this the first time a woman in your presence has taken control and made you succumb?"

Her smooth intimation did not go unnoticed.

Thomas stretched out his booted legs, crossed one over the other, and leaned back in his chair to plainly regard her.

"How did you learn to speak English so well?"

A subtle widening of her eyes told him she was surprised by the question.

"Are you trying to change the subject because you're losing?" she asked softly, raising her arm to lay it comfortably along the back of the sofa.

"No, I never lose," he answered wryly, his gaze locked with hers in candid arrogance. "I just think it's time to deepen our friendship." He paused for effect, then murmured, "Don't you?"

She waited long enough before responding for him to know she was slightly puzzled by his meaning and unsure how to answer. Her expression never changed.

"A close friend taught me English at my request."

"A close friend?"

She smiled and relaxed fully into the soft cushion; her lovely countenance filled with tender memories. "His name was Jacques Grenier, the disowned but wealthy son of a French count. He was also a magnificent poet, singer, and a brilliant man of the stage. He took special interest in me during my formative years and taught me . . . the ways of the world."

"Disowned because he was an actor?"

"Precisely," she replied with a tip of her head.

"He was your lover," Thomas added levelly, his insides churning because he knew this already but was suddenly irrationally jealous of it. What surprised him, though, was how much more he was affected by saying the words aloud.

Her perfectly groomed brows raised minutely, but she didn't try to hide anything. "Yes, he was my lover. I was fifteen and a virgin when he first bedded me, and I suppose he seduced me. We were together for almost six years, intimately for three of them, and in that time he was generous enough to teach me the English language. He was very well educated, and spoke it fluently."

"Why did you desire so strongly to learn it?" he asked quietly, although he also knew this answer.

She assessed him, hesitating for either her own recollection of events, or perhaps with curiosity about his interest, unsure how much to reveal. After a moment, her expression grew serious.

"My father was English, Thomas, a captain in the British Royal Navy. He died of cholera in the West Indies when I was twelve. I only saw him four very brief times in the years before his death, but our days together were wonderful—my happiest childhood memories. He told me once that he had wanted to marry my mother when he found out she carried me, but she wouldn't dream of it. The woman has always been manipulative and selfish, and she despised everything he was—a British subject, soft-spoken and conservative, a decorated veteran, second-born son of a middle-class but well-respected family."

Sighing, she folded her hands in her lap and turned to stare into the glow of the fire. "I'm not entirely certain, but I think he bedded her for only a short time while he was on duty and she traveled with the acting company somewhere near the Mediterranean coast. It was apparently a fast and torrid affair. He said he had truly cared for her, but my mother denies it. She early became addicted to opium, and was never more than a mediocre actress, raising me as her servant girl, toting me along from one smelly, crowded theater to the next, ordering me to do her bidding, while caring little for me. She considered me one of the stiff, arrogant English, and indeed I was—half English—but she refused to let me claim my English heritage or even come to England as a child to meet my father's family."

She paused, lost in memory. The fire crackled in the grate; the bitter wind and rain outside clamored with the force of winter, but she didn't appear to notice. Thomas didn't interrupt either, for fear that she'd cease her disclosure and change the subject. But after taking only a few seconds to collect her thoughts, she soberly continued.

"I was not informed of his death until well over one year after the event. I found a note from my father's family tucked into a side pocket of my mother's wardrobe that described his fate in detail. She, it seems, had forgotten to show it to me when it arrived because she was too self-centered to take the time. At the moment, Thomas, when Jacques read to me that crumpled letter informing me that my precious father had been dead for nearly two years while I waited each day with hope for his return, I decided that I would take my life, my future, into my hands. I was as much English as I was French. My mother was disgusted at the sight of me, so the French in me was of no consequence. It certainly didn't matter to her. She kept me only because she used me. My father had loved me and had wanted to raise me, therefore I would, from that moment forward, consider myself to be his English child. I would learn his language as my own, and I did, studying it for years, with Jacques and then after him. It became my work, my goal. My only obstacle, and the reason I do not pass myself off as an Englishwoman today, is that I cannot lose my thick accent. I also know France and its people and culture so well that I'm invaluable to the British cause there. For the first time in my life I am useful for something truly worthwhile." She let out a heavy breath and cocked her head. "Perhaps it is irrational, but in my heart it did, and still does, make sense to me. At thirteen,

I decided that outwardly I am French, inwardly I am and will always be English."

"And that's when you became involved with Grenier," he finally interjected, wanting to keep her on track by returning to the point of his original question.

She nodded and looked back into his eyes. Hers were weary, but, as Madeleine always did, she remained regal in her beauty, poised even as she remembered a tumultuous time in her young life. Thomas fought the overpowering urge to rise to his feet and take her in his arms.

"Yes, I met him during a very boisterous musical production in Cannes. He played a singing traveling salesman, and I was his costumer. I dressed him for the part and eventually I began undressing him as well. But I did not become his lover so that he would teach me the language," she clarified. "He was my willing tutor for almost two years before we became involved."

"You were still a child."

"Yes, and terribly naive."

Thomas stirred and closed his hands together over his stomach. "Were you in love with him?" he asked in a lowered voice, heart thumping, trying not to betray his concern through his demeanor.

The clock on the mantel chimed ten, and she smiled again, eyes sparkling as she attempted to lighten the mood. "All these personal questions during one game of chess? I think you are trying to distract me because it's late and I'm finally beating you."

"Your imagination is profoundly vivid, madam," he replied with feigned shock.

She tipped her head back and laughed faintly, closing her arms across her middle so that she unknowingly lifted her breasts up, the full, golden curves pushing over the top of her gown.

Thomas's gaze naturally dropped to the sight and lingered. When he raised it back to her face, she was watching him intently.

The corners of her lips turned up shrewdly, and she leaned forward to intentionally offer him more—a spectacular view down her magnificent cleavage.

"It's your move, Thomas."

His body went hard with those suggestive, silkily spoken words; perspiration beaded on his upper lip and across his neck. But he refused to let her know how just the thought of her affected him. For now.

He pushed his rook forward six squares to block her. "Answer my question."

She chuckled again then dropped her voice to a soft purr. "What is love, Thomas? I cared for Jacques, but I was very young, and he was twenty-eight years my senior. We had little in common beyond the theater, good poetry, and reading, speaking, and writing English. It would probably be more accurate to say we were there for each other at the time. Like most relationships, don't you think?"

He knew what she was implying, what she wanted from their relationship while she was in England, or at least what she thought she wanted. Fortunately for both of them he had no intention of ever being there for her for just the moment.

"Have you ever been in love, Madeleine?" he pressed, his voice caressing as his gaze penetrated hers. "I don't mean a passing, short-term love affair, or a strictly sexual love, but one that burns deep. One that is passionately real and immeasurably powerful." He leaned toward her so that the length of the chessboard was the distance between them. "A love that captures your imagination and takes your breath away."

The air between them thickened. He could sense that the question unsettled her, because her face flushed and she licked her parted lips as her smile faded.

Suddenly her eyes betrayed her wariness, and she dropped her lashes, reaching forward to caress the marble king at her fingertips. "Have you?" she asked in a tone barely heard.

Without the slightest hesitation, he whispered, "Yes."

The seriousness and finality exposed in his very forthright answer caught her off guard, and she fidgeted. Their discussion had become deeply personal, and she wasn't sure how to acknowledge his admission. He'd made her nervous, although she was doing her best to hide it. She just didn't know how intimately he knew her and how easily he could read her.

After several seconds she asked, "With your wife?"

And at that moment Thomas knew that he had her. The lightness was gone from the conversation, and she wanted to know. The attraction had instantly intensified at her demand, and he could hardly contain his grin of jubilance.

Huskily he replied, "With someone I met years ago, Maddie."

Very slowly she raised her eyes to his once more, and he immersed himself in those beautiful liquid pools of unsureness, the heat between them palpable, her breathing uneven as she tightened her grip on her king.

Then the corners of his lips turned up, his lids narrowed, and without so much as a glance to the board, he pushed his queen forward nine squares, confiscated her queen, then closed his palm over her knuckles.

"Mate."

She didn't move.

Her hand felt warm, the skin smooth, and he ran his thumb over her knuckles just once.

"I didn't see that coming," she said shakily.

"I know," he returned, conveying a far-reaching certainty. "Some of the greatest surprises in life happen when we least expect them."

She blinked, momentarily confused by his rather vague comment. Then she did the unexpected.

Regaining her poise, she straightened and turned her king on its side. "I am tired of the games, Thomas," she announced thoughtfully, her expression determined. "I think it is time for me to win."

Her eyes, brimming with confidence, shimmered in firelight, and his heart beat faster. She pulled her hand out from beneath his and gracefully raised her body from the sofa, taking two steps around the chessboard so that she stood directly in front of him.

"Madeleine," he drawled.

"Maddie," she corrected with a cunning smile, grasping the arms of his chair with both hands. Then, leaning over him, she placed her lips on his.

Thomas didn't immediately respond to her boldness or the sudden fullness of her warm mouth against his. Part of him wanted to wait to experience the physical between them, but that part was very rapidly losing the battle. He raised his hands and grasped her upper arms, but he neither pushed her away, nor pulled her in. He simply allowed her to stay in control.

She knew what to do. Expertly she began to kiss him, tilting her head and caressing his mouth with her own, applying more pressure as he began to reciprocate.

His breathing quickly grew shallow, and that made her eager. She pressed into him, though still keeping her body from touching his. Her hot, wet tongue traced the outline of his upper lip then drove past it, searching. Suddenly she was breathing as fast as he, and very slowly he began to draw her against him.

She wouldn't allow herself to close the distance completely. He remained in his chair, and she remained standing over him, off to the side of his thighs. Her tongue darted freely into his mouth, playing intimately with his, and when she finally raised a palm and placed it on his chest, he quietly moaned in pleasure and she sighed in understanding.

This kiss was better than the first, but he was also better prepared. She smelled of rose perfume; tasted of sweet wine and woman—a pleasure so long denied. He felt the heat from her hand through his fine linen shirt as she very slowly began to caress his chest in wispy circles. And then, indicative of her desire, she started to skillfully unbutton it.

This time he would let her have her way. At least for a few precious minutes.

Reaching in, she stroked his skin through thick curls as her lips continued to burn his with a marvelous torment. He responded in kind by gently massaging her arms, running his thumbs along the delicate underskin. That made her whimper faintly.

"Make love to me, Thomas," she pleaded in a whisper against his mouth.

His heart thudded soundly. Only in his dreams had he heard her asking for him to love her totally, and now, after long last, it was real.

She was real.

In desperation he couldn't begin to put into words, he finally did what he'd ached to do for years. With measured slowness, he lowered one hand to her breast, covering it completely as it burned his palm through thin layers of muslin.

She moaned, kissing him deeply as she pushed into his caress, giving him all, silently asking for more, allowing him the greatest physical fulfillment he'd experienced in recent memory. His breathing grew harsh, and his throat tightened as he glided his thumb across her still-clothed nipple, feeling it harden to a point in response to his touch.

She moved her hand lower until she ran her fingers over the waistband of his pants. He was erect to the tip, hard with an ageless need, and she certainly felt it. Boldly, her lips and tongue still teasing his, she closed her hand over the length of him, rubbed him once with her slender palm, and he nearly lost control.

In fear of embarrassing himself, he quickly grabbed her wrists, encircling them with his fingers and thumbs as he gently pushed her back.

A heady, dark arousal glazed her eyes as she looked into his. They were exquisite eyes expressing hope, passion, and the loveliness inside that she seldom revealed to anyone. He saw it all now, rousing the bittersweet memory of the first time he'd seen them, and he knew without question that he would never disappoint her when she looked at him like that.

Swiftly he was on his feet, taking control at last as he shifted her once again toward the sofa. She didn't say a word or glance away, but her moist, full lips pulled up in a knowing smile.

She sat upon the cushion and lifted her feet to stretch out across it, her head resting on a pillow at the armrest. Thomas released her wrists, extinguished the lamp next to them, then stood above her, watching firelight reflect off her golden skin and her thick, silky lashes create soft crescents on her glowing cheeks and brows. She stared at him, reached for him with an open hand, her raw hunger exposed. It took all that was in him as a man not to lift her skirts, climb above her, and enter her sweetness. It's what she wanted, probably expected, and that in itself was all the pleasure he needed for now.

"My gown," she said breathlessly.

He shook his head. He was desperate but not ready

for total exposure. That would come at a later time when he had much more to reveal. Yet like this he could still give her what she needed.

With a pounding heart, he awkwardly lowered himself to his knees between the sofa and the tea table, leaned into the cushion, rested a hand upon her forehead, and placed his lips on hers again.

Madeleine, for a very brief moment, thought she was dreaming. The man didn't take, he gave. She hadn't been prepared for that, or for the intensity she witnessed in his longing. She had seen it in his eyes all evening, and now she felt it in his extraordinary touch.

His lips lingered on hers, and she raised her arms, clasping them about his neck, entwining her fingers in the soft hair at his nape. The heat radiated from every pore, from her skin to his, even through clothing that she hoped he would soon remove, piece by piece, layer by layer, until nothing remained in the way of their joining.

She inhaled sharply when she realized he had taken her breast in his palm again and rubbed her nipple to a peak, wishing through this marvelous dream that he would take it in his mouth, that he would take all of her in his mouth.

"Thomas . . ." she whispered through an aching breath.

He remained silent as he began to kiss a trail across her cheek, stopping at her ear, stroking it with his tongue, causing her to tremble. He moved to her neck, down her throat and chest, until he reached the tops of her breasts, his hot, moist breath coming in uneven waves and setting her skin on fire.

Madeleine raked her fingers through his hair, clasping the back of his head as he kissed the top curve of both breasts then gently ran his cheek across them, his rough whiskers causing gooseflesh to rise on her arms.

"Maddie . . ." she heard him whisper.

"Don't stop, Thomas."

With that, his passion became fierce. He captured her mouth again with his own, his tongue thrusting inside until he found hers and began to tease, flick, suck, his palm on her breast, kneading the fullness with his large, warrior-like hand.

She whimpered and reached for him, but this time he grabbed her arms, forcing them above her head. Her fingers struck the chess pieces, knocking several of them over onto the marble board, but he didn't appear to notice the noisy intrusion. Instead he clasped both of her wrists together with his free hand and held them there.

Squirming, she tried to raise her skirts with her legs without much success, and he took to the task and finished it for her. She lay there exposed to him, only sheer linen drawers between them, and desperately she wanted him inside of her.

As if sensing her need, he suddenly released her wrists and mouth, and lowered his head to her breasts where he began to rub his cheeks, then his lips and teeth, across the tips of them, over her gown, striking her with the dull ache of pleasure as her nipples tightened against his ruthless caress. Finally, after what felt like an eternity of want, his hand took over at her breasts, and she felt him move farther down her body until his head rested on her belly at her hips.

She pushed up against him, her still-covered mound dusting his cheek, and she heard him inhale deeply, then moan and mumble something she could not understand.

With shaky fingers, he reached between her legs, urgently now, and she sensed the intensity in him rising. He fumbled with the soft material until he found the slit and parted it. At long last she felt his fingers touch her where she desired him most, at first timidly, then intimately as he began to stroke the wet, slick heat.

She gasped his name again, lifting her body just enough to meet his tender probing, but he didn't raise himself, or turn to face her, or kiss her again as she so anxiously wanted him to do. He made no move to enter her, but continued to stroke her breasts with one hand and her cleft with the other while he kneeled on the floor and leaned against the sofa.

Madeleine closed her eyes tightly, fingers in his hair, holding his head as she realized he wanted her to climax like this. And she was nearing it. It was so fast, so erotic to her, this man with his face in her feminine curls, inhaling and moaning and kissing her there while his fingers explored her at first cautiously, then bravely as he slowly pushed one of them deeply inside.

She sucked in a sharp breath, jumping involuntarily when his thumb touched that delicate center nub, but his pursuit was perfect. He didn't stop. He pushed his left hand down and inside the top of her gown to grasp what he could of her breast, massaging it while he continued to torment her below, his finger within, his thumb stroking her faster and harder, taking her to her crest.

She whimpered again, over and over, clutching him with firm hands when she felt the steady rise to that blissful point of no return.

He recognized it.

"Come to me, Maddie. . . ."

She obeyed the command.

Her belly tightened; her legs stiffened. And then the climax burst forth from the inside, tearing a cry from her lips as she clenched her fists in his hair and her hips jerked against his hand and cheek, and she in turn stroked his finger with internal spasms of pleasure.

"Oh, God." She heard him groan from deep in his chest.

Suddenly his palm gripped her breast, and his embrace became rigid as she arched into him. She felt his quick breath on her inner thighs, his enormous body shudder against her at her completion, and she held to him tightly until it subsided.

Gradually she quieted, and he calmed his movements. Neither of them spoke or moved for a minute or two as their breathing became regular and her body relaxed. At last he pulled his finger from her and turned his face so that his forehead rested on her hipbone. She caressed his silky hair and glided her palm along his neck.

"I want you inside of me, Thomas," she said very softly.

He inhaled with finality and stroked her intimately one last time. Then drawing back, he lifted his arms and hands from her body and awkwardly stood.

Without a word, or even a glance to her face, he walked away, his limp pronounced with every step of his boots on the wooden stairs that led to his room above the cottage.

Ten

When she awakened to an empty house, Madeleine knew she would find him by the lake. It was Thomas's favorite spot for thinking things through in peaceful silence, and it was quickly becoming hers as well. She would talk to him there.

Stepping onto the porch and into the clear morning, she breathed deeply of the frigid air and took a moment to close her eyes to the rising sun, just peeking above the thin layer of clouds on the horizon. Then she donned her gloves, clasped the neck of her cloak together tightly, and turned toward the path that led to the back of the cottage.

The night had passed slowly, and she had slept little. The wind had died down without so much as a drop of rain. What had kept her awake was the memory of Thomas's hands on her body, the look in his passion-filled eyes when they stared into hers, and the troubling memory of him leaving her—without taking what she wanted to give, without a single word.

She just didn't understand his actions. No man had

ever left her like that before, and although her experience with the larger sex wasn't exactly limited, she
wasn't so thoroughly seasoned that she could say she
understood male sexuality to any degree of perfection.
No man had ever made love to her and then not received
his own satisfaction at her request, although it was true
that Thomas was like few men she had ever known. Still,
at base level he was a man, and a man who desired her—
so blatantly, in fact, that it was almost charmingly humorous.

At first thought in the late night hours, as she'd lain
awake in bed staring at the ceiling, she'd decided he was
simply insecure. If his leg injuries were more severe than
she had earlier assumed, it was possible he was reluctant
to let her see them. Yet this didn't entirely explain his
silent departure. He could have had her without removing his clothing, and although his legs might be mangled
to some degree, he should know her well enough by now
to realize this would never repulse her.

Her second consideration centered on the question of
impotence. She had felt him briefly through his clothes,
and that part of him seemed to be perfectly formed—
well proportioned and long and very definitely hard for
her. He had certainly been erect, but had he been able
to sustain it? She couldn't tell after she'd stretched out
on the sofa, and with a little embarrassment, she realized
she hadn't thought of trying to touch him when he'd
started to bring her to orgasm. But then that was natural.
Still, he'd said he wasn't impotent, and one would suppose the man would know his own body.

The only other conclusion she could draw was one of
nonconclusion. He didn't want to be completely intimate
with her for reasons known only to him, which, she reminded herself, was exactly what he'd told her three
nights ago. This notion troubled her the most, and that,

in turn, amused her. She was reaching the point in their relationship where she was beginning to care for Thomas as a person, and she wanted him to want her. She wanted him to need her. She wanted him to make love to her, not just for the sake of sexual release, but for the sake of being intimate with her alone.

Madeleine pushed a long branch out of her way and stepped into the clearing beside the lake. As suspected, Thomas sat on the bench, staring out across the calm water, his legs spread wide, elbows on knees, hands clasped together in front of him. He wore his heavy twine coat, scarf and gloves, leading her to believe he'd been out in the woods for quite some time.

She walked toward him slowly, arms crossed over her stomach, her leather shoes crunching on the leaves and twigs at her feet. He undoubtedly heard her approaching but he didn't move his body or look in her direction.

"It's a beautiful morning," she said brightly.

He exhaled forcefully through his nostrils, nodding. "My favorite time of day."

"Mine, too." She stood behind him and off to one side, gazing down to his profile. Tiny lines spread out from the corner of his eye, his lips hard set and grim. He looked older this morning than his thirty-nine years, but distinguished and darkly handsome. She wished she could kiss the tension from his face but she didn't think she should be so forward. It was obvious that he needed the space.

"I have two questions to ask you, Thomas," she remarked after a moment of silence.

His jaw tightened noticeably, but he said nothing. Apparently she would have to do all the work.

"What do you think Baron Rothebury does with the books?"

Quickly he jerked his head around and stared at her,

his eyes wide, mouth slack. The fact that he appeared so suddenly surprised at the innocuous question made her suck in her cheeks to keep from giggling.

"Books?" he repeated, confused.

She raised a brow and rubbed her toe along the forest floor. "Lady Claire's books. Why is he buying them?"

He sat a little straighter, composing himself as he realized where her thoughts were heading, but he didn't move his steady gaze from hers. "I've been wondering about that, too. After meeting him I can't believe he's a collector or a dealer. It doesn't fit his personality, or at least what I know of him. He's an extroverted man, educated to the degree most nobles are, but he's not an intellectual."

Madeleine took a step closer and briefly scanned the baron's home on the other side of the water. "He also doesn't seem to be of need financially, which is exactly what was said at Mrs. Rodney's tea. Buying books just to sell them as a dealer wouldn't be especially profitable anyway. And that means," she reasoned solemnly, "he purposely lied to Lady Claire."

"Yes, I believe he did."

Thomas's voice sounded gruff to her ears. Masculine. She looked back into his lovely brown eyes, wanting him again. "Why?"

He shook his head, brows drawn together. "I don't know. Socially she's of his class, but I can't imagine him calling on her for anything. He might invite her to parties because it would be expected, but other than that I'm not sure why he'd want anything to do with her, or her extensive library."

"Maybe because she wants you, Thomas," she maintained smoothly, running the fingers of one hand back and forth along the top of the bench. "The woman certainly doesn't hide that fact, and he doesn't like you for reasons unknown. Maybe he feels you're intruding in Winter Garden where the opposite sex is concerned?"

His eyes narrowed carefully, his gaze piercing hers, and it suddenly occurred to her how that must have sounded. Like a jealous wife. How thoroughly unlike her. She could kick herself for making such a statement without thought or provocation.

"So he's buying her books to get even or attract her attention? That makes no sense at all. He wouldn't find her any more appealing than I do." He paused, then lowered his voice in calculation. "You're a better thinker than that, Madeleine. What are you really saying to me?"

She tried not to consider that an insult. He was right, naturally. She felt her cheeks flush hotly, which, of course, he noticed. But she didn't turn away. She needed to get to the point. He was waiting for an answer.

Straightening, she dropped her arms to her sides and daintily raised her chin. "I want to know why you left me last night."

He almost smirked. "I thought so. I'm sorry about that."

"I didn't ask if you were sorry, I asked why," she returned matter-of-factly.

He hesitated, rubbing his hands together nervously. "It's complicated."

That irritated her. His answers to personal questions always seemed to be purposely evasive, and she was tired of it. She tried to ignore the feeling; to remain cool was her persona. "That's a very common excuse for you, Thomas, but I really would like an explanation this time. I think I deserve it."

Shifting uncomfortably on the bench seat, he faced the lake once more. "It wasn't you."

"I should hope not," she agreed curtly. "You obviously made certain I would enjoy myself. And I also think it was obvious that I did."

His cheek twitched, and Madeleine wasn't certain if he was amused at her comment or annoyed. She couldn't see his eyes. But he seemed to grow more discomfited by the second.

"Are you afraid to become intimate because of the injuries to your legs?"

The words drifted softly through the morning air, but her question hit its target. Everything was out in the open now. He would have to talk of it.

Stiffly, palms to thighs, he pushed himself up to a standing position. With one shove of his gloved fingers through his hair, he walked forward several paces until he stood on the shoreline.

Madeleine waited, unmoving.

"I'm not in the least afraid to be with you, and that wasn't the problem last night," he said through a coarse breath.

She refused to be intimidated by his unnecessarily cool manner. "Then why did you leave me?"

Abruptly he replied, "I'm a man, Madeleine."

Was she supposed to be shocked? "Yes, I know. I felt the evidence of that."

"You don't understand." He thrust his hands in his coat pockets and stared at the water. "You were there, and I was ready. You were—hot, so hot. So . . . wet inside. Wet for me. I was making you that way."

Madeleine frowned and began to walk toward him. The conversation had immediately jumped from the evasive to the intimate. She supposed this was the perfect place to discuss it, though, as they were secluded, but she kept her response hushed nonetheless. "It's a natural physical reaction, Thomas. I desire you. I've desired you since the day we met."

"Why?" he whispered without looking at her.

She hadn't expected that, and it gave her pause to wonder if he were attempting to alter the tone of their talk. "You're a very attractive man," she answered candidly, standing close to his side. "I enjoy your smile, your quietness, your . . . thinking, rational mind. You are unlike any man I've known before, and every day I want even more than that last to be your lover. I think we could find enjoyment in each other's arms for the time we are together, but I don't understand your reluctance. If it's because of your physical problem, I can tell you now that I find you to be one of the most masculine men I have ever known, handsome of face and form, and very charming despite your private nature. You are robust and intelligent, and I think strongly attracted to me. Why do you keep protesting what is sure to take place?"

He exhaled loudly. "I don't think I've ever protested the desire, only acknowledged that our being intimate with each other could complicate our work."

Madeleine calmed on the inside and smiled broadly. "You will be my lover." It wasn't a question. She'd stated it without reservation or expectation, and he didn't deny it this time. He didn't say anything. She grew warm to her toes from his silent affirmation and confidently reached out to place a palm on his arm. "Why not last night?"

He breathed deeply and closed his eyes, stalling.

For the first time, Madeleine caught a glimmer of something else, another explanation for his quick departure, and her heart and body began to melt.

"Tell me, Thomas," she said gently.

He stood rigidly, eyes tightly shut as he faced the brightening sky. Finally, in a murmur of his own, he revealed, "You can't understand what it was like for me, Madeleine. You were there, so beautiful, wanting me, moaning my name, begging me with your eyes and body to love you, to touch you, to caress your breasts, your hard nipples. Then you let me put my face on your mons, so near where your need was greatest, to touch you there, and you were wet, so wet, and the dark hair between your legs rubbed my cheek and lips. I could— smell you, reach out with my tongue and taste you, and you were so sweet, Maddie, so sweet to taste. And then you let me put my finger inside of you and you were hot, and soft, and wetter still. And when you climaxed—"

His voice shook, and he swallowed hard, his body stiff at her side, his eyes squeezed shut. Madeleine silently watched him, partly in confusion, partly in wonder, while he recounted what sounded like a far-distant memory.

"When you climaxed," he continued, almost inaudibly, "I could feel you. Oh, God, it surrounded me, and I could feel it, feel your wetness cling to me, flow over my fingers, feel you squeezing me inside, stroking me, rubbing against my hand. You climaxed because of how I touched you, just touched you—" He shook his head again and clenched his jaw. "You can't understand what knowing that, what being there and experiencing that, can do to a man. You were moaning my name, responding to *my* touch, and I realized I was smelling and tasting and feeling the release of true feminine beauty. It was no longer a dream. It was real, *you* were real, and I couldn't—" He tensed and shuddered. "I couldn't contain myself, Madeleine. I haven't been with a woman in years."

The cold outside completely disappeared for her as a surge of exquisite warmth spread through her body and lingered. She didn't know if she was more stunned by his disclosure, touched by his honesty, or flattered. But it was true, she decided there, that a man had never been so open with her, especially about something that so affected his masculinity.

No man had ever described female sexuality to her in such lovely terms before, either. Even the French, who were, in general, more graphic about it, described it from a distance, as if it were a beautiful thing to admire and treasure, like a work of art. Thomas had described it as if he were a part of it and could feel it inside him, could feel her intimately with all his senses. As if he found *her* sexuality beautiful, and beautiful to him alone. Madeleine knew at once that this was one of the most unique moments of her life, if not one of the most wonderful.

So. What could she say to him now? That it was all right? That it didn't change her desire for him? That she understood, when in fact she was a woman and probably didn't? Could she ask him why his sexual life has been lacking for years, and how many has it been anyway? She did, however, understand that he was embarrassed, and the moment between them now, regardless of his honesty, had to be exceedingly awkward for him. This was probably not the time for a detailed discussion of his past. But she could, if nothing else, let him know how she felt.

Brushing breeze-blown hair from her forehead and lashes, she squeezed his arm once and released it. "Thomas, I have been with my share of men," she admitted softly, "but you are the only one who has ever made me feel like a beautiful woman with just common words."

He opened his eyes and slowly pivoted his rigid form to look at her.

She smiled faintly into those soft brown circles that bore a distinct hesitancy to believe, clutching her cloak with both hands to keep from reaching for him. "You are not poetic but you are sincere and descriptive in a very romantic way. Next time you will make me feel beautiful with your body, and I intend to share in it and make it last. I only hope that I can prove worthy enough for such a giving man."

The harsh contours of his face relaxed minutely; his gaze softened for her, sparking with what she could only describe as pleasure, and perhaps a shade of amazement at her response.

She straightened to carry on. "So. What do you intend to do today?"

A flash of amusement crossed his features at her quick change of topic, but she ignored that, keeping her expression blank and her chin lifted self-assuredly.

"I intend to call on Mrs. Bennington-Jones in the hope of visiting with, or learning something about, Desdemona," he said in a feather-soft drawl. "And you?"

Madeleine had the most difficult time keeping her lips from his, fighting the intense urge to seduce him right there on the bench. If she walked two feet forward she'd be in his arms.

"I think I will bathe at the inn then dress to call on Rothebury," she instead forced herself to say. "It is time for us to meet."

Without waiting for reply, she lifted her skirts and retraced her steps to the edge of the brush. Tossing a glance over her shoulder, she caught him staring at her, eyes narrowed in assessment, hands still in his pockets, his large, imposing body filled out impressively.

"Be careful," he cautioned in a husky timbre.

For the first time in her career, she wasn't offended by the edge of male superiority in a colleague's words and manner, because this time she sensed a flicker of emotional caring. He'd meant what he said, not because he was a man and she a woman, but because he liked her. Madeleine relished that knowledge, but she wouldn't give him the satisfaction of knowing how deeply, how strangely, he affected her.

"I think I should be warning you of the same thing. Mrs. Bennington-Jones could beat you to death with words." Looking him up and down, she lowered her voice to impishly add, "And I am very, very glad you are not impotent after all."

His deep chuckle reverberated through the trees.

Eleven

Madeleine had originally intended to surprise the baron at his home, knocking on his door and introducing herself to him in a neighborly fashion. The problem with that plan, however, was that she had no valid reason to do so. He might not be in residence, or, of even deeper concern, her visit might look suspicious. As a village newcomer, it would be more appropriate for him to call on her, and, of course, he would never do that. Her only alternative, then, was to stumble across him as he rode along the path beside the lake, making it appear as if the meeting were coincidental.

At ten o'clock she set out, wearing her morning gown, traveling cloak and gloves, her hair brushed into a long braid that she'd wound atop her head. She'd also added just a trace of color to her cheeks, lips and eyes. It wasn't enough to notice really, but she wanted to enhance what she could. First impressions were everything.

She had only traversed the path for a few minutes when she spotted the baron coming toward her through the trees. He sat atop his gray horse, dressed appropriately in dark brown riding clothes, his face taut with either physical effort or concentration, assessing the curves on the trail as he had yet to notice her.

Madeleine drew a deep breath and smoothed her hands over her cloak, assuming a casual air. It would only be a matter of moments until he saw her, and she wanted to be prepared.

And then he did.

Still some distance away, the baron pulled gently on the reins to slow his horse's gait. He didn't appear to be startled by her sudden presence, although he carefully studied her from head to foot, and obviously so, seemingly unconcerned whether she would take offense at his intense scrutiny. She pretended not to be aware of his indelicate behavior, giving him first a gentle look of surprise at finding him there, followed by a beautiful smile and a slight nod of her head as she continued to walk toward him.

He moved closer as well, likewise producing a grin on his mouth just as quickly as he saw hers. It was contrived, and she knew it. It never reached his eyes.

"Good day, monsieur," she said pleasantly, strolling to his side.

"And a good day it is, madam," he instantly replied in a heavy drawl, brazenly looking over every inch of her face. "Or at least it is now that I've come across such a lovely woman on my path. Are you a vision or reality?"

Such artificial, calculated words were meant to impress the insecure. Or the innocent. Did he think she would be so naive? Likely not. He had called her madam, which meant he either assumed she was or had been married, or he knew her identity already. He was smart, challenging her position here now with adulation and subtle seduction, waiting for a reaction. Madeleine felt the hairs prickle on the back of her neck.

"Goodness, monsieur," she returned through a soft chuckle, "you flatter a lady so. I hope you don't mind that I am walking on your property, but I didn't realize anyone owned it."

She let the words trail off into the crisp, calm air, expecting an introduction at last. He didn't disappoint, but neither did he dismount—an overt attempt to remain in a superior position as he looked down on her from above.

"I am Richard Sharon, Baron Rothebury."

He stated that almost boastfully, evidently expecting her to know who he was. She played to his vanity.

"Ahh, yes. You own the house in the distance," she replied sweetly. "Mrs. Bennington-Jones and her daughter Desdemona mentioned you at Mrs. Rodney's tea one afternoon."

He didn't blink or lose his smile, but she did notice just the slightest tightening of his lips. She carried on thoughtfully before he could interrupt.

"She even suggested that your home was so old it might have been a haven for those not afflicted with the Death. I found that fascinating."

"Fascinating, yes," he conceded quickly, "but only rumor. When ladies gather at tea, they can be drawn into conversations of the most amazing nature, don't you agree?"

She wondered how on earth he would know that. "I suppose so."

He tipped his head toward her once in approval. "Actually, I own much of the surrounding land—from the edge of the lake to several miles south of here, and, of course, as far east as the Hope cottage at the edge of the village." He lifted one corner of his mouth even as his

thickly lashed, dark hazel eyes narrowed with suggestion. "You are the Frenchwoman living with the scholar
there, are you not? I've seen you through the trees once
or twice, and have found myself staring. You're beautiful from head to foot, and such rare beauty is truly
difficult to ignore."

He tried to impress as he spoke, his voice deep and
velvet soft, suspecting, or at least hoping, she'd understand his seductive intent. He was an intriguing man in
a rather mysterious way, quite attractive to look at, and
he probably appealed to the smaller sex in a very gracious but sensual manner.

His face was hard of line, cheekbones high and defined, his skin clear, clean-shaven and smooth. His eyes
were arresting and intently focused, his mouth wide and
inviting. He wore new, polished boots and clothes expensively tailored to fit his muscular form, his sandy-red
hair and side whiskers trimmed to the fashion of the day,
only slightly tousled from his ride.

Yes, he was quite handsome, and a very sexual man;
he possessed an alluring presence that silently promised
erotic pleasures in the bedroom. An innocent would be
swept away if he chose her as his conquest. Madeleine,
however, was experienced in the art of seduction and
lovemaking, and understood his allure enough to guard
against it. Or use it.

Smiling vividly now, she sauntered closer to his
mount, even as instinct told her to back away. "Yes, my
name is Madeleine DuMais. I am in Winter Garden tem-
porarily while I translate Monsieur Blackwood's war
memoirs into my native tongue. He is a quiet but agreeable host, and the village is enchanting." She clasped
her hands behind her back. "I am very much enjoying
my short stay here but am anxious to meet others."

His brows rose. "Indeed. Then it is a pleasure to meet

you, Madeleine," he offered richly. "Perhaps the two of us can become better acquainted while you're in England."

His attraction was obvious, and so was his intent as he used her given name without awaiting the customary permission. She played on that.

Gracing him with an enticing grin, she reached up to pat the neck of his horse. The animal stirred, but the baron didn't respond to it and neither did he take his eyes from hers.

"I should enjoy that, Monsieur Baron," she intimated invitingly. "I've met several of the ladies from the village but none of the gentlemen."

He glanced out over the water, toward the cottage, and Madeleine hoped profoundly that Thomas wasn't watching conspicuously. She'd purposely avoided him in her last comment when referring to gentlemen of Winter Garden, and the baron seemed to grasp this. She didn't want him thinking she and the scholar were lovers.

Suddenly his cheek twitched, and his gaze met hers again. His expression had softened, but his eyes were hard as glass. Penetrating. "You are not familiar with your employer, Madeleine?"

The hushed question, spoken with such bluntness, took her completely aback. She hadn't expected him to be so straightforward in his approach. Then it occurred to her that maybe he was testing her to see just how virtuous she was.

Indecision sliced through her, but after only a second's hesitation, she decided to play the experienced.

Dropping her voice to a delicate murmur, she admitted, "No, Richard, we are not familiar with each other. Mr. Blackwood tends to keep to himself."

"Does he."

He sounded convinced, but Madeleine detected a suspicious undertone in his simple reply. He wasn't sure he believed her, and that gave her the very first advantage.

She was about to suggest they stroll, he on his horse, she beside it, back in the direction she had come, when he unexpectedly lifted his leg over the back of the animal and dropped to the ground to stand at her side.

He wasn't a tall man, but he was toned and hard of stature. Next to her he stood just above her in height, but somehow towered over her in feel. It made her nervous—the advantage once again his—and she countered it by starting to walk. He followed, pulling his horse by the reins.

"So, Madeleine," he continued jovially, "how long do you intend to stay in our lovely community?"

She shrugged negligibly, acutely aware of his presence at her side. "Until the work is finished, I suppose. I imagine I'll be here most of the winter."

"That seems like a rather long time to translate."

"Does it? I hadn't considered it, but then I've not translated war memoirs before."

"Mmm. What war, may I ask?"

She looked up to his face. "The Opium War. Are you familiar with it?"

"Oh, my, yes," he replied without pause, his eyes boring into hers. "England had much at stake in the opium trade. Still does. Did Mr. Blackwood become a cripple in the East Indies, then?"

His tone fairly dripped with condescension, angering her because she was nearly certain his tactlessness was deliberate.

"I believe so, during one of the many skirmishes with China, although we haven't reached that point in our work. I have yet to learn of his later war years, or earn his full confidence in the matter." That thought turned

her anger to sadness. She really had no idea how he had
acquired his injuries, since Thomas had yet to trust and
open himself to her as he had asked her to do. Soon,
though, she would insist on it.

"I see," the baron responded thoughtfully, adding
nothing more.

Suddenly he reached out and grasped her arm, bringing them both to a standstill. Madeleine felt the pressure
of his touch through her cloak and gown, and she fought
the desire to shake herself loose.

He didn't withdraw. She stared into his eyes, a forced,
partial smile upon her lips, her expression inquisitive as
she tried not to appear threatened. Thomas had said the
baron was as smooth as oil, and that description fit him
precisely. He looked at her frankly now, his gaze falling
momentarily to what he could see of the curve of her
breasts. When he raised his eyes to lock with hers again,
they were heated, and he made no attempt to hide that
fact.

For the first time that she could recall, Madeleine was
intensely unnerved by the advances of a man. She stood
alone with a stranger in a cold forest, the sun behind the
thickening clouds, the silence deafening, and the baron
understood her concern. He had to, and he was using it.
The man was a snake. No, not a snake. A spider. Creeping silently in and out of people's lives, his eyes calculating as they watched and absorbed many things at
once, drawing innocents into his web where they could
not escape. Now he wanted her and made no attempt to
conceal it.

His horse fidgeted again, and without looking at it,
the baron yanked on the reins to quiet it. Madeleine
didn't know a thing about horses, but she was certain
Rothebury was never gentle with them, and his harsh
approach at controlling the animal didn't seem to help.

"Perhaps, Madeleine," he proposed in a gruff whisper, "you would like to attend my annual ball the second Saturday after Christmas? It is a masked affair, but I would be honored to introduce you to local gentry and those of importance who will all, of course, be attending." Very slowly, he began caressing her arm with his thumb. "It would also give us a chance to become better acquainted."

Despite the brisk, still air and the restless horse, Madeleine centered her thoughts on only his words. Not their suggestive nature, but the fact that he wasn't inviting her into his home before the ball three weeks from now. That was remarkably strange. He didn't want her in his home, and yet it was more than apparent that he desired her physically.

His wrist brushed the side of her breast as he stroked her arm, making her shiver.

"Are you cold?" he asked with feigned concern.

"Extremely." She gave him a lucid smile and embraced herself, clasping her elbows with her palms, effectively cutting off his hold on her as he had no other option but to drop his arm. "I'm not used to such a chilly climate. My native Marseille has much more appealing weather."

"Of course." He stood back a little, and for a moment Madeleine feared he might take his leave in annoyance. As much as she desired it, she wasn't ready for him to depart just yet.

Against her inner counsel, she took a step toward him, lowering her lashes so that they half covered her fair eyes, tilting her head and toying with the buttons on her cloak.

"It would be my pleasure to accept your generous offer, Richard. I adore parties, and it would be the perfect excuse to get to know you better. But it would only be proper if I were escorted by Mr. Blackwood. I assume he is also invited."

A shadow of something fell across his face. Doubt? Irritation? . . . Alarm? But he played the gentleman by not arguing.

"He will also be welcome as my guest," he said with just a shade of reservation.

"Wonderful." Her lips twisted coyly. "And I do hope you will show me some of the rooms in your great house. Lady Claire has told me of your marvelous book collection and your interest in trading them. A library is the perfect place to . . . talk alone. Don't you agree?"

That startled him. He tried to hide it, but he was disturbed by her statement. He blinked; his forehead crinkled in the slightest of frowns, and she knew it wasn't because he was surprised at her suggestion of an interlude between them. He was concerned either about the books, or about Lady Claire discussing him. She had the upper hand again.

"So you've met Lady Claire," he maintained, his voice betraying his caution.

"Once a lovely woman, I'm sure." It was the best compliment she could think of.

Abruptly he returned to his slippery, charming self. "Yes, indeed, though her beauty could never compare to yours, Madeleine."

She hated the way he said her name. Caressingly smooth, pronouncing each letter as if he were making love to it. In its own way it repulsed her.

With that thought the image of Thomas came to mind—a man of integrity, so powerful, dark, and honest. She remembered his large body sexually hard for her; his moving reaction to touching her intimately. It had only been two hours since she'd seen him last, and yet she missed him. Now. Anxiously.

"Well, I suppose I should be on my way," she declared through a sigh.

He chuckled, an oily, aggressive sound. "Impatient to return to work?"

She laughed softly, as expected, inclining her head daintily. "No, not really, but I suppose it is my duty to do so. My employer is no doubt wondering where I am."

His features hardened ever so subtly. "I'm sure that he is," he said coolly.

It took everything in her to reach out and clasp his arm with her palm. But she did, and he didn't move. She felt the tightness of his body even through layers.

"It is such a pleasure to finally meet the man I have heard so much about in only the few weeks I have been in Winter Garden," she admitted softly.

"The pleasure is mine, Madeleine DuMais," he countered just as quietly, grasping her gloved hand with his own.

"Until next time, monsieur."

He squeezed her fingers. "Next time."

She turned, but he didn't let go of her hand.

"One more thing I forgot to mention."

Madeleine hesitated and glanced back to notice the deep crease in his brow, his sharp focus now on the ground.

"Monsieur?"

"Your employer, Mr. Blackwood . . ."

She waited. "Yes?"

"Where is he from, exactly?"

He had to know, and yet he asked her. Why? "I believe he is from Eastleigh, only staying here for the winter months. But again, I do not know his personal life and habits all that well." She paused for effect, then added, "Why do you ask?"

The baron shook his head briefly in apparent confusion, still looking at the twigs and dark mud at his feet, clinging possessively to her hand. "That's very odd."

He wouldn't release her until he made his point, and for no discernable reason, her pulse began to race. "Odd?"

He never raised his face, but he lifted his lids so that he peered into her eyes, his now hard, hazel-brown circles of triumph.

"I have asked about him in Eastleigh, and nobody has ever heard of a scholar named Thomas Blackwood."

Madeleine felt the cold seep into her bones. Rothebury was lying, of course, or he wanted her to think so. Had he actually suspected Thomas for more than he is and really investigated him? That was what she found most troubling of all.

"I'm sure there is an explanation," she insisted congenially, trying desperately to control the shake in her throat. "Perhaps he hasn't been there in so long the residents have forgotten him. He is, after all, a traveled man."

The baron's mouth curled shrewdly, and he squeezed her hand again, almost painfully. "I'm sure you're right. What I meant by odd was that nobody in the vicinity of Eastleigh has the surname Blackwood. That means his family is not from there. I only had someone check because I heard he is interested in buying the Hope cottage, and since it sits alongside my property, I was curious about the possible new owner. I'm sure you understand."

She stood quite still. "Of course, Richard."

"Maybe you could ask him about it sometime."

She didn't reply, and he didn't wait for an answer.

With that he dropped her hand, faced his large mount, and in one effortless action, raised himself upon it once more.

"Words cannot express my delight in meeting you

here this morning in the seclusion of the forest, Madeleine. I only wish we had more time to spend alone, getting to know each other." His intrusive eyes grazed her figure once more, slowly, down and up. "You are an exceptionally beautiful woman, and I hope we'll meet here again." He lowered his voice. "Perhaps even at night. It would be a physical pleasure to see your lovely skin illuminated by moonlight."

That struck her like a slap to the face, at several levels, from the base to the professional. But most jarring of all was that in a manner she couldn't explain, she felt molested.

"You have been most charming, Richard," she returned politely, her body unnaturally tense, mouth dry, unable to comment on his last remark. "And I'll look forward to my invitation to the ball."

"And I, too, will look forward to showing you my . . . library. Until then, madam," he promised with confidence. Then he was off, in the direction he had come.

Madeleine started trembling. Coldness oozed through her, and yet it was more than just a physical reaction to the weather. Baron Rothebury scared her, for reasons unknown. She had intentionally entered the web, and the spider had discovered her. Trapped her. Stalked her.

Turning, she walked calmly in the direction of the cottage until she knew he was out of sight. Then she lifted her skirts and began to run.

Twelve

Without intention, Thomas was gone most of the day. He, too, had bathed at the inn after Madeleine had left to meet Rothebury, partly because he was used to daily baths and refused to go more than two days without one while in Winter Garden, but mostly because he worried about Madeleine and knew he would probably watch her from the forest if he could. She didn't need that. She was perfectly competent, and the baron certainly wasn't dangerous, at least not at an initial meeting.

At late morning, Thomas called on Sarah Rodney, hoping to extract what information he could from her, as the town's historian, regarding Rothebury's property, only to learn she'd been in Haslemere for the last ten days caring for her daughter who had just given birth during a difficult confinement. She would likely be there until after Christmas, according to her butler. Unfortunately there didn't appear to be any other way to gain information about the manor house aside from asking Rothebury directly or traveling to London to do some investigation. Winter Garden didn't have a specific place

where legal records were kept that would date back to
the time when the baron's family didn't own it. He could
write the Home Office to begin checking, but he didn't
want to. He would wait for now.

His next stop had been to the home of Penelope
Bennington-Jones. Desdemona, who lived with her widowed mother while her husband was away serving his
country in the Army, was a trifle under the weather, or
so he'd been told. Penelope, though, seemed pleased
enough to receive him. Overly pleased.

Since Thomas's arrival in the village the summer
prior, he'd only called on her formally twice. During
those meetings she had been cordial but aloof, treating
him respectfully as a guest of both her home and community, as she must. This time, however, she was exceptionally sociable, which in turn made him highly
suspicious. She was a determined woman, inquisitive to
the extreme, and today she'd purposely kept him talking
for more than two hours. Her questions were direct and
about him personally—his background, his war service
and education, his reasons for bringing Madeleine to
Winter Garden. Of course, he and Madeleine knew their
roles and how to respond to inquiries, having discussed
them with each other, but what struck him was the
abrupt turnaround in Mrs. Bennington-Jones. She'd been
conversing with others in the village about them, and
most probably to Rothebury. Now she was taking it
upon herself to investigate. Thomas was sure of it.

By midafternoon he found himself in Lady Claire's
hot, uncomfortable, raspberry-colored withdrawing
room, sipping tea and consuming salmon paste sand-
wiches, listening to her endless chatter about her early
days of marriage, her younger years when she'd been
courted tirelessly by gentlemen from all parts of the
countryside because of her wealth and beauty. Thomas

believed it. The lady had probably been striking to look at at one point in her life, while she now wasted away from bitter loneliness, dying without heir or loved ones. He felt sorry for her in a broad sense, but did not pity her. She felt enough of that for herself, and if there was one thing Thomas understood, it was self-pity. He would have none of it.

But even during their lengthy afternoon together, he discovered nothing of any significance regarding the opium investigation. His initial intention had been to discuss Rothebury and her books, but the conversation continually drifted, no matter how much he attempted to keep it in line. In the end, he didn't think Lady Claire knew much of anything, except that the baron desired her book collection, which was indeed substantial, and that he paid a good sum for good books from time to time. Thomas found the whole business questionable, but he knew, as he left the lady's country house, that he would learn nothing more from Lady Claire.

Now, at nearly five, Thomas strolled through the village toward the cottage, unconcerned with the falling darkness and droplets of freezing rain that splattered on his bare head and neck. For all his social calling, he knew little more than he'd started with this morning except that he and Madeleine had become the targets of town gossip during the last couple of weeks. Perhaps safe targets for now, but targets nonetheless. Questions were being asked, the well-bred villagers were roused, and the hunted baron sensed the bars on his cage. Exactly as Thomas desired, except for the passing of time.

And Madeleine. Madeleine, the lovely, passion-filled woman who always hovered at the center of his thoughts, who remained the biggest question of all. Did he have an influence on her? Did she need him yet? For anything? He didn't know.

Frankly he felt far too restless about their work together. She hadn't considered it as yet, but he knew their
investigation shouldn't take this long, and eventually so
would she. She would wonder what he did each day to
move it along, why they were together so intimately on
a case that didn't really need both of them to solve.
Rothebury probably should have been arrested weeks
ago with solid evidence that could have been collected
much faster, by other means, but Thomas's need to have
Madeleine at his side was the greatest desire of all, of
any desire he would ever know. It had been his doing,
his idea to bring her to Winter Garden, and Sir Riley
had no standing when it came to his decisions. Thomas
was the superior, Sir Riley the subordinate, and Thomas
had chosen the path by which they would find the
opium, or at least its smuggler.

Madeleine had already deduced that Rothebury was
their prime suspect, and so had he, before she'd even
arrived. But he needed the time with her. He tried to
convince himself that their prolonged stay had little to
do with his feelings for the woman, but, of course, it
did. Selfishly he'd chosen this investigation to meet her,
to court her, to attempt the impossible, and that took
time. He had one chance, and this was it. He would take
all the time he needed.

Thomas smiled to himself in the darkness. She desired
him with a marvelous hunger. Last night's episode had
been indescribable, so unexpected, and his blood boiled
even now at the memory. When he'd admitted his failure
this morning, she'd neither laughed nor made light of it.
But then he knew she wouldn't, which was precisely
why he'd revealed it to her. She hadn't surprised him
with her concern, and had stirred him inside with her
tender desire to accept him as he was, to keep him from
feeling embarrassed. He never would have told another

human soul about his sexual inadequacy and lack of recent intimacy, but Madeleine had his trust, the pleasure of his life in her care. Madeleine had his heart.

He had hoped for a mutual attraction when she'd finally arrived in Winter Garden, but he'd never dreamed that she would be so giving, that her passion for him would be so fast and obvious. Knowing her as well as he did, he perceived her confusion about her feelings for him, the fascination she felt, and he wouldn't push her. If she were to want a future with him, her confusion would have to change to contentment and an inner longing greater than any she'd felt before. She had the strength, but it would be her choice. That's what scared him most of all.

Thomas spied the cottage up ahead along the road, wishing desperately he could run to it. He was soaked from the driving rain, his body numb with cold, and she awaited him inside.

Minutes later he opened the front door to the wonderful aroma of cooking food. With freezing fingers, he stripped himself of his coat and hung it on the rack.

Madeleine heard him then, for she rounded the corner at precisely that moment, wearing her simple traveling gown, unbuttoned at the neck, a white starched apron, and her hair down, tied with a ribbon at her nape.

Thomas stared as his heart began to pound. He'd never seen her so relaxed before and never lovelier. Always was she polished and . . . cultured. Composed. Perfectly poised and regal, like a queen on her throne. But now, standing in the foyer of this tiny, village cottage, she looked charming, young and untouched, pink-cheeked and adorable, a wooden spoon in one hand, a spot of flour on her chin, and her eyes shining with bashful contentment. Thomas knew this moment would stay embedded in his mind forever.

"I made an early dinner," she said sweetly, breaking the spell. "Fresh bread, roasted pork with carrots and gravy, and baked apples. I'm not a very good cook, especially with English food, so there are no guarantees that it will be edible."

Grinning, he shook himself from his thoughts and stepped forward. "I'm starved so I don't care what it tastes like."

She quickly assessed him from head to foot. "You're wet. Do you want to change your clothes?"

Shaking his head, he countered, "I want to eat." *And not leave your side.* Looking around the front room, he asked, "Why are you cooking? Didn't Beth come in today?"

Madeleine stiffened just enough for him to perceive it, and he glanced back to her face. She blushed now, averting her gaze.

"I sent her home several hours ago, Thomas," she replied, shoulders tight. With a slight toss of her hair, she turned toward the kitchen once more. "She's far too young and lovely to be flitting around the cottage. I'm sure she has more entertaining things to do with her evenings."

What did that mean? She couldn't possibly be using the right English word. "Flitting?"

She didn't answer him. He heard a pan rattling behind the door, so he followed the noise. The kitchen was comfortably warm, smelled heavenly. "Flitting?" he repeated.

Madeleine stood next to the stove, rubbing her cheek with the back of her hand, not looking at him. "I'm jealous of her, Thomas."

He nearly fell over. He really did. He had to grab the back of the chair to his right to keep himself steady, forcing his tongue to remain in his mouth long enough to think of something to say.

Madeleine was jealous of the vicar's daughter? Was she joking? Of course she was. Wasn't she?

No. She was being honest with her feelings, as always, and that awareness made him suddenly crazy with delight and satisfaction. But jealous?

"Why?" he managed to mumble in response, though it sounded like a croak in his throat.

Her back to him, she lifted her left shoulder minutely, stirring something on the stove that held her concentration. "She is young and innocent and far too devoted to you. I realize you would like to marry again, but I think she's too naive for a man of your experience. You would do better to look elsewhere. And I didn't dismiss her. I just didn't want her here tonight."

It was a fast and rambling explanation, which meant she was likely embarrassed by her concerns. Thomas sat heavily in the wooden chair, noting the curve in her spine, the soft swell of her hips, marveling in what he was witnessing. This dream was getting more and more breathtaking. Madeleine was jealous of a village girl. A girl who meant nothing to him. Beth was . . . seventeen? Eighteen? He was nearly forty. Not that age ever made much difference for men of his station, but why would he want a naive girl when he could look at and converse intelligently with and . . . play chess with a woman like Madeleine?

He shook his head in amazement. Madeleine was jealous. Incredible.

Thomas cleared his throat and ran his fingers through his still-wet hair. "Maddie, you're the only woman who holds my interest."

She turned very slowly, smiling coyly, gravy dripping off the spoon in her hand. "We work together, Thomas, but I am not young and innocent and certainly not the marrying kind."

He drew a long breath. "What makes you certain that's what I want?"

Her eyes opened wide. "Don't all gentlemen? If you want to marry again, you'll need to find someone like Beth, only I think it would be more appropriate for you to find someone older."

"You do," he stated blandly.

She swept over that. "What you do after I leave is your business, but I still don't want to watch you flirt with her while I'm staying in the cottage with you. For reasons I don't clearly understand, that bothers me."

Flirt? Him? She was being sincere, but irrational, and he ignored it even as he tried to keep from beaming. "She's nice to me, not devoted," he remarked without hesitation, boldly absorbed in her gaze. "And I would never court her because I don't want her." Sitting forward and dropping his voice to a dark whisper, he revealed the ache of his heart. "I want only you, Maddie. Only you."

Thomas took immediate notice of her reaction. She paled ever so slightly, her smile dimming with either confusion or disbelief, maybe both.

Then something changed in her. Very gradually she stood erect, her expression growing slack but thoroughly determined. She glanced away from him and placed the spoon back into the pot before reaching behind her to loosen the ties on her apron.

Thomas felt a rapid, rising tension in the air, thick and unexpected, the heat of the kitchen enveloping them. She focused on him again, brazenly, and he caught his breath.

Her eyes, blue as rain, caressed his, saturating them with contentment and pleasure and an unquenchable longing. He could feel it flow from her, and he didn't move, didn't say a word, refused to break the spell.

Silently Madeleine walked to his side, dropping her apron to the floor and reaching behind her head to pull the ribbon from her hair. That done, she lowered the top of her body over him as he sat in the chair, grasping the table behind him, straddling him with her arms.

She stared, examining him for minutes it seemed, taking in each feature of his face.

He felt her breath on his skin, and his body hardened with erotic thoughts, his pulse raced, his throat tightened.

Then she lowered her lashes and leaned into him. He closed his eyes, expecting her lips to take his in a molding kiss, his mind begging for it, body yearning. It didn't happen. Instead, she licked the side of his face, her gentle, moist tongue tracing a slow line up the scar at his mouth.

He inhaled sharply through his teeth. It was a surprise attack that filled him with the oddest combination of lust and triumphant joy. If this was a dream, it was the greatest of all dreams. If he was dying, it was a wondrous death.

"Thomas . . ." she whispered.

He could stand it no more. He lifted his hands and grasped her head, shoving his fingers through her thick hair at long last. Her glorious hair that he'd longed to feel for years. Silky strands that fell through his fingers and stroked his cheeks and neck.

He found her mouth and claimed it, pulling her against him, kissing her fervently as she kissed him back. She moaned softly as her tongue found his and their quick breath mingled. She tasted of apples and wine, making him dizzy, making him ache with need.

He needed her now.

Thomas reached for her breast, but she covered his hand and pushed it aside. He wanted desperately to feel her but she wouldn't let him. Gently he traced her lips with his tongue, and with that she pulled free to stare down to him once more.

Her skin glowed, eyes blazed, and without moving her gaze, she closed her palm over the bulge in his pants.

"Madeleine—"

"Shh . . ."

With remarkable speed, she worked through the buttons, watching him closely until she finished. He jumped fractionally when she touched him over his thin, cotton drawers, but she didn't withdraw her hand. Instead she turned her attention to the center of his desire, dauntlessly pulled his clothing down his hips and openly looked at him.

The moment burned in his mind. He was fully erect and well endowed, but she had been with many. Thomas, for all the pleasure this erotic encounter brought, was terrified of inadequacy.

For what seemed like hours, she studied him, up and down and to each side. Still, he couldn't bring himself to react, couldn't find his voice, which didn't matter since he had no idea what he would say anyway. Finally she looked up and grinned invitingly. "It is the perfect size for me, Thomas."

He swallowed painfully in an attempt to hold his feelings inside. She was just so bewitching of face and form, seductive in tone, purposely making him feel wanted whether or not she truthfully believed what she said. He clenched his jaw, his stomach tightened, his throat ached. And then she put her bare, warm hand on him, and he thought he would surely die.

She cradled him at first, skimming the sensitive skin up and down with only her fingertips. She rounded the

tip with her thumb, teased the dark, coarse curls at the
base with her nails, reached even farther below to place
feather-soft strokes on the cool sac between his thighs.
Then she knelt beside him and bent her head to kiss him
intimately.

Thomas could not believe what was happening to him.
Lights blaring, food cooking, he sat in the heated kitchen
on a small, wooden chair with the sound of heavy rain
splattering against the windows, while the woman of his
heart caressed him totally, unselfishly.

She placed tender kisses up and down the length of
him, stopping to glide her tongue across the tip. He
squeezed his hands in her hair, closing his eyes to the
feel, whispering her name.

She sighed softly, urging him nearer that blissful edge
of no return, and he knew it would only be seconds
before he lost himself. Gently he tried to lift her head,
but she resisted.

"Let me, Thomas," she said in a hoarse breath.

He did. Pleasure conquered reasonable thought, and
he knew he couldn't stop her now. It had been too long
for him. Too long—

She took him in her mouth. All of him. His body
tensed, and he moaned, his breathing erratic, eyes
squeezed shut, his head rested against the wall behind
him as he clung to her.

She stroked him with her hot, wet tongue, her lips
parted just enough to coax the seed from him, pulling
him ever closer to the brink of release. He wanted to
touch her, he wanted to be inside of her, he wanted her
to love him.

"Maddie," he pleaded, his voice raspy, "I need you.
Maddie . . ."

He climaxed in an explosion of white light and wonder, gasping, tightly weaving his fingers in her hair,

holding her firmly while she took him in and gave as he had with her. She stroked and teased and loved him with her mouth until the glow of satisfaction subsided and his rigid body slowly began to calm.

Seconds passed awkwardly. Finally she raised her head and laid her cheek on his thigh, facing him, he knew, although he had yet to open his eyes. He couldn't catch his breath, couldn't slow his racing heart, didn't want the moment to end.

Madeleine watched him carefully, examining every nuance of his face, the rugged lines and crooked scar beside his lips, the naturally bronzed skin, the bristles on his chin and jaw, his thick, dark hair and long lashes. He was a beautiful man, so powerful but for the flush in his cheeks from the release of passion that made him seem younger, exposed.

She kissed his thigh and caressed it with her fingertips. "I have a confession to make, Thomas."

He stroked her hair but said nothing.

She smiled contentedly, admitting softly, "I have only done that once before to a man, at his request, and I didn't like it. But tonight I enjoyed it because I did it to you—for you. Do you understand?"

At last he raised heavy lids to peer deeply into her eyes. "I understand."

His tone was thick and rough, but he smiled dreamily.

"I am not experienced with this form of lovemaking," she continued in a husky whisper, "therefore I, too, fear that I might have failed. I think we are now even."

He drew a long breath, running his fingers through her hair again. "This is not a contest, Maddie."

"Exactly," she quickly replied.

He thought about that for a second or two, searching her expression. "You could never fail me, in any way."

Her heart warmed from that. The man knew just what

to say to her to make her believe, to make her want. Suddenly she felt the most intense desire to curl up in his arms. "I feel the same way about you."

His eyes grew softer still, and his thumb grazed her cheek. Madeleine couldn't recall a time when a man had been so tender with her, so . . . absorbed in her.

"Will you now concede that we are lovers?" she asked gingerly.

He sat up a little, forcing her to raise her head, his lips twisting in a playful grin. "Yes, I will now concede that." He paused, then added, "But I don't want to move too fast."

She wasn't sure what he meant by that—possibly he was self-conscious about his appearance, his legs—but he would get over it eventually. She wouldn't argue about it now.

He shifted his body in the chair, pulling his hands from her as he seemed to become uncomfortable with his nakedness. She had only exposed him from waist to thighs, but he was limp now, and the lamps from the kitchen bared that part of him glaringly.

"I think I'll freshen myself," she said matter-of-factly, standing beside him while she looked only at his face. "Then we'll eat." She smoothed her skirt and lifted the apron from the floor to lay it across the back of another chair. "I had an interesting meeting with Rothebury in the forest. I'll tell you about it during dinner. The man is a spider, Thomas."

He chuckled as he pulled his rain-damp trousers over his hips. "A spider? I thought perhaps you'd find him to your liking."

Puzzlement lit her brow. "Aside from his illegal and immoral dealings, I suppose he is the type of man I would have preferred in France, in the city. But not here."

"Not here?"

Not now, she wanted to say, but didn't dare. Her insides were awash with confusion again because she didn't understand her thoughts regarding these last few weeks with Thomas. He made her think in different ways, respond differently to her feelings. Brushing the topic aside, she said instead, "Will you stir the gravy? I don't want it to burn."

"Of course."

She detected the slightest hint of amusement in his words but she let that pass. Tying her hair in place with the discarded ribbon, she turned and walked to the door, stopping short when she reached it. After only a moment's hesitation, she disclosed, "He's investigated you, I think. He says nobody in Eastleigh has ever heard of you."

She didn't pose that as a question really, not wanting to appear distrustful herself, but she did hope for an explanation. He said nothing until she put her palm on the frame and glanced back to him. Sitting forward in the chair, elbows on knees, he stared at the wooden floor.

"Madeleine, because of my injuries I have become somewhat of a recluse. I know few people and have even fewer close friends. That I am not well known in Eastleigh doesn't come as a surprise. I live in the country, not in the town proper, and I've kept to myself for years."

It was an extremely difficult thing for him to say. She sensed that and was content to let the subject rest. "Are you at all concerned that he's suspicious of you?"

He shook his head slowly. "No. He's getting nervous, but I don't think he knows anything, at least not enough to act on."

She paused again, listening to the pounding rain on

the rooftop, breathing in the satisfying aroma of pork roast and apples. "When will you tell me what happened to your legs, Thomas?"

He rubbed his palm harshly down his face. "Soon."

For a reason she couldn't at all understand, that simple answer liquefied her. Softening her voice, she asked hopefully, "Will you play a game of chess with me later?"

He met her gaze at last. "It's always the favorite part of my day, Madeleine," he replied in a silky murmur. "I want to see how many games it takes before you beat me."

"I'm beginning to think it might take a very long time."

He didn't respond, but the look he gave her made her stomach flutter, her hands tremble. It was so full of . . . something she couldn't define, something meaningful and lovely. He caressed her with his eyes, his slightly parted lips begging for her touch. *Her* touch. Only hers. Madeleine knew it, and the instant realization shocked her as new and wonderful thoughts filled the spaces in her mind where doubt had always been.

Thirteen

The Christmas season had arrived. An air of festivity and excitement drifted through Winter Garden as everyone prepared for the religious holiday. Carol singers stood in the square from time to time, entertaining those who chanced to walk by, bells rang from the church, and children popped crackers and collected evergreen pine and holly to hang from mantelpieces and doorways.

Madeleine had taken the last week to prepare bonbons—rich French chocolate balls wrapped in decorative paper—to deliver to several of the villagers. For those who were not suspicious of her as a Frenchwoman among them, the chocolates were accepted with pleasure and she well received. For others, including naturally, Lady Claire Childress and Penelope Bennington-Jones, the bonbons were taken by colorless butlers who thanked her cordially and informed her that neither lady was at home. Desdemona remained hidden it seemed, although being pregnant was, of course, a convenient excuse to shy away from visitors.

Madeleine and Thomas's investigation continued, albeit slowly. It had been two weeks since her encounter with the baron, and in that time neither she nor Thomas had learned anything new. On several occasions they had walked the lake path at night only to see nothing, hear nothing, in the dark coldness. Madeleine sensed that Thomas was stalling, although she couldn't explain that, even to herself. He seemed content to live in the cottage with her and learn things about the opium smuggling operation by chance, as they happened, rather than drawing them out. He had little desire to solve this investigation in haste; and with some misgivings toward her own laziness, if one could call it that, she realized she did, too. She enjoyed Thomas's company more and more each day, and, of course, England was a refreshing change for her. Although the focus of her work remained in France, this was her home, this was the place where she belonged, if only in heart and mind. She would use any excuse to remain on British soil for as long as possible.

She and Thomas had grown closer during the last two weeks as well, although only in the most superficial of ways, if she had to put a phrase to it. They usually spent their days together, reading or writing letters in companionable silence, walking in the village or paying social calls to a few, playing chess most evenings, or talking. He still kept his private life to himself, and she didn't pry, although he talked frequently of his son, whom he loved immeasurably. She ached to ask him about the ordeal in his past that had scarred him, but something inside that she couldn't explain compelled her to keep silent. She knew he would reveal more of himself to her in time. For some unexplainable reason, she felt they still had much of it together. She was certainly in no rush to escape his presence.

That troubled her, in its own way, very much. Although Madeleine was content to have a sexual relationship with Thomas, she couldn't allow it to blossom into anything more. She refused to miss him when she left, beyond the mildest sense, of course. She didn't want to be hurt or to hurt him, for that matter. She couldn't be certain of his feelings for her, but she was beginning to suspect that they went deeper than hers did for him. Sometimes she would catch him staring at her, an expression of intense longing in his complex and brutally masculine features, his eyes betraying thoughts and emotions he refused to verbalize.

They had yet to become lovers, at least in the fullest sense of the word, and her desire was growing each day. Since that eventful night in the kitchen when she had given without receiving, he hadn't embraced her, however much she tried to attract his physical attention. Twice he'd kissed her passionately, but both times he'd stopped the passion before it overcame them. She'd been anxious but considerate, and he hadn't pursued her.

Now she was tired of it. She wanted him badly, and tonight she would make sure they both received physical pleasure, regardless of what she had to do to entice him. It was the night before Christmas, the time for giving.

"I want to hear how you became a spy for the British government."

That statement, posed abruptly, jarred her from her thoughts. She and Thomas sat together on the sofa, in front of a warm fire, sipping brandy after a delicious meal of roasted goose with onion and sage stuffing, squash, plum pudding and iced chocolate fudge, the rest of which they would finish tomorrow after the Christmas church service. It was nearly midnight, and for the last two hours Thomas had been talking about several of his prior investigations for the Crown, all of them in England. She had listened raptly—when her mind hadn't wandered to his physique only inches away from the touch of her hands. He was a fascinating man for all his quietness, and had done a great deal for the English cause in the last decade. Now she supposed it was her turn.

She smiled into his eyes and strengthened her hold on the snifter in her lap to stop herself from reaching for him. "Compared to your stories, Monsieur Blackwood, I'm afraid mine is rather boring."

"Indulge me," he insisted, taking a sip of his brandy.

Madeleine eyed him directly. Thick, long thigh muscles pulled his black trousers taut; his wide chest bulged behind his silk shirt, making her wonder how, with such disabilities, he was able to remain so physically fit. Whatever he did, it worked, for she had such trouble resisting him, on any level—intellectually, physically— even emotionally, which worried her a little.

His lips twitched upward, drawing her attention, beckoning her. . . . She cleared her throat and looked to the warm amber liquid in the glass on her lap.

"I didn't have the best of childhoods, Thomas. My mother detested me in general, although I tended to be useful as her servant girl. At sixteen I began line dancing on the stage during my free time, which wasn't often, to earn what little money I could. I refused to consider prostitution, primarily because I had seen what it had done to my mother. I wanted to be able to support myself and I didn't have any other skills."

"Your mother was a prostitute?" he cut in softly.

She shook her head. "Not for money, and not intentionally as a form of employment. But she traded sexual favors for opium when she needed it and couldn't afford it. I was frequently in the next room and could hear everything."

He didn't say anything to that, so she carried on. "Initially my income as a dancer was very small, and I didn't care at all for the lewd comments I received from lustful men, but I was able to save almost every bit of it because my mother wasn't aware. She would have taken it for herself had she known. After four years I'd earned enough to comfortably leave, and at the age of twenty I walked out on her." She sighed at the painful memories. "She hated me for that, Thomas. She yelled expletives at me as I closed the door on her, not because she loved me or was afraid for my welfare, but because I wouldn't be there anymore to rouse her when she was drunk, or clean and mend her clothes, or cook her food and clean up after her. I haven't seen her in nine years, and I will honestly admit that in those nine years I haven't missed her one day."

He adjusted his frame on the sofa so that he sat a little closer, so that she smelled his clean, male scent a little more strongly, so that she could see the tightness of his pants stretch across his hips and thighs when he moved. She squeezed her snifter and took another sip of her brandy.

"You never had anyone to love you, did you, Madeleine?"

She paused, the glass tipped against her bottom lip, and then her heart skipped a beat when she met his honey-brown eyes, ignited with understanding and tenderness. He reached out with his fingers and took a few strands of her hair between them, rubbing them gently.

"The only person who ever truly loved me was my father," she replied steadily, subdued.

He studied her face. "I imagine that would be very hard on a child, to lose one's father at such an early age and then have nobody."

His quest for discussion of such personal issues made her a little uncomfortable. The topic was too upsetting, the memories too grievous. "I only saw him those few precious times, but I think the idea that he would arrive one day and take me out of France and back to England where I felt I belonged was what kept me happy all those years. When I discovered he had died, something inside of me died with him. It was as if my hopes and dreams were stolen from me." She tried her best to make the statement casual, to keep her anger in check, as she had done for years. "From that moment on," she concluded lightly, somewhat indifferently, "I took matters into my own hands. My life today is what I've made of it. I refuse to be unhappy."

He nodded, gazing at the tips of her hair as he held them up for his inspection under firelight. "My parents loved me," he said, his voice low and thoughtful. "But they've been dead for years, so I only remember a few good times, memorable times. William loves me more than words, but then I am his father and his only close, living relation. My wife cared for me very much, but our marriage was arranged. She was my distant cousin, and we both knew from a young age that we would marry each other. I loved her, too, in the same way. I took her death very hard because I had known her most of my life." His gaze grew vivid and intense as he looked back into her eyes. "I suppose I received a great deal more affection than you growing up, but like you, Maddie, I've never felt truly, passionately loved."

By a woman, he meant. Her stomach tied in knots again, and she took another long sip of her brandy. He was just so focused on her that it made her nerves tingle with an unusual form of anticipation and excitement.

He needed to understand who she was. He already knew *what* she was, but not who. The forces of her past had shaped her, molded her into a strong, independent woman, and that independence was more important to her than any love she might have lacked.

Not one to imbibe much, Madeleine placed her snifter, half full, on the tea table in front of her. He released her hair from his grasp but kept his arm relaxed across the sofa back, his hand next to her shoulder.

"When I left France at the age of twenty," she continued, attempting to revert to the original topic, "I came immediately to England, to meet my father's family. I was accepted with what I would call reserved warmth, but they could never embrace me as one of them. I am not only half French, but also illegitimate. They were courteous but . . . restrained. I stayed for three weeks, left without tears, and went to the Home Office in search of a position."

His mouth twisted fractionally, and it made her grin. "I know," she acknowledged, rubbing her palm along her forehead. "I look back on it now and wonder at my audacity. The men in charge nearly laughed me from the building. But I persevered, going to visit Sir Riley three times in as many weeks. When that final attempt failed at winning his . . . unconditional respect, and he again refused to hire a woman—and a French one at that—I returned to France vowing to continue my quest to help the English on my own. That was nine years ago, though it seems like yesterday.

"For three years I worked my way inside the French elite, learning what I could to help the British cause at home—little pieces of information that I would pass along to Sir Riley with the salutation, 'Warm regards from the Frenchwoman.' " Her eyes thinned slyly. "He knew who I was, and I enjoyed that little bit of power. I lived the life of a Parisian socialite by day, attending the appropriate parties, the devoted mistress to the right gentlemen when I so chose. I became someone I wanted to become, and nobody questioned it. I certainly learned to be a better actress than my mother."

Madeleine looked at Thomas frankly to see if he was shocked by her disclosures, but he remained expressionless, motionless, listening intently. She decided that she would tell all. He seemed to be truly curious, caring, and she knew without question that he wouldn't be judgmental.

"I continued to dance from time to time in filthy, smoky halls, where sweaty, drunken men would throw coins at my body and offer graphic sexual suggestions to my face in the hope of favors. I kept my identities separate, and fortunately for me those people of influence I socialized with by day were not the same as those who frequented dance clubs at night. I still needed the income, though, and I knew it would only be a matter of time before I received word from Sir Riley that I had been accepted as one of you."

He crossed a booted ankle over the other. "Rather naive of you, don't you think?"

She shrugged one shoulder. "Yes. I was very naive, but also extremely confident."

He matched her grin for grin, then sipped his brandy again. "Go on."

She hesitated a moment, relishing the companionable silence as she considered her next words. In the end she decided to be blunt.

"In early July, eighteen forty-three, while lying naked in bed with a widowed French diplomat, he unintentionally—and unfortunately—mentioned that Claude Denis Boudreau and Bernard Chartrand, two very high-profile political prisoners, were going to be transferred from trial in London directly to Newgate, and plans were in the making to free them while in transit, with force if needed." Smugly she straightened, her hands folded neatly in her lap, her smile turning devilish. "It was just the news I had been waiting for and I couldn't very well send such grave information to Sir Riley in a message. Time was critical, so I went to London myself for only two days, waiting hours in the cold and gloomy office building before he would see me. He was surprised and somewhat amused by my presence, but I think heavily persuaded by my tact and knowledge of the impending fiasco.

"When at last I learned that the Frenchmen involved in the conspiracy were apprehended, and Chartrand and Boudreau had continued to prison without incident, I knew I had proved myself to Sir Riley's satisfaction. Three days later, on August second, I was contacted informally near my home in Paris by one of our associates. Within twenty-four hours I had become Madeleine DuMais, widow of the mythical Georges DuMais, immediately sent to Marseille to begin my career as an informant in the field of trade smuggling." She flicked her wrist. "And for whatever else might arise."

"You're well known at the Office," he interjected, mildly amused, "and tremendously admired."

Madeleine had suspected this, but hearing it spoken aloud for the first time, with what she could have sworn sounded like boastful pride in his voice, caused her throat to close with emotion.

"Even as a Frenchwoman?" she asked with quiet diffidence.

"*Especially* because you're a Frenchwoman."

That was the greatest compliment of all. She leaned toward him, placing her palm on his upper arm, squeezing it gently, feeling hot skin beneath soft silk. Passionately she revealed, "I adore my work, Thomas. It's who I am, not merely what I do. If there is one thing I've learned in my twenty-nine years it's that love is fleeting, but who you are is not. I chose this path to live as a French spy for the British government because it's who I am and always have been. I will forever be comfortable with that, and I need nothing more to make my life worthwhile."

For a full fifteen seconds he said nothing, just looked at her, absorbing the meaning behind her comments, perhaps attempting to rationalize the women he knew with the past she depicted. Then he cocked his head as if he didn't understand something, his brows furrowing slightly, eyes gazing not into hers, but through hers, if that were possible, and Madeleine was struck with the distinct impression that he was attempting to peer into the deep recesses of her soul.

It made her uneasy, and she withdrew her hand, backing away from him a little.

"I think, Maddie," he said soothingly, "that for you love is fleeting because you have never truly allowed it in here"—he touched her temple with his fingertips— "or in here." His hand moved down her neck, slowly, gently, until he placed his palm over her heart, between her breasts. "Until you do you will be an excellent informant for the Crown, a good friend to those you care about, a respectable French citizen on the surface and a worthy Englishwoman beneath it, but you will never know *who* you are until you recognize that you are valued beyond the superficial, that you are loved."

Her body stilled except for the tiniest of tremors that shot through her belly and into her extremities. Of course, he didn't comprehend her longings and dreams, her ambitions, but then neither did she comprehend him. He talked in circles, as did most men of her experience, especially when discussing love.

"I'm not loved by anyone now, Thomas," she uttered grimly in explanation, "and I am happy and content. My work is my life. It's rewarding and fulfilling. I need nothing more."

He inhaled deeply then blew it out through tight lips, his hand still resting against her chest. "You will never know if you are loved, because you're not open to it. Your work means everything to you because it's safe, Madeleine. It can't disappoint and abuse you like your mother. It can't die and leave you lonely and afraid like your father did. Love does that, but a profession will not."

He leaned so very close to her that she felt his penetrating heat and saw firelight sparkle in the center black circles of his eyes.

"A profession pays your debts," he articulated in a gruff whisper, rubbing her collarbone with his fingers, "and satisfies your need to personally succeed and do something for the betterment of society. But love expands your soul with something inexplicably fulfilling. If you die without ever having experienced it, you will miss life's only true joy."

Madeleine felt her heart stop. For one second in time. And then it raced, which he certainly felt beneath his palm.

His seriousness was extraordinary, his look both evaluating and bold. Dangerous. A very small part of her wanted to run, to leave his presence and return to the safety of her room, maybe even her home in France. The larger part of her, however, the daring and irrational part, wanted to reach for him now, fold herself in his embrace, kiss him with a renewed power and the craving for something greater, and never let him go.

He sensed it, too, or saw the indecision in her shadowed expression, for quite suddenly he lifted his hand and traced her lips with his thumb, back and forth along the lush curves.

She faltered, swaying into it, losing the battle.

"I have something for you," he murmured, breaking the spell. "A Christmas gift."

She never glanced away from his beautiful eyes, so shaken by his mood and concern, his sheer maleness, and she had no idea what to say.

Reluctantly he withdrew from her and stood. He drained his brandy snifter in one swallow, then disappeared up the stairs to his room, returning momentarily with a large white box in his hands, tied with a blue satin ribbon.

A peculiar mixture of feelings darted through her as she reached for it—gratitude and amazement. Restlessness.

He hesitated before he let it go. "Promise me you'll keep it?"

His deep baritone timbre challenged her to deny him, and she took on a manner of total innocence, grinning broadly. "Of course. Why wouldn't I keep it?"

He half snorted, then released the box and sat next to her again, closer, his knee touching hers cozily, his arm on the sofa back, behind her neck and shoulders.

Swiftly Madeleine untied the bow, set it aside, then lifted the lid on the box. What she saw stunned her.

Inside lay a thick, woolen pelisse-mantle, as white and soft as swan plumage, trimmed in luxuriant black sable. She carefully lifted it from the box by the shoulder capes and stood, raising it to her chest and pressing it against her. Expensively tailored and figure fitting, six large black buttons closed it from neck to knees while the heavy fabric extended to her ankles. And not only did sable adorn the sleeves, collar, and hood, it lined the inside as well and covered a large, matching muff still sitting inside the box.

For a moment Madeleine was speechless.

"Do you like it?" he asked hesitantly.

"Oh, Thomas . . ." she whispered, incredulous. "It's . . ."

"Beautiful and elegant, and very much needed," he finished for her.

"Yes."

Huskily, he added, "Like you are."

She couldn't believe he said that, or that he intended to give her this marvelous cloak so generously. Thickly she mumbled, "You bought this for me?"

His reached out and stroked the fur. "You needed something warmer than a traveling cloak, and I had a little money saved. I wanted to spend it on you."

It had to be the most touchingly personal thing anyone had done for her in a long time. "Thomas," she started, then took a very deep breath. "Thomas, it's a wonderful gift—"

"And you said you'd keep it. I'm so pleased."

He'd backed her into a corner, but she had another reasonable excuse. "I'll only need a mantle like this in England, this winter. It wouldn't get any more use after that, I'm afraid."

Slowly his lips curved upward into a crooked smile, his thick hair curling over his forehead, eyes charged with fire. He looked like a pirate suddenly, cleverly estimating her value.

"Maybe you'll be in England much longer than you expected, Maddie."

The words flowed from his mouth like hot lava, making her breathless, stirring the heat within her. Now, sitting on the sofa, staring up at her, he exuded a sexuality so potent, so primeval, it seared her to the bone and refused to go unanswered.

"I have a gift for you, too," she said in a silky purr.

His brows rose in faint surprise. "You do?"

Meticulously she folded the mantle and returned it to the box, setting it gently on the rug beneath the tea table. Then she turned back to face him, hands on hips.

He waited patiently, watching her, and she decided to take the initiative.

Slowly she began unbuttoning the neck of her gown, and his eyes dropped to catch the movement. He squirmed.

"Aren't you rushing things a little?" he asked with a hint of dry humor.

Madeleine was quick to note that he didn't say no, or stop, or that he had something more engaging to do. She tilted her head to the side and let out a very soft, throaty laugh. "I promise not to take advantage, Thomas."

She had no intention of stripping completely; she sensed that this wasn't the time. Instead, she covered him with her body, straddling him on the sofa, her knees on the cushion beside his hips and her skirt hiked up to her thighs, pressing her sex against the long hard mass beneath his pants. Feeling that gave her plenty of instant satisfaction anyway. He was already hard for her, and they hadn't done anything yet.

"Someday, Mr. Blackwood, I intend to see you completely naked."

"Someday, sweet Madeleine, I intend to let you."

Smiling, she opened the top of her gown to expose her flimsy linen chemise. "My gift to you," she said invitingly.

She leaned over and kissed him then, hard and hot. He embraced her immediately, wrapping his arms around her body, pulling her in tightly as his hunger mounted quickly and his breathing grew harsh.

Running her fingers through his soft hair, she traced his lips with her tongue then inserted it into his mouth, deeply, teasing his until he grasped it and began to suck.

She moaned faintly from that as he caressed her back and hips. Then he drew his palms forward and cupped her breasts over her chemise, thumbing her nipples until they hardened into deliciously sensitive points.

Lust consumed her, and she began to move her body up and down his rigid erection, kissing him fervently, her hands in his hair, thumbs tracing his cheekbones. He gently squeezed and massaged her breasts as they fit snugly into his large palms, breathing fast, his quiet sigh blending with hers.

When he dropped his hands to her thighs, she loosened her hold on him in silent invitation, and he accepted, pushing them up and under her gown. The skin of his palms seared her bare legs at the moment of contact, and he jerked free of the kiss.

"Ahh, God, Maddie," he said through his teeth, "you're not wearing anything."

Not under her gown, and she beamed inside as she kissed his neck and jaw, his chin and lips. "Push your hands up, Thomas, and you'll discover your gift unwrapped," she whispered against his warm, stubble-coarse cheek. "It's been waiting there for you all day."

He groaned in unbridled pleasure but did as he was ordered, slowly, so slowly she thought she might die of want—or grab his hands and force him to cup her mound.

When at last his fingers teased the curls that beckoned him, she took his mouth again and kissed him deeply, whimpering softly, inviting him with her body to enter in and discover.

He welcomed it. Suddenly his thumb found her center nub, already so hot and wet, and he began to stroke it.

He shifted his body beneath hers so that he could feel her more intimately, then raised one hand back to her breast, kneading, pinching her nipple gently, running his thumbnail across the tip.

She toyed with his mouth, wove her fingers through his hair, then lowered her hands to his chest, feeling bunched muscles, lean, hard mass, and hot, hot skin beneath the silk.

Enough play. She was ready for more.

Madeleine pulled back and sat up, gasping for air, her body inflamed. She stared at him, only to witness his own inner heat as she rocked her hips against his erection and blissfully rubbing thumb.

His eyes were glazed, needy, begging.

She reached down to the buttons of his pants, and this time he helped her to quickly unfasten each one. She raised herself just enough so that he could slide his trousers down his thighs, exposing the stiff length of him, and then at last, very slowly, she placed her wet cleft on top of it.

That touch—burning, scorching, dripping with the scent and feel of sex—nearly pushed Thomas over the edge. But he refused to close his eyes and accept the pleasure without prolonging the enjoyment. He peered at her stunning face, so enticing and aroused, then put his thumb back where it belonged, on the tiny nub of her desire.

He stroked her again gently, slowly, as she towered over him, her cheeks flushed radiantly, her gaze luring him into the cresting wave of passion.

And then she did the unexpected. With one hand she reached up to loosen the braid in her hair, with the other she cupped one of her breasts, still hidden by only the sheerest piece of linen, and began circling her nipple with her own thumb and fingers, squeezing it, rubbing it, watching him intently.

Thomas had never seen a woman do that to herself,

and he caught his breath, swallowing painfully and biting down hard in an attempt to remain in control. He
intended to climax inside of her this night, to experience
her fully, not early, and not before he gave her something in return.

She reached for his free hand and placed it on one
breast while she continued to caress the other. She was
so wet where his thumb continued to tease, so beautiful,
leaning her head back and moaning as she began to
move faster against his erection.

"Now, Maddie," he insisted in a rough whisper. *And
my greatest longing will be nearly fulfilled.*

She knew what he meant. Lifting her hips, she
reached down and grasped him, encircling him with her
fingers and palm before she placed the tip of him at her
slick center.

"I've waited years," he murmured, closing his eyes,
not sure if he had said it loud enough for her ears but
unable to help himself.

Without sound, she very carefully lowered herself
onto him, drawing him inside inch by inch, to that place
in heaven where dreams come true. His dreams. She was
tight, heated, and ready. A small gasp escaped her lips
as she took him in.

"Perfect," she said wistfully.

The words touched his soul. "Perfect."

She enveloped him totally, her muscles snugly closing
in on him in a marvelous, caressing fit. He would stay
inside of her forever if he could. If she would let him.

Very cautiously she began to move. He followed her
lead, stroking her again between her legs, steadying the
rhythm. She leaned forward to kiss him soundly, drawing breath from him, heavy and ragged with desire.

She made tiny, petal-soft sounds at the back of her
throat as she picked up speed, moving quickly against

his thumb, his pubic bone, closing in on her release.

Then just as quickly she pulled back, and he opened his eyes, wanting to watch her this time, waiting to experience his own satisfaction so he could witness her loveliness in full when she climaxed.

It didn't take her long.

She began panting, whimpering over and over again at his exquisite assault, straining against his thumb while she cupped her own breasts and played with her nipples.

Thomas had never seen anything so erotic in his life. He was close to the brink, and she was guiding him to it without trying.

Suddenly her eyes flew open, and she squeezed his legs with her own. "I'm almost there, Thomas. Almost there. Oh, please, oh, please, oh, please—"

She screamed a low guttural sound that penetrated the cottage walls and shook him to the core. Then he felt her muscles contract around him, tugging at him, bringing him along with her to that wonderful, fulfilling edge. She jerked against him, but he never stopped the torment of his thumb between her legs. Her head tossed from side to side, her fingers pulled at her nipples, her palms caressed her breasts as she kneaded them, and he could take no more.

He gripped her thighs tightly with both hands. "I'm coming, Maddie, I'm coming with you—"

And just as he did, he moaned deep in his throat, and she pulled up from him so that he fell out of her, his seed spilling onto his stomach in pulsating waves. She placed her cleft on his erection and rocked against him, rotating her hips second after blissful second, until the pleasure subsided and he was thoroughly satiated.

At last her body movements calmed, and she slumped forward to kiss him, wrapping her arms around his neck, hugging him gently.

He kissed her in return and raised his hands to stroke her hair. Finally, wordlessly, she snuggled into him, her face in his neck, her warm breath brushing his skin.

Thomas stared into the dying fire. He held the woman he loved in his arms, and it was one of the saddest moments of his life.

Fourteen

Madeleine stood in front of the faded mirror in her bedroom, glancing over what she could see of her figure,
assessing detail to make certain all was perfect. She'd
donned her evening gown for tonight's ball, the only
dress she had yet to wear in Winter Garden, and she
wanted to make an impression.

Its cut was of typical design, though a stunning cre-
ation from shoulders to toes. Made of shimmery white
satin, neck rounded and low, sleeves long and fitted at
her arms, it pulled in tightly at the corset to then spread
wide and fall luxuriously over full crinoline. Royal blue
satin flounces near the bottom of the skirt, as well as
tiny rosebuds of the same material and color at the neckline, were the only decorations to adorn it. The style was
simple, elegant, and the effect truly spectacular. The
masked ball would be a huge event, both for the town
and their investigation. Tonight, for the first time since
her arrival, she and Thomas would be inside Baron
Rothebury's home.

Madeleine added only a trace of false color to her lips,

pinched her cheeks, then smoothed her hands over her hair. Instead of plaiting it as she usually did, she'd pinned it loosely to her crown, allowing only a few tendrils to frame her face and throat. Now she added the final touch—a dab of perfume and pearl ear bobs. She desperately hoped Thomas would be pleased by her appearance, for although reluctant to admit it, she realized she'd dressed to impress him most of all.

Inhaling deeply for confidence, she swept up her new, beautiful mantle in her arms, grabbed her muff and small reticule that contained nothing more than lip color and a linen handkerchief, then dimmed the light and left the confines of her bedroom for the parlor where Thomas awaited her.

The room was dark when she entered it, save for the glow from the lingering fire and one small lamp. Madeleine noticed him immediately, and the sight stopped her dead.

He stood by the grate, a slight frown on his mouth, gazing down to the mantelpiece and lifting the music box lid with his thumb, over and over, each time it dropped back into place. A nervous action, probably.

He wore black, all black from what she could see, and although conservative in style it suited his dark features perfectly. Hearing her enter, he turned to her just then, and the full sight of him made her sway with uncertainty and infinite delight.

He was devastatingly handsome, his hair combed away from his beautiful eyes and rugged face. She could see now that his waistcoat was a midnight blue silk, his cravat as white as her gown, and she wondered for a second or two if he had planned that. His clothes were expensive, and they matched hers, yet he couldn't have known what she'd wear. He hadn't seen this dress as far as she knew. Still, they would look like a couple, and she rather liked that idea.

His eyes traveled over every inch of her, lingering briefly at her bosom, and she felt herself blushing under his scrutiny.

"I have been to countless balls across England and Europe, Madeleine," he admitted pensively, breaking the silence in a voice both airy and resonant. "But never have I seen a lady as beautiful as you are tonight." He shook his head negligibly. "Words cannot describe it. You simply take my breath away."

Madeleine felt as if the sun broke free from the clouds to shine down on her in warm, golden brilliance. Men of quality so frequently commented on her beauty, but never had she felt—beheld—such sincerity in a compliment. If Thomas was trying to romance her into falling in love with him, his strategy was slowly chipping away at the shield of stone she'd built around her heart. He had to know that. She also once again recognized that glimmer of deep caring in his tone, and at last she melted into it, understood it. Suddenly she saw the challenge before her, before both of them. He was falling in love with her. That explained everything, and for the first time in ages she was scared to death.

"I think you just want me in your bed but are afraid to ask me bluntly to join you, Monsieur Blackwood," she replied through an exaggerated sigh, striding closer to him, covering her fears with congeniality. "But with better persuasion I won't even argue."

"What better persuasion could there be than telling you I find you more beautiful than words?" He put one hand on his hip, shoving his frock coat out of the way of his enormous chest. "I will admit, however, that I have been fantasizing for weeks about what you must look like without any clothes."

She pursed her lips in feigned contemplation, placing her mantle and reticule on the sofa as she passed it, only stopping when she stood next to him. "That's . . . a bit more persuasive. Perhaps I'll let you peel them off of me later."

He blinked, then grinned soundly. "Now you have me aroused, madam. An uncomfortable state before a ball. I certainly hope you're not teasing me."

She knew he was teasing her at the moment, but he charmed her nonetheless. Placing a palm on his waist-coat, she rubbed the smooth, costly silk. "I'm not teasing when I say that you've stolen my breath as well, Thomas. You look marvelous tonight, handsome and so-phisticated. Aristocratic. I'm so taken with you suddenly that I'm not sure what to do about it." She lowered her voice to a soft plea. "Any suggestions?"

"Other than making love? That depends," he reasoned darkly. Shifting his weight from one foot to the other, he asked, "How taken with me would you say you are?"

She almost laughed at his obviously anxious attempt to find out. But he'd posed the question in a serious manner, and she knew he needed to know. She didn't want to make light of it, either.

Reaching up to straighten his cravat that didn't need straightening, she nonchalantly admitted, "More taken than I've been with a man in a very long time. Maybe ever."

Madeleine sensed that he was acutely affected by her honest answer because of the flagrant way his gaze pen-etrated hers, his jaw hardened with a thick swallow. He wanted to embrace her but he held back for reasons un-known, as he had for days. He'd been somewhat aloof since Christmas, and as much as she wanted to deny it, she felt flustered and more than mildly disturbed by it. She tilted her head in question. "You've neglected me lately, Thomas. Why?"

He absentmindedly lifted the lid to his music box again, just a half an inch or so, then lowered it. "I don't think neglecting you is how I would phrase it exactly."

"Oh. You've just been busy, then?"

"Naturally," he quickly retorted.

"I see." She waited a few seconds, then decided to clarify. "Writing letters, making social calls, and walking in the village?"

"And thinking of you constantly," he whispered.

Those words had their effect. "Kiss me, Thomas, and prove it, before I start to think you're no longer interested in me as a woman."

That did it. For an infinitesimal moment he looked amused by the demand. Then he reached up with his palm and placed it on the back of her neck, caressing it lightly before he drew her lips to his.

His touch was gentle yet vibrant and nourishing, like a steady, misty summer rain. He smelled heavenly, felt both powerful and immense as he drew her into his arms. He didn't invade her mouth with his tongue in a rise to passion, but instead drifted along the current of soft sensation, of emotional tenderness, making love to her lips with his own. It was the sweetest kiss Madeleine had ever experienced.

When he pulled away from her seconds later, she had no desire to open her eyes. She clung to him, her head back, palms flat on his silk-covered chest, feeling dazed. He massaged her neck with his fingertips, then placed delicate kisses on her forehead and lashes, on her temple. She wanted the moment to go on forever.

"What are you thinking now, Maddie?" he murmured against her cheek.

"Mmmm . . . That it's wonderful." She leaned closer to whisper, "I've never felt like this in my life."

He stilled in mid-kiss to her jaw, and she noticed.

Gradually he lifted his head, and she opened her eyes to the striking dark depths of his. In all of her life she'd never seen a look like that from a man, and she couldn't begin to describe it if she had to. He wanted her sexually, he wanted her emotionally, he wanted all of her, and his longings were there before her, exposed to her view. Yes, he was falling in love with her, as no man had ever done, and not only was she frightened, she marveled at it.

She reached up and slowly traced his mouth with her fingers. "I'm scared of this, Thomas."

He breathed deeply at her husky admission and brushed his lips back and forth across her fingertips. "I know."

His warm breath teased her skin, his intensity unnerved her, but when he offered nothing more in response, she quickly took control of herself again and stood erect, stepping back to a safer distance. He let her go easily.

"We need to leave, Madeleine," he said before she did, straightening his frock coat, sweeping the sleeves down with his palms. "We need as much time as possible in Rothebury's house."

She nodded, suddenly shaken by the static in the air, grasping her throat with her bare hand because she couldn't think of anything appropriate to say. Of course, the work came first. Why had she forgotten that? She blinked quickly and turned away.

He waited for her to gather her things, then he helped her into her beautiful new mantle before he attended to his own twine coat. After pulling her reticule over one wrist, she stuffed her hands deeply into her sable muff, and they left the cottage in silence, stepping out into the cold, cloudy night.

Fifteen

Madeleine's first impression when she finally stood inside the Baron Rothebury's home was that the Winter Masquerade was truly the event of the season. Everyone of adequate social standing appeared to be in attendance, wearing formal party regalia, imbibing fine liquor, and nibbling delectable morsels that numerous polished footmen carried on silver trays to three buffet tables at the north end of the ballroom.

The house itself was smaller on the inside than it looked from across the lake, which surprised her. They'd entered through the large front doors, stepping into the foyer decorated with pale marble flooring and bare apricot walls that instantly drew attention to the marvelous crystal chandelier hanging from the ceiling. A large circular staircase in dark oak, straight ahead of them, presumably led to the private quarters on the second floor. To their immediate right, inside partially closed doors, appeared to be a parlor, then likely the library or private study behind it, followed by the dining area and kitchen in back. To their left, taking up most of the main floor as far back as she could see, was the ballroom.

Madeleine handed her mantle and muff to the butler, then walked gracefully toward it, Thomas following close behind her. At the stunning peach and emerald stained-glass archway separating the ballroom from the foyer, she paused long enough to tie a white satin mask to her face, given her by a very fastidious footman who nodded appropriately and gestured for her to descend the short staircase to the festivities below.

Quickly, she glanced around her surroundings, taking note of Rothebury's style. His taste was expensive and eclectic. She noted several furniture pieces of various colors and designs, and antiques of all sorts lining the walls or sitting atop marble and glass shelves. Like the rest of the house, the ballroom structure was old, but recently redecorated in woodland green and gold. Windows with ornate frames lined two walls, the others adorned floor to ceiling with mostly oil paintings from sundry artists. The majority of those invited had evidently arrived, as the room seemed crowded and rather stuffy; an octet played an unfamiliar, albeit lovely, waltz at the far west end as dancers took to the floor in growing numbers.

As she lowered herself onto the first step, Thomas now beside her, a slight but notable hush fell across the gathering below. Although masked, it was obvious who they were. Madeleine imagined they made a striking pair, but there was likely a great deal of shock at their appearance among the guests as well. She and Thomas had said little on their long walk from the cottage, taking the roads around the village instead of the path beside the water to spare dirt on her white gown, but now he leaned over to whisper in her ear.

"The baron is standing near the east wall, beside the window, talking with Margaret Broadstreet."

Madeleine tried to ignore the frictional heat from his body and the tingle on her neck where his breath lingered as she focused on the baron. Impressively dressed, he wore an impeccably tailored frock coat and matching trousers of deep purple, a lavender satin waistcoat, and a black cravat to match his mask.

As if on cue, Rothebury caught her eye, tipped his head, and graced her with an almost imperceptible nod, his lips twisting into a sly, knowing grin before he cocked his head and looked her up and down. Madeleine inwardly recoiled from the inelegant regard, but smiled to him warmly in acknowledgment. Just as quickly she felt Thomas grasp her elbow with long, firm fingers in an act of possession. At least she hoped it was.

"Let's move toward him first," he proposed quietly, being thoroughly practical as he began to descend the stairs. "We can make introductions and then perhaps part ways."

The suggestion annoyed her somewhere deep within. Contrary to her own practicality, she wanted to remain at his side all evening. But instead of arguing his point, she simply nodded and followed his lead.

"Not going to comment?" he asked wryly.

"Comment?"

"On the fact that you don't want me to leave you alone to the spider's attack?"

She stalled three steps down and flipped her head around to eye him shrewdly.

He grinned, devilishly, fully aware of what she was thinking. She fought an urgent need to verbally censure him—or kiss him again.

"I'm quite competent, Thomas, and he's a charming man," she replied ever so sweetly. "I'm sure we'll get on just fine, and with a little persuasion he might learn to . . . appreciate my presence."

He squeezed her elbow then rubbed his thumb along the bone. "Appreciate your presence? I think, Maddie, he'll probably appreciate your outstanding, milky-white breasts bursting up so beautifully from the top of your gown." Smirking, he admitted, "My fingers have been itching to remove your corset and let them loose in my palms since we left the cottage."

"So you *noticed* them," she remarked with feigned relief, tossing her curls with a lift of her chin. "I worked so hard to make them conspicuous."

"Did you?" he exaggerated.

She pressed her lips together to keep from laughing. "But I won't let the baron touch, if that worries you, Thomas. I'm reserving that honor."

He blinked. "Reserving it?"

A rotund woman in yards of gray silk marched up in front of them, her rosy face hardening beneath her white mask, irritated because they blocked her exit from the ballroom. Thomas took the cue and pulled Madeleine aside, then out of the way as he continued steadily down the steps to the main floor. He still clasped her elbow, and she made no move to break free of him.

Turning to face him at last, Madeleine nestled up as close as decency allowed under the circumstances, and lowered her voice to just above a whisper. "I want them touched and kissed and sucked by someone who makes me burn with a look, makes me hot with a simple caress, and makes me forget myself when he's inside me. In Winter Garden that could only be you, Thomas."

Although nobody could have possibly heard her, his eyes widened in shock at her outrageous comment in so public a place. For a second only. Then, disregarding all propriety, he fairly yanked her against his muscled chest.

"When you say things like that, it makes me hard, Madeleine, and as much as I enjoy the sensation when

I think about you, I don't want to attract attention from the ladies here."

She couldn't feel his erection, if indeed he had one, but she caught the endearing quality in his voice, the light pleasure in his eyes, and the sudden cold glances from those standing around them.

She pulled back a little to murmur gently, "You already attract a good deal of attention just by standing here, and frankly I think they're jealous because you are with me."

"Where I belong," he added simply.

She'd give anything to know just how seriously he meant that, but instead she said softly what was in her heart. "I wish I could kiss you."

His face grew markedly pensive in the course of seconds, his gaze burning with a vibrant hunger. "I wish you could, too."

They were words saturated with meaning, barely heard, and for Madeleine the chatter of gossip and high-pitched laughter, the sound of the lovely, melodic waltz, the heat of bodies and the parade of masked figures in fine jackets and swirling skirts faded around her. Suddenly she didn't care about the baron, or opium, or Winter Garden. All that existed in this crowded ballroom, in her lonely, singular universe, was Thomas.

"Will you dance with me instead?" she requested in a downy-soft breath, knowing it was a horrible substitute for kissing, but unable to think of anything else that would allow her to touch him.

His eyes grew stormy, and his shoulders dropped with his long exhale. "Nothing would please me more. But I cannot dance, Madeleine."

She never could have prepared herself for that. Like a cold slap to the face, his statement sucked the air from her, stung her, mortified her. He couldn't dance. His disabilities prevented it. And in her own fierce desire to understand him intimately, to engage him as her own this night, she had forgotten that.

But she wouldn't let him know it. Smiling beautifully, she remarked, "It doesn't matter anyway. Let's do the work we came to do."

His facial features relaxed, softened, and then he reached up with his free hand and ran his thumb along her chin. "How very tactful you are, my beautiful Maddie."

She shivered in the heavy ballroom heat. He'd never been possessive of her before, laying claim to her as his, and the thought made her suddenly uncomfortable which she hoped, for some very obscure reason, he didn't notice.

"Would you like champagne?"

She shook her head, erasing her troubled thoughts. "Not yet. I want to keep my head clear tonight. Let's go see Rothebury."

Quickly he turned, nudging her again in the direction of the east wall where they had first spotted the baron. The area had become quite congested and noisy, the dance floor overflowing, and Madeleine was forced to squeeze her way through whatever openings she could find, Thomas following closely just behind her.

She couldn't help but observe his limp now. For weeks she had given it little regard since he seemed to move around easily enough, a very strong and capable man, comfortable with his own form in his environment. But after bringing his injury again to light, his continuous stagger seemed pronounced, more than conspicuous to all, and her heart flooded with compassion and affection for the man who'd probably endured ridicule and revulsion from his contemporaries, from ignorant souls lacking grace. She understood this because she'd

lived with it herself through the years, from those like
Lady Claire who assumed she was a whore because of
her unusual beauty or her illegitimacy and apparent lack
of decent breeding. Thomas had said he was a recluse,
and the word had meaning to her now. In her own way,
although extroverted when it came to her work, she had
been a recluse all her life.

At last they neared the baron who stood elegantly
composed, a half-filled glass of champagne in one hand,
the other resting at his side while he listened to Mrs.
Broadstreet, a stout woman with fiery red hair wearing
a gown in the ghastly shade of pink flamingos, discuss
with some dramatics the horrid state of current local pro-
duce prices. Something of that nature was all Madeleine
could gather from the silly conversation to which only
the baron himself listened with scant interest. She could
see his head bobbing infinitesimally, the creases in his
high forehead where his thick brows met, but it was
obvious that he couldn't care any less about Mrs. Broadstreet and the cost of pickled beets. Still, he was smooth
in his attentiveness. Very smooth.

Almost immediately he noticed them as Madeleine
and Thomas approached, and he grinned broadly in a
cheerfulness she suspected was false. He turned away
from Mrs. Broadstreet's corpulent figure, who stopped
speaking in midsentence, and Madeleine smiled in return, reaching out for him with her hand.

"Monsieur Baron, it is such a pleasure to see you
again, and under such exciting circumstances. I am so
pleased we could attend your Winter Masquerade."

"Mrs. DuMais." He drew the title out in a very genteel
voice, ignoring Thomas as he reached forward with his
hand to clasp hers loosely. "The delight is mine. I've
been anxiously looking forward to the moment when

your supreme beauty would grace the halls of my humble home."

A ridiculous comment, but she gave an appropriate soft laugh. "Have you? I am charmed, Monsieur Baron."

"And Mr. . . . Blackwood, is it?" he carried on, now glancing up to Thomas. "I don't believe we've met."

He didn't reach for Thomas's hand, and Madeleine suspected he clung to hers so he wouldn't have to.

Thomas stood rigidly at her side and slightly behind her. "But you are wrong, Baron Rothebury. We met at Mrs. Bennington-Jones's garden party last September. Don't you recall? A small social gathering for her daughter Desdemona in celebration of the young lady's recent nuptials?"

Madeleine caught the faintest tick on the baron's mouth at the mention of Desdemona, but he hid any negative feelings well, smiling ever so craftily as was his nature.

"Ahh, yes. I now remember," Rothebury replied very slowly. "You remained at Lady Claire's side for the entire event, I believe."

If the baron had thought such a situation odd, or intended his remark to be a revelation of indecency, however slight, neither Madeleine nor Thomas reacted to it. Margaret Broadstreet, however, wrinkled her nose and stood back a step, her spine a little straighter, glancing down Thomas's large, dark form.

"You're very likely correct," Thomas agreed without explanation. "Is she here this evening, by the way?"

"Lady Claire? Oh, yes, of course," he rebuffed with a blasé lift of his champagne glass. "I imagine she's sitting, however. We all know about Lady Claire, and she did seem rather . . . fatigued."

An awkward moment passed, and still Rothebury had not released her hand. Others began to take notice of them in their small circle near the window, closing in to ogle her and Thomas as invited but highly suspicious and unusually intriguing guests. Many faces Madeleine recognized, some she'd met briefly, while there were still others she'd never seen before. All of them, though, were extremely curious about her position at the ball tonight.

"I also remember, Mr. Blackwood," Mrs. Broadstreet chimed in with only a trace of irritation at not being formally introduced. "But I don't think I've met this woman. She is the Frenchwoman who lives with you, is she not? We've heard all about her in the village."

This woman. Madeleine was growing sick to death of being given such a common distinction in an inflection that made it sound despicable. Instead of reacting, however, she did what she always did and bore it gracefully. With a little persuasion she was at last able to pull her fingers from Rothebury's, although not without some resistance and what she was certain was a purposeful stroke or two of his thumb.

"Yes, I'm here under Mr. Blackwood's employ," she said in her own defense, facing the lady directly. "But I'm sure I haven't heard of you, Mrs. . . . ?"

"Margaret Broadstreet," the baron offered congenially.

"We're from the north," she put in, "but we come to Winter Garden every year during the cold season, as my husband suffers."

Madeleine was beginning to believe it. "Is he here tonight as well?" she asked pleasantly.

"He is in the smoking room with several acquaintances discussing whatever it is men discuss in such places," she returned somewhat hotly. Then, with shoulders erect and a crisp lift of her thin, pink lips, she disclosed, "He is the second cousin once removed of the

Baron Seeley, you know." Forcing a chuckle from her throat, she lifted her thick, ringed fingers and splayed them across her chest. "But I'm sure you'd know nothing about English titles and such."

"Of course, she wouldn't. She's French."

The shrill voice came from behind her, yet Madeleine knew at once that it belonged to Penelope, and they all turned to regard her.

A large, sturdily built woman to begin with, she now looked enormous and thoroughly silly wearing a satin gown in dark purple, the full, swishing skirt covered in row after row of white lace. The high neckline pulled far too tightly across her expansive bosom, and the stiffness of her corset crunched her thickening waistline in to nearly bursting. She looked like a plump grape made ready to be squashed into wine. It was also amusing to note how her gown harmonized with Rothebury's attire almost to perfection. They were a matched set, albeit unintentionally, and from the look of coldness in the baron's eyes as he observed the lady joining them, it became clear to Madeleine that he was not pleased. No, it was more than that. Richard Sharon hated Penelope Bennington-Jones.

"The French are quite sophisticated, and certainly aware of titles and their historical and contemporary implications, Mrs. Bennington-Jones," Thomas said easily as she drew her heavily perfumed figure up to his side.

Penelope glanced at him askance, up and down, her cheeks puffing in silent indignation. "You're looking rather well, Mr. Blackwood," she replied brusquely, brushing over his comment as she opened her fan in front of her face.

"Thank you."

"And so are you, Mrs. Bennington-Jones," Madeleine offered politely.

Penelope shifted her feet and began fanning herself. "How thoughtful of you to notice."

Madeleine didn't know whether to laugh or compliment the lady on such a splendid reply. Penelope purposely avoided eye contact with her, but she'd come back with a tactful comment that, although meant to be rude, didn't really sound that way.

"The French often notice such things," Margaret cut in, reaching forward to pat Penelope on the arm. "They're very conscious of fashion and whether a person is well or not."

"Really?" asked the baron, taking a sip of his champagne and standing back on his heels. "How do you know this, Margaret?"

The impact of the seemingly innocent question was subtle, and yet Madeleine knew it was supposed to be condescending, to make the lady stumble in reply. Everyone knew it.

"This is a well-known fact, Baron Rothebury," came Penelope's tight rejoinder as all eyes turned to her. "The French are a rather . . . uncivilized bunch, of course, when they are together in a group, but generally they're also keen about appearances."

Rothebury's gaze iced over as he glared at the woman. Certainly it was beyond doubt that he had the superior position in his home, at his ball, and in title. But it was clear that Penelope also had some unusual connection to him. She wouldn't have otherwise made such a bold statement in defiance of his.

Margaret reached for a glass of champagne as a footman passed, jumping in to add, "I think you may be correct, Mrs. Bennington-Jones. Since we're speaking factually, however, it must be noted that while the French may care about appearances, they certainly have little taste when it comes to them."

Penelope shook her head. "No, the problem with the French is not that they have no taste, or style for that matter, but that they simply have no tact."

"Unlike the English, Mrs. Bennington-Jones?" Thomas asked in a hard near-whisper. When all eyes focused on him again, he smiled coldly and reached out to gently squeeze Madeleine's upper arm. "We've been standing here for five minutes, and aside from the good Baron Rothebury, not one of you *ladies* has offered a kind word to Mrs. DuMais—the Frenchwoman in our presence. She is a guest in our country, yet you have openly insulted her and her culture." He stood stiffly and folded his hands behind his back. "While under my employ I have found her to be intelligent, charming, and gracious. I have lived in Winter Garden for several months now, and I have yet to see such graciousness in one of the ladies from the village."

They all nearly gaped at him, an absurd picture beneath their masks, stunned into silence. It was truly a comical moment, and one that Madeleine would not soon forget.

Without waiting for rebuttal, Thomas looked once more at Rothebury who, most questionable of all, had narrowed his eyes in what Madeleine could only describe as appraising speculation.

"If you will excuse me, Baron Rothebury?" Thomas concluded, his voice fairly dripping with contempt. "I think I'd like to mingle." He turned to her. "Care to join me, Mrs. DuMais?"

Of course, she did. She wanted to hug him, too. "Actually I was going to be extremely bold and ask the baron if he would enjoy a dance or two."

Rothebury stepped forward instantly, closing off the other two ladies as he offered her his arm, his countenance shining with enjoyment that now appeared to be genuine. "It would be my pleasure."

Thomas nodded once. "As you wish." And then he left her staring at his large, broad back, disappearing into the crowd.

Sixteen

Richard was restless. Even as he danced a Bach minuet with the most lushly beautiful woman he'd seen in ages, he felt not relaxed and centered as he should, but tense and distracted.

His party was naturally a success, as it had always been in past years. He'd once again given great care to choosing the best food, drink, and music, sparing no expense. Lavish decorations abounded, the gentry mingled and laughed, and still he couldn't seem to concentrate on the affair with any ease.

At nearly thirty-three years of age he'd done many interesting things but none compared to his lucrative trade in stolen opium. He did it for the money, true, but also for the adventure. For months he'd enjoyed his success, spending the extra funds, refurnishing his study, library, and bedchamber with outstanding antique pieces bought at auction. But something in the last few weeks had started gnawing at him like a dull knife to the gut, and he couldn't exactly put his finger on the cause.

Now he held the alluring Madeleine DuMais in his

arms, peering at her through the eyes of her mask. She was truly a vision of unparalleled beauty, wearing an exquisite gown that accentuated her generous, pale breasts and a shapely figure that showed no sign of ever having borne a child. Her skin was incredibly flawless, her up-swirled, chestnut hair thick and shiny, her lips full and beckoning. Richard felt his body react as it did the day in the woods three weeks ago when he'd spent much of the time envisioning her naked in his bed. She was a cultured woman, experienced, and no doubt knew how to please a man. She'd all but said as much. He'd thought about her often since that fateful day, and now she was here, in his home, dancing and laughing softly at his wry wit.

He'd become immediately aware of her as she'd walked through the stained-glass archway into the ballroom. But when the scholar stepped in directly behind her, pausing at her side and allowing Richard a view of the two of them together, a measure of foreboding had struck him soundly. This is what roused his restlessness now. He was sure of it. Although it had stirred his uneasiness when Penelope had mentioned them weeks before, his sudden anxiety tonight was brought about by seeing them together. Unfortunately the marked coincidences that had lured both an unusually gorgeous Frenchwoman and a crippled, unknown English scholar to Winter Garden could no longer be denied.

They were an impressive pair, if Richard considered it objectively—Blackwood large, dark and commanding in appearance, Madeleine stunning to look at, true visual perfection. Aside from the man's obvious injuries, they presented an illusory, almost fairy-tale likeness as a couple, and everyone had taken note of it. Richard had even found it highly amusing to watch Penelope the bitch, Margaret the snob who was in actuality a nobody in station, the scholar, and Madeleine in their gauche exchange. Blackwood had settled the score, though, Richard had observed with clarity and some level of surprise, and not without noticing the subtle indications of admiration from the man's lovely escort.

They were attracted to each other. Very plainly, although they each did their best to hide it. But from each other? Or only the rest of them? Richard didn't know, and he also wasn't certain how it made him feel. On the one hand he wanted the woman, and badly. On the other, he couldn't afford to allow her into his life in any meaningful way. He had property to manage, a clandestine business to run, a house to maintain, and he wasn't at all interested in producing an heir at the moment. He would marry at the appropriate time, of course, and have a son eventually, but marriage for him lay in the distant future, and certainly not to a common, widowed Frenchwoman, regardless of her unusual beauty or how much she desired him. And he intended to discover the level of that soon enough.

The minuet ended, and breathlessly Madeleine smiled at him, fanning herself daintily with perfectly tapered fingers. He smiled in return and brought his mind to the present.

"Would you care to walk, Mrs. DuMais? I could use some fresh air and would be delighted to show you some of the treasures I've recently collected in my study and library."

His words had meaning beneath them, and she took the hint.

"Of course, Monsieur Baron—"

"Richard, please," he stressed, offering her his arm.

"And you must call me Madeleine," she insisted in a heavy, thoroughly titillating French accent, curling her fingers around his sleeve at the elbow.

He patted them with his free hand, her skin warm and soft. Suddenly, urgently, he needed those warm, soft fingers wrapped around him intimately, stroking him.

"The library first, Richard?" she asked in a velvety purr, fairly sparkling with impish intimation.

His bedchamber would be his choice, but the ballroom was crowded with neighbors and guests of relative importance, and many of them would observe the two of them leaving together. They couldn't chance being gone too long. The library would suffice for now, as she'd suggested during their first meeting in the woods, and later, with great hope, he could take her naked.

"The library it is, Madeleine," he agreed with a subtle gesture to the stairs.

They walked in silence, although the noise level in the ballroom had grown to a pitch too loud to converse casually. He climbed the stairs after her, watching her hips sway, the soft, light curls in her hair bob at her shoulders with each step. She fascinated him, which Richard found fascinating in itself. A woman hadn't unsettled him like this in years.

The foyer had grown a bit more crowded as well, but mostly with individuals on their way to the smoking room behind the ballroom, the ladies withdrawing room next to that, or a few brave souls who chanced a breath of cold air in the bitter night. Richard stopped three times to chat with certain guests that by mere influence required a greeting, introducing Madeleine only as a visitor to their country and their village. She charmed them with her sophistication, and with each passing minute, Richard grew more and more anxious to get her alone.

At last they proceeded down the corridor toward the rear of his home, passing his study. If anyone noticed the two of them isolating themselves from the others, nobody would comment openly about it. At least not tonight and in this house. Discretion would reign the conversations of nearly everyone invited to this affair. Richard knew them all, and his power among the villagers was essential to their welfare, if not their gossiping tongues. Let them speculate. They would learn nothing anyway.

Madeleine didn't speak when he finally escorted her into the library. Then he closed the door behind them and softly turned the lock in place.

Facing her once more, he noticed the briefest hesitancy in her eyes as she glanced to the bolt, but then it vanished as she drew a long breath and looked around the room.

"It's lovely, Richard."

He began sauntering toward her. "I think so as well." He'd meant her, of course, but he also knew that she had been speaking of his library. Newly decorated in burnt almond and evergreen, it was a beautiful room with vaulted ceilings of the original construction. There was elegant though simply designed Queen Anne furniture—two satin settees in dark green and two chairs in velveteen gold facing each other, and a cherry wood tea table between them all. Bookcases lined the walls, although they were mostly filled with priceless antiques he'd collected through the years, from Italy, Egypt, the Far East. He had pottery vases from ancient Rome, ivory jars from India, jade carvings from Japan, tapestries from Turkey, and plush rugs woven in Spain, all purchased with money collected by those in London who bought his opium for the needy elite. Yes, it was a marvelous business indeed.

"But where are your books?" she asked with a trace of confusion.

The question didn't surprise him; in point of fact he

expected it. It was a library after all, and his collection within it was scarce.

"Those few books of value are kept here, naturally, on the top shelves," he replied, reaching behind his head to untie his mask, "but I have others, ones I peruse on occasion, in my private quarters upstairs." He paused when he stood in front of her, dropping it on one of the settees, then lifting his hands behind her head to untie hers. "Perhaps you'd like to see them sometime, Madeleine?"

He'd posed that as a question while he removed the white satin cover from her face, but she didn't comment right away. Neither did she react to his forwardness, which he found exceptionally gratifying.

Tossing her mask on the settee beside his, Richard reached up and stroked her cheek with his palm. Her skin was warm and flushed, but her eyes, lighter than the summer sky, were steady as they remained locked with his.

"Where do you keep the books you buy from Lady Claire?" she asked softly.

That puzzled him a little. She drew him in with her impassioned gaze and brazen grin, asked for his advances by fairly fondling him with nothing more than a husky murmur, and posed a question having nothing whatever to do with sexual play. In fact, it was so far removed from the path of attraction they were following that it stumped him. For a moment only.

With a crooked lift of his lips and a stroke of his thumb across her cheekbone, he moved closer to reveal, "I'm a book dealer, Madeleine, remember? I buy what she's willing to sell and then I give them to a distributor who sells them to someone who is willing to pay more. It's simply a hobby that provides me the income to purchase lovely things such as these that line my bookshelves. If it must be known, I prefer owning priceless foreign artifacts to books."

"Oh, I see," she said airily.

Smirking, he leaned forward to add in whisper, "Please don't mention that to anyone. Everybody in Winter Garden thinks I'm an independently wealthy intellectual."

She smiled fully at the teasing remark. "I'll keep your secret, Richard. But do you have one person you deal with or many? And how do you send them, in boxes?"

She seemed genuinely eager to know, and Richard decided to quickly pacify her since the questions weren't altogether personal. "As I said before, I work with a distributor in London to whom I send the books directly, in crates, every few weeks. He takes the names of certain individuals from across the country, buyers who need a specific book or are looking for a specific author, then sells them as I send them in. He then gets a share of the profits and forwards the rest to me, part of which I then use to pass on to Lady Claire when I'm ready to buy more."

Her forehead crinkled in thought. "What did you do before you began buying Lady Claire's books? Did you buy from someone else or have a collection of your own to sell?"

He shook his head, chuckling. "Yes to both. You're quite an inquisitive lady, Madeleine. Or are you nervous to be with me?"

She blinked, and her delicately arched brows rose faintly. "Nervous? Heavens no," she protested a bit too fast.

She was nervous. Richard found it thoroughly arousing. He took a step closer.

"I've just never met a book dealer before and I find

it so very interesting. Have you been doing it for many years?"

He inhaled deeply, attempting to keep his countenance agreeable and his manner affable. He lowered his palm to her neck, feeling the steady pulse in the slight indentation. "Many, many years," he said quietly, smiling, refusing further explanation as he readied himself for their intimate encounter. He didn't want to talk about books anymore.

She shook her head in wonder and admired the library again. "I find it intriguing that you are a dealer of something you don't collect. If I were trading or dealing in books I'd be collecting them by the thou—"

Her words cut off in midsentence because he'd abruptly lowered his hand to her breast, covering it with his palm. Immediately she flipped her head around so that she faced him once more, staring into his eyes. It was a defining moment, one that would let him know just how seriously she took this meeting in seclusion, and likewise giving her the opportunity to understand just how seriously he intended to advance their acquaintance.

She didn't move, but her smile had vanished. In its place was a quizzical look of unsureness. She might be nervous but she wasn't about to run. Exactly as he would have hoped.

He began caressing her, very gently, over her gown, starkly scrutinizing the lines of her face, feeling the delicate peak come to life almost at once at his fingertips, even through layers. Her nipples had to be large and thick to do that beneath silk and satin, and that thought alone made him grow uncomfortably rigid with need.

"You're beautiful, Madeleine, but I think you know that," he whispered thickly.

She raised her palms and flattened them against his chest. "We shouldn't be doing this here."

Her words were factual, but her tone was quite inspiring in its provocative quality. She protested precisely as she should under the circumstances, but she didn't push him away, or slap him, and from that bit of encouragement, he raised his free arm, wrapped it around her back, and drew her into him.

With one more silent look of intention, he lowered his head and kissed her.

Madeleine's first thought was that the baron was stalling in answer, or perhaps attempting to dissuade her from continuing with her line of questioning. Kissing her would be an excellent way of doing either, and it was now apparent that he had something to hide. The kiss itself had no real effect on her, as she'd been kissed by countless men who had assumed her attraction to them and boldly took the first step. She'd frankly expected it from Rothebury, especially after he'd locked the library door. His soft caress of her breast, however, had surprised her—not because he'd actually done it, but because of her body's unwanted physical reaction to it.

Her nipples were hard, growing harder from the kneading of his hand, and she felt a rush of the familiar, tingling heat between her legs. Her breathing remained steady enough when he became a little more forceful in his approach and inserted his tongue in her mouth, but when he flicked his thumb over and over across the pointed tips beneath her gown and chemise, then squeezed and massaged them, her breath quickened with her building arousal. For the first time in her life, and for a reason she couldn't explain, Madeleine felt totally ashamed.

Yet a new, odd sensation coursed through her, too, as she tried to rationally understand her response to this man's touch. She wasn't the least bit attracted to Richard Sharon; in truth, she was repulsed by him in every regard. But her body simply behaved as it was meant to behave, as it would at the hands of any man and stimulating caresses. What really mattered was that the only man she wanted indisputably, *intimately*, was the one she hadn't yet had to completeness, the one she desired desperately, the only man she'd ever known who didn't tell her how physically beautiful she was before he kissed her each time, but instead commented on her ability to play an intelligent game of chess. The only man who cared more about her experiences in childhood, ignoring the bad parts and assimilating the good, than he did about her experiences in bed. The only man she had ever known who, before he made love to her, wanted to know her as an individual with a past she couldn't change, with hopes and dreams that counted for something. Several times through the years she'd been with men who didn't particularly attract her, but never before had she felt guilty about it. Now she knew why.

Richard released her mouth and drew back a little, moving to her throat where he left small, moist pecks, lowering his arm from her back so that he cupped her bottom and pulled her against him. As if a fierce gust of wind had blown through her, clearing her mind, she understood herself totally at last. Her newfound knowledge created its own broad smile across her just-kissed mouth, her eyes still closed as she tried not to push the annoying hound at her neck away too quickly, stirring suspicion. Yes, she wanted only Thomas, all of him, and this episode of becoming aroused by the stroking of Baron Rothebury's hand only validated her feelings, clarified them, and liberated her. She had trouble containing her laugh of pure joy.

"Richard, we can't do this here," she repeated in a

whisper, rubbing her palms across his shoulders as she felt him move his lips to her chest and begin to lift her skirt.

"We can if we're fast," he murmured, giving her an obvious nudge in the direction of the settee. "We need each other, Madeleine."

"I think so, too, but not here," she stressed, gently attempting to put some physical distance between them. "We have to meet somewhere else. Another time. Somewhere safer."

Madeleine gave thanks to a benevolent God when laughter rang out loudly in the corridor just beyond the library door, reminding them of their delicate position. The timing couldn't have been better.

Richard groaned and stalled his actions, raising his head at last and resting it on her shoulder until his breathing evened. Seconds later he lifted fully, his passion slowing as he looked into her eyes. His gaze was hot and hooded, his face was flushed with lingering desire, and he still had not removed his hand from her breast.

"You'll have to come at night," he said urgently, caressing what he could feel of her bottom through her petticoats, "when nobody will see you."

More voices erupted just outside the library, then faded. Madeleine glanced in the direction of the door, clinging to him as expected, her palms to his chest, licking her lips as if nervous. "I don't know, Richard. Someone will notice, a servant, a guest. And your reputation—"

"Nobody will know," he drawled, grinning in a manner that made her skin feel as if the spider had crawled upon it. "There are other ways of entering this house besides the large front door, Madeleine," he said smoothly, his composure returning.

Suddenly he grabbed her hand and pulled it down between their bodies, making her touch him, forcing her to cover his erection over his trousers. Never had Madeleine felt so sickened by such an aggressive gesture. She needed to get away.

"How long has it been since you've been with a man, Mrs. DuMais?" he mumbled, rubbing her hand blatantly over him.

Against every natural instinct within her, she wrapped an arm around his neck and leaned forward to kiss his lips again, briefly so as not to further arouse. "Far too long," she whispered against his mouth.

He chuckled. "I know how to please a woman. Remember that."

"I'll think of nothing else until the next time," she said shakily, running the fingers of her free hand through his hair. "But we need to get back to the ballroom now, before we are missed."

He kissed her cheek and jaw again, then sighed and stepped back. "I don't suppose you'll tell the cripple about us," he stated arrogantly, his sly grin returning.

Madeleine drew a deep breath, resisting the overpowering urge to strike him hard in the face with her fist. A horribly unladylike thought. But the comment did make her wonder if the man were afraid of Thomas, deciding quickly that he should be.

"I would never mention a word to anyone, Richard," she replied in feigned alarm that she hoped he witnessed in her wide-eyed expression.

He ran his palm across her breasts, deliberately and slowly, one final time before dropping it to his side. "Good. I would regret it terribly if you were sent back to France."

"As would I," she agreed, wiping the back of her hand across her forehead. The heat from the room had gotten to her, and she was starting to perspire. She needed air.

"I want to see you soon," he commanded quietly.

"I'll see what I can do." Reaching down, she collected their masks from the settee, handed his to him, then re-tied hers on her head. "No promises, but I'll try to meet you along the path again, if I'm able to get free."

"I'll bring you in at night, Madeleine, if you can get away without him noticing."

With a weary lift of her lips to a smile, she ran her index finger up and down his upper arm. "I'll try."

"Soon," he repeated.

She nodded.

He took her hand in his, and together they walked to the door, listening momentarily for sound from the other side. When quietness prevailed, the baron unlocked it, opened it slowly, then led her through to the cool, dimly lit corridor beyond.

From the end of the darkened hallway, where Lady Claire had escaped the crowds to drink her "medicine" without a prying gaze or word of reproach from those ignorant of her condition and need, she watched them leave the library in some haste, heading in the direction of the foyer.

Baron Rothebury had appeared first, smiling placidly. Then the French slut followed, her palm on his arm in a manner that to Claire seemed indecent. The woman's appearance was disheveled enough to reveal to all what they'd been doing behind the closed door.

She'd lured the good baron into the quiet seclusion of the library, no doubt. It was common knowledge that the French were far too liberal with their sexual views and levels of promiscuity. And men of any nationality, of course, could not help their base hungers. If approached they would, every one, fall victim to a woman's charms.

Baron Rothebury had unfortunately, and no doubt un-
wittingly, become a fly in this one's web. Still, the smile
of bland satisfaction Claire had seen on his mouth in-
dicated to her that he'd been able to properly reprove
the woman, though likely not before she had him
trapped in an intimate embrace. The French always did
such things at social gatherings, even in front of others,
or so she'd heard.

Claire tipped her flask of medicine to her lips for a
second swallow, then screwed the lid back into place
and stuck it into her reticule where she drew the strings
tightly against any who might have probing eyes. She
needed to return to the ballroom but she wasn't sure
what to do about what she'd just witnessed, if anything.
Bringing the slut's actions openly to light could also
tarnish the baron's good name, even considering that he
had nothing to do with the initial onslaught of affection.
Claire couldn't deal with the repercussions if the baron
turned against her, regardless of her good intentions.

Then she thought of Thomas. He was obviously taken
with the Frenchwoman, which, if Claire admitted honestly, stung her deeply. She quite liked Thomas herself,
and would be willing to bed him, under the proper conditions, of course, if he would only show half an interest.
Perhaps if he were made aware of the Frenchwoman's
obvious taste in seducing those with titles and money,
experiencing no shame to the consequences, he would
then find pleasure elsewhere, maybe even in her arms.
Convincing him was certainly worth a try. If nothing
else, she would derive immense gratification in watching
the slut's fall from grace in the eyes of the scholar who
held her in such esteem.

Straightening her aching body, Claire held her chin
high, clutched her reticule against her corseted waist,
and headed once again in the direction of the party.

Seventeen

Thomas strode quickly toward the main front doors of Rothebury's home again, shivering from the cold that had penetrated his body to his bones. He'd spent the last fifteen minutes outside without his coat, in the biting wind, studying the house at different angles and getting a much closer observation than ever before. No one would be suspicious of a party guest getting a breath of fresh air if he were caught, however frigid the night, and without a coat of some kind it would be apparent that he wouldn't be staying outside too long, wandering about, doing something he shouldn't.

His short time spent in the nasty January chill had been well worth the discomfort. He had learned something, and slowly the pieces of the Winter Garden opium-smuggling operation were beginning to fall into place. He wanted to talk to Madeleine but knew he would have to wait until their return to the cottage, partially because he didn't want to chance being overheard discussing the case here, but also because he needed to clearly think things through and make sense of all they'd learned in the last few weeks.

Right now, though, he simply wanted to see her.

Thomas suspected that she was beginning to fall in love with him, although he also knew that since this was exactly what he'd craved for so long his imagination could be playing with notions and hints of feelings that simply weren't there. Yet tonight, when he'd kissed her before they'd left for the masquerade, he'd witnessed a whirlpool of emotions in her that she had never allowed to surface, at least not in front of him. She was frightened of the intense attraction between them but she didn't attempt to leave him or even curb their sexual encounters—what few they'd had. Indeed, she seemed all the more anxious to build on them, which both amused and warmed him. He could only conclude that although somewhat bewildered by the heady tenderness of their deepening relationship, she wanted it, or she would have cooled the passion and distanced him from her life by now. They were almost there, to a place where he could tell her all. It scared him more than anything had in his life, but prolonging the lie would only make the secrets seem worse in the end. He knew Madeleine intimately and trusted her with his past, his necessary deceit, and especially his heart.

Finally he climbed the steps to the baron's front doors, which were opened at once by a conscientious footman. The heat inside knocked the breath from him momentarily, making his body shiver and his partially frozen skin tingle, but it was surely welcome. He avoided introductions to a small gathering of jovial guests standing at his immediate right by quickly tying his mask to his face again then heading toward the ballroom entrance.

He stopped short when his gaze suddenly fell upon Lady Claire Childress standing by the stained-glass portal, smiling at him cunningly, probably waiting for him. He groaned inwardly at what he could best describe as an intrusion into his privacy. It felt like one anyway.

He smiled in return, very formally, taking note of her ever-thinning figure in pale green taffeta that made her hair look sharply gray and her skin sallow. Although the appropriate length, the dress hung from her as if made for another, fuller figured woman, the beaded neckline and sagging sleeves falling loosely away from her small breasts and shoulders, exposing the edges of her white linen chemise beneath it. She was a ghost of a woman, and every time he saw her she looked less alive than the last. She surely didn't have much time left on this earth. The saddest thing of all was that her death was probably not now preventable.

"Lady Claire, I'm delighted to see you here tonight," he said with charming grace, forcing himself to walk toward her.

She laughed delicately, as a lady should, and extended her arm. "Thomas. It is such a pleasure to see you, as always, but I thought you'd said several weeks ago that you would escort me if you came to the Winter Masquerade."

He noticed instantly from her slightly slurred words that she was drunk and pouting, her bottom lip turned down and out just enough to express her disapproval and sustained hurt at being disregarded. Thomas loathed the pouting tactic from a mature woman. In Lady Claire it annoyed him more than her drunkenness, but he hid it well.

Grasping her bony, gloved fingers with his, he raised her knuckles to brush them against his lips, then quickly released her hand. "I apologize profusely, dear lady, but I didn't know until just a few days ago that I'd even be coming. My invitation arrived late."

"I see." She took in his entire appearance with shrewd eyes while she sipped her champagne. "I suppose you then came with the Frenchwoman you employ."

She stated that as fact, in a quiet, calculating voice. Thomas got the distinct impression that she knew this already and had a greater point to make regarding the matter. He played along.

"Yes. She also received an invitation from Baron Rothebury," he admitted, standing back on his heels and clasping his hands together behind him. "We walked here together, but I haven't seen her since early this evening. I imagine she's mingling or dancing in the ball-room."

"Likely so," Claire acknowledged, taking another long swallow. "The woman does seem to attract a good deal of attention, doesn't she? No doubt all the local gentlemen are surrounding her even now." She paused for effect, licking her lips, then asked slowly, "Have you danced with her yet?"

She'd put the question to him candidly, and Thomas caught the first whiff in the air of her malevolent objective in their discourse.

He never took his eyes from hers. "My legs are stiff tonight, and I don't care to dance, Lady Claire. Otherwise I would surely ask you."

"Of course. Probably due to the unusually cold weather."

She had to know, or suspect anyway, that his injuries prevented him from dancing altogether. Instead of explaining, he simply nodded once. "Probably."

One side of her mouth lifted slyly, and she tilted her head fractionally. "I saw Mrs. DuMais with the baron, and, of course, she looked beautiful this evening. But then, I'm sure you noticed."

The music and noise from the ballroom at his right had grown so loud he could barely hear the lady speak. To counter it, he took two steps to his left so that he stood next to the wall, beside her, giving him a better vantage point from which to view the foyer and all who walked within it as well.

"Most of the ladies here are as beautifully gowned and just as lovely, Claire," he rebuked in a manner that implied sagacity in his word choice but sounded like a scolding.

It had no effect on her.

After finishing off the contents of her glass in two long gulps, she lifted her face as close to his as she could get it. "But we all know she's an exceptional beauty, Thomas. To deny it now would be to make a mockery of me." She laughed bitterly, then dropped her voice to a near-whisper. "Actually, I saw her leaving the library with Baron Rothebury, and they looked like they'd had a very entertaining exchange, indeed. They spent a good deal of time locked behind closed doors, alone together, and by her mussed appearance I don't know just how proper the encounter was, although it was terribly clear that they weren't dancing. She is French, after all. A widow in need of a man, and he is a randy one at that. Everyone knows it. Quite a pair they make, don't you think?"

Thomas's heart began to pound, but he refused to react, because that's exactly what she wanted him to do. Naturally his instinct told him to smash his fist into the wall at his side, or better yet into Rothebury's teeth. As always, though, because of his very proper upbringing, gentility prevailed. He stood cool and composed, not a change in his features, staring down in well-hidden disgust at the drunken, wrinkled face a satin mask couldn't hide, only inches away.

Because he remained levelheaded by both nature and culture, he allowed her blunt words to sink in, to digest in his very rational mind before he replied. The anger he'd felt at the sudden and vivid picture of Madeleine and Rothebury making love to each other floated neatly from his body as he decided after a moment or two that such a conclusion made no sense at all. He knew Madeleine better than that. It didn't happen, not here at a party and not in the man's library. He suspected that Claire had seen them, and perhaps the baron had attempted to seduce Madeleine; but as certain as he was that there was a God in heaven, he knew Madeleine didn't instigate the liaison. Thomas knew that regardless of her feelings for him as her associate and lover, it wasn't necessary for her to gather information from intimate contact with the baron, and she was simply too smart to allow a casual affair with a suspect to interfere with their work.

Claire must have seen the resolution in his eyes, for at that moment her expression changed to one of vehemence.

"You don't believe me," she spat in a whisper.

Her outrage took him aback, and he blinked, looking her up and down. "I believe you saw them, but I'm not sure what that has to do with me," he countered flatly. "She is my employee and nothing more. What the woman does privately is her business."

Claire shook her head in contempt. "Don't treat me like a blind cow. You're in love with her. Everyone can see it, Thomas, because it's pitifully obvious. She is a slut, no matter how beautiful she is on the outside. You're an educated man who has fallen for someone who can give you nothing but heartache and disease. You *look* at her as if you haven't bedded a woman in decades. It's appalling, really, and you should be ashamed."

That absolutely infuriated him as nothing ever had. He closed his hands together in tight fists at his sides to keep from striking out. He'd never come so close to slapping a woman in his entire life.

"You are drunk, madam," he said in icy coldness, "and would do well to return home."

She scoffed, then snickered. "Afraid to tell me how you really feel?" she asked in a whisper thick with the influence of alcohol. "I could have given you riches for your attention, Thomas. Would have taken you to my bed should you have asked. Your being crippled means nothing to me. You didn't need to fall for a common woman who's likely been with dozens of men, who will leave you for the next suitor who offers something more, something better, perhaps just his perfect legs and the ability to dance a waltz with her when she asks." In a voice of sorrow, she stepped back to mumble, "She will break your heart and she will do it laughing."

Thomas had had enough. Regardless of the fact that Lady Claire's last words pushed deeply into the pockets of his only remaining doubts, he refused to have anything more to do with a woman who spoke from pure spite, who hurt him by mentioning something she knew mattered intensely.

Glaring at her now, he leaned very close to murmur harshly, "You reek of liquor and speak without thought. As a lady of quality, you should know better than to attack with words you can't prove, but because you're intoxicated, I'm ignoring them. The very funny thing, Claire, is that Madeleine DuMais, being lowbred and common, through no fault of her own, would never stoop to such coarseness by speaking so unkindly of you. She has outclassed you in every regard." He stood erect once more, glowering into her puffy, shocked eyes, his repugnance hopefully apparent in his. "You are a mess, and in time I hope that you can overcome your addictions. But just to clear the air, I'd like to end this pointless conversation by saying that I would never, under any circumstances, be interested in sharing your bed. The thought alone makes me shudder. Good evening, madam."

He brushed by her and entered the ballroom.

Eighteen

They left the masquerade ball just before one, deciding it best to take the shorter route home by walking the lake path due to the lateness of the night and the frigid air. Although muddier than the village streets, Madeleine didn't care about staining her gown when she would likely freeze to death if she went the long way home. Well, perhaps that was an exaggeration, but even with her fur-lined pelisse-mantle embracing her head to foot, she still felt the chill. Thankfully, though, the wind had died completely, and darkness prevailed now as the full moon of earlier had become hidden beneath a low cloud cover.

Thomas seemed overly pensive, and she didn't want to interrupt his thoughts until they were a rather good distance from the baron's home. He had, in fact, been quiet since he'd returned to her side nearly two hours ago, speaking only briefly about superficial things like the deliciously rich chocolate souffle, of which she herself had eaten two large servings, and the remarkably high quality of Rothebury's chosen champagne. She'd drunk almost a full glass of that as well, far more than she normally consumed at a party, and it had soothed her to the point where she'd actually enjoyed herself after being nearly accosted in the library by her host. Still, aside from a few meager words of a casual nature, Thomas had said little to her through the evening, regardless of the fact that he'd remained at her side at all times except when she danced.

Now they were nearing the eastern edge of the baron's property, where the path narrowed considerably, and the very still air and thick darkness made the going slow. She had to walk in front of him but decided they were far enough away for her to break the silence and discuss what she had learned in Rothebury's home.

"Did you have a good time tonight, Thomas?" she began ever so perfunctorily.

She thought she heard the faintest snort.

"I don't know if I'd call it a good time," he answered brusquely, reaching across her shoulder with his arm to shove a cluster of leaves from an overgrown bush out of her way. "But I will say it was somewhat enlightening."

She ignored his staid tone to remark agreeably, "I thought it was enlightening, too."

"Did you."

His statement was matter-of-fact, but Madeleine detected a hint of caution in his voice.

"For a book dealer, or trader, or whatever he wants to call himself," she carried on when he offered nothing more, "Richard Sharon certainly doesn't have many of them."

"He has no books?" Thomas asked in disbelief.

She ducked her head from an overhanging branch. "He has a few but not what you'd expect for a dealer, or even someone who only takes a mild interest in them.

His library instead is filled with unusual antiques and some very lovely artifacts. I'm not sure how this all ties in with smuggling but I'm certain it does."

"Interesting."

For moments she heard nothing more than the crunching of twigs and pebbles beneath their feet. Then finally the path widened again as they rounded the bend, heading in a northerly direction toward the cottage.

"The house is smaller inside than outside," Thomas mentioned very slowly, as if piecing together an intricate puzzle while he thought about it. "Did you notice that?"

Madeleine paused in her own musings to consider what he was implying. "Very briefly, I suppose, when we first entered, but I haven't really given it much thought. What are you suggesting, Thomas?"

He inhaled deeply of the crisp, night air, moving up to walk at her side again. "I'm not sure. Just thinking aloud for now."

A drop of rain hit her cheek, then another, and Madeleine lowered her head and raised her muff to her neck. "Maybe the rumors are true, then."

"Rumors?"

"The rumors of it once having been a refuge for those not afflicted with the Black Death," she expounded. "Maybe the structure is so old that the house has been closed in somewhat on its foundation, and there are spaces between rooms."

He chuckled at that, lightening the mood, for which she was grateful.

"Usually, I'd consider that the stuff of fantasy," he replied, "but in this case you may actually have a valid explanation. Don't forget, though, that the entire house can't be built that way. The ballroom, for example, is clearly open to the structure walls, and there are windows to other parts of the home that can be seen from the outside."

She slowed her pace and brought her muff higher, to her nose, to warm it for a second or two. "Yes, but windows to what? I remember looking at the house from behind the cottage in the early night and not seeing one blessed light on. That did seem very strange to me since it was only just after ten."

He shrugged. "Perhaps he retires early."

She scoffed. "Does the Baron Rothebury strike you as the type of man who would retire early, Thomas?"

"I see your point."

They were quiet for another minute.

"Let's assume," she continued solemnly, "that his home has been remodeled to accommodate certain . . . What shall we call them? Passageways?" She tossed him a swift glance even though she couldn't see much of his expression.

"That seems an adequate term," he concurred.

The notion of secret passages in Rothebury's home both confounded and fascinated her. "Why would he do that? For what purpose?"

Thomas hesitated before replying. "To smuggle? To move from room to room unnoticed so he can observe his indolent servants? To . . . bring young ladies into his bedroom at night without them being observed?"

She gradually stopped walking, pulling one hand out of her warm, sable muff to grasp his coat sleeve. He halted a pace ahead of her, pivoting to look down at her in question.

With increasing awareness, she whispered reluctantly, "He said that to me, Thomas."

Even in nearly pure darkness she saw him frown.

"Said what?"

"That he wanted to bring me in at night. For a lover's

tryst, although he didn't use those words. And when I protested by saying something he probably expected me to say as a cultured lady, about how I couldn't possibly meet him because I might stumble into a servant and speckle his reputation if I were caught, he quite casually informed me that there are other ways of getting inside the manor house than using the front door."

Thomas wiped his face with his gloved hand. "He said this while you were alone together?"

"In the library," she admitted, releasing his sleeve and inserting her hand back inside her muff, feeling only a trifle guilty for not immediately telling him about her and the baron's little escapade. She would get to that in a moment. "He wanted my . . . undivided attention, and I wanted to get him alone to talk, only suggesting that room because I'd get a good look at his book collection, which, as I just said, did not really exist." She clucked her tongue and shook her head in disgust. "Of course, he never mentioned a concern for *my* reputation, but then he's not the type of man who would."

Thomas smiled slightly at that.

"I suppose he could have meant the servants' entrance," she reasoned matter-of-factly.

"And chance meeting one of them? I doubt it." He stroked long, leather-covered fingers over his whiskers, slowly. "Do you want to know what I think?"

She grinned. "You have to ask?"

More droplets of rain tapped her hooded mantle, and Thomas glanced up to the dark night sky. "It's getting heavier."

"And I'm about to freeze to my death."

Without thought or comment he stepped toward her and wrapped a strong, comforting arm around her shoulders, pulled her tightly against his thick, broad chest, then began walking again with her at his side.

"I think this," he disclosed contemplatively. "I think that house is very old, perhaps even as old as local rumor suggests. Because of its age the inside has been remodeled through the years—to renovate it, to change the interior style for decorative reasons. I think there are hidden passages behind the walls that connect some of the rooms, maybe many of them, and that there are entrances into that house from the outside property."

It was all beginning to make sense to her, too. "Tunnels underground," she said in a quick breath.

"Maybe. Maybe only one. I'm beginning to suspect that's how he's getting crates of opium inside his home without anyone the wiser, including, perhaps, even his own servants."

"Servants would never talk, Thomas," she reminded him. "Not if they need their jobs."

"True," he agreed. "But remember that with a timely, illegal operation like this one he couldn't possibly take such a risk if he could help it. He's far too clever to chance bringing crates of stolen opium through the front door in the middle of the day."

She looked up to study the bold, rough edges of his facial features as he continued to stare straight ahead.

"He'd bring them in at night," she theorized aloud as amazing conclusions began to dawn on her. "He'd do it quietly, by lantern light, through tunnels that led into passageways in his home."

"That's precisely what I'm beginning to believe."

"And there he could hide everything from visitors and the authorities if he had to."

"Right again."

"Which is why he's cautious about inviting neighbors into his home socially."

"And probably why he holds the Winter Masquerade each year."

Her brows drew together. "That I don't understand."

"Think about it, Madeleine." He cleared his throat as he shook his head minutely. "If one looks at the house closely, as I did tonight, it can be deduced that the outside is larger than the inside, if only slightly and at certain observable angles. However, when he's filled it with people it would only *seem* small to someone who, although might notice a difference, would disregard the apparent size variation because it's crowded."

An incredible presumption, and perfectly plausible under the circumstances.

"So," she concluded for him guardedly, "he has to host a social event from time to time, or villagers would begin to wonder why they are not receiving invitations from the Baron Rothebury."

"Exactly. What better way to stay in the villagers' good graces than to invite them all to a masquerade ball each year, where the food is excellent and the expensive drink flows. Everybody has a marvelous time, he mingles with the local gentry, and the rest of the year he's busy. It's actually very clever on his part."

Madeleine plainly heard the disgust dripping from his voice at that remark, but because she knew Thomas liked the baron less with each passing week, she brushed over that as another thought of much more significance occurred to her.

"That's what Desdemona has seen."

He squeezed her once and pushed a branch covered with wet, clinging leaves out of her way with his free arm as they finally neared the clearing behind the cottage. "I imagine she's seen something, but fortunately for the good Baron Rothebury, he doesn't have to worry about a woman who can't say a word about it to anyone without ruining her family's fine reputation."

Suddenly Madeleine understood, and felt nauseated by it. "She was his lover."

"I would not be in the least surprised," he said coolly.

"So that explains the lights in the night that she mentioned," Madeleine surmised as her own mind began to bubble with possibilities. "But how much do you think she really knows?"

He shook his head again and slowed his stride as the bench came into view. "Impossible to say unless she talks, and it's doubtful she would help us if she could."

He guided her toward the entrance to the small tunnel of foliage that led to the cottage, but Madeleine pulled herself away from his grasp and continued strolling toward the water.

"I thought you were cold?" he maintained, confused.

She ignored the comment, hugging herself against the chill and sprinkling drops of icy rain, her hands in her muff at her chin as she stared out across the lake. "I think I know how he's getting the opium out, Thomas," she murmured at last.

Immediately intrigued, he followed her to the shoreline, stopping when he reached her side. "How?"

She tilted her head to glance at him sideways. Just as she did, the clouds in the western sky parted where the moon could shine through, illuminating his ruggedly handsome face in a hazy, blue glow. An eerie sight with the baron's darkened home silhouetted in the distance.

With a crooked lift of her lips, she quietly revealed, "When I was dancing on the line twelve years ago, I had to save my money somewhere, but didn't want my mother to find it. She would only have used it to fund her opium or alcohol habit. The first little bit I earned I stuck in my shoes, but found out fairly quickly that I wouldn't be able to save it there because my mother often wore my shoes. I then stuck it in books—my English reading books that Jacques had purchased for me—because I knew my mother would never open them when she didn't speak the language. But I still had the problem of the money piling up. It was stuffed inside and began to show." Her eyes sparkled as she dropped her voice to a murmur of intrigue. "So I cut out the pages."

That stumped him for a moment. Then the image of all she was implying hit its target and his shaded expression turned to one of astonishment. "You think Rothebury is hiding the opium inside Lady Claire's books?"

Madeleine nodded succinctly in a manner of clarifying her jumbled ideas before she explained what she was starting to suspect. "I think he buys them for a fair price, as any good dealer might, opens each book individually, cuts or saws a square or circular insert out of the pages—probably a good twenty or thirty pages within and ten to fifteen pages deep—then places the opium inside for shipment. Then he stacks the books in crates and sends them to a distributor in London, who is waiting patiently with a client list for disbursement." She laughed into her muff with excitement she could no longer contain. "And think about it. Who would look *inside* a book? Especially if the baron isn't suspected of anything."

"A remarkable theory," he said seconds later, sounding a bit unconvinced.

"Any way you look at it, Thomas, the baron wins," she articulated jubilantly. "He likely pays pennies to have the opium stolen at the docks and delivered here, probably by thugs who would never reveal the source of their income. They wouldn't be believed over the word of a baron anyway. He then brings it into his house himself through at least one underground entrance of

some kind to avoid servants or even guests if he has
them. He cuts the pages from the books with his own
hands then burns the remaining paper in his own fireplace, inserts the opium and ships it to London. Ingen-
ious, really, except for the fact that we know about it."

"And he doesn't know about us," Thomas added in a
heavy whisper.

The deepening of his voice struck her. The double
meaning behind his words caused her to waver and consider them, and it once again tuned Madeleine's mind to
the present.

"Do you think he's shipping it in jars?" he questioned
softly when she didn't respond.

A very gradual grin tugged at her mouth as she looked
into his eyes, now large black circles of amusement, of
dark thoughts and wonder. His closeness warmed her
heart and radiated through her body to the tips of her
toes.

"No," she whispered in return. "That would be too
awkward and costly. I think he's shipping it mixed with
tobacco."

"But tobacco would smell," he argued hesitantly.

She leaned closer to him. "Not much if he concealed
it in newspaper or cloth, and not deep inside a book.
And if somebody did question a slight odor, just to look
at a crate of old books would explain it. Sitting in a
home for years in a private library they would naturally
take on the lingering smell of tobacco." She bit her lip
with her smile of satisfaction. "Think also how convenient the opium would be to be ready for smoking upon
purchase. It could demand a higher price."

Thomas simply stared at her, marveling at her cleverness, drinking in the unparalleled beauty of her pale
face surrounded by rich black sable and bathed in moon-

glow. He ached to reach for her but restrained himself for the moment.

Her hypothesis, crazy as it sounded, made sense. It all made sense. From bringing stolen opium into his home through an outside tunnel, to mixing it with tobacco, to hiding it inside books of all places before he shipped his books to his London distributor. Who would ever think of doing such a thing? Nobody but the baron, probably, and that's why the man was so incredibly arrogant. The entire procedure was clever, deceitful, profitable, and inconceivable to the average man. Thomas couldn't begin to imagine how they were going to prove it, either, even if they could, although he could leave that to Sir Riley and the appropriate authorities if he wanted. Time was crucial only to him and Madeleine right now, but what made him feel so wonderfully satisfied was knowing the two of them had deduced the entire scheme together.

Slowly his lips curled up to match the level of hers as they stood there, side by side at the beautiful, moonlit lake. He wanted to laugh, and so did she. Instead, he grasped her head with soft, gloved hands and drew her mouth up to meet his.

Her nose and lips were cold, but they didn't detract from the warm supple feel of her, and without any persuasion on his part she pulled herself into him, withdrawing one hand from her muff so she could wrap her arms around his neck to kiss him back with fervor. She jutted the tip of her tongue in his mouth then traced his top lip with it. The sprinkling rain felt lighter on his skin now, warmed at once by the heat generated from his quickening pulse.

Finally she drew back a little, their lips disengaged, and he proceeded with small, tender kisses on her cheek and nose, lashes and brows.

"The baron kissed me tonight, Thomas," she said through a ragged sigh.

"How could he not?" he muttered in reply, his hot breath at her ear. "I expected him to try."

She squirmed in his arms, then dropped her head back to expose her neck to his loving assault. "Are you jealous?"

"Terribly." He ran his tongue over her pulse point, feeling the up and down movement in her throat as she swallowed.

"He also touched my breasts."

"Then I'll have to kill him," he whispered at the hairline just above her ear.

She pushed solidly against him with her hand. He raised his head, though only enough to view her face, refusing to move his hands as they cupped her temples over her hood. She kept her eyes closed for a moment, then reluctantly opened them,

"I'm serious, Thomas. He touched them, without permission and only over my gown, but . . ." She drew a very deep breath. "But my body responded, and he noticed it."

His heart raced with his fading passion. For seconds he said nothing, then huskily whispered, "Noticed what?"

She groaned and closed her eyes again, biting down hard. "That my nipples were hard."

"From his touch?"

"Yes."

"I see." He waited, hating the baron, of course, but loving this rather amusing exchange. "Are they hard now?" he asked in a sensual whisper, stroking her cheek with his gloved thumb, his nose nearly touching hers.

"I—I think so," she murmured, suddenly captivated. "But it's freezing, Thomas."

"It's snowing, Madeleine."

Very, very slowly she raised her lashes once more, unable to at first comprehend his soothing words. Then she looked above him, into the sparkling night sky, and her expression turned to one of luminous wonder.

"It's snowing, Thomas," she repeated in a voice barely heard.

He witnessed the joy in her eyes as the cold, crystalline drops fell and clung to her forehead and cheeks and the sable on her hood. She backed away from him with her hands in the air, one covered with her muff, the other palm up. And then she twirled around once, twice, laughing, eyes closed.

He grinned as he watched her, thoroughly charmed. "Have you never seen snow?"

She fairly giggled, slowing her body to focus on him again in pure delight. "Yes, but not in years. And never like this—falling heavily in bright moonlight on a crystal-clear lake." She reached for his hand, squeezed his fingers, then turned her body out so that she faced the water. She raised her face and arms toward the heavens, and sighed. "It's beautiful."

And it was, he agreed silently, observing the queer force of nature that prompted a snowfall, growing heavier by the second, on a cold night of utter stillness, clouds just above them and a full moon in the western sky that shined off the lake and brightened the flakes in the air like specks of floating white cotton. No, not cotton. Diamonds.

Madeleine turned her head and gazed into his eyes, smiling. "Are you mad because I kissed him, Thomas?"

He raised her knuckles to his lips, grazing them with his mouth. "Only if you enjoyed it more than kissing me."

She lowered her arms, and her hood fell from her

head, freeing strands of shiny, dark hair that clung to her cheeks. She never released his hand and never took her eyes from his. After a long, full breath, she admitted, "I didn't enjoy the kiss very much, but all the fumbling he did with my breasts did tell me something about myself."

He shifted from one foot to the other, angling his body closer to her, supremely frightened to know. "What was that?"

"That I'd rather kiss you more than anyone I've ever known," she confided in a passionate tenor. "That I'd rather spend one night with you in your bed than spend forever in the arms of someone else. That I wish France was not so very far away."

The moon shone like blue mist upon the water lapping quietly near his feet, the snow descended from the heavens in silence, and yet the greatest miracle to ever enter his lonely, painful world was the giving, gentle woman at his side.

"Are you mad at me for allowing him to touch me?" she asked again modestly.

"Ah, Maddie . . ." He shook his head and brought her palm to his lips, kissing the warm, delicate skin of her fingers, one by one. "I'm in awe of you."

A whimper came from her throat, and she faltered, blinking quickly, lowering her lashes and shifting her eyes to the lake. She stood like that for moments, and his heart pounded as he waited.

"I want to give you a special gift, Thomas," she said resolutely, attempting to hide the flow of overwhelming emotion in her voice.

"Madeleine—"

"Shhh . . ." Without another word, she stepped past him, her hand wrapped in his, pulling him toward the cluster of bushes that led to the cottage.

Nineteen

The air had grown cold inside the cottage, and in darkness Thomas strode to the grate to add coals to the dimly glowing embers of what remained of their early-evening fire. Madeleine unbuttoned her mantle and hung it and her muff on the rack near the door, then walked into the parlor and over to his side.

For seconds she looked into his eyes contemplatively, searching, and then she straightened her shoulders and resolutely glided around him, her skirts sweeping his legs, so that she stood to his left in front of the mantelpiece, staring down at his music box.

Thomas remained silent, battling unsureness with each breath. The moment was so poignant, rousing untold feelings deep within him, but he couldn't bring himself to move a muscle.

Very slowly, and with great ease, she lifted the music box in her hands and carefully turned it from one direction to the next, examining its size and structure. Then she raised the top and peered inside to the glass-covered brass player and empty contents.

Thomas kept his gaze keenly riveted on her. He knew she couldn't help but see the inscription on the inside of the lid—*My beloved. Your beauty is my sunshine; your strength is my torch; your love is my joy. I will forever be yours. C. T.*—and there was nothing he could do to prevent it should he try.

"Who does this belong to?"

Her soft question was like a silky, mesmerizing caress to his ears.

"It's mine now," he answered factually as he pulled his gloves from his hands and began unbuttoning his coat, "but it was originally my mother's. I suppose you could call it a family heirloom."

"Who is C. T.?"

"My father, Christian Thomas. He and my mother both died soon after my marriage to Bernadette."

"He gave it to her?" she asked sedately, lifting it higher to look at the underside.

"It was a wedding gift," was his rather undefined answer.

"And a perfect one at that. So romantic." Finding the small dial, she wound it several times, fully, so that the music began to play. "It's beautiful," she said with a wispy sigh and a pleasurable smile into his eyes.

"Beethoven's Sonata in C Minor, or *The Pathétique*," he informed. "My family has always been quite interested in music, obsessed really," he added with a shy, crooked grin. "I play the violin and viola myself."

That surprised and delighted her. "You do?"

He nodded.

"And now your son studies it in Vienna."

"But he is gifted, I am not."

She hesitated on the verge of saying something more. Then, apparently deciding against it, she instead turned and placed the music box back on the mantelpiece so that the deep base expanded in sound and deepened in tone, chiming through the room. Taking a step closer, she stood directly in front of him.

"Dance with me, Thomas?" she requested, her voice deliciously honey-sweet and innocently encouraging.

He didn't move. The air stilled around him, and for a timeless moment, he tensed to the ends of every fired nerve in his body.

"Madeleine—" he started, his unspoken thoughts catching in a wave of turbulent emotion.

"Dance with me," she urged again, her conviction strengthening as she held out her hands, palms up.

Thomas knew that this would always count as one of the most profound memories of his life, and possibly the only instance in his life when he would ever come so close to breaking down into tears in front of a woman.

He couldn't verbalize his thoughts, though, and she apparently understood. Without further hesitation she reached for his coat and gloves, pulling them easily from his grasp and tossing them in his chair. Then she wrapped her arms around his neck, smiled knowingly into his eyes, and hugged him tightly, tucking her head into the crook of his neck.

As in a gentle, drifting tide, she began to sway to the music, her body pulsing with each beat of the enveloping melody. Thomas embraced her cautiously, one palm to her back and the other resting on the silky flesh at her nape. She held him securely, feathering her fingers through the curls at his collar. He felt her breasts against his pounding heart, her curves becoming a part of him as he rested his cheek on her head, inhaling the clean, flowery scent of her hair.

"You're magnificent," he said, his words floating above the entrancing music.

She pushed herself closer in his arms, molding her

form against his to the extent that her gown would allow. "I was going to say the same about you."

"I don't want you to leave, Madeleine."

He didn't know where that statement had come from, only that he'd said it aloud. But his pulse sped up with uncertainty when seconds ticked by and she had no response. The first hints of fear tugged at his heart when it wasn't forthcoming.

"Make love to me, Thomas," she whispered, still gazing into the fire, still swaying to the soft melodic tones from the music box as the tempo began to slow.

It was time, he knew. He could wait no longer to reveal more of himself. Denying her now would only pose troublesome questions, perhaps even growing suspicion on her part.

He stood a little straighter and drew in a deep breath. "There are certain things I have to tell you—"

"Shh . . ." She cut him off, raising her head to gaze into his eyes. Hers were a vivid, melting ice blue, shamelessly suggesting all the thoughts he was finally allowing himself to express. The passion she silently communicated made his blood boil in his veins, his skin prickle with excitement and anticipation of the unknown he was about to explore with an ageless hunger.

Pulling back from his embrace, she began to unfasten the buttons of her gown behind her. Without consideration to the contrary, he helped her with trembling fingers, one by one, until the top of her dress fell away from her shoulders.

She let the bodice hang forward, exposing the sheer silk chemise that clung to her breasts. Then her beautiful white gown dropped to the brown rug in a swirling heap at her feet, and she stood before him in the sheerest of stockings, shoes, petticoats and her tightly waisted, white corset.

"Oh, God," he heard himself whisper, his throat suddenly dry and painfully clenched, his hands at her shoulders, thumbs stroking the curves at her neck.

"It has been a long time, hasn't it, Thomas?" she remarked with an amazed little grin of enjoyment. "You're shaking."

"It's—" He swallowed harshly and tried again. "It's more than that. You don't know what seeing you like this does to me, what making love to you means to me."

"I know what it means to me." She reached up to free the pins in her hair, dropping each one on the mantelpiece. "I want you to enjoy this night slowly, Thomas, remembering every second of the passion. I will give you everything you want."

He paused, his fervid gaze melding with hers, then whispered, "All I want is you, Madeleine. All I've ever wanted is you."

He noticed the subtle change in her expression as he said the words, her eyes filling with a confusion of thought so obvious it drove deeply into him, connecting to his soul, thrusting into it, slicing it open for exposure to her intense probing of his desire.

I love you, Madeleine. Do you know that yet? Can you feel it?

She took his hands in both of hers, lifted his fingers to her mouth and kissed them, one by one, her hot breath and moist lips coaxing another shiver from his body. Then she placed them on her silk-covered breasts, rubbing his palms over her large, pointed nipples that came alive to his touch and seared his skin.

"Unfasten my corset, Thomas," she pleaded in a raspy breath, shaking her hair loose from her head to fall down her back while she in turn began to untie his cravat.

Sexual need struck him hard, overtaking soft emotions as the sudden, wondrous thought of seeing her naked for the first time chased momentary doubt away.

Quietly he did as she bade him, pulling at the fasteners one by one, quickly, though, in an effort to release the visual beauty that awaited his starving view and pleasure-seeking feel. She did the same, dropping her fingers to each button on his shirt, working through them as she exposed his chest to her waiting caress. It had been years since he'd touched a lady's underthings, and he stumbled along the path, although she didn't appear to notice his ineptitude.

Thick, charged air surrounded them suddenly. Silence, save for the smoldering fire, pervaded their privacy as the music finally ceased playing. Snow fell silently in the outside world, enclosing them in a cottage of warm, beautiful dreams, encouraging a joining that would erase the anguish of wait from his lonely, isolated world. He wanted to give her all, everything, but mostly he knew it was time to give her himself.

Her corset fell to the floor at her feet. She slipped off her shoes as his hands rested at her shoulders again, drawing small circles on her shoulder blades with his thumbs. Then he hooked them through the thin, silk straps of her chemise and pulled them down, exposing her breasts to his waiting gaze for the very first time.

Large, pointed, perfect nipples the color of dark, ripe cherries begged him to devour as they protruded from the smoothest, most translucent skin he had ever seen.

"They're so beautiful," he commented wistfully, captivated as he reached forward to touch. His thumbs stroked them once, again, and then he groaned and covered them with his palms, rotating them to knead and stroke and sweep over the tips that grew harder against his sensitive skin.

"Kiss them," she whispered, jutting them out just

slightly as she closed her eyes and dropped her arms to her sides.

She sucked in a sharp breath when his lips brushed over one, then the other. Then he took one into his mouth, swirling his tongue over it, and her knees buckled.

He encircled her waist with his arm, holding her tightly against him as he made love to her breasts, standing on the rug beside the fire, sucking and kissing and tasting.

He moaned when she did, giving equal time to each nipple. "You like this, don't you?" he managed to murmur.

She wrapped her arms around his neck. "It's heaven, Thomas."

His shirt fell away from his chest, and she tipped her body up and into him, rubbing his erection purposely with her belly. That movement fanned the fire, making his self-control weaken and his need burn anew.

Suddenly she pushed away from him and stood back, lashes lowered as she reached for her stockings, removing them and the remainder of her clothing with intentional slowness, forcing him to watch the annoyingly prolonged process. Moments later she stood fully nude before him, and his focus shifted to drink in her grace and unusual loveliness as the woman he'd wanted for so very long.

Its beauty unmatched, her pale, smooth skin glowed golden from firelight; her breasts, large and slightly uplifted, begged for his undivided attention. Lingeringly his gaze traveled down and up the length of her, to her narrow waist, her tiny protruding navel and long, shapely legs, to her hipbones that spread out from the dark thatch of curls leading to—

He dropped to his knees, awkwardly and most pain-

fully, to put his face directly in front of the glorious
center entrance that made her a woman.

"Thomas?" she murmured breathlessly, unsure of his
intention.

So was he. For only a moment. Then the scent of her
startled his senses, and he raised a finger to push through
the crease beneath the curls.

She moaned again, grasping his head with both hands.

"You're wet, Maddie," he said through a shiver of
impatience and longing and wonder.

He stroked her back and forth for seconds, then slid
in even deeper to find the hidden opening.

"Oh, God . . ." he said hungrily as his finger easily
slipped inside. Then he pressed his face to her feminine
softness and inhaled deeply before he forced his tongue
through the folds and began licking the sensitive nub
that would drive her to the heights of bliss.

She widened her knees minutely, pushing gently
against him, whimpering softly as he picked up speed.
He held his head steady and paced the rhythm of the
back and forth action of his tongue, grasping her bottom
with his free hand to hold her firmly. He coaxed and
teased and continued his blissful action without pause
while her breathing grew heavy and fast and she began
making little grinding movements with her hips.

"I will climax too quickly, Thomas," she said rag-
gedly, worriedly.

He held her against him, never ceasing in his pursuit
of her pleasure.

"No," she whispered again in an attempt to stay her
release, but it was too late. "Oh, Thomas," she whispered
seconds later, clutching him tightly. "Oh, Thomas. Oh,
Thomas—"

And then he felt her orgasm with his finger and his
mouth; heard it with his ears as she rocked into him and

cried out, her hands now tight fists in his hair.

The juices flowed from her in quivering waves, tasting more succulent than the finest French champagne, and he devoured it as if a feast for the starved, wine for the soul. When she at last began to calm against him, he kissed her thighs quickly and hungrily, back and forth, then put his face in her curls again.

"Maddie, what you do to me," he fairly growled.

Her breathing came out sharp and abrasive, and after only the briefest moment she gently lifted his head until he withdrew a little. She lowered her body to his level, on her knees directly in front of him, and without a look she placed her hands over the jumping pulse points on his neck, and kissed him deeply, passionately, surely tasting the sweetness of herself on his lips.

"Thomas . . ." she whispered against his mouth. "Thomas, Thomas, Thomas, Thomas . . ."

He encircled her waist with his arms, caressed her soft back with his fingertips, felt her exquisite bare breasts against his chest.

"I know, Maddie . . ." he whispered with conviction, his lips brushing her cheek and jaw and throat. "I know."

She had never felt like this in her life, Madeleine realized, never experienced a rush of such incredible heights of passion and pleasure as she did with this man. This marvelous man who made her sigh with a look from his dark, dangerous eyes, tingle with a word from his resonant voice, and climax with such ease and complete abandonment from his exquisite touch. It had never been like this with another, and she was almost as certain that it never would be again. Thomas made her feel beautiful without telling her so, made her feel so very wanted by only his presence at her side. Now she wanted to give him everything.

With a sudden nervousness she couldn't explain,

Madeleine reached for the buttons of his trousers, fumbling with them quickly, until she felt his palms wrap around her wrists.

"Madeleine, we have to talk first," he murmured huskily, his lips once more meeting hers.

Talk? *Talk?*

"Maddie," he tried again, pulling back a bit and raising his hands to weave his fingers through her hair. "There's something I need to show you, some things I need to tell you."

Desire still burned within her like a soaring flame, never extinguished, but she forced herself to do what he wanted and wait for him.

His gaze penetrated hers with warmth, as well as a level of anxiousness she not only saw, but felt within. Curiosity mounting, she reached up with her hand and ran her thumb once across his chin. "Talk to me, then."

He inhaled deeply, then turned to his side and, pushing her discarded gown and underthings beneath the tea table, sat upon the soft rug, his long, muscular legs spread wide and around her body. She sat when he did, as daintily as she could between his thighs, warm from the fire at their side, staring at the rippling muscles of his unclothed, chiseled chest, relishing the comforting closeness that only this man had ever seemed to give her unconditionally.

He hesitated, scrubbing his face with one hand before beginning.

"I told you once that I was injured in the war," he said quietly.

"Yes," she answered, meeting his gaze.

His jaw tightened, and his eyes bore into hers. "I was injured badly, Madeleine."

She wasn't sure how to take that, how he wanted her to react, so she simply replied, "How badly?"

He dropped his gaze to her breasts, then her belly and exposed pubic area, then shifted his attention uncomfortably to the fire. Stalling.

His uneasiness, coupled with what she could only term mild insecurity, melted her inside, and she reached for him, her palm to his cheek. "Tell me, Thomas," she insisted as sternly as the situation allowed.

He squinted, and she had a difficult time discerning whether it was due to mental or physical pain. She decided it was the former but chose not to comment, waiting for him.

After wrestling with his thoughts uncomfortably, he finally revealed, "A burning, wooden pillar fell on top of me in a shipyard in Hong Kong, pinning me beneath it and breaking both of my legs below the knees. They didn't heal properly."

Questions immediately filled her mind. Why? How? "Show them to me," she demanded softly instead.

With resolve, he reached for his left leg, rolled up the cuff of his trousers to the top of his black leather boot, and very slowly pulled it by the heel, twisting his foot until his leg gave way and came out of the rim. He rolled down his sock and exposed it to her view.

Madeleine looked at it curiously, carefully withholding a reaction due to his penetrating focus on her, noting the badly burned and mangled flesh from knee to toes, two of which—the two on the end—were missing. The color of the injured area was hard to distinguish in dim firelight, but she could tell it was an odd mixture of dark red and purple—the shade of a day-old bruise. The muscles of his calf had been torn and healed over incorrectly, and scars abounded from top to bottom, from the deep to the superficial, which undoubtedly accounted for the pain in his walk.

"Oh, Thomas," she whispered, reaching out to touch

it. He let her, sitting still as death, watching, anticipating
her resistance, though she only felt his gaze on the side
of her face. The skin was rough and knotty, but she
skimmed the area with her palm, up and down in a
soothing motion.

Silently he reached for his right leg, pulling up on the
cuff of his pants as he had with the left. This time, however, she noticed a difference in his boot. At the top,
near the knee, were two buckled straps, one below the
other and an inch or so apart, which he unfastened very
slowly. That finished, and with a tug of one hand at the
heel, one at the calf, the boot gave way, exposing the
core of his fear.

Madeleine stared, her body numbing, heart twisting
with overwhelming compassion and sadness. Two
inches below the scarred and deformed knee, his right
leg had been expertly cut off.

"Will you love me now, Maddie?" she heard in a
tender, hoarse, far away voice.

The words struck a chord within her, and her mouth
went dry as she gaped in obvious shock at the forever-
wounded part of a tortured soul that belonged to a beautiful man. She raised tear-filled eyes back to his, unable
to speak, aching to hold him, to prove to him she didn't
care, to convince him her affection went far deeper than
the superficial. She understood so very vividly how the
world judged appallingly by physical beauty and so little
by character and goodness. Oh, how she needed him
now—to show him, to be with him.

His eyes remained locked with hers, boldly probing
while they fearfully hoped. With a harsh swallow to control the powerfully intense rise of confusing but wonderful emotions seizing her, she leaned over and placed
her lips on the sight of his injury.

She heard a rush of air escape his chest, and then his

hands were in her hair, fingers weaving through it as he gently massaged her scalp while she left tiny kisses in a circle at the end of his leg, at the tip where the prime scar had closed over what used to be healthy muscle and tissue, bone and skin.

Madeleine placed her palms on his thighs, over his pants, and pushed them up until she reached the crease at the top of his legs. Leaning up at last, she hooked her fingers over the waistband and pulled, and this time he lifted his hips, allowing her to move forward in her approach. She tugged at the woolen fabric until she'd removed it, underclothes next, and then he sat beside her as naked as she.

Thomas watched her, she knew, but she had yet to look back into his eyes. She stared at his body—his magnificent body—so strong and large and aroused. That amazed her most of all. He was still so aroused, even after the moment just shared where he'd revealed his gravest concern to her, afraid of her repulsion.

He wanted her, and he was ready for her in every regard.

Madeleine stared at his erection as it extended upward—hard and long and thick, the base surrounded by a mass of black curls that thinned to a tiny line ending at his navel. Placing her hands on his bare thighs, she leaned over and skimmed the length of it with her lips, up and down, then kissed it heartily over and over to tease, to enjoy and give enjoyment.

He groaned, tensing beneath her caress, and that gave her encouragement as she continued on her journey. She leisurely explored his body, kissing his navel, stroking it once with her tongue, then his chest and neck, finally stretching out fully upon him as she silently revealed her intentions and he reclined on the rug beneath her.

Madeleine lay atop his hot, hard body and looked into

his eyes, now dark pools expressing an infinite yearning for her alone.

"I have never wanted a man more than I want you right now, Thomas," she said very slowly, observing the changes in his face with each calculated, sincere word. And then before he could summon a comment, she at long last captured his mouth again with hers, kissing him fully and fervidly, and in total knowledge of the flame of something undefined but obviously blazing between them, something she didn't now dare to determine.

Desire sparked anew, and he kissed her back forcefully, his tongue thrusting deep with returned hunger, his hands in her hair, taking the weight of her body with ease as her breasts flattened against his chest and her sex rested upon his as if made for it, the perfect fit, the perfect closeness.

She rubbed against him once, then again, and he moaned his pleasure, cupping her bottom, stroking her back and waist with long fingers and large warm palms. Madeleine understood his need and quickly she raised herself so that she sat upon him, her moist, ready cleft smothering his erection with intentional, indulgent care.

Then with a sensual narrowing of her lids and an impish lift to the corners of her lips, she began to move, back and forth and in slow circles on top of him, watching the longing in his eyes turn at last to centered lust, and reveling in it.

Thomas didn't think he'd ever been so aroused in his life. Her erotic movements entranced him; her small whimpers and short, quick breaths held him under a spell of torturous bliss. And when she raised her hands, threaded her fingers through her own hair to shake it loose, then suddenly began caressing her own breasts and nipples, he had to close his eyes momentarily to keep himself under control.

It was the most sensual thing he'd ever seen a woman do. She'd touched herself on Christmas Eve, but that episode certainly didn't compare to watching her now: flickering firelight dancing on golden, shiny skin—skin that she herself stroked and teased as she moved her sex against his, slowly, evenly. Perfectly.

Thomas placed his hands on her thighs but didn't move them, just held them there. He didn't want to change the intimacy as it was. His breath quickened, his chest ached, his need neared explosion, and still her moans grew louder and her breathing more shallow as she massaged her breasts and tugged at her hardened nipples.

"You feel so good," she whispered, eyes closed, rotating her hips above him, against him.

He raised himself slightly to match her movements. Then she dropped one hand and placed her own fingers at the center of her desire to stroke and pleasure herself as he watched in absolute fascination that took him to the brink of his own release.

"You're making me crazy," he said gruffly.

She didn't reply, but panted, whimpered, lost in her own sensual world as she rubbed her wet, hot cleft against his engorged erection, caressed the satiny skin of her breasts and nipples, and moved her fingers rhythmically between her legs, faster and faster.

When she dropped her head back, Thomas could feel her long, luxuriant hair on his knees, on his injured, mangled legs that she'd accepted without revulsion, that lay exposed to a woman for the very first time.

"I want to watch you climax," he whispered. "Nothing is more beautiful to me, Madeleine."

He wasn't sure if she heard him, or understood, for she was so close now. She stretched and moaned as she neared the ultimate satisfaction, and he smoothed his palms over her thighs and hips and waist, letting her experience it the way she wanted.

Suddenly she lifted her head, raised her lashes, and looked down at him, her eyes glazed over, unfocused but sharply intense.

"Thomas," she whispered again.

"I'm watching, my love," he returned in a voice barely heard.

Her eyes opened wider. "Thomas . . . Oh, God, Thomas—"

She reached her crest with a small cry of fierce pleasure through her lips, smothering his member with flowing moisture, touching herself with one hand, stroking herself with the other, and Thomas could take no more.

As soon as he sensed the tension draining from her, he grasped her waist and lifted her easily, turning over quickly so that he could enter her from above.

She didn't protest in any way as she spread her legs for him, welcoming him when he slid into her slowly, gradually, filling her to an ideal fit. She cushioned him warmly, accommodating his size as if made for him. Thomas stilled his body and braced himself when he came to rest deeply within her, his forearms laying flat on the rug on either side of her head as he peered down to her lovely, flushed, satisfied face. He'd done that, without doing a thing. He'd pleasured her twice tonight and he would do it again, as she needed it, coaxing her along to that marvelous brink of oblivion. But first he needed gratification himself.

In a drugged haze, her lips curved up contentedly. "I want to watch you this time," she murmured thickly, caressing his chest with her hands, grazing his arms and neck with her fingers.

He slid very gently out of her once, then back in again. "This is my heaven. You are my dream."

She raised her hands to cup his face, her smile fading, expression intense. "I've never known lovemaking like this. Do you believe me?"

Her question was spoken timidly, although she tried to hide that. He leaned forward and kissed her chin, her cheek, her lips, and forehead with absolute tenderness. "I believe you," he whispered, voice strained, heart pounding, "because neither have I."

She inhaled unevenly, and he lifted himself a bit to look into her eyes once more. They were shiny and brilliant blue and charged with love. For him. He knew it, as suddenly as if he had been slapped with it. To discover it now, like this, naked and warm against her, enveloped inside of her during the greatest physical intimacy, made this without doubt the most extraordinary moment of his life.

Perspiration beaded on his brow, but still he refused to move, holding back, giving himself time to adjust physically, emotionally.

She didn't want to wait any longer. She ran her thumb across his lips and squeezed her inner muscles that surrounded him, urging him to orgasm, and that was all it took. He withdrew from her once more, waiting, holding back, the tip of him only just inside, ready to pull out completely and let himself go against her leg with one more stroke. Then the unbelievable happened.

She grabbed his hips with her hands, tightly, and wrapped her legs around his thighs.

"Yes," she whispered possessively, from the depths of her heart to his.

His jaw hardened; he flexed his body, and then he drove himself completely into her as she wanted, as he felt himself coming to the edge.

"Maddie—"

He spilled himself inside of her then, during wave

after wave of the most intense rush of pleasure he had ever felt, his eyes opened wide to the startled depths of hers, giving himself to her in body and spirit, revealing to her own wounded soul the love he felt inside for her, the beautiful woman who had let him in.

For the first time in his life, Thomas didn't feel the pain in his legs or brood over the unfairness and harsh realities of life. He heard birdsong and the laughter of children, the crescendo of music and cascading waterfalls, and he felt the marvelous warmth of total contentment.

His joy was unspeakable.

Twenty

I don't want you to leave, Madeleine.

The words kept ringing in her ears like an endless bell, sometimes beautifully, sometimes annoyingly. Like those chiming now in the distance as she walked in haste through a half-inch of snow, carefully put together in her morning gown and mantle, toward the church for Sunday morning service.

Madeleine had awakened in his bed only an hour ago, snuggled into his arms as if she'd belonged there her entire life, feeling as if she might never leave, realizing at once after the glow of the night had faded that such an idea was dangerous.

Of course, she would leave. Eventually. She had to, for she couldn't stay in England only to do . . . what? Marry him? That was a preposterous thought, though not necessarily an unpleasant one. Still, she was surprised that the notion had occurred to her at all, as she had never considered herself the marrying kind of woman. Could she settle for just being his lover in Eastleigh as they worked as spies together? That seemed laughable

to her. She would never be accepted in this country, as
his wife or mistress, and her work was in France. That
was where her talents and expertise were needed most,
not here. Not permanently. Thomas had to know that,
had to have known at the beginning that any relationship
they might have had would be short-lived. She just
wished the knowledge didn't tear into her so deeply, as
it did each time she thought of it, which was constantly
of late.

Last night had been incredible, she reflected, beaming
in a manner she couldn't help and that she hoped would
not be observed by the many Winter Garden ladies she
was bound to encounter only a few minutes from now.
Thomas had desired her so much, had been so attentive,
so tender, so . . . energetic. He'd made love to her four
times in as many hours, and at nearly forty years of age,
that had to be a record of some kind. Going more than
half a decade without a woman had certainly made him
anxious to make up for time lost. She had given in to
his need, finding her own satisfaction more times than
she could count—or wanted to, for that matter. Finally,
though, satiated and content, they'd slept in his bed,
molded together as one, absorbing each other's heat and
total devotion, until just over an hour ago when she'd
awakened with a curious thought, a theory plaguing her
suddenly that she wanted to clarify by attending church
of all places on this brisk, overcast winter morning.

The idea itself had come from considering her own
selfish stupidity. Her first thought upon waking, after
only three hours of sleep or so, which came after hours
of blissful, restless lovemaking, was that she never
should have allowed him to climax inside of her. He had
been prepared to withdraw himself, and would have each
time, but she had yielded for a reason, or reasons, unclear. She had wanted to give him a marvelous time

because of the pain he had suffered, because of the inadequacy he'd felt all these years due to disabilities he assumed would disgust female companions. And yet, if she pondered it honestly, her reasons also included feelings far more complex in nature, that she couldn't yet define, and possibly never would.

He still would have enjoyed himself even if he'd been outside of her at orgasm. It was her own selfishness that had wanted him to penetrate her when he'd reached it. She had experienced a sudden, inexplicable need to watch him find pleasure inside her, and she'd basked in the moment when he had. She'd never given in like that with another man out of her very real fear of getting pregnant with a child she'd never wanted, but last night with Thomas it simply hadn't mattered.

Now, as the morning coldness weighed heavily on her shoulders and common sense took over, she had to face the fact that she could be carrying Thomas's child. Right now. Inside of her. The thought made her shiver, but not with aversion, surprisingly. It made her shiver with an unusual kind of warmth, because his feelings for her went far below the surface, to the hidden place within her that needed him, that longed for something to hold him there, and he knew that place existed. He knew it. If she were pregnant with his child, he would love it unconditionally, regardless of their unmarried status, her illegitimate birth and past. She also knew this beyond question. If she gave birth to his baby, Thomas would forever be a part of her, loving that part. That was what she'd felt from the heat of his eyes at the moment of his physical release when he'd left his seed deeply within her. It was the only reason she'd allowed him in more than once last night.

Of course, there was always the possibility that she hadn't conceived, but she was, nonetheless, frightened of the prospect. In theory, the idea of pregnancy was romantic and splendid. In reality, what she'd likely done was allow one night of extraordinary passion to ruin her life as she knew it.

Stupid, stupid, stupid!

Madeleine kicked the snow in front of her with the toe of her shoe, creating a mist of fine, white powder that clung to the sable fur at the base of her mantle. Rounding the final corner on the relatively deserted street, she spied the vicarage in the distance, the small church behind it now filling with locals in Sunday best, and she raised her chin with her graceful walk, trying to think of something else. It didn't work.

Thomas's baby. If indeed she carried it, she would keep it, and probably come to love it. What else could she do? It would be a child born of her own mistake, which would make it her responsibility. And *that* was the thought that had so stirred her to seek out Desdemona this cloudy, bitter morning, by herself because their conversation was going to become personal, and in a place where the lady would undoubtedly be, and where ignoring Madeleine would be unlikely and rude should she try.

She didn't know why she hadn't thought before of confronting the lady after church, as she'd wanted to speak with her for weeks now. Maybe because a conversation in Desdemona's home seemed more practical, more intimate, and, of course, Madeleine rarely attended the small English church. But after the spark of clarity striking her this morning, she knew she didn't have time to waste by calling on the woman and being told, again, that she was out or under the weather or resting. Talking on the street wasn't the ideal situation, but at this point she really had no choice. Her only hope was that Desdemona would be there and would be able to escape her mother for a few minutes.

The service was amazingly full, considering that the party of the season had been held only last night. Many of the gentry were absent, Madeleine noticed as she sat in the back of the congregation, listening with not a shade of interest at the sermon droned by the very proper Vicar Barkley who had, upon their first meeting, made it clear without comment that he found her a fascinating addition to the Winter Garden community, but disapproved appropriately of her living with the unmarried scholar. It was curious that he allowed his daughter to work for them, but that was irrelevant apparently. And, of course, she was Catholic by birth, which didn't endear her to anyone.

She did, however, take the time to observe the attendees now, looking at the backs of heads until she spotted the subject of her search in the second pew on the far right side, near the small, untalented but diligent choir. She wore a large straw hat in royal purple that sported three tall plumes of the same color, tied with a wide satin bow at her chin so that the hat slanted sideways to allow just enough of her fair hair to show becomingly. Penelope was nowhere to be seen, although Desdemona whispered to a larger girl with the same hair coloring sitting to her right whom Madeleine assumed must be one of the lady's two sisters.

Madeleine waited until the choir finished singing for a final time, then stood as Desdemona did, watching the woman turn in her direction as she made her way toward the exit at the back of the church.

For the first time, Madeleine took special interest in the lady's appearance, studying her critically. Desdemona was a slight, well-groomed and well-dressed but somewhat unattractive young woman, made more so by her dour expression and light blue eyes that had lost their excitement, even hope, in life. Her pregnancy was showing now, although only to the most observant as her woolen, dark gray and fox-trimmed mantle covered it well. She wore a gown the same color as her hat, but Madeleine could only see the lace cuffs as they extended below the sleeves.

So sad. That was the feeling she exuded. Her eyes were wide but vacant as they stared straight ahead; her skin, though fair, waxed more pale than it should, considering her youth and the natural blush that was reported to come with pregnancy. Madeleine suspected the reason, and it doused her with an uncommon sense of compassion and empathy for this young woman who had succumbed to temptation she wasn't prepared to handle.

Desdemona, her sister following, spoke to no one on her way from the sanctuary as she headed toward the snow-covered vicarage garden, lost in her own thoughts. Madeleine cut through the disassembling crowd until she strolled up to Desdemona's side as if it were an accidental meeting.

The lady blinked quickly when she turned her head and realized who walked beside her, slowing her stride though not stopping to visit.

"Good morning, Mrs. Winsett," Madeleine began pleasantly, rubbing her hands together in her muff.

For a second or two Desdemona seemed confused at seeing her there. Then she smiled faintly. "Good morning, Mrs. DuMais. Have you met my sister Hermione?"

Madeleine shifted her focus to the girl now walking slightly behind Desdemona and to her left, and tipped her head in formal acknowledgment. "It is a pleasure to make your acquaintance, Miss Bennington-Jones."

"Likewise, ma'am," came the hesitant reply.

Sturdily built, taller, and even more homely than her

sister, Hermione had a round face and rounder hazel eyes that implied a sheltered child within, though she was clearly near an age suitable for marriage.

"Where is your mother today?" Madeleine asked to clear the air quickly before she got down to the business at hand, peeking over her shoulder with the near expectation of seeing Penelope bustling in their direction, pointing her finger in irritation at Madeleine's audacious attempt to seek her daughters' company.

Desdemona snorted and stared forward again, her slim shoulders erect, mouth curled. "Mother is slightly under the weather today after the festivities of last night and, of course, the busy time she's had lately preparing for my sister's coming out."

"Oh, I see. I hope she'll be feeling better soon," Madeleine replied as expected.

"Thank you. I'm sure she will."

They walked side by side for another few seconds in silence, but Desdemona didn't seem at all desirous of escaping her presence. In some fashion, Madeleine decided the girl wanted her companionship, if only for a little while.

"Do you hear from your husband?" she asked congenially.

Desdemona hesitated in answering, though she tried not to show it. "He has written me twice in the last month. He's in Poland now, with the twenty-second infantry, as their chief weapons inspector." She looked at her askance. "It may not seem important to you, Mrs. DuMais, but it's important to the English cause. I'm also very proud of him."

Madeleine stepped around a mulberry bush at the edge of the vicarage garden and headed out into the lane, uncrowded as those who had chanced the service quickly returned home to avoid the frosty air. "I'm sure it must be a comfort for him to know that you're safely in England with family while you await the birth of your child."

It was altogether subtle, but Desdemona stiffened at the remark. Directing her attention to Hermione, Madeleine suggested, "Perhaps you wouldn't mind if I speak with your sister alone?"

Desdemona paused in her stride as the younger girl's brows drew together in a frown.

"Mother is expecting us," Hermione replied reluctantly, shifting her gaze from one to the other.

"And I shouldn't be out in the cold air while I'm carrying," Desdemona added with a great deal more confidence.

"Nonsense," Madeleine scoffed. "Fresh air is good for you and the baby, and I really would like to discuss something with you privately. It's important."

Desdemona didn't argue, but she and her sister exchanged another look that implied a suggested restraint on both of their parts—Desdemona toward Madeleine, and Hermione toward Penelope.

"I'll tell Mother you're on your way, Desi," Hermione mumbled, a trifle flustered. "Good day, Mrs. DuMais." Then she lifted her skirts and quickly crossed the road, treading as lightly as possible over snow and ice.

Desdemona watched her for a few seconds, then continued strolling along their original path, heading down Saderbark Road toward the village square.

Madeleine waited until Hermione was clearly out of earshot, then chose to delve straight into the issue that brought her to this imperative discussion on this particular morning.

"I was wondering about something," she started, her voice suggesting an air of both concern and puzzlement. "You mentioned at Mrs. Rodney's tea several weeks ago that you'd heard rumors of lights at night and ghosts on Baron Rothebury's property." She clucked her tongue. "I happened to be out taking a late-night stroll recently and saw that light. Can you believe it?"

Desdemona stopped short and glowered at her with eyes a soft, innocent blue—and brimming with trepidation. "What do you want, Mrs. DuMais?" she asked coldly.

Madeleine caught the alarm in the young woman's voice, and she pursed her lips, tipping her head an inch to the side in apparent contemplation. "You're carrying the baron's child, aren't you, Desdemona?" she inquired very softly, without pretense or pleasure from bringing that out in the open.

Desdemona not only paled significantly, but also flinched as if struck. Her eyes grew to wide pools of a secret fear, a repulsion of their own kind, and something more. Something like hatred.

A lone horseman trotted by, advising them in a loud, terse tongue to take their conversation out of the center of the street, but neither she nor Desdemona looked his way, nor did they move as they stood staring at each other.

"That's slanderous, Mrs. DuMais," the lady said in a frigid voice. "I recommend you take your loathsome comments back to France."

Madeleine wasn't the least daunted or unnerved by Desdemona's threatening rejoinder. She had, in fact, expected it. Smiling vaguely, she dropped her gaze to her feet and began shuffling the snow with her already frozen toe.

"It is, however, quite true, isn't it? You met the baron several times during late-evening rendezvous when he took you into his home as his mistress through a tunnel that leads to his bedroom." She lifted her lashes only, just enough to view the tangled cloud of disgust and apprehension on Desdemona's ashen face.

Suddenly the younger woman stood stiffly erect, lips thinned, and then she lifted her skirts with a return of self-possessed dignity and swept by her.

Madeleine remained unfazed. "I have a proposition for you, Desdemona," she called after her.

She didn't stop.

"I will keep your secret if you will keep mine."

That got her. Desdemona slowed her pace until she came to a halt, although she didn't turn around.

Madeleine sauntered toward her once more, regarding the lady's tight shoulders and properly rigid back, her perfectly coiled ringlets that hung from beneath her hat.

Desdemona didn't look at her, or speak, but stared straight ahead.

Madeleine lowered her voice although it was unnecessary as they again stood side by side on the vacant road. "Baron Rothebury is likely to be arrested for smuggling stolen opium, and this could happen within days."

The lady's composure weakened fractionally. Her gaze shifted briefly to Madeleine's face, for only a second in time, then back to the village square.

When no comment was forthcoming, Madeleine asked wryly, "Would that please you?"

Desdemona swallowed and lifted a gloved hand to her belly, covering it gingerly. "How do you know this?" she whispered without looking at her.

She shrugged minutely. "Tell me the truth about your pregnancy, and I will tell you the truth about Rothebury."

A gust of icy wind stirred up the loose snow on the ground in front of them, and Madeleine shielded her face with her muff, noticing at once how Desdemona did not.

"You've never been in love, have you, Mrs. Du-Mais?"

Madeleine had never been so surprised by a faintly spoken question, and she feared it showed in her immediate expression, though the woman probably didn't notice because she still refused to look at her.

"Have you, Desdemona?" she countered, feeling better to avoid her own confusing feelings altogether when they didn't apply. "Are you in love with Rothebury?"

Unexpectedly Desdemona smiled and turned her body to confront her at last, color returning to her cheeks. "I thought so, for a while," she admitted candidly. "But in actuality I was naive and allowed myself to be seduced by a snake who took advantage of my innocence and left me carrying a child he would never acknowledge as his."

It wasn't exactly a direct confession, but it told her the truth as she expected it. And because Madeleine had experienced the baron's charm and seductive manner firsthand, she believed it of him. But what mattered now was that this information gave them power, if they could find a way to use it.

"Would you like me to testify to the authorities about his illicit operation as I've seen it?"

Madeleine blinked, incredulous, unsure if she'd heard correctly, or even if the woman knew exactly what she offered. She'd never expected it and frankly wasn't sure how to respond.

Desdemona guessed her surprise and sneered. "It's why you're here talking to me, isn't it?"

She composed herself to utter, "Would you be willing to do that?"

The Englishwoman's thin blond eyebrows rose with the deepening crease in her forehead. "And risk social ruin and family disgrace?"

Madeleine's heart sank. She had been so hoping, but, of course, a lady of quality would never purposely soil her reputation so blatantly. If Desdemona provided information to the authorities, even under total secrecy, word of her conduct would eventually filter through the village and blacken her and ultimately her family's reputation forever. Irreversibly.

Desdemona laughed bitterly, shaking her head so abruptly the ringlets framing her face bounced across her cheeks. In that instant she looked twelve years old, and Madeleine felt not only sorry for her, but also a sharp pang of resentment on her behalf.

"I would be happy to help you, Mrs. DuMais. On one condition."

That statement nearly knocked her over. "What condition?"

"Tell me who you are."

For the first time Madeleine hesitated in answer, quickly scanning their immediate surroundings. They were alone, for all practical purposes, and nobody could hear them speaking. Telling Desdemona an abridged account of her mission in England really wasn't a concern. Her true misgiving was the very real possibility that she might in some way jeopardize Thomas's identity because he lived here, at least for now. But she could probably get around that for the sake of putting a devious spider in prison for a long time to come. It was worth the attempt.

She drew a long breath and faced Desdemona again, squarely. "You won't mention this to anyone." It was a shrewdly spoken statement, not a question.

"I believe," Desdemona reminded her articulately, "that you were the one who said we'd keep each other's secrets."

"Quite right," she agreed. Then, "I am a French native, brought to Winter Garden at your government's request to learn what I could about an opium smuggling operation in this vicinity. I soon began to suspect the baron, and I think I've discovered how he's doing it and why." She paused, then whispered, "Now, will you tell me what you know?"

Desdemona absorbed the information, her features growing taut with assessment. "Why you?" she pressed, nonplussed.

Madeleine was afraid she would ask that. "I work for the British government abroad," was all she said, hoping it would be enough.

"As Mr. Blackwood does in England," Desdemona remarked as the light began to dawn.

"Yes."

The younger woman bit her bottom lip, head cocked, very nearly smiling now, and then she straightened and looked to the snow at the foot of her gown.

"I only saw the opium once, wrapped inside two crates that he carried through the tunnel one night when he wasn't expecting me," she murmured. "I didn't know what it was initially, but he told me in his usual arrogant manner when I challenged him. I'm sure he thought I was safe to confide in since I couldn't very well reveal his operation without also announcing that I was on his property alone at night, or at least that I knew him far too intimately." She laughed again, nervously. "He was so furious when I surprised him, entering the tunnel on my own, hoping to seduce him. Of course, he took advantage of me even then, knowing it was the last time we were going to be together. I was aware that I carried his baby, but I didn't want to tell him until I had an assurance that he loved me and wanted to marry me. I'm from a good family, after all, and would make a respectable wife. He bedded me knowing he might get me with child. I naively assumed he would want me."

She raised her lashes, and this time her eyes were crystal clear and tear-filled. "He laughed at me when I confessed my love, Mrs. DuMais. I told him I loved him and wanted to marry him, but instead of being overjoyed at the prospect, or even just gentle with my feelings, he laughed at me and called me *loose* as he put his pants back *on*."

She hugged herself, her soft jaw tightening with supremely controlled rage as she boldly announced, "I never told him about the baby and I never will. He would only deny that it's his, and I refuse to be humiliated again. The Baron Rothebury is no gentleman. He is a viper, and I will do whatever it takes to see that he rots in prison if I cannot see him burn in hell."

Madeleine fought the urge to reach out to her, to wrap her arms around the lady's sagging shoulders in comfort. But decorum exhorted her to hold back. At least for now.

"What will you do?" she carried on very gently.

Desdemona knew she meant when the rumors began, when her family was socially disgraced after she divulged to the proper authorities her intimate involvement with a respectable baron in his home. In that instant, Madeleine pitied the woman.

"Let me tell you about my husband, Mrs. DuMais," Desdemona began in a clear, earnest voice. "He is an old family friend, someone I've been extremely close to for years. My mother never liked him because he is effeminate, preferring the pursuits of girls over boys' as a child. I never cared, because he is a tender soul who always listened to my complaints without judging and caught my tears when they fell on his shoulder. He and I were so much alike as children, typically the naughty one in the family, the disappointing one, though for different reasons, neither of us ever able to please our par-

ents and live up to their expectations." She inhaled
deeply and raised her hands to her face, prayer position,
speaking into her gloves. "I'm sure you'll understand
when I ask that you not repeat this."

"Of course," Madeleine replied at once.

"My husband is . . ." She squeezed her eyes shut and
then opened them again. "My husband prefers the company of men. Do you understand?"

Madeleine wondered if Desdemona expected her to
be shocked, or perhaps disconcerted by this news. Instead of questioning it, she simply nodded and admitted,
"I understand."

That seemed to satisfy the woman, as she wouldn't
have to explain. She began tapping her fingers together
at her mouth to carry on. "After the last night with Richard, when he mocked my love so shamelessly, I went
immediately to Randolph. I thank God every day that he
was still in Winter Garden and could console me. I was
desolate and"—she wavered—"and considered taking
my own life. He, being the greatest friend I've ever had,
suggested marriage to each other, saving both of our
families disgrace. He would no longer be ridiculed for
what people suspected were his sinful indulgences. I
would have a father for my child. It took me only two
hours to agree."

Madeleine felt admiration for both of them through
every pore, though she really had no idea how to express
that exactly. But Desdemona continued without waiting
for a reply.

"In one week I am leaving Winter Garden, Mrs.
DuMais. My husband has invited me to live with his
family in the northern country as they recently relocated
to Belford, near the Northumberland Coast. They are
quite affluent, my husband's father having just retired
from the textile industry, and they've shown an interest

in our residing with them. Randolph may be gone
through the years on duty with the Army, so it's best
that I stay with family who will take me in gladly and
help me care for my child. My mother, as you know, is
not altogether fond of me now, and will likely despise
me when she learns of my betrayal. Randolph's family
will probably, and hopefully, never hear of it, being so
far removed from life in this village. That is the only
reason I will consent to speaking with the magistrate."

Madeleine didn't comment on the fact that the arrest
of a baron would be very serious, widespread, and scandalous news. With any luck, Desdemona could remain
rather anonymous in the whole affair, and perhaps only
be known to a select few.

Madeleine reached out for her at last, taking one of
Desdemona's hands in hers, somewhat assuming that the
lady would jerk herself free of any comforting embrace.
She didn't. If anything, the simple touch relaxed her,
and she sagged even deeper into her large pelisse-
mantle, the wisp of a genuine smile of gratitude threatening to cross her pale lips.

"What does your mother have to say about your leaving, Desdemona?"

The younger woman shook her head and closed her
eyes for a second or two, as if to shield out the enmity
to come. "She doesn't yet know, but I intend to tell her
soon. It doesn't really much matter now, though. My
sister will never find a husband, my father's name will
be tarnished, and the very respectable Penelope
Bennington-Jones will be ruined along with her loose
daughter who defiled them all by laying with Richard
Sharon, the great Baron Rothebury—"

"Who seduced an innocent while he stole expensive
opium and smuggled it into the country illegally," Madeleine interjected as if to soften the brewing storm await-

ing the residents of Winter Garden. "He is not a saint, Desdemona, remember that. Your family will survive, and you'll be fine. You're a strong woman and you have a husband who is willing to provide for you, who obviously cares for your safety and comfort. Many a lady should be so fortunate."

As if caught in a sweet memory, Desdemona smiled at that and squeezed her hand once. "I will never know physical intimacy again, never feel passion—"

"You don't know that," Madeleine cut in.

Desdemona shook her head sadly in denial and pulled her hand away, turning once more toward the village square. "I do know that, but I will have my child to love and my husband as my friend. It is enough."

Madeleine sighed, unable to argue such practicality, and started to walk down the road again, stepping away from the gutter filled with muddy, melting snow. Desdemona followed at her side.

"When are you returning to France?" she asked her quietly, in mild contemplation as she changed the subject.

Madeleine didn't particularly want to think about that. "I'm not certain. Soon, though."

Desdemona eyed her carefully. "What do you intend to do about Mr. Blackwood?"

She felt her pulse quicken but she tried to ignore it. "I'm not sure what you mean."

For the first time since they'd met at the church, the young lady at her side gave every indication of being the enlightened one, the mature one, the one with the knowledge as she smiled cleverly and shook her head very slowly.

"He's in love with you, you know."

Madeleine paused in her stride, her mouth going dry. "I beg your pardon?"

"In love," Desdemona repeated, "and very deeply, I think."

The woman was clearly mistaken. "I don't think so."

"No?" Desdemona chuckled at that. "Everybody in the village is aware of it, Mrs. DuMais. It is so extremely obvious I was certain you knew or at least suspected. But then I suppose where love is concerned we're all a little blind, especially when we don't want to see what is before us."

Madeleine stilled from head to toe, awash with numbness, feeling trapped suddenly. Like a doe running head-on into her hunter.

"May I offer you a suggestion, Mrs. DuMais?"

The words sounded sharp and shrill to her ears, echoing loudly. Coldness blanketed her, and a wisp of wind swept snow crystals into the air to strike the bare skin on her face.

But she was a professional and refused to notice these things, refused to acknowledge a remark that was clearly unfounded. Attempting to remain dignified, she responded politely, "Of course."

Desdemona scrutinized her, up and down, then admonished, "I would never forgo a chance to be with someone who loved me passionately. That will never happen to me now, because I will not leave my husband. I take my marriage vows very seriously, and we have a child on the way whose protection must be considered." She stepped closer and dropped her voice to just above a whisper. "But I saw Mr. Blackwood look at you once, while the two of you were walking together in the village, and I read his feelings for you on his face like an open book. He loves you desperately, Mrs. DuMais, the word is spreading rapidly through Winter Garden, and I am envious. He is a cripple, true, but I would follow him, or any man, to the farthest edges of the earth to have him look at *me* like that. Just once."

Madeleine had never been so disconcerted by a disclosure in her life. She stood there, stunned, gaping foolishly, head spinning. Suddenly the words she'd been hearing in her mind all morning no longer sounded beautiful, but loud, raucous, piercing.

I don't want you to leave, Madeleine.

All I want is you, Madeleine. All I've ever wanted is you.

Will you love me now, Maddie?

He had asked her that with a tangible fear in his eyes, and at the time she'd assumed he'd been referring to lovemaking. Now the specifics of his phrasing took on a grave new depth that she could no longer ignore. What Desdemona suggested she had, in fact, considered herself, but not so carefully. Perhaps she just hadn't wanted to see it at all. She could deal with his lovemaking, a casual affair with a definite conclusion to which they both aspired. But she didn't think she could accept his love. Not real, passionate, desperate love. She didn't know how to handle it or return it. Madeleine felt herself begin to shake. She clutched her hands tightly together in her muff, trying to remain collected.

Desdemona stood erect once more and wiped her palms down her mantle nonchalantly, no longer looking at her. "I'm sure you're aware that my mother hates you," she confided frankly.

Madeleine didn't know whether to laugh or scream or thank the lady politely for such a quick shift in topic. "I suppose she does," she managed to reply, her mouth as dry and grating as carpenter's sandpaper.

Desdemona brushed a ringlet from an icy-pink cheek. "Do you know why?"

She searched the younger woman's round, innocent

face for a moment, uncertain how she was supposed to answer. "I imagine because I am French."

Desdemona smiled satisfactorily and peered into her eyes. "But you are wrong, Mrs. DuMais. My mother despises you because you are so very English."

Madeleine felt the blood drain from her face, and Desdemona snickered delightedly when she noticed it, hugging herself again and rocking back on her heels.

"You weren't prepared for that, were you?"

She couldn't move or speak.

Desdemona guessed this apparently and carried on with a casual lift of her shoulders. "Aside from your very thick French accent, you are the epitome of all that is respected in an Englishwoman, Mrs. DuMais. You are cordial when others rudely defame you, educated for your class, reserved as you should be, graceful and sophisticated in style and manner, and your grasp of the English language is superb. My mother abhors seeing those qualities in a Frog."

Desdemona's gaze became intense. "It's possible there are many Frenchwomen like you. I wouldn't know. The point is, although we place so much value on breeding and class, it's obvious that the place or status of one's birth is highly irrelevant to the person one becomes. You could be an Englishwoman should you choose to be, and others would learn to respect you as one. Perhaps that's what Mr. Blackwood admires about you, and wants you to see in yourself while you're here."

Desdemona turned her attention to the village square, so empty and bleak and white. "You know, I have lived in Winter Garden my entire life and I have never seen it snow. Everything changes, and I suppose this is a sign that it's time to move on." She glanced a final time to Madeleine and nodded once formally. "I will do what I can to help you, but I am leaving Saturday. The magistrate must call on me before then. Good-bye, Mrs. DuMais. I wish you well in your endeavors."

Then with a tug at her wide skirts, Desdemona whisked past Madeleine and continued down the quiet road toward the home she was soon to leave, her shoes crunching noisily on the narrow, ice-covered street.

Twenty-one

Madeleine returned to the cottage in a daze, walking blindly, slowly at first, mindless to the fact that her extremities were freezing, her nose, cheeks, and lips numb from cold.

She couldn't decide if Desdemona was thoroughly insane or incredibly wise beyond her years. The facts remained that, yes, things change, times change. Her life was not now the same as it was last night before she and Thomas had made love. Nor was it the same as it had been even early this morning when she'd gone to Desdemona, fully in control of her mind and emotions, with a professional purpose, only to return dumfounded, uncomfortable, and scared of the unknown.

She needed to see Thomas, she decided, picking up the pace and praying she wouldn't slip on the ice. She needed to feel his lips on hers, his skin next to hers, to feel him inside her. She wanted desperately to be with him, to run from him, wished suddenly that she had never met him. Mostly she just wanted to look into his eyes and witness for herself what Desdemona said was there for all to see.

But could *she* see it? If indeed he loved her, shouldn't she have recognized it before now if others had? Had she been blind to it intentionally? Or was the notion of some endless love he felt for her pure folly on the part of an impressionable young woman with romantic dreams?

Life was so complicated when feelings were involved. She had never been passionately in love with anyone so how could she know how it felt? Jacques had loved her, and she had loved him, she supposed, but that was somehow different from what she felt for Thomas. Her feelings for Jacques had been comforting, soothing, companionable, simple, and their lovemaking had been pleasant and, in general, fulfilling. Indeed, with the few men she'd bedded over the years, sex had ranged from the enjoyable to the routine, satisfying a mutual lust and allowing for a measure of brief closeness. Nothing more and nearly always forgettable.

From the moment she'd met Thomas, however, her reactions to him as a man had been unusual—remarkable, really—and thoroughly unexpected. With Thomas the air crackled when they touched, her stomach fluttered when they kissed, her heart pounded erratically when he walked into the room and looked her up and down with his dark, narrowed, direct eyes, drawing her in with his irresistible mouth. Their lovemaking was like nothing she'd ever experienced with anyone, though she couldn't say exactly why. It was just . . . magnetic.

What *did* she feel for him, exactly? She really didn't know him all that well. She knew many of his likes and dislikes, his social and political views, his aspirations and devotions because they'd had a great deal of time to discuss them, and yet much of himself he kept secret. Could she possibly be in love with the part she knew, love him as he was?

More significant, though, was the idea that he might be deeply in love with her. She really didn't think it was possible. No man had ever loved her deeply before, and she supposed she was partly to blame for that. She just didn't allow anybody to get emotionally close enough. She respected herself, enjoyed and admired the woman she had become, but time could not forget that she was the illegitimate daughter of an opium-addicted actress, who had danced in music halls and lost her virginity at the age of fifteen with the first of many lovers, and Thomas very well knew all of this. She was also nearing thirty. Many a man might want her as a mistress, but no respectable gentleman would ever want her as a loving wife. Not when they knew who she was, which was precisely why her work came first above all things. It was all in the world she had that was truly hers, that she had earned using her own cleverness, sagacity, dedication, and determination. It was the only thing that would get her through life with a measure of pride and happiness, as well as a sense of accomplishment. She would never give it up for love or marriage. Never. Thomas knew this because she'd told him so.

Did he love her anyway? After a few minutes of serious reflection she concluded that he probably did not. He was likely infatuated, as she'd paid him undivided attention, made love to him by pressing him into it when he had denied it would happen, had become his friend and working companion, but they had only known each other for a few weeks. Surely love took longer to bloom. Still, it left her with few answers and many troublesome questions.

The wind had stirred the loose snow so that the porch was covered with a thin layer of ice when she finally stepped onto it a few minutes later. She unlatched the door and walked inside the cottage, the heat of the coal

fire and the scent of furniture wax and toasted bread
hitting her soundly with the rustic feel of home. This
wasn't her home, though, and she would do well to remember that. She would be leaving shortly, to return to
her life in France, to sunshine and warmth and her private residence on the Rue de la Fleur in Marseille, to
her maid, Marie-Camille, and her extensive wardrobe
and food that she missed. And her work in France. It
was where she was needed. Regardless of the looming
sadness at the thought of leaving Thomas, she must remember where she was needed.

With renewed resolve, she unbuttoned her mantle with
cold, stiff fingers, then hung it on the rack with her muff.
She shivered, quickly rubbing her hands up and down
her upper arms to help them warm, then smoothed a
palm over the coiled braid at her nape to make sure it
was still in place. That done, she straightened her spine
and fairly glided into the parlor, and then the kitchen
where she found Thomas, pen in hand, head bowed,
mulling over paperwork scattered across the table. She
paused at the door and stared, warming to the bone at
the rugged, masculine, arresting sight of him, her resolve
instantaneously deserting her.

The cloudiness of the day made lamplight essential,
and the glow from it created a thin, wavy streak of silver
down the center of his dark hair that fell without his
notice over his forehead. He wore plain, black trousers,
a white linen shirt rolled up at the cuffs and unbuttoned
at the neck, and, of course, his expensive, specially made
leather boots with the gold buckles and the wooden,
right foot insert that he'd shown her in detail this morning. His face, unshaven since yesterday, gave him a
scruffy appearance, tempting her to slide her palm across
it, to feel the tingling roughness against her skin, which

in turn reminded her how those bristles had sensually grazed her inner thighs last night.

Just looking at him, thinking about that experience, made her weaken inside. Her belly quivered, her breath quickened, and as she considered it now, she realized she'd never felt any of these feelings for another man. Just Thomas.

Abruptly he glanced in her direction and jerked his body upright, startled to see her, having been so engrossed in his paperwork he hadn't heard her come in.

Her gaze met his, melded with it, and she leaned against the doorjamb, arms crossed over her bosom as her lips curled up ever so slowly in a soft smile of contentment.

He noticed it and grinned boyishly, showing polished teeth and blushing skin.

Blushing. Thomas was blushing. From thoughts of last night? From embarrassment at their heated, uncontrollable passion of only hours ago? She ached to know, but wouldn't ask. His reaction was just so charming, so wonderful and endearing, making him look years younger and utterly content.

"I sent an urgent note to Sir Riley," he said after clearing his throat. "I explained the situation in detail, and expect to hear back from him as early as tomorrow."

She said nothing, just watched him intently—the fullness of his mouth, the tiny, almost indistinguishable cleft in his chin, the way his eyelashes curved out long and thick, his refined, aristocratic nose, the way that ever-present piece of hair that never seemed to bother him fell down between his dark brows.

"Did you learn anything?" he asked when she didn't respond, resting his pen in the inkwell on the table, his voice a bit more sober.

"Yes," she murmured, never taking her eyes from the

glimmering, honey-brown recesses of his. "I think I did."

And then without further remark she drifted toward him and gracefully sat on his thighs, ignoring the surprise on his face as she pulled her legs up and under her gown, curling into him. She snuggled against his massive chest, wrapping her arms around his neck and clinging to him as she began to kiss his jaw and cheek, inhaling the scent—Thomas's scent—that she'd come to know so well.

His response was predictable and fast. He embraced her without comment and began kissing her in return, small pecks of affection to her cheeks and chin and brow, his lips feather-soft.

Immediately she'd had enough of the preliminary. Heat rising, she quickly took his mouth with hers and kissed him deeply, possessively, aching, needing, and he sensed it all, felt everything. He raised his hands behind her and unpinned her braid, letting her hair fall loosely down her back and then threading his fingers through it until it began to come apart. Then one hand was on her breast, kneading it through her gown, caressing her nipple to a point of delightful sensation. A whisper-soft moan escaped her mouth.

She felt his erection just barely through the layers of clothing, and she adjusted herself on his lap a little, moving as close as possible, spreading her legs for his probing hand. He obliged her unspoken demand, taking advantage of her position by inserting his palm up her gown to caress her calf, stroking it over her stocking. She wove her fingers through his hair and then pushed her hips up, begging tacitly for his touch.

He groaned then, coming alive with a burning raw hunger, and suddenly there was fire—searing heat—between them. She clawed at his shirt until the first two buttons popped, and then her mouth found his chest and she traced his nipples with her wet tongue. He groped for her petticoats and pulled at them until he was able to shove his hand inside, fingers searching, finding the slit then probing it.

He stroked her, slowly at first, and then quickly, more intimately as she became wetter and slicker against his hand.

She moaned softly at the back of her throat, stealing quick breaths when she could, kissing the muscles of his chest, raising her lips to his neck, his jaw again, tracing his scar and then his mouth with the fine point of her tongue.

His breathing grew shallow, but he never gave up the relentless pursuit of her pleasure as she grew closer to it.

It was so fast, so hot, so charged.

Magnetic.

Within seconds she felt herself rising to the edge of satisfaction as his fingers explored, stroked, his mouth took hers, his tongue plunged inside to suck.

Yes! her mind screamed as she kissed him back fervently, squirming and pushing against his hand. *Yes, Thomas, yes!*

Love me!

And then she experienced that glorious explosion within. She jerked her head back and closed her eyes to the intensity of his, crying out her pleasure, savoring the wonderful, rich moment as she never had before.

Bliss enveloped her for seconds, and then she raised herself, held tightly to his neck, and snuggled into his chest.

"I want to stay here forever," she heard in a far-off whisper, realizing only partially that the words came from her.

He didn't ask for clarification. He withdrew his hand from under her gown, lifted her in his arms, holding her close as his aching, tired, damaged limbs carried her slowly from the kitchen, up the stairs, and into his bedroom.

Twenty-two

Dreamily Madeleine awakened to a dark, gloomy morning and the sound of steadily tapping rain on the rooftop above. It had been falling for two days, melting all the snow, which naturally made the roads a muddy mess that iced over during the night and turned the village an ugly brown color. Madeleine detested the unusual cold spell outside when she needed to brave it, but she cherished the warmth within the cottage, so much so, in fact, that she was not looking forward at all to this afternoon's meeting with Sir Riley that was bound to be the beginning of the inevitable end of her stay in Winter Garden.

Although she hadn't felt him leave, Thomas had already risen from her side and was probably preparing tea for them downstairs. She took the moment by herself to snuggle deeper under the covers, avoiding the chill in the air until she was forced to confront it.

She'd slept in the nude for the last two marvelous nights in Thomas's large bed, in Thomas's arms, on Thomas's pillow that smelled of him, in Thomas's room that so perfectly fit his personality. The room, in fact, was rather subdued in point of function but carried conspicuous traces of his personal elegance, such as his wardrobe of four fine woolen suits and complimentary silk shirts, his carved, ivory jewel case that sat atop a finely crafted, gold handled, mahogany highboy that matched the headboard and a decorative chest at the foot of his bed—a larger bed than hers. And most striking of all, most captivating of all, was the notable oil painting—very old and surrounded by an expensive, gilded frame—of a large, peach-colored country estate at the bottom of a sloping hill. Emerald green grass and lush oak trees filled out the terrain encircling the two-story house. Colorful peonies, chrysanthemums, and roses lined the gravel path that circled around to the front marble white steps rising between two graceful pillars. Thomas had brought the painting with him from his home in Eastleigh, and it was the only item to brighten the four dark walls.

Sighing, accepting the inevitable, Madeleine finally dragged her body upright and shivered as the cold air came into contact with her skin. At the very same moment Thomas entered the bedroom carrying a tray and looking devastatingly handsome in a worn, ecru linen shirt, unbuttoned at the neck, and navy trousers.

He smiled at her mischievously. "I brought you breakfast, but if you're trying to seduce me, it's working."

She followed his gaze and realized at once that her nipples were hard from the icy air. "Yes, I rather enjoy keeping a room cold on the outside chance of seducing the next gentleman who enters."

He closed the door behind him with his left booted foot. "You'd seduce someone other than me?"

He sounded hurt, in a wry manner that made her smile. Propping up the pillows behind her head and lean-

ing back on them, she said, "Only if he had more
money."

"Oh, I see . . ." Tray in hand, he walked to her side
of the bed and, without looking at her, placed their food
in the center of the mattress, beside her legs that were
still beneath the blankets. "Funny, though, I would only
expect a statement like that from a virgin. Or perhaps a
widow. You are neither." Before she could respond, he
placed both hands on the coverlet, one on each side of
her hips, quickly lowered his head, and took one of her
nipples into his mouth, sucking it gently, expertly.

It had an obvious effect on her body, but she resisted
with a little laugh and a push with her fingers through
his hair. "You have made your point, sir. Now kindly
let me eat before it gets cold."

Groaning, he pulled back, then dropped a quick, solid
kiss to her closed lips. "I brought enough for both of
us."

He stood again and grasped the handles of the tray as
she positioned herself against the headboard, leaving her
breasts bare to his view should he forget how much he
enjoyed them. It was the least she could do, she thought
with some self-centered amusement.

She turned her attention to the food. He'd scrambled
eggs, fried ham, spread what appeared to be blackberry
jam on thick slices of toast, and completed the meal with
a generous portion of canned pears. He'd divided the
food between two china plates, and added two mugs of
tea with cream and sugar. Undoubtedly delicious, and
her stomach growled.

"This smells heavenly," she praised with convincing
honesty.

"Thank you." He sat beside her, spreading his own
napkin on his thighs. "Madam," he offered with his
palm.

She grinned and lifted a fork. "You're the only man I've ever known who cooks, Thomas."

"Ahh, but you're the only woman I've ever cooked for, Madeleine," he replied jovially.

"Really? So why do you cook for me?" she asked after swallowing her first bite of steaming eggs.

He shrugged a shoulder and studied his ham while he cut it. "Someone has to do it. Beth can't be here for every meal, and you're obviously too pampered to cook for me, at least for breakfast when you prefer lounging in bed."

"Ha!" She fairly giggled, then leaned forward and kissed the side of his lips. "That's an excuse if I've ever heard one, Mr. Blackwood. I have yet to lounge in your presence."

He grinned but added nothing more as they both focused on the food.

"Sir Riley should be arriving by four," Thomas disclosed matter-of-factly, after a few moments of silent eating. "I imagine he'll be punctual."

Madeleine tried to ignore the sense of unhappiness that managed to creep its way under her skin, while recognizing at the same time that this was the opening she needed to discuss the central issue facing just the two of them.

After swallowing a spoonful of pears and taking a sip of her tea, she dabbed the corners of her mouth with her napkin and delved bravely into the subject of their real concern.

"You know I'm going to be leaving England soon, Thomas," she reminded him quietly, although she knew he had to assume as much.

He didn't look at her but took a large swallow of his tea. "I don't know why we need to be discussing that now. Our work here isn't completed."

That was true, and yet he didn't exactly say he wanted her to stay, which, by so evading the issue, had put the burden of explanation on her shoulders.

She had to be strong in her stand to bring their affair to a satisfactory conclusion, and now was as good a time as any. She didn't want to part enemies, because truthfully she didn't really want to part at all. What she'd said to him after her talk with Desdemona was true. She *wanted* to stay here forever—detached from the outside world and encircled in the comfort of his arms. But she'd confessed that want in the heat of passion, and he should know that such wants, while desirable, weren't practical. Leaving was simply something that must be done, however unpleasant for either of them, and under the circumstances, she couldn't see an alternative.

With a long breath, she pushed her unfinished eggs and toast away from her. "Thomas, our relationship has been wonderful—"

"I think so, too," he remarked casually, lifting his fork, piled with eggs, to his lips. "And far too involving to give up after such a short time. We have lots to learn about each other, Madeleine."

She watched him fill his mouth and chew, regarding his food, not reacting at all as if she were serious. Setting a firm tone, she clarified her statement. "It's been a wonderful few weeks, Thomas, but affairs like ours always end. I'm not happy about it, but let's let it end satisfactorily, shall we? As friends and companionable colleagues? Don't make this harder than it has to be."

He swallowed and wiped his lips with his napkin, looking at her again, quiet and evaluating for a moment, though his expression had intensified. He no longer appeared quite so congenial.

"Classifying what we've shared intimately as a simple affair is awfully convenient for you, isn't it?" he returned dryly, becoming disinterested in the remainder of his breakfast as he lowered his plate to the tray. "It allows you to return home, your time in England neatly tied up into a little package of delightful memories that you can tuck away in the back of your mind while you revert to your private, uncomplicated life."

That irritated her, perhaps because he was all too close to conveying the truth, though she would never admit that to him. She also didn't want to argue the point. Regardless of their personal feelings, she needed to remain pragmatic.

Folding her hands primly in her lap, she tried again to clarify. "I didn't mean to imply that what we've had between us has been fanciful or unimportant, only that it hasn't . . ." Her forehead creased as she attempted to find the right words. "It hasn't been very practical in terms of finality. We both knew this love affair would end sometime."

"Did we?" He looked at her blankly, features flat. "So this relationship, to you, is impractical because you thought of it as temporary?"

The more he talked in circles, the more irritated she became, and all the more flustered. "The relationship itself has been practical in that we both found comfort and companionship in each other's arms for a time. *Continuing* it would be impractical."

"I see."

When he said nothing more, she decided to add in explanation, "I think it would be more accurate to describe our relationship as a short, enjoyable . . . escapade, with memories we'll both treasure for years to come."

He remained silent for another second or two, but he peered into her eyes, almost intrusively. It made her uncomfortable.

"Tell me, Maddie," he murmured, his voice becoming resonant in the small room, "how do you feel about France?"

That bothered her tremendously, although she wasn't sure why precisely. She did her best to hide it by stalling. "I'm not sure what you want me to say—"

"Just answer the question," he insisted.

After a moment of edginess, she fairly announced, "I enjoy its warmth, of course. I miss that and my home in Marseille, my personal things, my work—"

"That's a very superficial answer," he cut in rather sharply, "and not what I asked you."

She squirmed a little and dropped her lashes to avoid his gaze, studying the tight weave of the dark blue sheets, refusing to respond to a query that concerned very complex and deep-seated feelings of anguish and longing and resentment—toward her mother for ignoring her goodness, her father for leaving her time and again and finally forever, for her childhood of which she had been robbed, and her past in a country that offered her, in itself, nothing.

Instead, she whispered, "Desdemona thinks you're in love with me."

The air between them shifted violently, like a fierce, blustering thunderstorm. She could positively feel the abrupt static charge as the blood began to surge through her veins and her words, and fears, hit their target.

"Is it true?" she urged in a silky wisp of hope, her apprehension about his forthcoming answer probably apparent in her somewhat ill-confident voice.

Huskily, seconds later, he whispered, "Would you stay in England if I said I was?"

Her eyes shot up to meet his, and were suddenly seized by his flagrant, torrid gaze.

She caught her breath; her skin flushed and her heart

fluttered. Then the truth revealed its ugly self, and all flickering hope died within her. She understood his desires all too clearly. "Would you lie to me to keep me here? I make a marvelous plaything, don't I, Thomas?"

He shook his head slowly and sneered with disgust, leaning back on his palms, though he never glanced away. "Is that what you think I want? You've insulted me by insulting my opinion of you, my feelings for you, but I'm going to ignore it," he maintained grimly, his dark, heated eyes steady as they blatantly challenged her. "I have more at stake by answering your question about love than you do in hearing that answer, Madeleine. So I'll ask you again: If I professed a great love for you, would you stay in England?"

His continued ambiguity made her truly frustrated and angry to the point where she could no longer avoid revealing it. "Remain in England to do what? Be your ready mistress? Marry you? Become the devoted wife to a . . . a . . . middle-aged, intellectual spy, while we roam the countryside solving crimes together when we're not entertaining our neighbors at tea? Where would we live? A small cottage in a tiny village in Eastleigh? How would we spend our days? Our evenings?" Her voice became frigid. "I do not knit, garden, or mother children, Thomas. Regardless of love, there has to be more substance to an extended relationship than enjoying one another's company while playing chess."

His eyes grew caustic and stormy, narrowing to thin slits. "I suppose there's nothing more to say since you seem to find the idea of a future with me repugnant—"

"I do not," she seethed in a quiet, controlled vehemence, sitting forward, mindless of the sheet and blankets falling to her waist, exposing her. "Do *not* twist my words to take the easy way out by making me the villain. What I'm saying is that I find all of *this*"—she flung her hand wide—"a fairy tale, and fairy tales may be marvelous, but they are for children, Thomas. In a few short years I will be middle-aged as well, and losing my appeal. What gentleman will want me then? Would you? Let us be very candid here. I am a used woman, a woman who has lived on my own, supporting myself and doing what was needed to provide for my necessities while at the same time attempting to keep what dignity I possess intact. When I was twenty, I found that opportunity in my work for your government and I took it. I won't give it up for love, for you, for anything or anyone, not because I don't want to, but because I *can't*. The only way I can protect my future is to save as much of my income as possible while working at a profession where I am valued, where my position is secure. What I do is vitally important to my life in later years, my self-preservation, my commitment to my father's homeland, and most importantly my self-respect. My work is all I have, and I am needed—*needed*—in France."

Although she knew it would hurt him deeply, she sat erect and squared her shoulders defiantly, adding tersely, "I believe you are infatuated with me, Thomas, not in love. Lots of men have felt the same way before you, and there will probably be others to follow, before I become old and undesirable to all of them. It is an illusion, and illusions are easy to put aside when they are honestly faced. This is what you will do when I leave."

For an endless moment all that could be heard was the pattering of rain on the roof above and his slow, steady breathing as he sat only a foot away, eyes hard as glass, jaw rigidly set, his body like stone. Then when she thought her pounding heart might explode through her chest, he slowly looked away and stood, walking tensely to the door.

Pausing with his hand on the knob, and without a

glance in her direction, he said brusquely, "I don't see how expressing my feelings is relevant when you've obviously decided they don't matter."

He left the bedroom, slamming the door behind him for good measure.

Twenty-three

Madeleine bathed at the inn for a final time, plaited her clean, wet hair and set it in two hoops around her ears. She then dressed in her plum silk day gown, bundled herself into her mantle and muff, hood over her head to avoid the chill, and walked swiftly back to the cottage.

Her heart was breaking, she supposed, and yet her mind was firmly set. She would not give in to irrational feelings or harsh persuasion or the sight of Thomas looking at her as if he were losing his greatest friend. She hadn't seen him since their row this morning, and that was probably for the best. He had left the cottage, and alone she had cleaned the breakfast dishes, tidied up, dressed, and packed some of her things for her return trip which would likely be a day or two from now. She'd visited with Mrs. Mossley and Lady Isadora for the last time, extending her good wishes and promising to write, explaining that her work with the scholar was almost finished.

She hadn't cried in years, and didn't intend to at her departure from Winter Garden. It was a necessary part-

ing, and she would make the best of the sadness to follow. The snowfall had been magical three nights ago, as
had her and Thomas's feelings for each other when
they'd made love beside the fire. Since then a gray
bleakness had fallen on the village, and reality on them.

She would get over the pain of her departure, and she
would not cry.

She would not cry.

Madeleine strode briskly onto the porch and opened
the door to the cottage, her heart dancing nervously because she knew Thomas would be back by now. She
didn't want to argue, but she wasn't sure she could resist
him if he tried to make love to her, and she was fairly
certain he would try. Giving in to him would be disas-
trous, for the act would only unmask how she felt deep
within her, exposing the lie she'd so emphatically proclaimed just a few hours ago.

But Sir Riley was due to arrive at four, and it was
already half past three. Hopefully the time would keep
her safe from revealing what was in her heart.

She heard deep male voices as she entered the foyer,
however, coming from the front room, and she quickly
realized that the Londoner had arrived early. Her agita-
tion increased with every step as she walked into the
parlor. She should have been here to welcome him at
his arrival, as Sir Riley was her employer, and all that
she did was under scrutiny while in his company. Even
now she must look and act her best, her most confident
self, and that would be a terribly difficult thing to do
with Thomas standing only a few feet away, watching
her, thinking about the intimate conversation they'd
shared where they'd separated so hastily and on such
uncertain terms.

She noticed him first, dressed rather formally in a
charcoal-gray suit, black and gray diagonally striped

waistcoat, white silk shirt, and black cravat. His hair was combed away from his face and he had recently shaved. Her stomach clenched again at just the sight of him, for as usual, he was impressive to behold, his handsome, commanding presence pervading the room.

Sir Riley, the younger man by two or three years, was just as imposing as Thomas, and almost as tall and firmly built. He had raven hair and hazel eyes that absorbed detail rather than looked it over, and the intelligence to match the finest scholar. He also possessed a keen sense of truth that gave him the natural ability to discern either a flagrant lie or the slightest prevarication, from the common individual to the well-bred. This made him the perfect man for his position in national security, and Madeleine admired him tremendously for his talents. He maintained a shrewd bearing, but his personality was altogether charming. Also an extremely handsome man, he was someone she might have taken an interest in at another place, in another circumstance. Now such thoughts seemed irrelevant, even laughably adulterous.

Both men noticed her at the same time—Thomas standing squarely in front of the mantelpiece, a small fire burning in the grate behind his legs, Sir Riley leaning against the north windowsill, gazing out to the gray stillness of the midafternoon. They became silent immediately and turned her way when they heard the clicking of her heals on the foyer floor.

Thomas's eyes grazed her figure once, thoroughly, his expression neutral, and at that moment she would have given her life savings to know exactly what he was thinking, what he thought of her, how he felt. That sudden realization staggered her with an incredulity so great she nearly began to cry on the spot. She refused to stay in England because of the life she'd created for herself in France; and yet it was amazingly clear to her now that her future meant very little if Thomas couldn't be happy. *She* could make him happy, and there was no one alive who deserved it more—

"My dear, Madeleine!" Sir Riley fairly bellowed, breaking into her troubled thoughts. "How lovely to see you again, and under such engaging circumstances." He moved toward her, his gait formal, but a smile of unaffected pleasure lighting his face.

She blinked quickly to recover herself, yanking her mind back to the present situation, planting an enchanting grin on her lips and extending her hand. "It is always a pleasure, Sir Riley, and how well you look. Was your trip to Winter Garden satisfactory?"

"Thank you, it was, quite," he replied, drawing her knuckles to his lips then swiftly releasing them. "A frigid ride on the train as I forgot a hot-water bottle, and there wasn't one available. But at least the snow had melted, and the roads were once again passable by coach when I journeyed into the village." He shook his head, brows drawn in consideration. "Rather unusual for this part of England to see such snowfall."

"So I've been told," she acknowledged politely.

He stood back on his heels, hands clasped together behind him. "I took a room at the inn upon my immediate arrival. It seems to be warm and comfortable enough for my needs. I intend to get a good night's rest before the events of tomorrow unfold."

She glanced to Thomas, who stood unyielding in front of the small fire, head bowed, gaze down, arms to his sides, though he nervously tapped his fingers against his thumbs.

"Perhaps it would be best, Sir Riley, if we all sit so that you can explain what is to take place," she submitted warmly. "Or have you two already been discussing it?"

His eyes widened as if he couldn't imagine that. "Oh, no, not really," he insisted. "Our conversation has centered mostly around the unusual weather and everyone's health, of course. That sort of thing. And I'm very glad to know you've both managed to escape the nasty influenza that's so recently struck. But, no, we were waiting for you before we began an in-depth discussion, Madeleine."

Madeleine suppressed a laugh of delight. The man was highly charming in an extremely adorable way, reminding her of a favorite stuffed doll a child might cuddle with and carry by the throat.

No, not a doll. A large, stuffed bear.

"Would you care for tea?" she asked sweetly, wondering why Thomas hadn't offered it.

"Oh, no. Thank you, no," he declined with a wave of his hand. "I'm saving my appetite for stew and ale at the inn very shortly. I won't be here long, as I'm sure you and"—he shot a quick glance to Thomas—"and Mr. Blackwood have much to discuss."

That statement struck her forcibly, though she wasn't exactly sure why.

How much does he know?

"Of course, Sir Riley," she said as expected, refusing to give her discomfiture away as she ushered him to the sofa with her palm. "Please be seated."

Thomas had yet to say a word upon her entering. She tried not to let that bother her as she walked around the tea table, her skirts sweeping across his booted legs even when she tried to avoid them, seating herself at the farthest end of the sofa, away from his chair should he choose to occupy it.

He didn't appear to even notice her, remaining transfixed on the rug at his feet, his hands behind his back now, the slightest of frowns crossing his complex face.

Sir Riley sat beside her, one leg crossed over the knee of the other, maintaining a relaxed demeanor as he cleared his throat to begin.

"Well," he started, attempting to chip away the ice, "let's get down to the business at hand, shall we? I . . . um . . . think I have a plan in mind that will entrap the baron and expose his unlawful doings as he carries out another illicit theft."

Madeleine's eyes widened in surprise, and pride. English pride. How clever this man was. "You're going to set him up to be caught in the act," she whispered aloud. "How marvelous. I cannot wait to see the shock in his eyes when he is arrested. What an arrogant man."

Thomas looked at her for the first time, betraying nothing. "It's the only way to be sure we can convict him," he remarked evenly. A small smile tugged at the left corner of his mouth, momentarily hiding his scar, though she wasn't certain if it was a smile of genuine or sarcastic pleasure. "Desdemona, although a magnificent witness, could turn on us and decide not to testify at the last minute." He lowered his voice to a meaningful murmur, "We need proof, and she is, after all, a fanciful young lady."

The hidden significance of that did not go unnoticed, and Madeleine squirmed on the sofa, turning her attention to Sir Riley. "I'd like to be involved, then. He wants to take me through the tunnels, and with a note to him, I'm sure it would be easy for me to gain access. Perhaps I can . . . *accidently* discover something, catch him in the act of lying. Maybe unnerving him is enough." She shrugged. "Then again, maybe I can see the opium and witness the rest of his operation."

Sir Riley became immediately uncomfortable, his gaze shifting from Thomas to her and back again. He shuffled his feet by changing their positions, his hands rubbed his trousers over his thighs, and with that, Madeleine got the first real hint that things were not as they appeared.

"Is there something you're not telling me?" she asked cordially, her pulse beginning to speed beneath her calm, professional manner.

Sir Riley adjusted his posture and studied the tea table. Thomas, as he had since she'd arrived, appeared composed, and very definitely in charge.

"I think, Madeleine," Sir Riley admitted at last, "we've developed a plan that would allow the Baron of Rothebury to be taken without force."

We? Who is we? "You *think* so?" she repeated as respectfully as the situation allowed.

Sir Riley tapped his fingers together in his lap. "Three nights ago our operatives allowed two crates of opium to be stolen from a ship that docked at Portsmouth. During the week before this theft, we had men working the dock, spreading the word quietly that the opium would be arriving." He beamed and lowered his voice. "Tonight, or tomorrow night, if his schedule remains the same, the crates should be delivered to the baron, and he'll be taking them through the tunnel. We plan to have several men awaiting him inside it when he arrives."

She blinked. "Inside the tunnel?"

"Yes," he returned. "Inside and out, and additional men interspersed among the trees so there can be no escape. If we catch him in the act, along with Mrs. Winsett's testimony, there can be a firm conviction."

Madeleine shook her head, puzzled. "I don't understand. How can you position yourselves if you don't know where the tunnel is precisely? Even Thomas and I couldn't find the entrance in the forest."

"I spoke with Desdemona," Thomas revealed without a shred of pomposity.

That stunned her, and she turned her head sharply to stare at him. "When?"

"This afternoon. We had a rather long conversation, and she gave me very specific information about its location, some of which I've already passed on to Sir Riley. She's a very expressive and opinionated lady when engaged in direct conversation," he drawled with a wry lift of his lips, his eyes challenging.

Madeleine refused to be baited by the innuendo and forced herself to ignore it, looking back to Sir Riley. "Why use the additional resources when I can enter the tunnel for you? I've all but been given permission to do so by the man himself."

"Because I don't want you in the tunnel, Madeleine," Thomas stated flatly.

Her confusion slowly turned to offense, then outright anger, though she refused to let it show.

"I don't think that's for you to decide," she argued just as articulately.

Sir Riley cleared his throat again. "I think, Madeleine, that what Mr. Blackwood is saying is that it's not necessary for you to put your life in danger by entering the tunnel unguarded and alone."

"Because I am a woman," she maintained with little inflection.

"Precisely," Sir Riley agreed with a satisfied grin. "We have others who can enter quickly now that we know where it is, and we think we've developed an excellent plan that will put no one in peril, least of all you."

One of the most disappointing moments of her life was happening right now as Madeleine realized that Sir Riley, possibly the man she admired most in the world, was lying to her. To *her*, his most dedicated, trustworthy subordinate on the Continent. And she knew this suddenly because her gender had never before been an issue in her assignments. Never. She and everybody else involved knew the risks one took in this kind of work, and it was accepted unconditionally if one wanted to continue in the field. She had previously, without question, been given responsibilities that put her life in danger. Indeed, she was the only woman she knew of who worked in her capacity, and for the last six years she'd been under the extreme scrutiny of others to perform as a man would, bravely and confidently, because she was expected to fail. She hadn't, and that's why she was so admired. Nobody had ever doubted her strength before now, especially Sir Riley.

No, her arguments for entering the tunnel herself were sound and created the least risk for the baron discovering their intentions. Thomas and Sir Riley knew this, which meant conclusively that something here, in this room, was very definitely wrong.

Gracefully, spine stiff, she stood, though she didn't move from her position. "Well, then," she uttered as her palm brushed her skirt. "I can see that my usefulness and talents are no longer needed. I suppose there is no reason I cannot return to France immediately."

Thomas said nothing, but her words clearly flustered Sir Riley, who stood when she did, gazing to the other man as if needing direction in such an awkward moment.

Thomas remained where he was, rigidly set, features hardened. Madeleine sensed the first real stirring of a momentous occasion about to take place.

"I think it's time for me to speak with Madeleine alone, Sir Riley."

Her employer actually sagged with his exhale, appearing visibly relieved as he tipped his head toward her once without argument. "Indeed, and I am famished and ready for a pint or two. It is always wonderful to see you, Madeleine, and I'm sure we'll be in touch very soon."

He bowed to Thomas. "Good evening, sir."

Then a hush fell over the cottage while he walked to the foyer, lifted his twine coat from the rack beside the door, donned it, and exited hastily.

Madeleine didn't know what to do or say. She just stood there, waiting for something to happen in the uncomfortable silence. She glanced to Thomas, who had yet to move from where he'd been positioned when she'd arrived a few minutes ago, but he looked unsettled now, as if he wasn't certain how to begin a lengthy, vital discussion.

"Why did he call you 'sir'?" she asked bluntly, beginning it for him.

"He was nervous to be here," he readily replied without so much as a look into her eyes, lifting a hand to rub his chin with his fingers.

She folded her arms across her breasts, undaunted. "Yes, I know. I also found that odd." When he said nothing in reply to that, she insisted, "I think it's time for you to explain it to me, Thomas. What is going on here?"

The mood surrounding them intensified abruptly. She could feel his sudden uneasiness like a punch to the gut in her own unmistakable pangs of fear.

He turned around so that he faced the grate, studying the slow-burning fire for a moment or two. She waited, uncertain but refusing to move, feeling her heart pound in her temples and perspiration break out between her breasts.

"Do you love me, Maddie?"

The softly, gently spoken question was the last thing she expected to hear from his lips, and it caused her knees to give as her legs weakened. She sat once more, ungainly, grabbing the armrest to her left to help her.

"I—I'm not sure how that's relevant to this discussion."

"Do you?"

She couldn't avoid the topic, she supposed. He didn't seem about to let her. "I think we have become very close during the last few weeks, yes."

He shook his head. "That's not what I asked you."

She shifted her feet under the tea table and smoothed her moist palms along her thighs over the silk of her gown. "I'm not certain what you expect to hear," she countered very matter-of-factly. "I'm returning to Marseille in a day or so, and—"

He laughed harshly, cutting her off. It was a bitter laugh overflowing with pent-up resentment, irritation, and obvious exasperation. Then he grabbed the mantel with his hands and pushed himself away forcefully, turning quickly in her direction again. He crossed the space between them in two strides, grabbed her upper arm, and yanked her to her feet at his side.

Before she could attempt a protest, she read in his eyes what he intended to do. They were dark as a moonless night, hard as steel, and desperate.

"Thomas—"

His mouth came crushing down over hers, roughly, aching, pleading. She inhaled his scent, tasted him, absorbed all that he gave. She fought him initially, for a second only, or maybe it was hours, she couldn't possibly know. Then she clung to him as his kiss deepened and grew more tender, his hands came behind her back to caress, to mold her against his hard form. Oh, God, how she wanted to be with him, needed him.

A soft sound escaped her throat, and with that he rapidly withdrew.

She stood wavering, hands and body shaking, lips hot

and yearning for more as he looked down into her eyes again, his own expressing a profound confirmation and sublime satisfaction.

Rage filled her instantly, and she wanted to slap him hard across the mouth for taking advantage of her weakness for him. But slapping him wouldn't accomplish a thing, because it was nothing but an act of desperation. She'd never break down and strike him, and he very well knew it. Instead she relaxed her features and waited for him to release her, hoping he couldn't feel the hammering of her heart in her breast.

He never moved, nor lowered his intense gaze.

Suddenly he grabbed her cheeks and lifted her face to within an inch of his. "Tell me you don't love me."

Features as bland as she could muster, she pushed against his chest, though it did no good as his strength far exceeded hers. A scream welled up inside of her, but she fought it, choking it down, choking the tears back because she refused to cry in front of him.

"Why are you doing this, Thomas?" she whispered steadily.

He shook his head very slowly, his thumb rubbing her cheek. "Because I want you to admit that you *feel* something, Madeleine, for me, for us. Anything."

She gaped at him. "Of course I feel."

He gripped her harder. "I want you to admit you feel *passion*, not physical passion, but *emotional* passion, an emotional attachment to me and what we've had together."

She tried to shake him loose, but he wouldn't budge. "Our relationship has been very passionate. I don't know what more I can give you."

She didn't understand, or didn't want to, and Thomas decided at that moment he would simply have to tell her everything to make her see. He wanted her to admit to

loving him first; it would make the pain to come that
much more bearable for her. But she didn't comprehend
what he needed to hear, and it was altogether possible
she hadn't yet realized how deeply her feelings for him
went.

He released her abruptly and stood erect. She pulled
away from him at once and stepped backward several
feet, until she reached the other end of the sofa.

Turning away from her, he walked to the far side of
the room and stared vacantly out the window to the
growing darkness of late afternoon, at rooftops and one
or two smoking chimneys in the distance, seeing nothing. Only silence invaded their world for minutes as she
waited for him, probably dazed and certainly angry, although she did very well at hiding it. He knew he would
feel exactly the same way were he in her position. He
could hear her uneven breathing, but nothing else, and
it affected him tremendously. He was so focused on her,
only her. Regardless of her continuous denial, Thomas
was almost certain Madeleine was in love with him. If
she realized it herself, they might have a chance.

"I haven't been completely honest with you about myself, Madeleine," he disclosed quietly.

After seconds that seemed like hours, she murmured,
"Again you have bewildered me, Thomas. I don't understand."

He drew a deep breath, squeezed his hands into fists
at his sides, and briefly closed his eyes. "My name," he
revealed in a steadily building tension, "is not simply
Thomas Blackwood. It is Christian Thomas Blackwood
St. James, Earl of Eastleigh."

Her breathing stopped. Silence roared, or perhaps that
was only the blood in his veins. He couldn't be sure.

"An earl?" she repeated, her voice whisper-soft and
shaky, barely heard in its disbelief. "An earl . . ."

When at last he detected the noise of rustling skirts, he swung around again slowly to watch her sit with great difficulty once more on the sofa, clutching the armrest with tight fingers as if to keep herself from reeling. Meeting her gaze then was one of the hardest things he'd ever done, for she was bewildered and deeply stunned, staring at him with desolate, crystal-blue eyes, silently pleading that is wasn't true, that he had never deceived her at all.

Deciding to get to the heart of the matter before the sight of her broke him into pieces, he revealed, "And I don't work for Sir Riley, he works for me."

"Wha—what?"

Now she shook visibly, paling markedly, her composure failing as she sagged into her corset, her beautiful eyes so lost in an astonished flurry of confusion and complex emotions she couldn't begin to deal with right now.

There was no turning back.

He removed his jacket and waistcoat with trembling hands that he hoped to God she wouldn't notice. Next, he untied his cravat, pulled it from his neck, then carried everything to his chair, folding his discarded clothing over the arm before walking behind it to rest his hands on the soft back, for comfort, for stability.

"I want to tell you a story, Madeleine," he began soothingly, digging his fingers into the cushion to prevent himself from going to her, forcing himself to stand his ground while he revealed his hidden past.

She never moved, but her wide eyes peered into his, clear as glass.

"After the death of my wife, and before my accident, I was a rather gregarious man, and a randy one. I lived in the city most of the time, when I wasn't on the Continent with some investigation or another. I played

loosely with the female sex because I had the power and
money to attract them. I was a widowed earl, after all,
with a title and a fairly large estate. Women also found
me attractive physically, so I was able to pick and dis-
card them at my choosing. It was a game, and I enjoyed
it immensely."

She showed no outward response to that, to any of it,
so he turned his attention to the glowing embers in the
grate, concentrating on his phrasing, his words that had
never been more vitally important.

"I told you I injured my legs in the war, and that was
essentially true. But they weren't injured in the fighting,
however much I wish they had been." She probably
didn't understand that, nor was she likely to comment
on it, so he carried on. "The Home Office sent me to
the bay of Hong Kong in early October of 'forty-two,
just after the signing of the Nanking Treaty. My mission
had nothing to do with the war itself, but was to investigate two high-ranking naval officers, Charlie Dunbar
and Peter Goodfellow, both stationed on a warship near
the Kowloon Peninsula to keep the peace during the
tense few weeks after the initial signing. These men
were rumored to be trading spices, opium, silks, and
other goods on their own with high officials in the Chinese government, misreporting the goods as pilfered by
the Chinese, lost at sea during heavy fighting, or simply
stolen, and then keeping the money for themselves.

"I reported for duty to Captain Dunbar on the *Royale*,
a newly christened steamship, the second of November,
posing as a shipbuilder hired by the government to over-
see the construction of a shipyard near Hong Kong
Harbor. My false identity remained intact, and all went
fairly routinely for about six months, but in that time I
learned nothing regarding the men and my mission. I
could not find one solid piece of evidence that suggested

either Dunbar or Goodfellow was involved in illegal activity, and yet there was still an occasional report of missing cargo from the ship or fleet. It was a baffling case, and one that, over the course of several months, began to unduly distress me."

Thomas paused and passed her a fast glance. She gazed unblinking at the chess pieces now, hands clutched together in her lap, clinging to her plum silk skirt as she balled it in her fists.

His voice grew weary as he carried on. "The worst part about this story, Madeleine, is that discovering how covert operations like this one operate, then putting myself inside of them to bring an end to the illegal activities, are the two things I do best. It's my job. Yet in Hong Kong I couldn't accomplish my objective by doing the task others were counting on me to do. At the time I arrived in China I'd been working for the Crown for four years in the same capacity, and never had I had such a difficult time finding the proof needed to implicate the offenders as I did on that assignment. I should have found the evidence to have them arrested, but nobody would talk, I had no clues, and I could not find one shred of solid, usable evidence against them. For the first time in my career I was failing."

He squeezed the back of the chair even harder as the memories of the fateful day of his accident came flooding back. "On May tenth, eighteen forty-four, I committed the gravest error of my entire life," he confessed in a husky tenor. "I walked alone one evening on the edge of town, taking the time to think through my options, my caution for my safety undermined by my usual arrogance, as well as the resentment and desperation I was starting to feel for my work. As I headed toward the dock, I remember hearing footsteps behind me on the vacant street, and as I turned to look at the source,

I was clubbed in the back of the head. The next thing I remember was waking up inside an abandoned shipyard, trapped under a smoldering wooden pillar as the building burned to the ground."

Thomas hesitated in his disclosure. He couldn't even discuss the smoke that made his lungs ache with each breath and his throat burn for weeks, the vomiting and unbearable pain. The torment and hopeless fear he'd felt when he'd tried to use his legs, only to realize they'd been crushed.

"I managed to pull myself to safety, though I don't know how," he mumbled shakily, in a far-off voice. "I spent three weeks in hospital in China before I could return to England. When I finally arrived at home I spent two months recuperating and adjusting to the world as a man whose life, to my mind, had just been destroyed."

He couldn't stand still any longer, and with hands clenched into fists at his sides, he began to pace the room from the north windows to the fireplace, hearing nothing from Madeleine and unable to look at her.

"You have to understand what this accident did to me," he stressed fervently. "All of me, not just physically. Before I left for Hong Kong I was a much-sought-after gentleman in society, admired by the ladies, pampered, wealthy, and established with friends and colleagues. Then suddenly I was nothing. Nothing. I left to do a simple task and returned a cripple, Madeleine, and I'm sure you now know how we're treated by society." He chuckled acrimoniously, stopped where he stood on the long, brown rug in front of the tea table, and squeezed his eyes shut. "On May tenth, eighteen forty-four I became a cripple, and for what? For what? I didn't do anything noble. I didn't save a life, or find myself in a dangerous place while exposing the thieves I was sent to observe and have arrested for the good of my country.

I didn't even lose my legs in the goddamn war." Through his teeth, jaw clenched, he articulated, "I lost my legs because of my inflated arrogance and stupidity, probably when someone who was hired to kill me failed. That's it. Nothing was ever proven, and my investigation was never solved. Quite the joke on me, really."

Thomas opened his eyes again, his gaze fixed on the rug. The room had grown warm. The right side of his body was hot from the heat of the fire, but he didn't care. All that mattered now was Madeleine, and he couldn't look at her yet. Not yet, though he knew she hadn't moved an inch or a muscle.

"When I came back from China everything had changed for me," he proceeded, trying to detach himself from the lingering outrage and horror that still managed to unsettle him to the bone. "I was burned very badly on my legs, and to some degree on my chest, back, and face, though most of that healed quickly where the scarring is now practically invisible. But I could not walk. In early July, when I was able to climb out of bed for the first time in weeks, I was forced to spend my waking hours in a wheelchair. Can you imagine what that was like for me? Me, the proud, extroverted aristocrat, doomed to a wheelchair and maybe, if good fortune befell me after months of physical effort and exhaustion, to a world where I would walk with the help of a crutch. A crutch. I was never again to know a life of sensual indulgences and entertaining social enjoyment, a life with sexual contact unless I purchased it, which we both know satisfies lust but offers no meaning. And I knew with certainty that I would never again be truly desired and intensely loved by a woman. As you said so well this morning, Madeleine, 'who would want me?' "

He scraped his face harshly with his palm. Then no

longer able to stand still, he paced once again to the window, his legs like lead, aching.

"My fears were well founded," he detailed, resting his hip against the sill, arms crossed over his chest, gazing out at blurred shadows through increasing darkfall. "During the first few weeks following my return to London, I became the subject of polite gossip and quiet pity, and I was generally ignored when it wasn't socially required to visit me. Many a man came back mangled from war, but only very rarely one in my social position. It made me an odd sensation, something less than human to be ogled and discussed openly among those who had once called themselves my friends. The refined Lady Alicia Douglas, a somewhat obtuse and whimsical beauty I courted and once considered marrying, called on me formally at my home in early July. She didn't offer a kind word that wasn't trite, or a kiss to my mouth—and before that time we had certainly done our share of passionate kissing. Instead, she sat across from me, on a wicker chair in my beautiful garden, visibly repulsed by my disfigurement while she flatly announced without misgiving that she was very sorry but, regardless of my wealth and title, she couldn't possibly marry a man who could not waltz with her on a ballroom floor."

Madeleine winced at that. He saw it from the corner of his eye and turned to face her fully, at last ready to reveal all. She had lowered her lashes now and was ever so slightly shaking her head in negation.

"I wanted to die, Madeleine," he whispered, his voice low and scratchy and wavering, reaching out for the ice-cold windowsill to hold himself steady should his knees give way beneath him. "My life was over as I knew it, and I didn't want to exist anymore. I had nothing left personally—no self-worth, no wife, no friends. Everything I knew and cared about before I left for Hong

Kong was gone from me, taken from me by my own stupidity. How could I work? How could I live the life of a cultured gentleman? Ride a horse or dance? Nobody wanted to spend time with a cripple in a wheelchair, walk with him while he limped profoundly on a crutch. I had only my son, nine years old at the time and so *alive*, and I felt like I'd shamed him somehow. He would do better to inherit my estate at my death, be raised by my wife's brother, his very able and prosperous uncle, rather than to give constant care to his lonely, invalid father for years to come. I was suddenly an obligation, only to grow more dependent on his company over time, and I didn't want that for him. I didn't want that for anyone. I just didn't want to live anymore, and by the middle of summer I'd convinced myself that I had the courage to let go.

"On July twenty-ninth, trying to ignore the rude gawking and embarrassed whispers of those I passed, my private nurse wheeled me into Sir Riley's office in the city so that I could conclude my assignment on paper, sign any lingering documents, and visit with him again for a final time. It was a dismal day, severely cold and wet, which I decided would be perfect for my last outing, my last few hours on this earth."

The cottage was almost dark inside now, the fire dying in the grate, lamps unlit from lack of concern or notice. Thomas's mouth became dry as his heart began to beat hard and fast with trepidation. For the first time in ages, he desperately needed a whisky. But he refused to move, refused to curb his revelations now, to keep the secret any longer, to take his eyes from her beautiful, elegant form.

"Instead of pursuing my cowardly death, the greatest miracle of my life occurred that unforgettable afternoon. As I sat waiting in my chair in Sir Riley's outer office,

the pain excruciating, my head and face partially bandaged as my sewn wounds slowly healed, my mind and
heart bitterly accepting of my fate, the door opened, and
this lady, this . . . breathtaking vision, glided into the office in a flurry of daffodil-yellow silk, shining like a
brilliant rainbow after a spring shower."

His throat constricted as the memory of that momentous event came back to him in lashing waves, forcing
him to stumble in his detail, the scene in his mind as
real to him as if it had all happened yesterday. But as
difficult as it all was, he never looked away from Madeleine.

"I was awestruck by her beauty," he continued in a
trembling whisper he could no longer control. "I
couldn't think coherently when she turned her exquisite,
pale blue eyes in my direction and noticed me, although
I vividly remember cringing inside because of what I'd
become, knowing that at another time I might have made
an impression on this incredible woman, but by then it
was too late. I was ready to bow my head in humiliation,
when this gentle soul smiled radiantly into my eyes and
walked toward me. And not only did she smile at me,
she purposely sat beside me. I was a hideously ugly,
broken mess of a man, and yet in an otherwise vacant
room, this angelic creature chose, *chose*, to sit beside
me.

"She spoke to me," he whispered huskily as if back
in the dream. "She ignored the deep, sewn gash beside
my mouth, my cuts and burns, never recoiled from my
grotesque, missing leg. She so sweetly related her trip
to London, told me about her home in France, all the
while smiling, touching my arm, her voice velvet-soft
and caring.

"She fascinated me, this unusual Frenchwoman," he
said passionately. "So when she left two hours later and

I had some time to discuss her business with Sir Riley, I was astonished to learn what she'd come to England to do. Was it possible? Could a Frenchwoman be a British spy? He informed me of all that she'd done up to that point, with no direction or funds, and although Riley was amused and took her ambition somewhat lightly, I was enthralled. He remained skeptical of the idea of placing a woman, a Frenchwoman, under his employ, but I found the notion as intriguing as the woman herself."

Thomas knew this was the critical moment, but he had to get the rest of it said. Pulse throbbing erratically in his temples, his stomach squeezing him hard from the inside, legs like jelly, he forced himself to lower his arms to his sides and stand perfectly still.

"I insisted that Sir Riley hire her, and he did. Four days later. Her work was immediately praised, and the most interesting thing of all was that I was so captivated with the woman and her sudden burst into my life that my self-pity had vanished. I had a purpose, even if it was only to see her succeed.

"I sent two men to France to discover what they could about her, from her past to the present, her likes and dislikes, her heartbreaks and joys. In this way I learned of her lonely childhood at the hands of a beautiful but selfish mother, her devastation at the loss of her father, her determination to learn the English language and then accomplishing it. I learned of her first lover, and then the next, and then the ones after that, of her experience as a common stage dancer to provide for her future."

Thomas could see the tears streaming down her cheeks now in two thin lines, reflecting what remained of the firelight. It tore through his gut, making his chest ache, and he wanted so badly to touch her, to hold her and tell her it would be all right. It had to be. That thought alone gave him the fortitude he needed to finish.

"The hardest part of all, Madeleine," he whispered intensely, no longer able to control his grief as his voice began to shake with it, "was when I realized, six or seven months after I'd met this beautiful, unusual woman, that I was falling in love with her—not the cultured, physically exquisite image she portrayed to all, the only part every other man she had ever known had loved and desired. But with her fighting spirit, her hidden talents, her gentle goodness and bravery and passion to make the best of the harsh life she'd been given through no fault of her own. Within a year of our meeting I'd come to know everything about her, admiring her tremendously for the woman she was inside, understanding how she'd used her beauty and charm to position herself in the world, because that's the part of her people judged."

He leaned toward her and tapped his chest hard with his fist. "*I* know how others judge the physical beauty. *I* know how their ignorance damages and scars a person inside far worse than the scars on the outside. The very same judgments this brave woman had faced *I* was beginning to face, and I understood. Of all the things I had ever understood about life, Madeleine, I understood the pain this physically beautiful woman had endured inside because she could not help the way she looked."

Madeleine bowed her head and put her face in her palm, her body shaking violently, although she had yet to make a sound. Any sound. If she cried, she cried silently.

Thomas felt himself succumb to her misery, and it nearly tore him apart. He stood only five or six feet away from her, and yet he couldn't go to her. In all of his life, he'd never known such fear as he did at this moment, wondering if she would lash out at him for trying, despise him eternally. But he couldn't stop now.

"For years I waited, giving her work as she needed it, loving her from afar, enormously proud of her accomplishments, accepting but so deeply hurt each time she took a lover who was not me. I ached inside when she was alone, wanting to comfort her, to be a friend she could trust and talk to when she was lonely. I couldn't expect anything in return for my efforts, and yet for years it was enough because I had no idea how to meet her again, how to get to know her without others around, to engage her intimately in conversation, to allow her the opportunity to get to know me. And then last summer I had an idea. If I brought her to England to work with me, just me, outside her world in France, I would have a chance, one chance, to see if she held any attraction to me, a common scholar, if she would want me as a man disabled, if she could learn to love me."

Thomas stiffened, fists at his sides, and swallowed forcefully. "I love you, Madeleine," he said brokenly, looking at her silent, crying form. "I am not infatuated with your beauty, or your charm, or the sensual pleasures you have given me in bed. I love the little girl who witnessed opium addiction and sexual perversion, who had no mother to love and cherish her but one who abused her. I love the child who lost her father, the only person she had ever loved, when she was so young, who at only fifteen found comfort in the arms of a man twice her age. I love the manner in which you achieved greatness by avoiding prostitution when that was your easiest option. I love your laugh and your dignity and your cleverness. I love your elegance and your style and your disregard of the physical ugliness surrounding you, because you see innocent beauty in all things."

He lowered his voice with profound conviction. "I will love you when you are old, Maddie, when age finally takes your youthful glamour. I will love you when your face is wrinkled and your hair is gray and your breasts are no longer firm and your waist has thickened. I love you more than I have ever loved another living soul, but more importantly, I value you because you are so very worthy. You gave me back my life, and I will live it to make you happy."

The silence became deafening when he finished speaking. For several long, excruciating moments he was aware of nothing but the woman before him, her shiny hair coiled up into perfect braids, her day gown smooth and silky as it draped over her legs, her straight, trembling back, her face in her hands as she cried. Darkness loomed, coldness intensified as the fire died slowly in the grate, but he remained focused solely on her. Only her. Hoping.

"Madeleine—"

"Why?" she asked in a breath of anguish.

Tears filled his eyes then, tears he could no longer control. "Please—"

"I asked you why!"

Her scream of vehemence startled him, rocking him to the core. She looked into his eyes as last, and it was then that he realized his confession had shattered her.

He took a step toward her, and in that instant she flung her arm wide and put every ounce of strength she possessed into scattering the chess pieces across the room, each of them striking the floor with a sharp piercing stab as a knife to his chest.

"This is a lie! Everything is a lie! All of it!" She stood, rage enveloping her, hands fisted at her sides as she faced him. "You are the greatest lie, Thomas, and the greatest liar! Do you know what you've done? Do you have any idea? You manipulated me to *your* advantage. I am a lie created by you, an identity created as easily as those you created for yourself, the shipbuilder, the simple scholar. I am now the person *you* wanted, not the woman I chose to become. I believed for years that I was admired for what I did, that I was wanted, *needed*, for something other than how I looked. Now I learn, through some . . . some . . . selfish scheme of yours, that I am laughed at, probably ridiculed constantly because I am really nothing more than an audacious French-woman attempting in vain to be an English subject. How absurd I must look each time I contact the Home Office. How much fun it must be for all the men to mock my feminine qualities as I parade them around France in the name of British national security."

"That's not true," he said harshly, trying desperately to control his rising panic, feeling the walls around him closing in. "None of that is true. Nobody has ever laughed at you or scorned your abilities while you've worked for the Crown."

She hugged herself, crying out in a wail of agony. "Oh, God, don't you understand? You've humiliated me, not just now, but in front of others, in front of my su-periors, my colleagues! Can't you comprehend how dif-ficult it was for me to get here? How exhausting it's been to stay in this position all these years? How hard it is even now to be accepted? I believed what I did was worthwhile and highly regarded, but now you tell me it has all been a lie. You've made me a fool and my work meaningless! You've played with my life, Thomas, and I am nothing! Nothing!"

He stared at her, stunned and dazed, blinded by her pain. "I *gave* you a life, Madeleine. You would have had nothing to support you if it hadn't been for me."

"You arrogant *bastard!*" With that she lashed out, crossing the space between them in the course of a sec-ond to slap his face soundly, to hit him squarely in the chest with palms and fists, over and over, crying, wailing. It was the first time he had ever witnessed her out of control, clawing, striking, and after a moment he grabbed her arms, holding them to her sides while she used all of her strength against him to attempt her release.

He refused to let her go. He deserved her rancor, her hostility, and the unrestrained sobbing that ripped his dreams into shreds.

Eventually she calmed, and he wrapped his arms around her and held her tightly, listening to her uneven breathing, inhaling the clean scent of her, feeling the thundering beat of her heart against his chest.

"My life for the last six years has been a lie, Thomas," she whispered against his shirtfront, standing now stiffly in front of him, "and I will never forgive you for what you've done. I have nothing now, can you understand that? My work isn't mine, it's yours. I didn't secure it by my own cleverness, you did. I feel nothing for you but contempt."

A sob tore from his throat as tears welled up again in his eyes, and he closed them to the wetness on his lashes.

"I have loved you for six years, Madeleine, six *years*," he whispered fervently, his lips against her forehead. "I had one chance to give it to you openly, without constraints and interruptions. Please—oh, God, *please* believe that every feeling I've ever expressed to you has been the truth. I never wanted to hurt you. I only wanted to bring you happiness."

For moments she didn't move, didn't speak. Then she gradually pulled away from him, and he let her go.

"I am leaving England tonight, Thomas, for good, and I don't expect to see you again," she stated coldly, spine erect and tight, face to the window, her features taut with misery, but her facade of grace and undaunted composure returned. "Since you carry such an interest in my future, let me assure you, sir, that I will be fine. You need no longer concern yourself with it." She didn't look at him as she stepped past him and around the sofa. "If you'll excuse me, I think I'll retire to pack my wardrobe now. I wish you well, Lord Eastleigh. Thank you for your work on my behalf."

He watched her retreating back as she turned the corner, the soft click of her heels on the wooden floor like a slowly ticking clock, the bolting of her door like the strike of a chisel into his heart.

He couldn't go to her, couldn't argue anymore. She would only converse with him coolly, superficially should he try. How ironic life was that he knew her better than anybody.

Thomas put his face in his palms and wept.

Twenty-four

Madeleine sat alone on a wrought-iron bench, across from the large round duck pond at the center of the Parc de le Papillon near the waterfront. Springtime had arrived at last. The surrounding olive trees shaded the sun, daffodils and roses and wild flowers bloomed. Children played contentedly, loudly, on the grassy areas off the busy roads, birds chirped and sang on all sides of her. It was a peaceful time, a time of renewal and excitement toward the warm season dawning. But as if in contradiction, in resistance to change, her soul remained troubled.

Casually she slipped off her shoes and lifted her legs so her bare feet rested on the bench seat, tucked under her gown. Then she rested her forearms on her knees, chin on her arms, and stared at the crystal blue water and splashing ducks in front of her.

Despite Marscille's temperate climate which she generally preferred, she missed England. She missed the frost on the windows of all the old English dwellings, she missed the chimney smoke, she missed the quiet lake and the villagers, and the cottage where, after twenty-nine years, she had truly lost her innocence. But more than all of it, more than everything combined, more than she ever thought she would, she missed Thomas.

Life was really so ironic and ridiculous in a very humorous way. She should hate the man for what he'd done, and part of her did—a very small and gradually diminishing part. Mostly she just felt angry at him for remaining silent all these years then expecting her to approve of his actions of so long ago when he finally announced them. What did he think she'd say to it all? *Thank you for your amazing care and generosity? For giving me something I didn't earn but thought I did? I love you, too?* His naivete was rather alarming, but in its own way charming, she supposed. She'd had two months to think about it now, since the horrible night of her departure, and she'd come to terms with it, even understood his point of view to a degree.

She really didn't hold any animosity toward him any longer, and that was likely because, after careful consideration on her part all these weeks, she'd come to the conclusion that he had meant every word he'd said that fateful night in January. Whatever he'd done six years ago, he'd done so that she would have a better life, so that she would be happy. That alone meant so much to her because nobody, not even her parents, had ever cared about her happiness before.

She also realized that although her initial feeling that her work had been rendered meaningless was well justified, it was probably incorrect. Thomas had given her the job of informant for his government when nobody else wanted to, but if she hadn't performed to top expectations she would have been pacified with simple tasks through the years. She hadn't. Her work had been very risky and difficult, her assignments professionally compiled and of the highest security. In fact, as she thought about it now, the easiest assignment she'd received in all her years working for the Home Office had been the one on which she'd worked with Thomas.

Madeleine smiled to herself as she considered that case. Her mind had to have been totally focused on the sensual pleasure that arrogant, charming, quietly intelligent, wonderful man had smothered her with from the moment of her arrival for her not to realize they could have set up a scheme for Rothebury to be arrested immediately. Or at least within the first few weeks. Truthfully, she hadn't been *needed* for the task at all. Thomas could have done the work himself with his false identity intact and believed by everybody in Winter Garden. He could have completed the case long before she'd ever arrived.

To acknowledge these things made her jubilant in a manner she didn't exactly understand. Never in her life had one person spent so much time, money, and effort on her behalf. If Thomas made her feel nothing else, she would always remember him giving her a sense of her own value above all things. She only wished, on lovely days and melancholy moments like this, she could tell him that.

She'd remembered him immediately when he confessed who he was. Their conversation of six years ago remained vague at best, and she imagined it was mostly frivolous. But she would never forget the sight of him, the flat hopelessness she'd seen in the swollen eyes of the defeated, bandaged man without a leg, who sat in a wheelchair in Sir Riley's dim office and introduced himself as Christian St. James. What a beautiful, refined name, she had thought. She remembered him trying to smile at her, in so much pain from the brutal cut at his mouth, of stroking his hand once and feeling uneasy about being so forward but wanting to comfort him anyway. He had been a stranger to her, but she had taken to him because of the way he had looked—not handsome and powerful as he did now, but incredibly deformed and weak—because she knew how much beauty mattered to the outside world. She knew exactly how being judged by something you cannot change affects everything you are inside.

She would never see him again. Every time that popped into her head she got that ever-painful lump deep in her throat as her nose tingled and her eyes filled with tears. She hadn't heard from him in all these weeks and she had refused to write him. What would she say? She had been furious when she'd left, but she couldn't be sorry for that. Her fury had been justified. He was so hurt, though. He had loved her more than anyone ever had, and she had hurt him desperately that night. It would tear at her heart for the rest of her life.

But that same life, however difficult, went on. She just didn't know exactly what she wanted to do with it now. Marseille held no deep meaning to her. She liked it because it was her home, but she could only count social acquaintances. She had no real friends. Thomas had been right about that. She'd never let anyone in for fear that they would leave. Marie-Camille was here, and would probably go anywhere she did in France, but the woman was her maid, and as such she'd remained in a subservient position to her and likely always would. She supposed she would keep working for the government, but even that had lost some of its attraction now, and would feel to her like work for employment, not excitement. That saddened her a little. Everything had changed when she left for Winter Garden, and nothing would ever be the same again.

She closed her eyes, listening to birdsong, ducks

quacking, splashing in the pond, the bustle of traffic on the surrounding streets, children laughing.

Suddenly the overwhelming anxiety she hadn't felt in weeks reappeared, and her heart began to pound heavy in her breast. She put her legs down slowly, pulling her arms from her knees and wrapping them around her belly. Disbelief filled every pore in her body then quickly fled as the tears began to flow, first filling her eyes, then rolling down her cheeks uninhibited. She bowed her head and closed her eyes in wonder, in joy, for above every noise in the park, above every sound in the city square, she recognized the tapping of his boots and his slow, uneven stride on the sidewalk behind her.

Thomas had come to Marseille. He had come for her. Suddenly she didn't care about past deceptions or their individual struggles. All that mattered was them, together. Thomas had come to Marseille for her, and her world was once again beautiful.

Seconds later she felt his presence behind her, and with a choke of longing and a tremble in her voice, she said softly, "I've been waiting for you, Thomas."

For all the fear the moment brought, for all the hardship he'd endured in the weeks since she'd left him, every single second of the torment had been worth it to hear those spoken words, the same words, in fact, that he'd said to her all those months ago when he'd met her in the backyard of the Winter Garden cottage. She remembered them, understood them now, and was using them as a sign of her forgiveness. In all the years to come she would never know what that meant to him.

His legs were weak and throbbing, his mouth dry, his eyes scratchy and tired from days of travel, but he stood behind her, unsure what to do next.

"It's a beautiful day," she offered, with only the slightest catch in her throat as she took control.

"Beautiful," he repeated, his tone somewhat raspy.

She breathed in deeply and tilted her head toward the sun.

The urge to touch her was unbearable now, and so he reached out gingerly and placed his palm on her bare shoulder, bare skin, so warm.

Just as quickly she lowered her cheek and brushed it against his knuckles, back and forth.

"Madeleine—"

"Come and sit with me, Thomas," she urged quietly, adjusting her body a little on the bench, her poise returning in full. "I've missed you so much."

They were the sweetest words he had ever heard in his life, and he hoped desperately she wouldn't see just how much of a puppy he was in her hands.

He stepped around the bench conveniently made for two, and then without a glance to her face, he sat heavily next to her on the hard wrought iron, staring out to the ducks in the pond.

For minutes they didn't speak, just sat closely beside each other. He felt her warmth against him, noticed the way her yellow silk gown clung to his legs complimenting the dark blue color of his morning suit. But most of all he sensed the coming of a certain attainable peace for the first time since his accident six years ago.

"I'm still so mad at you," she started confidently, breaking into his thoughts.

He inhaled sharply. "I know."

After another silent moment, she whispered, "What are we going to do?"

"What would you like to do?" he replied at once.

He felt the heat of her gaze on his skin at last, and he bravely turned to face her. Her eyes were misty and afraid, longing so much for everything to be right as they entwined with the depths of his. He restrained himself from moving forward two inches and kissing her fears away. It was too soon.

"I can't possibly marry you," she said weakly.

His heart nearly stopped beating. "Why?"

She shook her head and glanced down, picking at a loose string on his jacket. "You are an earl, Thomas. An *earl*. To marry you would make me a countess. I can't be a countess."

"Whyever not?" he asked a bit more sternly than he'd intended. "Nobody I know is more suited for the title, Madeleine."

The possibility, or perhaps just his manner, made her uncomfortable, and she moved her fingers to her skirt to play absentmindedly with a flounce of pale yellow lace while her eyes shifted to the grass, away from him.

"I will be laughed at, and certainly not respected. I am a Frenchwoman, and to hold an English title . . ."

Her concerns were valid, he supposed, but they didn't matter to him in the least.

With a fast exhale through his teeth, he turned his attention briefly to the pond. "Madeleine, if you married me you would not be *a* countess, you would be *my* countess, and I don't give a damn what people think. Frankly, I'd enjoy watching the likes of Penelope Bennington-Jones curtsy to you. Such a vision would instill in me the knowledge that all is right with the universe. I just want you to be happy. I want us to be happy together, and I have never wanted anything more in my life."

He felt her turn back to him and he did the same, capturing her tear-filled eyes once more with his.

"I love you," he murmured passionately, reaching up to place his palm on her soft, wet cheek. "I've loved you for so long I don't remember *not* loving you, so I don't suppose that's likely to change. And because I love you so deeply, I'm willing to do what it takes to be with you. If you don't want to be an English countess, I will relinquish my title to my son with fond memories and live out my middle- and old-age years with you in France. Or America. Or Turkey, for that matter. I have plenty of money, Madeleine. All I want is to be with you, conversing with you, playing chess and loving you, for the rest of my life. Nothing else matters."

"I'm carrying your child, Thomas."

That statement took time to register, and when it did Thomas wasn't sure he could manage to keep his aplomb intact. For a second he was certain he would cry in front of her. He stared at her, stunned, his heart banging against the walls of his chest, throat aching, clutching at hope.

"Do you want it?" he whispered, knowing it would shatter him if she said no, but realizing he had to ask. It could be their final barrier.

She smiled tenderly through the tears that sparkled on her lashes, her lips trembling. She kissed his palm once, but she never looked away.

"How could I not want and love something so precious that you have given me? I felt your love for me when I conceived this child. Even if you had never come here today, I would cherish it always."

Speechless, Thomas knew he was very close to losing his composure. She sensed it, too, for at that moment she reached for the hand he still held against her cheek, tucking it between her own warm palms, sharing her strength.

"I love you," she whispered. "I knew that before I left Winter Garden but I wasn't sure why. It took me all these weeks alone, without your imposing presence, to realize that I loved you so much not only because of your giving soul and intelligence and charm, but for no other great, complicated reason than because you love me." Her eyes became fierce. "Nobody has ever loved me unconditionally, Thomas, accepting me for who I am. You do, and I can feel that love whenever I'm with you. I never want to be away from it again."

It was all as he had ever envisioned, had ever dreamed. He couldn't possibly speak after such a declaration. Instead of trying, he reached for her and pulled her against his chest, holding her close when she willingly came to him. Sunlight reflected off her hair, and the scent of it touched him with wonderful memories and the belief in new, joyous ones to come.

"I bought the Hope cottage, Maddie," he whispered, his lips against her temple.

She sniffed. "I'm so glad."

Seconds later, he explained. "The real reason I didn't want you entering Baron Rothebury's tunnel and getting involved was not because I think you're incompetent as a female investigator, but because I didn't want either one of us to be involved with his arrest. I didn't want the villagers to learn that either of us works for the government because I wanted us to not only continue with our work, as a team of sorts, but also to be able to retreat to Winter Garden through the years. I'd like to live for months at a time in that little cottage where you fell in love with me, to play chess and then make love to you over and over again on the old brown rug in front of the fire, to sit together by the lake at sunset."

"I can't wait," she whispered, without arguing his reasons for being secretive. "Still, you lied about your identity," she added. "That's sure to raise a few eyebrows."

He smiled, gazing at two boys and a girl fighting over a ball. "I am a recluse, Maddie, and I have been for years. Nobody in Winter Garden will be surprised to learn that I kept my identity as an earl hidden from the local gentry so that I could retreat to the village in peace. I'll eventually tell them. You can continue to be who you are. Nobody will know you didn't actually translate my war memoirs."

"Only if they ask to see them," she said wryly.

"We keep them at Eastleigh."

"Oh, I see. How convenient."

"Maybe we'll spread the word that they burned in a fire. I love to lie."

She giggled adorably at that, and he squeezed her tighter against him.

Suddenly she tipped her face and looked up at him. "What am I supposed to call you? Christian?"

It was his turn to chuckle. "I didn't care much for arrogant bastard, but Christian is too formal. My family always called me Thomas. That's why I saved it for you."

"You planned this all very well, didn't you," she maintained a bit sharply, trying to suppress a grin.

He touched his lips to hers, kissing her softly, briefly, marveling in the warmth and taste of her mouth, knowing he would treasure this moment forever, knowing now beyond all things that there would be many more to come.

"I hoped, Maddie," he whispered against her. "I only hoped."

Madeleine DuMais, the illegitimate daughter of an opium-addicted actress and a British naval captain, married Christian Thomas Blackwood St. James, the most distinguished Earl of Eastleigh, on April 14, 1850. Her wedding was a formal enough affair arranged on rather short notice, but it was the celebration afterward that she cherished the most.

Thomas had taken her to the cottage so that they could

spend their honeymoon in Winter Garden, among the villagers who were most ready to accept her as Madeleine St. James, Countess of Eastleigh—even Mrs. Bennington-Jones, who indeed curtsied to her because, Madeleine assumed, she was one of the few who bothered to call on the woman after the disgrace of her daughter, Desdemona.

Richard Sharon, Baron Rothbury, had been arrested for the importation of stolen opium, and his ultimate fate was as yet unknown. He would be gone from Winter Garden for years, though, and probably for the rest of his life. Madeleine held little sympathy for him, and instead found the villagers all the more congenial and relaxed at his departure. Most thoroughly did she enjoy the bantering and speculation between them all as they placed their wages on what was to become of the baron's estate, his home that was filled with secret tunnels and mysteries from the past.

People were only learning now of her pregnancy, which had been progressing as it should. Their baby would arrive a little more than two months early, according to their wedding date, but scandal had always been a part of her life, and she would take the talk as it came. Most of their acquaintances were unaware that she and Thomas had only recently married anyway, assuming instead that they'd married the week she'd left in January. Beyond everything, however, remained the fact that she was the highest-ranking subject in Winter Garden, aside from her husband, and in Eastleigh for that matter, and nobody would dare say anything remotely rude to her person. They could think what they would. Like Thomas, she had learned early not to care about the snide conjecture and gossip of others.

On the first night of their honeymoon, Thomas had given her the music box as a wedding gift, adding her name to the inscription, which he said had been his intention all along. They had dined with her only real friends in England so far, Jonathan and Natalie Drake, who had worked with her on a previous assignment in France. The talk had been wonderful between them all; Thomas had known Jonathan for many years. Natalie, expecting her own child—their first—one month after Madeleine's was due to arrive, surprised Jonathan with the news that he was to become a father during a dessert of apple cobbler. Poor man. The look on his face at his wife's casual confession had been matchless.

Life was indeed ironic. Her journey and experiences in Winter Garden had all happened so quickly and unexpectedly, and yet it seemed like a lifetime ago when she'd met Thomas. She had trouble remembering an existence before him.

Madeleine loved him so much, for all that he had done for her, for all that he was. He knew it, too, which was the most wonderful feeling of all. He had given her the dream of a lifetime, and the chance to be English—everything in the world that she had ever wanted.

Now she and her husband of two weeks stood together, embraced in each other's arms, beside the hard wooden bench in front of the lake, watching the sun set across the water as they danced to the soft, melodic tune of Beethoven's Sonata in C Minor.